WHEN WOMEN WERE WARRIORS

The strong, supple prose on display in all three novels, the intelligence of the plotting, and the skillfully varied pacing make this a standout trilogy — highly recommended.

— from a review by The Historical Novel Society

★ ★ ★ ★ ★ *A Journey of the Heart* shows the same strong storytelling ability of the first book. The language is still almost musical and wraps its sweet spell around you.... Storylines that were just starting to grow in the first book are also very well developed here. Intrigue and conflict are fleshed out and take some surprising twists. All that I had hoped for, reading the first book, begins to bloom.... Someone get me the third volume, quickly. It's a beautiful story.

—from a review by Kate Genet, *Kissed By Venus*

Catherine Wilson creates a magical sense of place, and of belonging to that place. Within that, she also tells how it feels to not belong. ... Ms. Wilson's is a tale of bone wisdom. It whispers of what we remember when we sleep at night and dream. It calls us to remember that women had, and still have, a wise and powerful place in the world.

—from a review by Baxter Clare Trautman,
author of *The River Within*

In this book we see Tamras' world open from the House of Merin and its immediate environs into the lands beyond its borders. She meets other peoples, whose ways are different from those she knows. Similarly Tamras' inner life expands as well: the feelings within her blossom into the romantic love that will be the linchpin her life will hinge on.... In my review of the first book in this trilogy I compared Wilson to Le Guin, Holland and Rosemary Sutcliff. I can only additionally compare her second book to Mary Renault's Athenian books as Wilson explores the passionate love between people who are very distant from us in their cultural assumptions.

—from a review by Charles Ferguson, *Goodreads*

ALSO BY CATHERINE M. WILSON

WHEN WOMEN WERE WARRIORS
BOOK I
THE WARRIOR'S PATH

WHEN WOMEN WERE WARRIORS
BOOK III
A HERO'S TALE

WHEN WOMEN WERE WARRIORS

BOOK II
A JOURNEY OF THE HEART

CATHERINE M. WILSON

SHIELD MAIDEN PRESS
BOULDER CREEK, CALIFORNIA

Publisher's Cataloging-in-Publication
(Provided by Quality Books, Inc.)

    Wilson, Catherine M., 1944-
      When women were warriors / Catherine M. Wilson.
      v. cm.
      CONTENTS: bk. 1. The warrior's path -- bk. 2. A
    journey of the heart -- bk. 3. A hero's tale.
      LCCN 2008901689
      ISBN-13: 978-0-9815636-1-9 (bk. 1)
      ISBN-10: 0-9815636-1-9 (bk. 1)
      ISBN-13: 978-0-9815636-2-6 (bk. 2)
      ISBN-10: 0-9815636-2-7 (bk. 2)
      ISBN-13: 978-0-9815636-3-3 (bk. 3)
      ISBN-10: 0-9815636-3-5 (bk. 3)

      1. Women heroes--Fiction. 2. Lesbians--Fiction.
    3. British Isles--Antiquities--Fiction. 4. Feminist
    fiction. I. Title. II. Title: Warrior's path.
    III. Title: Journey of the heart. IV. Title: Hero's tale.

    PS3623.I57785W44 2008   813'.6
             QBI08-600093

Library of Congress Control Number: 2008901689
ISBN-10: 0-9815636-2-7
ISBN-13: 978-0-9815636-2-6

Cover photo by Donna Trifilo

Published by Shield Maiden Press
P. O. Box 963
Boulder Creek, CA 95006-0963
www.shieldmaidenpress.com

For my mother

Acknowledgements

Many people offered advice, support, and encouragement during the "quite some time" it took to finish this project.

It is an extraordinary piece of luck for a writer to find someone who is willing to discuss a work in progress, someone who can enter the world of the story and gossip about the characters as if they were real people, who will question their motivations, scrutinize their actions, complain when they step out of character, and cast a light on a side of them their creator may have missed—someone who will take the work as seriously as the author does. For me that person is my friend and editor, Donna Trifilo, who, in addition to all of the above, pushed me through the hard times.

To everyone who was willing to read a work in progress, sometimes more than once, I offer my gratitude and the assurance that everything they had to say about it mattered.

Susan Strouse helped me overcome a major stumbling block at a crucial turning point. Lisa Liel, whose enthusiasm for the story rekindled my own enthusiasm, showed me how I could take a good idea and make it better. Ann Thryft's considerable knowledge of the time, place, and culture deepened my own understanding of the story and its characters. Jo Trifilo's insightful comments and careful critique gave me a new perspective on the story.

In ways too numerous to mention, significant contributions were also made by Jen Davis-Kay, Katherine Gilmartin, Rebecca Hall, Rob Field, Carmen Carter, Kate Maynard, the late Dr. Susan Barnes, Judi Miller, Jack Contento, Ru Emerson, the members of my first writers' group—Morgan Van Dyke, Barbara Murray, Cooper Gallegos, Sandralee Watters, Marlene Michaelson, Rebecca Morn, and Eileen Thompson—who suffered through my early attempts to get my story started, and Heather Rose Jones, who helped me find my characters' names.

And many thanks to George Derby and Marissa Holm for keeping me well fed.

CONTENTS

CONTENTS

28

TRUTH

Maara took the sword from my hand.

"What is this?" she said.

"It's a sword," I replied, as if she couldn't see that for herself.

"What are you doing with it?"

"Practicing." I wiped away the sweat running down my face. "I'm not used to its weight anymore."

We were standing on the practice ground, where I had been giving a wooden post the benefit of my clumsy blows. I was discouraged. Although I had grown a little taller in the last year, I still had to use both hands to wield the heavy sword, and it had been so long since I'd practiced with it that I felt like a beginner again.

"Did I say anything to you about practicing with a sword?"

Maara leaned the sword against the post and beckoned to me to follow her. She found us a place to sit in the shadow of the earthworks where it was cooler.

I waited for her to speak. I had thought she would be pleased with me. Instead she sat frowning down at the ground.

At last she said, "I don't want you to practice with a sword. Not even with the wooden ones."

"Why not?"

"When will you be strong enough to wield a sword one-handed?"

It was a question I didn't know how to answer.

"Someday," I said.

"I don't think so."

What dreadful thing would she tell me next? Was she saying I would never be a warrior after all?

"You don't believe I'll ever be strong enough?"

"No."

I couldn't comprehend what I was hearing. Why would she have apprenticed me if she didn't believe she could make a warrior of me? I almost suspected her of accepting me because she knew that I would fail and so release her early from her obligation.

"I thought you believed. . ."

"What?"

"That I could become a warrior someday."

"Of course you can," she said. "You will."

"A warrior without a sword?"

"A warrior with a weapon she can use."

She reached for something that lay hidden in the tall grass. I recognized at once the bow she took from the man who killed Eramet.

"The bow and the sword are very different weapons," she said. "A sword takes both strength and endurance. A bow takes a different kind of strength. It also takes great skill and more patience than most people ever have."

I was only half listening to her. I was grieving the loss of my dream of myself with sword and shield, standing with my comrades, as I had imagined my mother and her sisters standing, shoulder to shoulder, against the enemy.

"A bow is a coward's weapon," I said. I was mouthing words I'd heard somewhere without understanding what they meant.

My warrior frowned at me. "Any weapon is a coward's weapon in the hands of a coward."

I blushed with shame and looked away, but my pride was wounded, and I refused to understand her.

"Why did you accept me if you thought so little of me?"

"So little?" She waited for me to meet her eyes. "I think the world of you."

A lump in my throat prevented me from speaking.

"If I did not," she said, "I would hang a sword from your belt and a shield from your shoulder and pray that you never had to use them."

If she was making a joke, I didn't find it funny.

She turned the bow over in her hands, admiring it. Her fingers followed the carvings, swirling spirals that meandered up and down its length. When I had first seen it, it had no bowstring. Now a new string wound around the shaft of the unstrung bow.

"Do you know what kind of bow this is?" she asked me.

I shook my head.

"It's a forest bow. Powerful, but meant to be used at close range. Easy to carry among the trees. Small enough not to get in its own way."

"Small enough even for me?"

I couldn't keep the bitterness out of my voice. She answered me in kind.

"Yes," she said. "Small enough even for you." Then in a kinder voice she said, "And like you, it is powerful and clever. Like you, it has strengths that are easily overlooked, but they are many nonetheless."

The sweetness of her words was meant to help me swallow a bitter truth, but I was not yet ready to give in.

"If a bow is such a wonderful weapon," I said, "why is it that you carry a sword?"

"For the same reason you want so much to carry one. A sword is a symbol of power. A hunter may carry a bow. Even a child can make a bow to shoot at birds that would scratch the farmers' seed out of the ground. Only a warrior has the right to bear a sword." She gave me a long look. "I understand your disappointment, but you must face the truth about yourself."

"And the truth is that I'm too small and always will be."

My words tasted bitter in my mouth. Nothing she could say would sweeten them.

"Too small?" she said. "Too small for what? Too small to wield a sword? Yes, I believe you are. But the whole truth is that you are small of body. That's all."

She stood up and took several steps away from me, then stopped and turned around. She still held the bow, and she shook it in a gesture of impatience.

"There is great power in this truth you can't accept, and I don't know how to make you see it."

Now she had my attention.

"If you insist on acquiring the trappings of a warrior, that's all you'll ever have. A sword can't make you something you were never meant to be."

"What was I meant to be?" I wondered aloud.

"I have no idea," she said. "Nor do you, but you'll discover that only when you can face the truth about yourself."

Although nothing could make facing the truth any less painful, she had made it a little easier. She had held out to me the hope that, by letting something go, I might be able to take hold of something better.

Maara came back and knelt down in front of me.

"You once told me that every warrior's heart is different," she said. "I never thought of it before, but you showed me that it is a warrior's heart that matters, more than her size or the weapon she carries."

Surely it was the power of the oak grove that had given me those words. I could never have thought of them myself.

"A woman with a warrior's heart shouldn't fear the truth," she said. "No weapon in the world is stronger than the truth."

I closed my eyes and tried to find the courage to face the truth about myself. I would have to let go of a dream I'd dreamed since childhood. For a little while grief filled my heart. I had no choice but to bear it. Then the pain subsided, and I put that dream away.

"It can't be done."

"Yes, it can." She was trying not to smile.

With all my strength I tried to bend the bow, so that I could slip the loop of the bowstring into its notch. It stubbornly refused to bend.

"Let me see it."

I handed Maara the bow. She placed one end on the ground and braced it against her foot. While I had been tugging hard on the other end, which only drove the bow straight down into the soft ground, she held it lightly, her fingers ready to guide the bowstring into place. With her other hand she grasped the belly of the bow and pulled. The bow bent, and the string slipped easily into its notch.

"Nothing about a bow is obvious," she said.

She unstrung it just as easily and handed it back to me.

I didn't succeed right away, but after struggling with it for a while, I was at last able to string the bow. She had me practice stringing and unstringing it until I was drenched with sweat and my arms trembled. Then she let me rest.

"That's all for today," she said.

"Oh."

I was disappointed. She knew why.

"You're not strong enough yet to draw a bow like this," she said. "When you can string it without effort, you'll be ready to learn to draw it."

"If I were strong enough to draw a bow, wouldn't I be strong enough to wield a sword?"

"A bow takes a different kind of strength," she said. "To wield a sword, you must have the strength to lift it and to strike with it. Once you've drawn a bow, you must hold it drawn while you take all the time you need to find your aim. I've seen many who had no trouble wielding a sword in battle shake like an aspen in the wind after they had held a drawn bow for only a short time."

Day after day I practiced stringing the heavy bow. After several weeks went by, it did seem to be getting easier. Maara found a lighter bow for me in the armory, and after I had strung and unstrung the heavy one until my arms were limp, she let me try drawing the lighter one. She had me hold the drawn bow as she circled around me, adjusting the placement of a foot or the angle of an elbow until she was satisfied.

I was impatient. If I was going to become an archer, I wanted to get on with it. Every day the other apprentices practiced with sword and shield. I watched them enviously, wanting to believe that someday my skill would be a match for theirs, though mine was a different weapon.

The day came at last when my warrior met me on the practice ground carrying a few arrows in her hand. She saw my eagerness and smiled.

"Let's go down the hill a little way," she said. "We don't want to hurt anyone."

She found a place where I could shoot the arrows into the side of the hill. I was more than ready to begin, but she sat down in the grass and patted the ground beside her. I resigned myself to waiting a little longer and sat down.

"Look," she said, showing me the fletching of one of the arrows. "Like the feathers of a bird's wing, these feathers control the arrow's flight. They are as delicate as a bird's wing, and you must be careful of them."

She showed me how to hold several arrows loosely in my hand so that the fletching of each arrow didn't rub against the others. Then she showed me that by putting a finger between each shaft I could hold them more tightly and still keep the arrows separated from one another. She sighted down the shaft of each arrow. None of them was perfectly straight, and she explained that each would fly a bit differently. At last she stood up.

"I don't want you to try aiming at anything yet," she said. "Just shoot the arrow and watch its flight."

She handed me the light bow and watched me string it. Then she handed me an arrow and showed me how to lay the bow flat to nock it, how to align it in the bow, how to set the tips of my fingers against the bowstring. When I turned the bow upright, the arrow fell away from the bow and dropped at my feet.

After several tries I could keep the arrow more or less in place while I drew the bow. Maara had me hold the bow drawn while she examined my stance. I resisted the urge to find something to shoot at.

"Straighten your fingers," she said.

I did, and the arrow tumbled out of the bow and hit the ground a few feet in front of me.

"Good," she said. "Try again."

I couldn't believe how difficult it was. There were so many things to remember all at once. Draw the string with the fleshy part of the fingertips, not at the joint. Hold the bow upright. Don't let it tip to the left, or the arrow will fall away from the bow. Don't let it tip to the right either, or the arrow won't fly true. Let the hand that grips the bow support the tip of the arrow without restricting its flight. Keep the elbows down, head up, back straight, feet well apart.

By the time Maara took me home, my shoulders ached. My fingertips burned from the bowstring brushing over them. The inside of the arm that held the bow was red and sore where the bowstring sometimes struck it. Worst of all I had succeeded only in sending arrow after arrow in every direction but where I wanted them to go.

Maara saw that I was discouraged.

"You're doing well," she said.

I didn't believe her.

29

THE WILLOW TREE

One day, when Namet invited Maara to spend the afternoon with her, I thought I would pass the time by watching the other apprentices sparring on the practice ground. I found Sparrow and Taia there, using wooden swords and wicker shields. They were well matched. Taia was a head taller than Sparrow and had a longer reach, but Sparrow was more agile, and much more skillful.

While Sparrow was clearly enjoying herself, Taia appeared to be half-hearted. She didn't seem to mind that time after time Sparrow's sword found its way past her guard. At last she tossed her sword and shield aside and wiped the sweat from her brow with the tail of her shirt.

"Shall we try with real swords?" Sparrow asked her.

Taia shook her head. "It's too hot," she said, and went to join a few of the other girls, who were resting in the shadow of the earthworks.

Sparrow turned to me. "Will you practice with me?"

"I can't," I said.

"Why not?"

"My warrior doesn't want me to practice with a sword."

Sparrow knew, of course, that I had been learning the bow, but I hadn't yet told her what Maara had said, that I would never be strong enough to fight with sword and shield. I was ashamed to admit that to anyone.

"Let's go for a walk then," she said.

We went down to the river. Sparrow undressed and waded into the water, to wash off the sweat and dust of the practice ground. Then she joined
me on the riverbank. The cold water had made her nipples shrivel up, and
I thought briefly about taking one of them into my mouth.

"What does your warrior think she's doing?" Sparrow asked me.

I knew what she meant, but I didn't know how to answer her.

"She's putting you at a disadvantage," Sparrow said. "Whether you're
any good with a sword or not, you must carry one if you're going to be a
warrior."

"Maara doesn't think so," I replied. "She wants me to have a weapon I
can use."

Sparrow sighed. "What does the Lady say?"

"She hasn't said anything to me."

"She will."

As much as I had protested Maara's decision, I found myself defending it
as if it were my own. "It is Maara who is under an obligation to teach me.
She'll teach me what seems best to her, and the Lady should have nothing
to say about it."

Sparrow pursed her lips, but she held her tongue. She knew better than
to remind me that Maara wasn't one of us, although I knew that was just
what she was thinking.

"I'm not saying you shouldn't learn the bow," she said. "We all train with
the bow a little. But why not learn to use a sword as well?"

"Maara says I'll never be strong enough to wield a sword," I admitted at
last. "She's right. I'll always be too small."

"Listen," Sparrow said. "Small has nothing to do with it. You saw Taia
just now. She's the tallest woman in Merin's house and as strong as an ox,
but she has no skill with a sword. She doesn't work at it. She doesn't have
to. She'll never be called upon to carry a sword into battle herself. Next
year she'll go home with her sword and shield and hang them on the wall
and be done with them."

"Taia will never go into battle?"

"Taia is the first daughter of her house," said Sparrow. "She'll wear a sword
like the Lady does, as a symbol of her authority, but I doubt she'll have to
use it any more than the Lady has used hers."

"But the Lady fought in the war."

"Who told you that?"

No one had told me in so many words. "My mother sometimes talked about the war. She said that the Lady, young as she was, commanded warriors twice her age."

"Yes," Sparrow said. "She commanded them, but how could she have commanded them if she had been in the melee alongside them? She would have stayed where she could watch the battle, and her guard would have protected her."

How was it that I knew so little of war when my own mother had been in the midst of it? By the time she earned her shield, the fighting was over, but she must have known the things that Sparrow was now telling me. The more I thought about it, the more I realized that my mother spoke very little about what had happened to her during the war. She had told me how terrible it was and how afraid she'd been, both for herself and for those she loved. She had shared her grief with me, but she had never told me about the things she'd seen and done and seen others do.

"How did you learn so much about the war?" I asked Sparrow.

"Eramet told me. She heard the stories from her mother and from Vintel."

"How would Vintel know about the war?"

"Vintel was here. She spent her childhood here. She was young then, but she must have been aware of what was going on."

"Oh." I lay back in the grass. "I have so much to learn."

"So have we all."

I looked up at her, and the curve of her breast caught my eye.

"You can touch me if you like," she said.

I blushed, embarrassed that she had understood what I wanted before I was aware of it myself. She took my hand in hers and held it against her breast. I forgot my embarrassment. I supported the soft weight of her breast in the palm of my hand and brushed my thumb over her nipple, to watch it shrivel up again. She closed her eyes. Her face showed me the pleasure my touch gave her, and seeing it gave me pleasure too.

She opened her eyes and caught me watching her. She smiled at me, then stood up and held out her hand. I took it, and she pulled me to my feet. When she started to undress me, I tried to help her, but she stopped my hands and made me stand still, as if I were a child.

Sparrow led me naked into the river and began to bathe me. Her hands slipped over my skin with a light and teasing touch. She caressed my breasts, and I felt my nipples harden. She drew her fingertips down my spine, over my hips and belly, and through the curls between my legs. Then I felt a more intimate touch.

"What are you doing?"

She was the image of innocence. "I'm giving you a bath."

I laughed and let her do as she pleased. After a little while she embraced me and whispered in my ear, "Come with me." Then she lay back and let the current take her.

We splashed ashore not far away, where the branches of a willow tree trailed their leafy fingers in the water. Sparrow pulled the branches aside. There was just room enough for the two of us to lie together under the tree. The ground was soft with moss, and the drooping branches hung like a curtain about our own private bower.

Sparrow lay down and would have pulled me down beside her, but I resisted her. I sat beside her and gazed down at her body. I found it beautiful in a way I didn't understand. Beauty, I thought, is for the eye, but the beauty of Sparrow's body demanded to be touched. Her beauty demanded to be held and kissed and changed by my caress into something yet more beautiful.

My fingers traced the line of her collarbone. She shivered, and I thought I'd tickled her, but when I glanced at her face, I saw that my touch had pleased her. I let my hand explore the hollow of her throat, the curve of her shoulder, the roundness of her breast and belly, the softness of the skin on the inside of her thigh. All the while she lay still, her eyes closed, her mouth half-open. Sometimes a certain kind of touch made her catch her breath or caused her body to move in a way that showed me the pleasure she felt.

I lay down beside her and propped myself up on one elbow so that I could continue to caress her.

"Show me how you like to be touched," I said.

She reached up and took my face in her hand. "Kiss me."

When I bent down to kiss her, she pulled away from me a little.

"Lightly," she said. Her lips brushed mine, then retreated. "More than anything, I like to be kissed."

"Why?"

"A kiss will always tell you how someone really feels about you."

She kissed me again, and I thought I understood what she meant.

She took my hand and guided it to her breast.

"Show me," I said.

She smiled. "I will."

And her body did show me. By the way she moved and by the sounds she made, I discovered what gave her pleasure. I found the places where her body was most sensitive. I kissed her throat and felt her pulse quicken under my lips. I took a nipple into my mouth and felt it change.

Her skin grew warm. She took my hand, and I thought she would put it between her legs, but she had me touch her everywhere but there. She wanted me to stroke her belly and the insides of her thighs. Then she opened her legs for me.

I touched her lightly. Her body demanded more, but when I touched her more strongly, she put her hand over mine to stop me.

"Now you must stop listening to what my body asks of you," she breathed into my ear. "Make it last."

I caressed her more gently, and her body became less impatient. She moved in enjoyment of the pleasure I gave her. For a time it was enough. Then she put her arms around me and drew me into a close embrace. I felt her hips lift, and this time I didn't tease her. I gave her body what it asked of me, and her cries of pleasure echoed in my ears like music.

For a long time neither of us moved. I held her close, while my heart overflowed with tenderness. When I brushed her hair back so that I could kiss her brow, I saw that her face was wet with tears.

"What is it?" I asked her. "What's the matter?"

"Nothing's the matter." She brushed her tears away.

"Why are you crying?"

She snuggled into my arms. She didn't answer me.

Sparrow woke me with a kiss.

"Why did you let me fall asleep?" she said. "I wanted to take my time with you. Now it's almost too late."

I looked for the sun and saw that it would soon be time for supper. Maara would be wondering where I was, and no doubt Vintel would be looking for Sparrow.

"It is too late," I said. "We should get back."

When I started to get up, she pulled me back down beside her and rolled on top of me. She gave me a long kiss, and I forgot what time it was.

"Can you come here tomorrow?" she asked me.

"I don't know."

Sparrow grinned down at me. "I won't let you up until you tell me when you can spare a little time for me."

"Soon," I said.

She was satisfied with my answer. She kissed me again. Then she got up and dived through the willow branches into the river.

While we were getting dressed, I worried that we would be late for supper. Vintel would be angry, and the thought of Vintel's anger made me afraid for Sparrow. Would Vintel ask her where she'd been? Would she be unhappy with the answer? I looked up to find Sparrow watching me.

"What is it?" she asked.

Without stopping to think, I blurted out, "Does Vintel know?"

"Does Vintel know what?"

I didn't answer her. She knew what I meant.

"Whether she knows or not, it's none of her business."

"Vintel may not agree with you."

Sparrow finished tying the laces of her shirt. When she looked at me, her eyes revealed her anger and her disappointment. She turned away and started back to Merin's house.

I ran after her. "What's the matter?"

She stopped and turned to face me. "If you're afraid of Vintel, then you had better stay away from me."

The anger in her voice hurt me more than her words. "How little you must know me if you think that Vintel could frighten me away from you."

"Then why do you care what Vintel knows?"

"Because I'm afraid for you. I'm afraid she'll be angry with you. I don't want to be the cause of trouble between you and Vintel, and I don't want you to be sent home."

The anger left her eyes. I was about to tell her that if spending time with me was dangerous for her, I would understand and be glad for whatever she could give me, but she spoke first.

"I don't know what Vintel would think," she said, "but I doubt she'd be glad to give me the afternoon off whenever I wanted to spend some time with you." She gave me a wry smile. "I ought to be more careful, I suppose. I'll try. But I won't let anyone, not even Vintel, tell me what I can or cannot do with my own body. Or with my heart. Never again. Even if Vintel breaks my apprenticeship and they send me home. Do you understand?"

I nodded. I admired her courage, but at the same time it frightened me.

"Let us both be careful, then," I told her, "and perhaps the world will leave us alone."

But the world did not leave us alone. The next day Sparrow stole a moment to tell me she would have to spend the entire day, and most of the next few days as well, making preparations for a journey. In three days' time, on midsummer's day, Vintel intended to travel with a band of warriors who would be returning to Arnet's house. Eramet's people had not yet been told of her death, and Vintel wanted to bring the news to them herself. It would be a journey of several weeks. She intended to take Sparrow with her.

"We won't have much time together before I have to go," Sparrow said.

I nodded that I understood. I tried not to show my disappointment.

"What will it be like for you to go back there?"

Sparrow shrugged. "I didn't expect to see Arnet's house again until I returned with Eramet. I don't much like the idea, but perhaps I'll find my mother there. I hardly knew how much I missed her until I thought I might see her again."

"Why would you doubt that she'd be there?"

"One never knows what may happen to a slave. I don't even know if she's still living."

A hard knot of anger formed deep in my belly. If my mother were to die, someone would be sent to tell me, so that I could go home and say my farewells to her before her spirit traveled beyond the sound of our tears.

"May you find her in health and power," I said.

Sparrow smiled at the familiar words of the ancient blessing.

"Health I may hope for. Power I never will."

"She will find her power in you," I told her.

30

MIDSUMMER'S DAY

On the morning of midsummer's day I woke early. Sparrow lay at my back, her arm around my waist. I kept still, waiting for her to wake. More than anything I would miss this closeness to her. I smiled to myself, remembering how impatient I had been with my mother when she would approach me silently from behind and slip her arms around me. As much as I needed to free myself from her embrace, I missed the comfort of being in her arms. I relaxed against Sparrow's body and opened my heart to her, to draw this sweet feeling into me against the time when she would be far away.

Sparrow's arm tightened around me, and her lips brushed the back of my neck.

"I have to get up," she said.

"I know." I turned in her arms. "I'll miss you."

Sparrow reached for something that lay hidden beneath her pillow.

"Maybe this will keep you from forgetting about me while I'm gone," she said, and handed me something wrapped in a ragged shirt.

I sat up and unwrapped her gift. It was a bit of soft leather with a thicker piece sewn onto it and a few thongs that I thought must be meant to tie it to something, but I couldn't imagine a use for it. Sparrow took it from me. She held it against the inside of my left forearm and tied it in place.

"This will keep that bow of yours from taking the skin off," she said.

Once she saw that I understood its use, she started to untie it. I stopped her and pulled my shirtsleeve down to cover it.

"Let me wear it a while."

She smiled with pleasure.

"Your gift is in the kitchen," I said.

I took Sparrow into the cool pantry where meat and milk were kept. There I found the package I had made up for her the night before. Sparrow unwrapped it to discover a loaf of the sweet honey bread I knew she loved, a thick slab of cheese, hard and fragrant with age, and some dried fruit. One of the kitchen servants had baked the bread for me in exchange for three rabbit skins. The cheese and the fruit were an afterthought.

"For your journey," I told her.

She was as pleased with my simple offering as if it had been a feast.

We hardly had time to exchange a few words of farewell before we heard Vintel and the others of their party clatter down the stairs. After a quick breakfast, they started on their journey, and I watched them out of sight.

Midsummer's day was not a holiday in Merin's house. The elders withdrew from the household to conduct the ritual of the longest day, but for the rest of us a bustle of activity marked the turning of the year. The warriors who had completed their time of service to the Lady would leave for home, as well as many of the young women whom the Lady had fostered. Others, like Vintel, would travel with them to visit the households of friends. By early afternoon all the travelers had left. The house felt empty.

Maara found me sitting in the shadow of the earthworks by the practice ground. I had gone there hoping to find someone to keep me company, but the field was deserted.

"We shouldn't waste the day," she said.

She took me by surprise. My mind was far away, thinking sad thoughts and missing Sparrow and my other friends who had left the household. All around me were the empty places where they should have been, at the companions' table, in the bower, here on the practice ground.

"What's the matter?" Maara asked me.

I shook the lonely thoughts out of my head. "Nothing."

"Come on, then."

She started down the hill. Then I noticed that she was carrying my bow and a handful of arrows. She had brought only the heavy bow. After I had strung it, she handed me an arrow. It was different from the arrows I had used before. The fletching was small and tight. It had a small stone tip, and the thick shaft was almost perfectly straight.

It took all my strength to draw the heavy bow. I drew it as she had taught me, with a steady pull until my thumb brushed the hinge of my jaw. I couldn't have held that position for more than a moment. As soon as I had the bow fully drawn she said, "Let go." The arrow flew straight and true and buried itself half its length in the sun-baked earth of the hillside.

I could hardly believe what I had done. Although I practiced with the light bow every day, sometimes for hours, I had never before done everything exactly right. This time was different, and my body knew it. For the first time everything had been in the right place. Elbows, shoulders, feet, all had been perfect. A surge of excitement went through me, and my body hummed with pleasure at what it had just accomplished.

Maara was as pleased with me as I was with myself, but when I reached for another arrow, she shook her head.

"That's enough for today," she said.

"Why?"

"Let your body remember what perfection felt like."

She reached for the bow, and I unstrung it and handed it back to her. Then I pulled up my sleeve and started to untie the thongs of the leather guard.

"What's this?" She took hold of my wrist and examined the guard.

"Is it all right for me to wear it?"

"Of course," she said. "It's a very good idea."

"Sparrow gave it to me this morning, for midsummer's day."

"For midsummer's day?"

"Midsummer's day is a gift-giving day."

"There are special days for giving gifts?"

"Yes," I said. "The days when the year turns, at midsummer and midwinter, are gift-giving days. Year days too, at least for children."

"What are year days?"

"When a child starts another year of life," I said, "each member of her family gives her a gift."

"And on midsummer's day? Do members of a family exchange gifts on midsummer's day?"

I nodded.

"Then I should have a gift for Namet."

I was surprised that Namet hadn't given Maara her gift already. Then I remembered that Namet would have been with the elders in the place of ritual since before dawn, and she might not emerge until late that evening.

"What does one give to one's mother?" Maara asked me.

When I was small, I used to pick my mother a bouquet of flowers or give her something I had made myself. One year I gave her a lumpy sheep made of clay. Another time I wove a scarf for her that unraveled a bit every time she wore it. When I was bigger, I more often did things for her to make her day a little easier.

I couldn't think of anything for Maara to give to Namet. Maara had so little, and everything she owned she needed.

"Well," I said, "the reason for gift-giving is to let someone know you care for her, and if you care for someone, you pay attention to the things she likes. What does Namet like?"

Maara considered that for a minute.

"She likes the night sky," she said.

"The night sky?"

"Her room has no window. Several times she's come into my room in the middle of the night. When I asked her why, she told me she liked to look at the night sky."

I remembered how my mother used to come into my room when she thought I was asleep. She would watch by my bed for a little while before she tucked my blankets around me and kissed me good night.

"I doubt it's the night sky she comes to see," I said.

"What do you mean?"

"She comes to see if you're all right. It's something mothers do."

"Oh," she whispered.

I smiled at her. "What else does Namet like?"

"I can't think of anything else."

"Well," I said, "you'll think of something, but it will pop into your head when you're not trying to think of something."

She chuckled. "You're probably right."

While she went to retrieve the arrow I'd shot, I tried to come up with something for us to do that would keep us outdoors a while. I was in no hurry to return to Merin's house. It felt too empty.

"We could go swimming," I suggested when she returned.

"All right," she said.

After our swim we lay in the sun on the riverbank until we were dry enough to put our clothes on. Once we were dressed, Maara was content to stay where we were. She sat cross-legged in the grass, gazing off into the distance, lost in her own thoughts. I lay on my stomach and watched the river go by.

At last Maara broke the silence. "I have a gift for you," she said.

I turned to her, surprised. "You do?"

"A very small thing," she said. "But it's a gift you gave to me, in a way, and I want to share it with you."

I didn't understand. I had never given her a gift. And what gift could she have for me? Only an hour before she had never heard of our custom of gift-giving on midsummer's day.

"When Namet took me into the place of ritual," Maara said, "she made me a child again. She has a power in her eyes. When she looked at me, she saw the child, and I became the child."

I nodded that I understood. I too had felt the power of Namet's eyes.

"She touched me as a mother touches her child, and I understood that it was Namet, but at the same time there seemed to be another pair of hands that I remembered. Namet put her arms around me, and there was also another pair of arms. I felt her heartbeat and remembered the beating of another heart. She brought back to me the mother who gave me birth at the same time that she became my mother."

While Maara spoke, I kept very still. I had forgotten all about the gift she'd promised me. It was gift enough that she would share these things with me.

"For a long time," she said, "there were two women with me, and I was in two different places, and I was both a child and a woman. The child heard strange words she understood and smelled food cooking on the hearth and waited to be called to supper. She ate her fill and was put to bed, and her mother's voice lulled her to sleep. Her mother told the child a story that the woman remembers."

Deep in the heart of the forest, a little man lives. You may see the feather in his hat sticking out from behind the trunk of a forest oak, but if you look behind the tree he will be gone. You may hear him call his dogs to the hunt, and you may hear the voices of the pack baying in the night, but they will run past you unseen like the wind. You may wake in your own bed in the middle of the night to hear the softest footfall, and in the morning you may find a single leaf lying on your new-swept floor.

Deep in the heart of the forest, a little man lives. Ask him his name. He has none. Offer him bread. He eats none. Pour him good ale from the pantry keg. He will pour it out upon the floor. Water from the spring he drinks, and on his table you will find venison and quail. He lives in a house of twigs, the gift of trees that never knew the ax. He lives in a house of grass that never knew the scythe. He lives in dens dug by badgers under the roots of trees. He lives in the open air.

Deep in the heart of the forest, a little man lives. Go out singing to sow a field, and from the hedgerow you will hear him sing. Go out dancing to tend your flock, and you will see his shadow dancing by your side. Go out into the rain, and where the water pools, gaze at his reflection gazing back at you. Deep in the heart, a little man lives.

Maara looked at me. I met her eyes. They asked me if I would accept her gift. I couldn't answer her. I could find no words that wouldn't break the spell.

"I wish I had a better gift for you," she whispered.

When I opened my mouth to speak, she silenced me with a wave of her hand.

"When you found me in the oak grove," she said, "I know you were afraid. You could have told the Lady what you saw, and she would have broken the tie between us and set you free if you had wanted it. Instead you brought me Namet, and Namet brought my mother back to me, and my mother gave me back that story. It's just a small thing, but it's all I have of my own."

"I wish I had a better gift for you too," I told her, "but this is all I have."

And I took her hand in both of mine and kissed it.

We walked back to Merin's house in silence. I was still wrapped in the power of her gift. Someday I would tell her how beautiful it was, but at that moment no words of mine could be enough.

When we'd had our supper, Maara sent me off to bed. She waited up for Namet.

After Sparrow left that morning, I moved my bed from the bower back into the companions' loft, and I lay where I could watch Maara sitting alone by the cold hearth in the great hall. She'd had no time to find a gift for Namet, but if she had thought of anything like the gift she'd given me, Namet would be delighted.

I fell into a heavy sleep. I may have slept for an hour or more. When I woke, the last of the long twilight was fading. Maara was still sitting by the hearth. I was about to close my eyes again when she stood up, and I saw Namet approach her.

They spoke a few words to each other. Although the murmur of their voices reached me, I couldn't hear what they said. Namet took something from around her neck, a token of some kind, and placed it around Maara's neck, and Maara took it in her hand and admired it. Namet turned to go, but Maara reached for Namet's hand, took it in both of hers, and brought it to her lips. When she let it go, Namet stood quite still for a moment. Then she took Maara into her arms.

THE LADY

When I thought about how Maara and I had spent our first summer in Merin's house, I wished that we could be as carefree now as we'd been then, though of course only I had been truly free of care. This year I had new responsibilities.

It was the task of the apprentices to teach the new girls their duties as companions. I tried to be both as kind and as demanding with them as Sparrow had been with me. Although they could be exasperating, I enjoyed teaching them. In them I saw myself as I had been the year before, and it reassured me to see how far I had come since then.

I spent time with the other apprentices too, mindful of the Lady's charge to find new friends among them.

I also spent many hours practicing with the bow. I never again that summer made a shot as perfect as the one I made on midsummer's day, but I was steadily improving, and each day I grew stronger.

I was beginning to come to terms with the choice Maara had made for me. Perhaps I finally saw the wisdom in it. While I could never have held my own against even as poor a swordswoman as Taia was, I believed that I might become as skillful with the bow as any archer in Merin's house. I hoped in secret that someday I would surpass them all.

As Sparrow said she would, the Lady found an opportunity to speak to me. She chose a day when I went out alone to practice with the bow. Maara had set stakes into the ground all over the hillside, to teach me to judge distance. When I made a shot that sank into the ground inches from one of the stakes, I heard a voice behind me.

"Well done," it said.

I turned to see the Lady standing there.

"Are you making progress?"

"I think so."

"Good."

Her eyes wandered over the hillside, taking in the broken ground around the stakes, as well as the evidence of many arrows that had gone astray. It must have been obvious to her how much time I spent there.

When she had finished her examination of the place, she turned back to me and said, "Come sit with me a while."

I walked with her up the hill. We took shelter from the sun in the shadow of the earthworks.

"So your warrior is an archer too," she said.

Although I had never seen Maara draw a bow, she must be a fine archer, or she couldn't have taught me so well.

"Yes," I said.

The Lady watched her hands as she carefully smoothed the wrinkles from the skirt of her gown. "Someone has mentioned to me," she said, "that your warrior has forbidden you to touch a sword."

"No," I said. "That's not true."

"Have I been misinformed?"

"Forbidden is too strong a word."

"So she intends to teach you the sword as well?"

Then I had to admit that Maara intended to do no such thing.

The Lady looked puzzled. "Why not?"

"I believe it's her opinion that I shouldn't waste my time on a weapon I can never master."

"Master?" she said. "What does mastery have to do with war?"

I didn't understand her question, but the Lady wasn't waiting for an answer. She gazed past me into the distance with such a look of concentration on her face that I almost glanced over my shoulder to see what she was looking at.

"When I first set foot upon the battlefield," she said, "I was not much older than you are now, but I was the daughter of my house, and it was my responsibility to lead our warriors into battle. How could I shelter safe inside the walls while others died?"

The Lady gazed up at the earthworks and the palisades that crowned the hilltop. "My mother's archers stood on the walls and rained arrows down upon the enemy. They did a lot of damage, but in the end it was the courage of our warriors who went out and fought them hand to hand that won the day for us."

She had put into my mind a picture of the battlefield. I saw the archers on the walls and the warriors on the ground advancing on the enemy behind a wall of painted shields. I remembered how my mother had described the din of battle — the war cries and screams of pain, the clash of sword on shield, the shouting, the confusion, the roaring in the ears that comes from fear. I imagined myself there. Would I be the archer on the wall who after the battle is joined can be of no further use, but must watch her friends fight the enemy face to face and hand to hand?

The Lady turned her eyes to me again. "Your warrior may not know what will be expected of you when you inherit your mother's place," she said. "You too will have warriors to command someday. What will you do then?"

I had no answer for her.

The Lady leaned toward me. Her eyes held mine. "I believe you still covet your mother's sword."

I looked away before she could read the answer in my eyes, but she knew what was in my mind.

"If you like," she said, "I will speak to your warrior on your behalf. Perhaps I can make her see that when your mother's sword comes to you, it would be well if you could use it."

For a moment I was tempted. Vivid in my memory was the day my mother claimed that sword. For nine days, while we mourned her death, my grandmother's place remained empty. On the tenth day, my mother took her mother's sword down from the wall. Then she took her mother's place at the head of the table, and by doing so unchallenged, she took the place of leadership. It seemed as if I were remembering myself taking the sword from the wall, as if I were remembering the future.

But an unseen force was pulling me in another direction. As much as I wanted to be worthy to inherit the weapon that was the symbol of my house, something new had begun to stir in me. Every time I had taken up a sword, I felt a sense of hopelessness, but the bow had given me hope, and it was my warrior who had given me the bow. Allowing the Lady to question Maara's decision on my behalf would be a mistake. It would be a betrayal of the trust between us.

"I need no one to speak for me," I told the Lady. "I can speak to her myself."

"Certainly you can, but will you speak to her of this? Somehow I doubt that you will."

"There's no need," I said. "She and I have spoken already, and I'm satisfied that she has made the right decision."

"You're as stubborn as your mother."

The Lady's voice was light, but her eyes flashed dark and angry.

My own anger loosened my tongue. "If I were apprenticed to any other warrior here, would you question how she was teaching me?"

"And impudent as well," the Lady said, "which your mother never was."

"I mean no disrespect, but it's Maara's place to decide these things for me, and if there are things she doesn't understand about our ways, it is her mother's place to teach her."

The Lady was silent for a long time. She kept her eyes on mine. They made me uncomfortable, but I refused to be the first to look away.

"I will admit that Namet surprised me," the Lady said at last. "She sees something in your warrior that others have missed. She seems to share your high opinion of her. I've known Namet almost all my life. I respect her, and I must take seriously her opinion."

The Lady looked away from me and frowned. "I hesitate to say this to you," she said, "but you're no longer a child, and you have an understanding beyond your years. Namet is wise. This house depends upon her wisdom. She is also powerful, and I trust her power to see and understand things that I cannot. But you should also be aware that she can be as blind as anyone to the faults of those she loves."

As are all mothers blind to their children's faults, I thought to myself.

"Will we see your mother in the spring?" the Lady said.

She had changed the subject so abruptly that it took me a moment to understand what she was asking me.

"Next spring my sister will come of age," I told her. "If nothing prevents her, my mother will bring her here."

"I'm looking forward to seeing her again," the Lady said. "Aren't you?"

I nodded, but to be truthful, I hadn't thought much about it. While I'd had a moment of missing her when Sparrow spoke about seeing her own mother, another part of me was apprehensive. I had grown up so much since I had been in Merin's house. I was afraid my mother's presence might make me feel like a child again.

"Your mother will be looking forward to seeing what her daughter has achieved since she saw her last," the Lady said.

Before I understood her meaning, she got to her feet. "I know you doubt my good intentions, but I want what's best for you. I want your mother to be pleased when she sees what you've accomplished here. I want her to be pleased with you, and I want her to be pleased with me for the care I've taken of you. Your warrior may still have enemies here, but I am not one of them, nor am I your enemy. I wish you would believe that and have a little trust in me."

And she turned on her heel and left me there.

I spent the rest of the afternoon by myself, trying to understand my feelings. The Lady's last words to me had left me feeling guilty, but I didn't know what I was guilty of. I had done nothing more than affirm my right to choose my own teacher. While I had been angry, I didn't think I had been disrespectful. I still believed it was the Lady who had been disrespectful, both of me and of my warrior, but for some reason I didn't understand, I had wanted to run after her and tell her I was sorry.

That evening after supper I asked Maara to go for a walk with me.

"What happened?" she said, when we were on our way down the hill and out of earshot of the others who were enjoying an evening stroll.

"The Lady spoke to me today," I told her.

Maara nodded. She didn't seem surprised.

"She offered to speak with you on my behalf," I said. "She objects to the way you're teaching me."

"What does she object to?"

"Someone told her you'd forbidden me to touch a sword."

"Someone?"

I hadn't stopped to wonder who had spoken to the Lady about me.

"She didn't tell me who, and I didn't think to ask."

"Just as well you didn't," Maara said. "She wouldn't have told you."

"The Lady has no right to interfere with the way you're teaching me."

"No, but she must have her reasons, and I'd like to know what they are."

I thought about it for a minute. "She said she didn't want my mother to be displeased."

"Your mother's displeasure shouldn't concern the Lady. You became Merin's responsibility when your mother chose to foster you here."

"My mother and the Lady are shield friends," I said. "They trained together here when they were young, and they have been fast friends ever since."

"I see."

We had reached the river, and we sat down on the riverbank. Maara slipped her boots off, rolled up her trouser legs, and dangled her feet in the water. I sat cross-legged beside her.

"Tell me everything," she said. "Tell me everything you can remember of what the Lady said to you."

I told her everything but one. I left out what the Lady had said about Namet. It felt wrong to me to say such a thing to someone Namet loved.

When I finished, Maara smiled at me. "So the Lady offered you your heart's desire."

"She offered me what I thought I wanted, but I must have changed my mind."

"Why?"

"I don't know."

"What if we give the Lady what she wants? Would you like to put away your bow and take up the sword again?"

My heart fell.

"Don't worry," she said gently. "I won't let anyone take that from you."

I didn't need to ask her what she meant. She wasn't talking about the bow. She was talking about hope.

"When I told you not to practice with the sword," Maara said, "it was because I wanted you to let go of it. I wanted you to give yourself every chance to feel the power that comes from having a true belief in yourself. It will take time, but mastery of the bow is something you can achieve. You believe that, don't you?"

I nodded.

"I might have convinced you with words alone, but I wanted you to come to this knowledge through your own experience. Now you understand, and now I think it will do no harm for you to practice swordplay with the others. In fact, in light of what the Lady said to you, I think it would be wise."

I wasn't so sure of that. It felt too much like giving in.

"Wouldn't that be admitting she's right?" I said.

"In a way, she is right."

"She is?"

"If your mother's sword will come to you someday, you should know how to use it."

Something else was bothering me. I couldn't put my finger on it. Maara waited in silence until I understood.

"Even if I do what she wants, she won't be satisfied."

"Very good," Maara said. "Now tell me why."

That knowledge may have been hiding somewhere at the back of my mind, but I couldn't put it into words.

"This wasn't about your choice of weapons, was it?" Maara said.

"No."

"What was it about?"

"It was about you and me."

Maara nodded and waited for me to go on.

"The Lady gave me what I wanted," I said, "but I don't think she means for me to keep it."

Once I had spoken that idea aloud, I suspected it was true.

"Why are you surprised?" Maara said. "You knew you'd acted against her wishes. Her wishes aren't just idle whims. She wanted to make your choice for you because she believed it was the wisest choice. You insisted on making what she believes to be a foolish one. I imagine she's waiting for you to see that you made a mistake."

The Lady was doing more than that.

"Today the Lady was trying to get me to make a mistake. And yet she tells me she's not my enemy."

"Why would you believe the Lady is your enemy?"

"If she's trying to take my choice away from me, how can I believe that she's my friend? It's my right to choose my teacher, whatever her opinion may be about it."

"But your welfare is her responsibility."

Tears of frustration stung my eyes. "Why are you taking her side?"

"I'm not," she said, "but I want you to see her side. I want you to understand why she does what she does."

"I think she doesn't like to lose," I said bitterly. "I think she wants everyone to do what she wants them to do. I think she's angry with me for choosing for myself."

"Do you truly believe the Lady is that petty?"

I didn't know what to believe.

"Tell me what you believe," I said.

"I believe it all," she replied. "I believe the Lady doesn't like to lose. I believe she wants to be obeyed. I believe she can be petty. And I believe she wants what's best for you. I believe she cares very much for your mother's good opinion. I believe it all."

"It can't all be true," I said.

"Perhaps it can. People may have many reasons for what they do."

I spoke my worst fear out loud. "What good reason could she have for wanting to break my apprenticeship to you?"

"I can think of many," Maara said. "She may fear that I will make you too different from the others. Your choice of weapon has already set you apart. So will other things. My experience has been different from hers and from the experience of the other warriors here. Because of that, I intend to teach you things they won't understand, but I would be wrong not to teach you those things, because I think they're important."

Maara leaned forward and gazed down into the river. I watched her face reflected in the moving water.

"And that's not all," she said. "The Lady may still mistrust me. She would be foolish to trust me as she trusts her own. For all she knows I may make off with you and go back to where I came from."

I laughed at that.

"Or she may think that you're going too much your own way. You have the right to choose your own way in life, but you also have responsibilities to others. She may worry that you've tipped the balance too far in one direction."

"She's wrong," I said. "And what she did today was wrong."

"No one does the wrong thing believing that it's wrong. The Lady believes that what she does is right and necessary."

"How can I show her she's mistaken?"

"You can't."

"Then there's nothing I can do?"

"You have a choice," she said. "You can oppose her. You can resist her at every turn. And if you do that, you'll make her believe all the more that what she fears is true, and she'll try all the harder to control you. And if you challenge her openly, she will defeat you, because she's much more powerful than you are."

Her words filled me with despair. "Are you saying that I must always give in to her?"

"No," she said. "But instead of making her your adversary, you can try to understand her. You can listen to her with respect, believing she has your best interests at heart. Think over what she says until you understand why she said it. Let her know you understand. Then do what seems right to you."

"There's only one thing wrong with doing that," I said.

"What's that?"

"What if she cares nothing for me, but only for having her own way?"

"Whether she's right or wrong, whether she means you well or ill, what have you to gain by treating her as your enemy? What have you to lose by treating her as your friend?"

It was almost dark. Maara picked up a handful of pebbles from the riverbank and began tossing them one by one into the river. I watched each one send circles of silver across the black surface of the water. I felt my anger fade.

"After the Lady left me today," I said, "I wanted to apologize to her, but I didn't know why."

"How do you feel about it now?"

"What would I say to her?"

Maara tossed the rest of the pebbles into the river, and the surface of the water sparkled as if she had cast into it a handful of stars.

"Do you remember when Vintel tried to take your brooch?"

"Of course I remember."

"You said you knew that giving it to her would appease her, but you couldn't do it, because your anger prevented you. Do you remember what

I told you then, that you were right to pay attention to your anger and that giving her the brooch would have been a sign of weakness to Vintel?"

I nodded.

"I also told you that sometimes making such a gesture could be a sign of strength. I think this is the time to make a gesture to the Lady, and I think that doing so will make you stronger."

The house was quiet when we got home. A light still burned in the Lady's chamber. Her door stood open. She was sitting by the window, looking out at the night. I waited in the doorway until she saw me.

"Come in," she said.

Her voice was cool and distant. She looked tired, and her dark eyes glittered in her pale face like the eyes of a hungry child.

"Sit down," she said.

I sat down on the edge of her bed.

"I owe you an apology," I said.

She raised her eyebrows in surprise.

"I spoke to you with disrespect today," I said. "I was angry with you, because I believed you disapproved of my teacher, but I thought over what you said to me, and I spoke to Maara about it. She agrees that I should take up the sword again, although she still expects me to master the bow."

The Lady hardly knew what to say to me. She sat looking at me for a while, then rose and came to sit beside me on the bed.

"What brought about this change of heart?" she asked.

"When you left me today," I said, "I wanted to run after you, to tell you I was sorry. I didn't understand why I felt that way. I had to take some time to think about it, but I didn't want this day to end before I'd made things right between us."

"I see. Does your warrior mind that I spoke with you about your training?"

"No, Lady. Not at all."

"And have you forgiven me for interfering?"

"I'm here to ask for your forgiveness, Lady."

"You have it if I have yours," she said. "Do I?"

I nodded.

Gently she took my hand. "I'm glad you came to see me. You've been in my thoughts all day." She clasped my hand between both of hers and held it tight. "I've been trying to understand how to end the estrangement between us."

It was my turn to be surprised.

"I've made mistakes with you," she said. "I realize that, and I've tried to make it up to you. I wish I could discover how. It seems that everything I do only increases your distrust of me."

I wanted to protest that I didn't distrust her, but it would have been a lie, so I kept silent.

"I see your mother in you," she said. "I see many of the things I loved in her, and I also see her stubbornness and her pride and her insistence that she was always right." The Lady smiled at some private memory. "I have loved you for your mother's sake, but perhaps I was mistaken to look for so much of her in you, because you are your own person. I should have spent more time learning to know you, not as your mother's daughter, but as yourself."

More than her words, her eyes persuaded me. Instead of the keen look I was used to, the look she gave me was soft and questioning.

"Is it too late?" she asked.

I didn't know how to answer her. Although I was unsure of what she wanted, for the first time I felt that she was not trying to put into my heart the feelings that would suit her purposes. She was asking me an honest question.

Before I could think of a reply, she spoke again. "I wish I had told you long ago that many of the things I admire in you have nothing to do with my regard for your mother, but I said nothing, because much of what I admire has also been a source of pain to me."

"I don't understand," I said.

"For one thing," she said, "I admire your loyalty. I see your loyalty to Maara, and I envy her, because I wish you could be as loyal to me. I also admire your ability to see the good in others. That's something I can seldom afford to do, because for the safety of us all I must be looking for their darker side. If I miss the good in someone, no harm is done, but if I fail to see the evil, it may someday overwhelm us."

I put that idea away to ponder later. I wasn't certain I agreed with her.

"It's late," she said, "and I'm very tired. I've probably said too much, but it means a great deal to me that you came to see me tonight."

"I'm glad I did," I told her.

I had never felt toward her as I did then. The truth was in her voice and in her eyes. Ever since she had shown me her own darker side, whenever I was with her a part of myself would stand aside and watch, waiting for her to reveal herself. This time I knew it wasn't necessary.

"Do you believe I care for you?" the Lady asked me.

"Yes," I said, and at that moment I did believe it.

"We made a bad start, you and I. I would like it if we could wipe out the past and start again, from this moment. Do you think we can?"

"We already have," I said.

The Lady gave me a tender smile and gazed into my eyes. It seemed that her eyes were open windows, and I looked into them and saw the one who dwelt within the house. Then the Lady stood up and went to stand at the window, to gaze out at the night.

"Look," she said.

I rose and went to stand beside her. The window was barely wide enough for the two of us to stand side by side. The Lady clutched the windowsill with both hands. She looked like a child who keeps watch, awaiting the homecoming of someone she loves.

I didn't know what she wanted me to look at. There was no moon, and clouds hid the stars. My eyes refused to see anything but vague shapes. They soon gave up the effort and saw only the velvet softness of the dark. The smell of rain lingered in the air.

"The night is full of ghosts," she said.

I saw nothing that she might have mistaken for a ghost, but as I stood beside her, with my shoulder against hers, I felt envelop me a wave of sadness that brought tears into my eyes. It took a few moments for me to understand that this sadness wasn't mine, but hers. It flowed from her body like blood from a dreadful wound, and soon I was awash in it. Deep in my breast I felt my heart break.

Late as it was, I knew I wouldn't sleep, and I didn't want to go alone to the companions' loft. If Sparrow had been there I would have taken refuge in her arms. Instead I went to Maara's room, hoping she was still awake. I found her sitting up in bed. Namet was with her, sitting just as my mother had sat on the edge of my bed when she came to tuck me in at night. When I came into the room, Namet got up.

"I'm sorry, Mother," I said. "I didn't mean to interrupt."

"Nonsense," said Namet. "It's long past my bedtime. Maara has been worried about you. Sit down and set her mind to rest."

She turned back to Maara, bent over her, and kissed her brow. Even in the lamplight, I saw the color come into Maara's cheeks. Namet turned to me and pretended to whisper, though she spoke loud enough for Maara to overhear.

"Eramet wouldn't let me kiss her good night after the age of twelve," she said, "but don't tell Maara that."

That made me smile, but at the same time I couldn't keep a tear from rolling down my cheek. It was impossible to hide anything from Namet's sharp eyes. She took my chin in her hand and turned my face to the light.

"What is it, child?" she said.

I couldn't speak. The feeling that came over me when I stood beside the Lady had faded, but my heart still ached with it.

"Close your eyes," she said.

When I did, she set the palm of her hand against my breastbone. A warm glow began in the center of my chest. When she took her hand away, my heart felt lighter.

"We'll talk tomorrow," she said. Then she left us.

I sat down at the foot of Maara's bed. If she understood what Namet had done, she gave no sign of it.

"Did you make your peace with the Lady?" she asked me.

"I think so."

"Good," she said.

Another tear escaped and ran down my cheek. I turned away from the light and brushed it away. When I looked back at her, I saw Maara's eyes turn dark.

"Did Merin hurt you?"

"No," I replied. "I'm fine. I think I'm just tired."

My own words surprised me. I never hid anything from Maara. This time I wanted to think about what had happened before I spoke to anyone about it.

As if she'd heard my thoughts, Maara said, "Is there something you want to talk to me about?"

I shook my head. "Not tonight."

"All right." She hesitated. Then she said, "Just tell me if all is well between you and the Lady."

"The Lady and I have agreed to start over with each other," I said. "All is well."

Maara's body relaxed, as if she had been guarding herself against a blow she feared might fall. "That's all I need to know."

"Namet said you were worried."

"I shouldn't have been," she said. "I should have trusted that you would make the right gesture."

"My mother should have trusted me to climb trees, but she never did."

Maara laughed. "I'm glad you understand. Now go to bed. Tomorrow you and I are going with Namet to a special place."

A ripple of excitement went through me. Of course I badgered her to tell me where we were going, and of course she only smiled and said, "You'll see." And at last, feeling much better, I went off to bed.

The Council Stones

We walked for half the morning, high up into the hills to the east of Merin's house. The higher we climbed, the more difficult the trail became. Maara led the way. I followed a few paces behind her. Namet followed me, and more than once I turned to give her a hand over a rough place only to find her right behind me.

When we left Merin's house at dawn, great black clouds filled the eastern sky, but Namet assured us that we would have fair weather, and by mid-morning the clouds had blown by.

Although we had eaten an enormous breakfast, I was soon hungry again, and I was anticipating the good things to eat that Namet had packed for our lunch—a joint of mutton, a wheel of cheese, sweet plums, and a whole loaf of bread, baked that morning. I sometimes caught a whiff of it that made my mouth water.

We had been following a cattle trail that wound through the hills. Then Maara left the trail and scrambled up a steep embankment. I followed her up the embankment and into a dense thicket where there was a faint, though overgrown, trail. People must have made it, because cattle would not have taken so difficult a way.

When we emerged from the thicket, we had only a short climb to the hilltop. We all stopped there to admire the view. The grass on the surrounding hillsides waved and billowed in the wind like an immense cloak shaken by an unseen hand.

"This way," said Namet, and she led us over the crest of the hill.

We were now facing north. Here the view was even more beautiful. Forest covered the hills to the northeast. In the distance I could just see, through a veil of mist, the mountains that guarded our eastern border. White clouds hung over them, bright against a deep blue sky.

I was too enchanted by the beauty all around me to watch where I was going, and my foot caught on something that sent me sprawling to the ground. I picked myself up and turned to see what had tripped me. It was a stone, hiding in the grass.

"Well done," said Namet. "Your foot has found the path."

I thought she was teasing me until I saw her face.

"Lead on," she said.

I had no idea what she meant. I looked again at the stone. Then I saw another a few feet away from it. Beyond that was another one. As my eyes followed them, they showed me the way. I followed the stones, and Namet and Maara followed me in single file.

The path led me in a circle around the hilltop until I passed the place where I began. Then I saw that we were treading a spiral path. When we started down it, the path had been invisible. As we trampled down the grass, the way revealed itself. Soon the grass would spring up again and all trace of it would vanish.

Then the path ended. As hard as I looked, I couldn't see where I might find the next stone.

"Now you must take your eyes off the ground," said Namet.

I looked up. From where I stood, through a narrow cleft in the hillside I saw a standing stone. A shiver ran down my backbone. I knew that Namet meant for me to approach the stone, but my feet felt rooted to the spot.

"Go on," said Namet, "before I starve to death."

I convinced my feet to move, but when I stood before the stone, I couldn't take another step. Namet slipped past me and laid her hand upon the stone in greeting. I half expected it to move aside to let us pass. Namet went past it on the left-hand side, and Maara and I followed her into the circle.

Although they are said to be quite common, I had only once before seen a circle of standing stones. I was a child then, and the stones were no taller than I was. The stones of this circle were smaller still. Except for the first one, which came up to my shoulder, the tallest stood not much above my knee.

"These are called the council stones," Namet told me, "because there are thirteen of them, as if they were placed here for the members of some council to sit on while they made their deliberations."

"Is that what they were used for?" I asked her.

"What do you think?"

"Why would anyone hold a council meeting out here?"

"I suspect no one would," said Namet.

"What were they for then?"

"That secret died with the people who set them here, but the stones most certainly have their uses. I've found a number of excellent uses for them."

"Like what?"

I expected her to tell me they were magical in some way. Instead she said, "It's a wonderful place for a picnic."

Namet found a smooth, sun-warmed stone to sit beside and unpacked our lunch. While we satisfied our hunger, no one spoke. Afterwards, we were too full to talk. Namet leaned back against the stone. Maara and I lay in the soft grass.

It was a perfect day. I closed my eyes. The sun warmed my body, and the cool breeze ruffled my hair. Comfortable and content with the two of them beside me, I felt we all belonged together in some special way. I was certain we would have found one another though worlds had separated us.

I might have dozed a little. I heard the murmur of voices. The three of us were talking about a journey we had made together. When I opened my eyes, Namet was talking about something else.

"I was living in my sister's house," said Namet. "I had just given birth to Eramet."

Maara saw that I was awake.

"Namet is telling us about the war," she said, and I sat up to listen.

"It started that same year," Namet said. "At first we didn't notice that anything was different, though the spring raids went on a bit longer than usual, and there were skirmishes in which people were badly wounded and sometimes killed. We killed their warriors too, but they sent more. No one understood how things were for them."

"Did their harvest fail?" I asked her.

"No," she said. "The year before everyone had had a wonderful harvest. Our granaries had never been so full. That's why it was so difficult to understand. It almost seemed they took pleasure in the fighting for its own sake.

It wasn't until two years later that we learned about the painted people, the strangers from across the sea."

A delicious shiver of fear went through me as I remembered the stories I'd heard about the painted people when I was small. Huddled on my mother's lap, safe in her arms, I had listened fascinated to the tales of people with painted bodies and animal faces who crept out of the forest when the moon was dark to do dreadful things. The painted people had gone back to where they came from and were no longer a threat to us, so they didn't really frighten me, but everything about them seemed dark and mysterious and strangely exciting.

All I said was, "I remember the stories."

Namet suddenly leaned forward so that her face was close to mine. "What do you remember?"

"Not much," I said. "I'd nearly forgotten about the painted people until you reminded me. My mother didn't like those stories. She hated the painted people for the suffering they caused. When I was older, she wouldn't let me listen to the stories anymore. Whenever someone would start to tell one, she would send me off to bed. That only made me more curious, and I slipped out of bed and hid in the shadows to listen."

"What did you hear?"

"In one of the stories the strangers came across the sea riding on the backs of fishes. In another they were shape-shifters. They turned themselves into fishes and swam across the sea."

"Have you ever seen the sea?"

I shook my head.

"I have."

She paused for a moment, remembering. Then she said, "What else?"

"They said that when our warriors found the remains of the strangers' camps, in the fire pits, along with the charred bones of animals, there were also human bones."

"I remember those things," Namet said. "But we're getting ahead of the story." She settled back against the stone. "It was some time before those of us in Arnet's house understood what was happening. We were protected by Merin's mother in the north and by our allies in the east. We never feared the fighting would reach us. Of course Arnet sent warriors here, as was her obligation, and they brought us back reports of the fighting.

"At first no one paid much attention. I paid even less. I cared little about fighting that was happening so far away. I had a husband I loved and our little child. I was too caught up in my own concerns to let the bad news trouble me, but the next year things grew worse. The raids went on all summer. Merin's mother asked for as many warriors as we could spare."

"Were they fighting the painted people?" I asked.

"Not then," she said. "I don't believe the painted people ever came close to Merin's house, but they had harried many of the northerners out of their own homes. The displaced tribes had no choice but to live as best they could in the wilderness. What they couldn't hunt or grow they stole from one another or from us. The strangest thing was that they were more careless of life, both ours and their own, than they had ever been before, possibly because of what they suffered at the hands of the painted people, but we knew nothing of the painted people then."

She paused for a moment, and a troubled look came into her eyes. "At the end of that summer, my husband came here to see for himself if things were as bad as we'd been told. He didn't return before the snow fell, and because of my young child, I couldn't try to join him here. The following spring, as soon as it was possible to travel, I left Eramet with my sister and came to find my husband."

As Namet spoke it seemed to me that her white hair had turned the honey gold it must once have been, the lines in her face had softened, and her plump figure had become that of a young matron. In her eyes I saw her grief for a man who must be long dead. I felt too the longing of the child Eramet for the mother who had left her behind.

"When I arrived here," Namet said, "I was told my husband was dead. When I demanded his body, they admitted he'd been taken by the northerners. While the warriors who were with him believed he had been killed, no one saw him die, so I made up my mind to find him. I swore to myself I would either bring him back or die with him."

Namet paused, to see what I thought about what she had said.

"I was wrong to do that," she went on. "I had a child who needed me. She was barely two years old when I left her and nearly four when I returned. I don't think she ever forgave me, but I was young and headstrong, and I refused to believe that the Mother would take my husband from me. It seemed too cruel."

My heart grew heavy. The brightness of the day began to dim. I thought I knew what she was going tell us, and I didn't want to hear it. Maara moved restlessly beside me. I didn't think she wanted to hear the next part of Namet's story either.

"That spring when the raids began," Namet said, "I went out with a war party. I don't know what I was thinking. I had no idea where I might find my husband. I may have trusted that the Mother would lead me to him. In any case, as soon as I could get away, I left the others and went north alone."

"What happened?" I asked.

"I was captured, of course."

"By the painted people?"

"No, by the northerners. They took me into their homeland. There I saw the painted people and their handiwork." She frowned. "I was appalled by what I saw. It was clear to me that the painted people were a savage people who had no compassion in them."

"What did you see?"

"I hardly remember it anymore. For years I remembered everything about that summer. I couldn't get the images of the things I'd seen out of my head. I had to undergo a difficult healing, and then the memories began to fade. Now when I look back, it's like searching for a dream I dreamed years ago."

"You don't remember anything?"

"I remember odd things. I remember the northerners cooking their meat with strange-smelling herbs. I've never tasted anything like it since. I remember the sound of their strange talk. Their speech had a sharp sound and a choppy cadence to it. I never understood it very well, but I did grow to like the sound of it. And I remember the day I saw the sea."

"What was it like?"

"It was vast," she said. "Nothing but grey-green water everywhere, constantly in motion. Watching it made me dizzy. It curled up onto the land as if it would devour the earth from under our feet, and the sound as it beat against the shore was deafening."

"Why did the northerners keep you?" Maara asked.

"I have no idea. They may have thought I would be useful as a hostage. In any case, I went with them willingly. If my husband was alive, I hoped I might find him a captive among their tribes."

"Did they mistreat you?"

"No," said Namet. "They thought I was a witless fool. I certainly acted like one. Going alone into their territory was a foolish thing to do, but grief can make us do very foolish things."

"Why were you grieving?" I asked her. "I thought you believed your husband was alive."

"I hoped," she replied, "but I don't think I believed. A kind of madness had come over me. I had been so happy, and like all young people, I thought I had a right to my happiness. I told the Mother that I would refuse to live if my husband were no longer living. It seemed such a small thing then, to throw my life away."

Namet's talk of the sea and the northerners and the painted people had distracted me. Now I knew that soon we would hear the story of her loss. She must have loved her husband very much to leave her child to go in search of him. What must it be like to lose someone so beloved? My heart ached for the young woman she had been.

Namet leaned toward me and brushed a tear from my cheek. "Why are you crying?"

"For your grief, Mother."

"And last night?"

"Last night?"

"Whose grief caused your tears last night? Was it the Lady's?"

By then I was convinced that Namet must know everything that happened under the sun. I nodded.

"You brought her into Maara's room with you last night," she said. "I felt her there as if she'd followed you and was standing by the door. Did you know she was still with you?"

"Yes," I said. "No. I don't know."

"What did Merin say to you that hurt you so much?"

"Nothing." Then I remembered. "She said the night was full of ghosts." Namet thought that over for a while. "Is that all?"

"Yes."

"What do you know of the Lady's grief?"

"Nothing, Mother, unless you're speaking of the grief that comes to everyone in time of war."

"Surely that's grief enough," said Namet.

She reached for me and lightly touched my cheek. "You have a gift. You have compassion for others because you have the gift of understanding how life feels to them. If the world were filled with more joy and less pain, I would envy you." She smoothed the hair away from my face and smiled. "I'm teasing you a little, but yours is a gift you must learn to master or the pain may overwhelm you."

"Will you teach me, Mother?"

"My dear," said Namet, "you already have a teacher."

I looked at Maara. Her eyes went from Namet's face to mine.

"How can I teach her?" Maara said. "I know nothing about this gift of hers."

"You know enough to let it be," Namet told her. "And you're the one she chose, so you will teach her well enough, whether or not you understand what that teaching is." She turned to me. "All I can tell you is this. Some hearts break from grief and some from joy. Some even break from love. But hearts break because they are too small to contain the gifts life gives us. Your task will be to let your heart grow large enough not to break."

Namet leaned back against the stone. She folded her hands in her lap and waited, watching me, as if she expected me to ask a question. Although her words had filled me with questions, I couldn't find a way to ask any of them.

"My husband died," said Namet gently. "He didn't die that summer. He died of a fever five years later, and I still grieve for him, as I grieve for Eramet."

I didn't know whether that made me feel better or not. I was glad for Namet's sake that nothing terrible had happened to him at the hands of the northerners or of the painted people. I had feared that one of the memories Namet had been unable to forget was the memory of watching him die a cruel death.

While a part of my mind was still thinking about the task she had set for me, I listened to the rest of Namet's story. I learned that there was much more to the war than anyone had told me. It had begun long before anyone was aware, and by the time it overtook our people, there was no stopping it.

Our people and the northern tribes had been enemies for as long as anyone could remember, but we were enemies who were respectful of each other. The painted people respected nothing. They would drive a tribe from its land, then plunder everything of value they could carry. The most terrifying thing about them was that they laid waste to everything they left behind. They slaughtered every animal they couldn't take. They burned homes and fields and stores of grain. When the northerners raided us, they had the sense to leave us enough to go on with, so that when they returned there would be more to plunder. The painted people left a wasteland behind them.

"My husband had spent the winter with one of the northern tribes," said Namet. "He was a gifted healer. He nursed the hurts and fevers of the people who had captured him. Because he was useful to them, both as a healer and a hostage, they let him live. When he learned of the painted people, he saw a way to save his own life and many other lives as well. He thought that if our people could make common cause with the northern tribes, together we could drive the painted people from our lands once and forever.

"My husband had learned a great deal about the northerners, and he hoped that an alliance with them might also put an end to the raids and skirmishes that every year brought grief to both sides. After he had lived with them a while, when he had begun to understand their language, he spoke to their elders of the possibility of an alliance.

"All summer their councils met and debated, but they could come to no decision. They feared the idea of an alliance was a trick, that my husband had proposed it as a ruse so that they would allow him to go home. They didn't want to lose a hostage who might someday prove valuable and be left with nothing to show for their misplaced trust. Then my husband heard that a woman of his people was held captive by a neighboring tribe."

Namet smiled, remembering one happy day from that unhappy time. "One morning he walked into the village where I was. I thought he was a ghost. I was sure of it when he spoke to the village elders in their own tongue. They talked for a long time. Then my husband came to me and took my hand. When I felt his warm hand in mine, I knew he was no ghost, but even if he had been, I would have followed him.

"We had only a little time together before he persuaded the northerners to send me home, to speak with our elders while they kept him as a hostage against treachery. With one of us to send and one to keep, they were willing. At first I refused to go. I told him I hadn't traveled all that way to find him only to leave him again, but he persuaded me that both our lives and many more might depend on this alliance. So I came home.

"I arrived here just as the first snow of winter began to fall. With my husband's life at stake, I used all my powers of persuasion to convince Abicel and the elders to join with the northerners against the painted people. I told them the dreadful things I'd seen, to make them fear the painted people more than they distrusted the northern tribes.

"All winter it seemed that no one spoke of anything else. Many said we should leave the northerners to their fate, that if the Mother favored us, we might never have to deal with the painted people at all. Others feared that when the northerners' strength was gone, the painted people might overwhelm us too. Others had grievances against the northerners they would not forgive, and they refused to lend warriors to the alliance. When the decision was made to send our warriors to join the northern tribes, those people were greatly criticized, but in the end, it was they who saved us.

"In the spring, I returned north, to tell the northerners that our people had accepted their offer. The northern tribes gathered their strength together. Warriors from Abicel's house and from many of her allies joined them. Together we went out to make war on the painted people, but when we searched out their winter camps, we found only the dead. A plague had visited them all. The dead lay in their beds as if asleep, and the few survivors we found hiding in the woods weren't fit to fight. They asked no mercy. The northerners, remembering their own dead, put them all to the sword. A few may have found their way to their boats and gone back to where they came from, but the painted people never again returned to trouble us."

The unexpected ending of Namet's tale confused me. Where were the battles outside the walls of Merin's house that my mother had told me of? When did her sisters die? Namet saw the questions in my eyes.

"Yes," she said. "There's more."

She closed her eyes and leaned back against the stone. She was silent for a long time, until I began to wonder if she would tell us the rest. At last she opened her eyes.

"Our people rejoiced at their easy victory," she said. "They believed the painted people had brought their misfortune upon themselves, that their disrespect for life had angered the one whose labor gave birth to the world. They said it was she who took the painted people back into the dark.

"While we were in their country, our warriors saw how much the northerners had suffered. We felt pity for them. In gratitude that we had been spared their suffering, we thought it only right to offer them our friendship and our help. They had been our comrades in arms. We felt we knew them, and we could no longer regard them as our enemies. Some thought, as my husband did, that we should build on this alliance. When we came home, we brought with us many warriors of the northern tribes.

"Those who might have spoken out against this plan had stayed at home. It was the young, the adventurous, the inexperienced, who had gone to fight. It was they who brought a northern army to our door.

"Whether the northerners had treachery in mind from the beginning no one knows. Perhaps they saw their chance to make good their losses at our expense. Perhaps they felt that, after all their suffering, the Mother might favor them and would give them what they had coveted for so long — our crops, our animals, the land itself. Or perhaps it started with a drunken brawl over which warrior should take the best cut of meat. No one living now knows."

Namet said no more. There was no need. I knew the rest. I knew the stories of the battles almost by heart. Namet's story helped me to understand things I had never thought about before — how the northerners had come unchallenged so far into Merin's land and why the fighting had been so fierce. The northerners would have fought with the desperation of those who have closed the door behind them. They had little to return to and much to gain from our defeat.

What I had missed I saw in Maara's eyes.

"No," said Namet, answering the question Maara had not yet asked. "No one blamed me, at least not publicly, but that didn't prevent me from blaming myself."

"Many shared the blame," Maara replied. "It wasn't yours alone."

"I alone brought about that dreadful alliance," Namet said. "But for me, none of our misfortunes would have happened. The painted people would never have been a threat to us, so in the end we lost much and gained nothing."

She turned to me. "And if not for me, your mother's sisters would not have died. Your mother would not have gone home to take her mother's place and you might never have been born." She smiled. "So you see, it is possible to pluck good fruit from an evil tree."

My mind was a confusion of questions. How could just one person be responsible for a war? I didn't see how she could blame herself for the decisions of so many people.

Maara spoke aloud what I was thinking. "How could you blame yourself? You could not have known what the result would be."

"No," Namet replied. "No one could have known."

Her eyes softened as she returned Maara's gaze. "I understand what you're saying, my child. I was only one link in a chain of events that led us into disaster. But you must look deeper for the truth."

She turned to me. "Do you think I did wrong?"

"No, Mother," I replied. "You thought you were doing what was best for everyone."

Namet turned back to Maara. "Do you share her opinion?"

Maara said nothing. The two women sat looking at each other until prickles began to run up and down my spine. The silence went on so long that I had to resist the urge to break it.

"If I had known the outcome, would I have done differently?" Namet said at last. "That's the question behind the question. And the answer is, I don't know. Because of what I did, I had my husband back. I had five years with him I would not have had otherwise. I can't wish that undone. What I've never been able to decide is if I would have urged the alliance on our people even if I had known the consequences, to save my husband's life."

"The answer to that question doesn't matter," Maara said. "It's a question you were never asked. You will never bear the guilt for even the most treacherous answer to it."

A tear slid down Namet's cheek. Maara looked away, embarrassed, but Namet reached out and took her hand.

"You are a gift," said Namet.

The shadows of the stones stretched across the circle. I lay back in the grass and thought about Namet's story. Namet fell into a doze, still sitting up, with her back against the stone. I caught Maara's eye.

"When you spoke of the question she was never asked," I whispered, "what did you mean?"

"Has life never asked you a question?"

"I don't think so."

Maara chuckled softly. "Life asks you questions every day," she said.

33

I<small>NNOCENT</small> B<small>IRDS</small>

T he next day Sparrow came home. I was practicing with my bow when I heard the soft footfall of someone approaching me from behind. I thought it might be Maara, coming to see how I was doing. When Sparrow slipped her arms around my waist, I caught the scent of lemon grass.

"Don't you know how to use that thing yet?" she asked me.

I paid no attention to her teasing. I turned in her arms and hugged her tight. "I've missed you," I said.

She let go of me and held me at arm's length. "Have you grown taller?"

"I don't think so."

She pulled me toward her, as if she were measuring my height against her own body. Then she bent and kissed me. "Will you come down to the willow tree?"

"Now?"

"Yes, now. When did you think?"

I hesitated.

"If you don't want to —"

"Maara might come looking for me."

"Will she be angry if you're not here?"

"No."

"Then come on."

She took my hand and led me down the hill. We slipped through the curtain of drooping branches and settled ourselves on the soft moss under the tree. I leaned my bow against the trunk. Sparrow had never paid any attention to it before, but the carved designs caught her eye, and she ran her fingers over them.

"Where did you get this?" she asked me. "I've never seen a bow like it."

"My warrior gave it to me."

"Did she make this?"

Although Sparrow's guess provided a reasonable explanation, I couldn't bring myself to lie to her.

"No," I said. "She found it."

To my relief Sparrow didn't question me further. I couldn't tell her the truth about the bow without telling her about finding the body of the man Vintel had murdered. Then she would know that this was the bow that had killed Eramet.

"How was your journey?" I asked her.

"Better than I expected," she said.

"Did you see your mother?"

She smiled. "I did, and I actually heard her say that she was proud of me."

"Why wouldn't she be proud of you?"

"She used to tell me I aimed too high. She used to be afraid for me, afraid I wanted too much."

"Surely she would want as much for you as you would want for yourself."

Sparrow gave me an indulgent smile. "You're such an innocent. Slaves who fly too high are often brought back down to earth in most unpleasant ways."

"But you were not."

"No," she said. "I was not. I was lucky."

I knew she was thinking of Eramet.

Sparrow caressed my cheek. "Don't be jealous."

"I'm not jealous."

And I realized that I truly was not jealous of Eramet. I would have wished her back again in an instant, both for Sparrow's sake and for Namet's.

Sparrow pouted. "Not even a little?"

I laughed. "Well maybe just a little."

"I suppose that will have to do."

We sat looking at each other. Suddenly I felt shy. So, I think, did Sparrow.

"Tell me about Arnet's house," I said.

"Well," she said, lying back on the mossy bank, "nothing much has changed there in the time I've been away."

I lay down beside her and listened as Sparrow told me about Arnet's house and the people she grew up with. Many of her old friends had rejoiced to see her. She hadn't expected such a warm welcome from people who had known her as a slave and who now must accept her new position in life.

When she finished telling me about her journey, Sparrow turned to me.

"I missed you too," she said, and took me into her arms.

That evening the sunset was so lovely that Maara and I joined many of the others who went to sit on the hillside outside the earthworks to watch. When the light had faded and the others had gone in, I would have stayed on to enjoy the twilight, but Maara surprised me by sending me to bed.

"We're going to be up well before dawn tomorrow morning," she said. "We're going hunting."

"Hunting?"

"Bring your bow," she said.

Her mention of the bow reminded me of Sparrow's questions.

"This afternoon," I said, "Sparrow asked me where my bow came from."

"What did you tell her?"

"I told her you gave it to me. When she asked me how you came by it, I said you found it."

Maara nodded. "All quite true."

I hesitated to ask my next question, but it had worried me all afternoon.

"What if Vintel were to recognize the bow?"

Maara shrugged. "Even if she does, I doubt she'll say anything about it."

"But then she'll know we found that man's body."

"Does it matter?"

I thought it over. Could anything make Vintel more our enemy than she was already?

"I suppose not," I said, but that wasn't what was bothering me. "Would she tell Sparrow, do you think?"

"I don't know. She might." Maara saw the worry in my eyes. "Sparrow can't fault you for being less than completely honest with her. The Lady asked us to keep our knowledge to ourselves."

"That's not what worries me."

"What is it then?"

"My bow killed Eramet."

I had never before said it out loud. I remembered how I felt when Maara first handed me the bow. How could I have used it all this time without once thinking of the loss of Eramet?

Maara turned to face me. "That troubles you?"

I nodded.

"Why?"

Why couldn't she see what was so obvious to me? "My bow took the life of someone Sparrow loved. When I couldn't tell Sparrow the truth about the bow today, it was more to spare her that knowledge than because the Lady told us not to tell."

"You would spare Sparrow the knowledge that the bow that killed her warrior is now in the hands of her friend?"

"I would spare her the reminder of her loss."

"Do you believe she doesn't remember her loss every day? Does she need to be reminded of it?"

"No."

"Your bow has taken life, a warrior's life. That makes it strong. If I were to choose a sword, I would choose one that has tasted blood over a blade brought new from the forge."

"Why?"

"Just like a person, a weapon that has been tested can be relied on."

"So I can trust my bow because it has taken life?"

"You must first trust yourself," said Maara. "But you can trust that your weapon has at least as much courage as its master." She looked at me appraisingly. "When you set your foot upon the warrior's path, had you not considered all that it entails?"

"All the women of my family were warriors. It's the path I was always meant to take."

Maara frowned. "Was it not your own choice?"

"It was the path I wanted. I never wanted anything else."

"You never considered anything else?"

"What else is there?"

"There is more than one path to power," Maara said. "You could have become a healer or followed the path of wisdom like Namet."

"Namet was first a warrior," I reminded her.

"That's true," she said. "And like Namet you may find that your true path lies elsewhere but that you must take the warrior's path to find it."

I couldn't imagine that someday I might be as wise or as powerful as Namet. I thought I would be satisfied just to become a warrior, something that until only a short time ago I had suspected might not be within my reach.

"In the meantime," Maara said, "you must understand that at the heart of power is the willingness to use it. At the heart of a warrior's power is the willingness to take a life, in order to preserve her own life and the lives of others. The taking of life is a responsibility you will have to bear, and before you become a warrior, you must decide if you're willing to bear it. When you go into battle, there will be no time to ask yourself that question."

When you go into battle. A shiver of anxiety went through me.

"Of course every path carries its own responsibility," said Maara. "A healer takes responsibility for the lives in her care. And Namet has certainly made choices that meant life or death for many. But to stand before a living person and take an action that may end that person's life is not something everyone can do. To be unable to do it is not a shameful thing, but you must be honest with yourself about it before you put lives at risk. Do you understand?"

I nodded.

"Every time you draw your bow, I want you to feel the power in it. Let your weapon guide you into an understanding of what it means to wield the power of life and death."

She saw that I didn't understand.

"Never mind," she said. "It's too soon for you to think about that."

The next morning I was still sound asleep when Maara came to the companions' loft. I slipped out of Sparrow's arms without disturbing her and followed Maara down to the kitchen, carrying my clothes with me so that I could dress without waking the companions.

"Wait for me here," Maara said, and she went back in the direction of the great hall.

It didn't take me long to dress. While I was waiting for Maara to return, I made us each a bowl of nettle tea with honey. I usually had no trouble waking up in the mornings, but the night before I had stayed up later than I should have talking to Sparrow, and the sweet tea cleared my groggy head.

"Who's there?" Gnith's voice came from the direction of the hearth.

"It's me, Mother. Tamras."

I went to sit beside her and offered her a sip of my tea.

"You're up early," Gnith said.

"I'm sorry I woke you, Mother."

"Wasn't sleeping." She took a long drink of my tea.

"My warrior got me up early today. We're going hunting."

"Hunting? Hunting for what?"

"I don't know."

"Then how will you know when you've caught it?" She cackled at her own joke.

I couldn't help laughing with her. "Maara knows what we're hunting. I imagine she'll let me know."

"Mmmm," said Gnith, as she finished the last swallow of my tea. "Bring some more."

I set another bowl to steep and brought her the tea I had brewed for Maara.

"Would you ask a blessing?" she asked me. "A blessing on your bow perhaps?"

I don't know what surprised me more, that she remembered my asking for her blessing or that she knew about my bow.

"Little birds," she said.

"What?"

"Little birds come and tell me things."

"Oh." Then I remembered that I had left my bow upstairs. I started to get up, to go and fetch it, but Gnith put her hand on my arm to stop me.

"Your stranger's idea, was it?"

"Yes," I replied. Before she could tell me I should learn to use a sword instead, I said, "It was a good idea."

"Yes, indeed," she said. "A very good idea. How did she come to think of it?"

"You'll have to ask her that."

Gnith's thin lips puckered into what might have been a pout. "She never comes to see me."

Just then Maara entered the kitchen carrying an armload of weaponry. She came over to the hearth where Gnith and I were sitting and set everything down on the floor. She had brought my bow, as well as another for herself, along with an assortment of arrows and two quivers.

Maara sat down cross-legged on the cold stone floor and handed me one of the quivers. Then she picked up an arrow and inspected it, sighting along its length to see if it was reasonably straight and making sure that the stone tip was securely fastened. I followed her example and began to fill the quiver she had given me.

"Is she the one?" Gnith's eyes were on Maara's face.

"Yes, Mother."

"Dark," said Gnith.

Maara's hand paused for the briefest moment before proceeding to slip an arrow into her quiver. She gave no other sign that she had heard what Gnith said.

It was the first time I'd known Gnith to be unkind.

"She can hear you, Mother," I said.

"Of course she can," said Gnith. "She has ears on her, doesn't she?"

"What's that?" said Maara. She cocked her head as if she were listening for something. "A wind through dry leaves? Black water whispering down a cave wall?" She turned to look at Gnith. "No, just the voice of a foolish old woman."

I hardly believed what my ears had heard. When I turned to look at Gnith, I was astonished to see that she was staring wide-eyed at Maara, her face alight with a delighted grin. Then she began to laugh. Her laughter started as a whisper that did sound rather like the wind in dry leaves. Soon it was a chuckle, and then a cackle, and then full-throated laughter that I feared would wake the entire household.

"Why was she laughing?" I asked Maara when the kitchen door had closed behind us.

"She was laughing at my calling her a foolish old woman," Maara said.

"But why did she think that was so funny? Didn't she think you were insulting her?"

"She found it funny because she knew that I know better."

"Oh." I still wasn't certain I understood her.

"Do you believe she's foolish?"

"No," I replied. "I think she's very wise."

"Why?"

"She's given me wise advice. More than once."

"Oh?"

I tried to think of an example to give her. I was going to say that Gnith had given me the binding spell, until I remembered that Maara didn't know about the binding spell. I doubted that I could explain it to her very well, so I said, "She told me how to ask the Lady for the apprenticeship I wanted."

"Did she?"

I nodded.

"Then I am in her debt," she said.

Whatever I had been about to say flew out of my head. Before I got over being surprised, I felt a foolish grin spread across my face and a warm glow begin around my heart. A nagging voice at the back of my head tried to spoil the pleasure her words had given me. The voice whispered, *It's Namet she's thinking of.* I ignored that voice. I wanted to believe something else.

When we reached the bottom of the hill, we turned into a narrow lane. On either side of the lane were fields where the grain had just been harvested, and the hedgerows were alive with birds.

The first light of dawn appeared over the eastern hills. The birds began to wake. The way they sang and twittered almost made me laugh out loud, when I thought of how like they sounded to the voices of the girls in the companions' loft.

We came to a break in the hedgerow. Maara strung her bow and motioned to me to do the same. Her quiver hung from her belt at her left side where she usually carried her sword. She drew an arrow from it, but she didn't nock it. With the bow in her left hand and the arrow in her right, she slipped through the gap in the hedgerow.

Birds were feeding on the grain that had fallen from the sheaves, and I wondered if Maara intended them to be our quarry. I saw several quail, but they would provide no more than a mouthful, and the other birds weren't big enough to be worth the plucking of them.

When we approached, they scurried away from us. As if they knew the reach of our arrows, they stayed just out of bowshot. Maara kept to the edge of the field. I thought she was using the hedgerow for cover, but it didn't seem to be an effective tactic. Every bird feeding in that field knew we were there.

Suddenly, with a desperate flapping of wings, from right under our noses a large, brown bird flew up out of the tall grass that grew along the hedgerow. It startled me. Before I could take a breath or say a word, I heard the singing of Maara's bowstring. The bird stopped in mid-flight and dropped to earth a dozen feet in front of us, where it struggled to free itself from the arrow that had pierced its wing. Maara walked over to it, picked it up, and wrung its neck.

I stood staring at her. I hadn't seen her nock the arrow or let it fly. I hadn't seen her move at all. She withdrew her arrow from the bird's wing and slipped the bird into her game bag.

Within the hour she brought down half a dozen birds. I tried to watch her, to see how she did it, but always the bird flying up startled me and drew my eye. Then she signaled me to take the lead and do as she had done.

Time after time, a bird flew up out of the grass and took wing before I could do more than watch. I couldn't react quickly enough to nock an arrow, much less let it fly. After several failures I kept an arrow nocked and ready. At last I loosed it more or less in the direction of the next bird to fly out of the grass. I missed the bird by yards.

It was midmorning, and by now every bird on Merin's land had filled its belly and was attending to other business. The day had grown quite warm. Maara took me to the river, where we bathed and cooled ourselves.

"If you'll make the fire," she said, "I'll share my game with you."

It had never occurred to me that she wouldn't share whatever food she had. We had brought nothing with us, and we'd had no breakfast. I was ravenous.

"The next time we hunt," she said, "you must feed yourself or go without."

I nodded. I knew why.

We shared one of the birds between us. All the rest but one Maara gave to a boy who was herding geese out to the fields where we had hunted that morning. The last bird she gave to me.

"For Gnith," she said.

That evening I cooked the bird for Gnith. She hadn't many teeth left, so I stewed it until it fell off the bones and gave her the broth with the meat in it.

"My warrior sent you this," I told her.

"It's good," she said.

When she finished, she set the bowl aside.

"You should have let me bless your bow."

I was only a little surprised that she knew about my failure as a hunter.

"Next time I will," I said.

The next morning I rose before dawn and took my bow down to the kitchen. Gnith was waiting for me.

"Let's see this strange bow of yours," she said.

Gnith closed her eyes and ran her fingers up and down its length.

"Strong," she said.

She opened her eyes and looked at me. I thought she was going to ask me where the bow had come from. Instead she said, "Not one of ours."

"No," I admitted.

"Not your stranger's either."

"No."

Gnith closed her eyes again and sat still and silent for so long that I thought she might have dozed off. Just as I was about to touch her, to see if she was sleeping, she looked up at me and gave me back the bow.

"The bird your warrior sent me did me good," she said. "Bring me another."

I had an arrow nocked and ready, but three birds flew up before I got over being startled. The fourth didn't surprise me quite as much. The next few times, I sent an arrow in the general direction the bird had flown, but I never came close to hitting one.

I sat down under the hedgerow and tried to understand what I was doing wrong. A little voice in the back of my head was grumbling about the impossible task my warrior had set for me. My grandmother had taught me not to listen to that little voice. I thought instead about taking a bird home for Gnith.

A bird flew up. Almost of itself the bow followed it. I loosed the arrow. It missed, but I saw that it had flown just behind the bird, so the next time I let the bow anticipate its flight, and the bird fell to earth. I picked it up still living. The arrow had only torn a few feathers from its wing.

The bird's frantic heart beat against the palms of my hands. I hesitated, undecided. Should I take this bird to Gnith or should I try again? I was making progress, and I didn't want to stop until I had shot a bird properly. On the other hand, it was getting late, and soon the birds would have finished feeding.

I set the bird down. It didn't move. When I reached for it again, it leapt into the air and flew away.

For another hour I walked the hedgerow. The birds were gone.

I was angry with myself. I wondered if I had let the bird go for lack of courage. I hadn't liked the idea of killing it when it was whole and uninjured. If I had wounded it, I would have felt differently, but there had been so much life in it that I hadn't the heart to end it.

"I'm sorry, Mother," I said.

Gnith looked disappointed. "I feel a fever coming on."

"I can bring you some beef broth."

"Don't want it." She pouted like a child.

"Shall I fix you some tea?"

She shook her head.

"You need to eat something, if you're feeling ill."

"I want a bird."

"I'll bring you one tomorrow, Mother."

"Might be dead by tomorrow."

"Surely not," I said.

But she turned away and wouldn't say another word.

The next day it took me several hours, but at last I shot a bird. The arrow went through its body, and I took it to the river and cleaned it right away before the ruptured organs could contaminate the meat. I brought it back to Gnith and made her some soup out of it.

"About time," she said. She reached eagerly for the bowl and took a long drink of the broth. Then she looked up and grinned at me.

"Am I forgiven?" I asked her.

"What for?"

"For letting you go hungry yesterday."

"Didn't."

"I thought you did," I said. "You wouldn't let me bring you something else."

"You're not the only one who brings me good things to eat."

With her fingers she picked a chunk of meat out of the bowl and put it into her mouth. "It gets easier," she said.

"What gets easier, Mother?"

"Killing things."

"I've killed animals before." My defiant words slipped out before I could bite them back. Of course we had butchered animals at home, and Maara and I had spent the winter snaring rabbits for both their meat and their fur. That kind of killing hadn't bothered me since I was a small child, but I was still a little angry with myself for failing to kill the bird I caught the day before, and it puzzled me that I should suddenly be so squeamish.

Then Gnith caught hold of my hand. I felt in her fingertips the echo of her heartbeat and remembered how the living bird had felt in my hands.

Every morning I rose before dawn to hunt. When the birds had gleaned the last bit of grain from the fields that had been harvested, I had to work harder at finding their new feeding places. Every day I managed to shoot at least one bird. Some days I brought back two or three. There were days when I had to walk so far afield that I would have given up but for Gnith, who continued to insist that my soup was doing her a world of good.

One evening, as I handed Gnith her bowl of soup, Namet came into the kitchen. "That smells wonderful," she said. She came over to the hearth and sat down on a low, three-legged stool. "Is there enough for me?"

I was about to get up, to bring another bowl so that she could share Gnith's soup, when Gnith handed her bowl to Namet.

"Have it all," she said. "I'm sick of it."

I stared at her, astonished.

"You might have told me," I said. "I would have eaten it myself."

Gnith took my hand. "Would you find it so easy to kill a little bird? Just to make yourself a bit of soup? You have lots of other things to eat." She made a tut-tut sound. "Such a tender-hearted child." I tried to withdraw my hand from hers, but she held on to it with surprising strength. "To bring an old woman a little treat is not the same as using living things for target practice."

Gnith's words chilled me. She gently stroked my hand, then let it go and settled herself on her pallet for a nap. In a few minutes she was snoring.

"What did she mean?" I whispered to Namet.

"It's her gift to see these things," Namet replied. "She saw your reluctance to take the innocent lives of birds."

The next morning when I went out to hunt I found Maara waiting for me just outside the earthworks. She was carrying her bow.

"May I come with you?" she asked me.

"Of course," I said.

I waited for her to lead the way. Instead she gestured to me to go ahead. It felt strange to have her following me. I kept wanting to turn to her, to ask her if I should go this way or that, but I understood that she wanted to see what I would do.

I couldn't make up my mind where I might have the best luck. I tried several places along the hedgerows where I had found birds before. That day there were none.

Then I remembered that a few days before I had noticed a field of barley that was almost ready for harvest. When we approached it, I saw that more than half the grain had now been cut. The sheaves were still standing in the field, bound and ready for the cart.

As soon as I started out along the hedgerow a bird flew up. I took a hasty shot at it and missed. I missed the next three birds too. That didn't bother me. For every bird I hit, I usually missed at least a dozen, but after many more failed attempts, I knew something was wrong.

Another bird flew up. Before I could react, Maara's arrow brought it down. We went to the river, and while she built a fire, I cleaned the bird.

"Did it make you nervous to have me watching you?" she asked me, as we sat by the fire waiting for the bird to cook.

I shook my head. She never made me nervous. One of the things I loved about her was her infinite patience with me.

"Do you know what you were doing wrong?"

"What?" I asked her.

"I have no idea. I wondered if you did."

"No," I said.

Maara took the bird from the fire. She broke it in two and handed half to me. I hesitated, remembering what she told me the last time she shared her game with me.

She smiled. "Don't be silly."

Hunger won out easily over pride. While we ate, I thought about what had happened that morning. I wasn't troubled by my failure. I was hardly surprised by it. I knew the answer lay close at hand, and I waited patiently for it to show itself.

"The innocent lives of birds," I said aloud.

Maara looked at me with curiosity.

"That's what Namet said," I told her. "She said I was reluctant to take the innocent lives of birds."

"What do you think she meant?"

I thought the meaning was obvious. "I suppose she meant that I don't like to kill things."

"No one likes to kill things."

"But we do it anyway," I whispered.

"Yes."

"Why?"

"To live," she said.

Neither of us was thinking about the killing of innocent birds.

When I woke the next morning, Sparrow's arms tightened around me.

"Do you have to get up so early today?" she whispered.

I was lying on my side with my back to her. She blew gently on the back of my neck just above the hairline, knowing how my body would respond. A shiver of pleasure ran down my spine, tempting me to stay where I was, but that day I needed to prove something to myself. Reluctantly I slipped out of Sparrow's arms. When I got up, Sparrow got up too.

"If you won't stay with me," she said, "I suppose I'll have to come along with you. I'll never get to see you otherwise."

We took our clothes down to the kitchen. Gnith was snoring on the hearth. I took my time getting dressed, hoping she would wake. She didn't stir. I took up my bow and quiver, and Sparrow and I slipped out the back door and walked together down the hill.

I first thought of going back to the field where Maara and I had seen so many birds the day before. Then I saw that a mist lay heavy on the river and long tendrils had drifted up onto the shore. There would be birds feeding there. Hidden by the mist, they would be scratching for insects in the grass along the riverbank.

With Sparrow following a few paces behind me, I nocked an arrow and held the bow ready. Step by cautious step I walked into the mist. A bird flew up. It startled me. I raised my bow, but the bird had vanished.

I stopped and collected myself. Today, for the first time, I was hunting with full awareness of what I was doing. I felt the power in the bow, and at last I understood what Maara had been trying to teach me. As the hunt was teaching me mastery of the bow, it was also teaching me to bear responsibility for wielding the power of life and death, not only over the lives of birds, but over the lives of others like myself, the lives of women and men, the lives of warriors.

A bird flew up, and the bow followed it, moving in an arc, anticipating the bird's flight. As the bird vanished into the mist, I let the arrow fly. I heard a fluttering of wings and found the dying bird by the sounds of its struggle. I picked it up and wrung its neck.

When I turned around, Sparrow was right behind me, on her face an expression of wonder and delight.

"How did you do that?" she whispered.

I shrugged. I didn't really know myself. I felt both satisfaction and regret.

"Are you hungry?" I asked her.

"Now that you mention it, I am."

We walked a short way uphill, until we were clear of the mist. While I built a fire, Sparrow cleaned the bird. The early morning air was cool, and we were both chilled from being in the damp. We huddled close to the fire as we waited for the bird to cook.

"I've never seen anyone do that before," said Sparrow.

"I don't usually bring down a bird on the first try."

"Maybe I brought you luck."

"You should come with me every morning."

She shook her head. "You get up too early for me. Besides, there are other things I'd rather be doing that early in the morning."

I blushed.

"Sleeping for one."

"Oh."

She laughed at me. "And other things." She reached across the fire and let her fingers drift down my thigh.

For once I didn't know how to respond to her teasing. I looked away.

"Have you changed your mind?"

I looked up at her and saw that I'd hurt her feelings.

"I thought we were something more than friends," she said, "but I'll be your friend and nothing more, if that's what you want."

"I've been happy as we are," I said.

And then I wondered what I meant.

"As we are," she said. "You have no time for me as we are. You're up too early in the morning, and by the time I've finished my work and come to bed, you're asleep and snoring."

There was justice in her complaint.

"I didn't realize. We need to find time to be together."

"We're together now," she said.

She took the bird from the fire and tested it to see if it was done. Then she handed me a piece of it.

As we ate, I was aware of how close she was, sitting only an arm's length from me across the fire. My skin tingled where she had touched me, and I wanted her to touch me like that again. I remembered the day I had made love to her under the willow tree.

Is this what love is like? My body was restless with wanting her, but where was my heart in this? I thought about Gnith's blessing. Was this the love she thought I'd asked her for? I cared for Sparrow. I cared for her very much, but I had expected something else of love. Something more. The bitter taste of disappointment filled my mouth. I set my food aside.

"What's wrong?" said Sparrow.

"When I was little," I said, "I used to ask my mother what love is like. I never understood her answer. She said that love always brings with it the unexpected."

"That's true," she said.

A shadow crossed Sparrow's face, and a look came into her eyes that told me her heart was far away from me. She was thinking of someone else. In her face I saw her love for Eramet, and I knew she would never love me, nor would I love her, with that kind of love. I felt at the same time both a pang of jealousy and a flicker of hope, hope that such a love might some-day come to me.

"Tell me what it's like," I whispered.

"I always loved her," Sparrow said. "I loved her first as I would have loved an older sister. When I was small, she teased me and played with me and protected me, just as a sister would, but I never expected to feel for her as I do now."

Now.

"I certainly never expected her to love me back," she said. "When she took me as her lover, I thought she wanted me as Arnet wanted me, as Arnet's son had wanted me."

"Did you want her too?"

"I was willing. I cared for her. What harm to give her a little pleasure? And perhaps to receive something back. I missed her so much when she was gone, and I wanted to be close to her. I thought that was all I wanted."

Sparrow smiled. "She was the first to touch me. No one else had ever touched me like that, to give me pleasure. In the beginning I thought that was why being with her was so different from being with anyone else."

I thought about Sparrow's tenderness with me and saw what a gift it was.

"When I began to understand what I was feeling," she said, "I was afraid to reveal myself. I was afraid that if she knew, she would make fun of me, or, even worse, turn away. I hid my feelings so well that she complained I didn't love her anymore." Sparrow chuckled. "I had dreams when I was younger. Just like every other girl, I thought about what it would be like to love someone. But your mother was right. Nothing ever happens the way you expect."

I blushed, remembering my own childish dreams.

"I used to say, 'Of course I still love you.' I said it in such a way that she couldn't tell what kind of love I meant. Then one day she told me."

"What did she say?"

"She told me I was beautiful."

"You are beautiful."

Sparrow laughed. "At the time I was up to my elbows in bread dough. My face and hair were covered with flour and soot from the ovens. In the kitchen heat the sweat was pouring off me. I must have been a sight."

Sparrow brushed away the tears that had come into her eyes.

"I'm sorry," I said. "I didn't mean to make you unhappy."

"I'm not. Really. It's nice to talk about her with someone."

I had noticed that Namet too seemed to want to talk about Eramet. I wondered again why these two who both loved her couldn't share their memories with each other.

"You could talk about her with her mother," I said.

Sparrow shook her head. "I don't think so."

"Maybe Namet needs to talk about Eramet too."

"Maybe."

We were silent for a while. Then I asked her, "Do you think you'll ever love someone else like that?"

"Why would I want to love someone else like that?" she whispered. "Nothing has ever hurt me more."

Her words shocked me. "I know that losing her was painful, but wasn't it worth the pain to have loved someone so deeply and to know that she loved you?"

"Losing her was the worst of it, but loving her hurt almost as much sometimes."

I didn't understand at first. Then I remembered the harvest festival the year before, when Sparrow told me that Eramet was with Vintel. Sparrow would have lain with me then, to ease the pain of her hurt feelings and her loneliness.

"I didn't mean it," she whispered. "I didn't mean it."

34

RUNNING AWAY

The raids began on the farms along our northern border. Every day bands of warriors left Merin's house. Some would stay at the farms while the farmers were bringing in the harvest. Others would go beyond our borders into the wilderness, hoping to find the raiding parties and turn them back before any harm was done.

I wondered if Maara and I would be asked to go. Some of our warriors would have to stay behind, but the younger ones, the ones most fit to fight, were almost sure to be sent north. Still I remembered that the year before Maara had gone alone to the frontier and disappeared. The others too would remember. Only Namet and I trusted her completely. Although she was bound to me by my apprenticeship and to Namet by the most unbreakable tie of kinship, to the others she was still a stranger.

For several days our warriors had been busy making preparations, seeing to their weapons and their armor, while their companions cleaned and repaired warm clothing for their warriors and themselves. Maara and I had also made ourselves ready, but none of the leaders of our warrior bands had yet asked us to join them.

Maara shook me. "Get up," she whispered. "Now."

It must be the middle of the night. "What?"

"Get up."

I got to my feet and fumbled in the dark for my clothes. Maara was already heading for the stairs.

"What's happening?" I asked, when I caught up with her in the great hall.

"Where is your bow?"

"In the loft."

"Come with me," said Maara.

As I followed her through the darkness of the hallway that led to the kitchen, I wondered if I would have time to brew some nettle tea, but she went past the kitchen doorway to the armory.

"Bring a light," she said.

I went into the kitchen, found a lamp and lit it, and brought it back to Maara. In a far corner of the armory was a pile of bows and some quivers filled with arrows, all lying in a careless heap. She rummaged through the pile until she found a bow case. It was empty. She handed it to me.

"Go upstairs and put your bow into this case," she said. "Then bring it to me here."

I did as she told me. When I returned, Maara took the case from me and put it back where she had found it, piling some loose bows on top of it until it was well hidden. My scalp began to prickle with fear, but her actions were so calm, so deliberate, that I convinced myself there was nothing to be afraid of.

Maara sorted through the hunting bows until she found one of the smaller ones. She handed it to me, along with a quiver of arrows, and took another bow and quiver for herself.

"Come on," she said.

We went out the back door and down the hill. There was no moon. From the position of the stars I saw that it couldn't be much past midnight. I didn't ask Maara why she had brought me out into the countryside in the middle of the night. She was thinking something over, and when she was ready, she would talk to me about it.

We turned south and followed the river road until we were well away from Merin's house. In a copse that stood close by the riverbank, Maara lit a small fire. I sat down and huddled close to it. Walking had kept me warm enough, but once we stopped I felt the chill in the night air.

Maara squatted down across from me and gazed into the fire.

Finally I asked her, "Are we hunting?"

She shook her head. "We may have nothing to fear," she said, and then I began to be afraid.

"Laris came to speak to me after everyone had gone to bed," she said. "She's taking her band of warriors north tomorrow morning, and she asked Vintel if you and I could join them. Vintel refused her."

"Why?"

"I don't know. It worries me. It worried Laris. That's why she came to tell me."

I felt more kindly toward Laris than I had for some time.

"When Laris asked her why, Vintel became angry. She too is leaving with her band tomorrow morning, and she told Laris that if we went north with anyone, we would go with her."

"With Vintel?"

She nodded.

"Why would Vintel want us to go with her?"

"I don't know."

"Surely she doesn't think——"

"Think what?"

"That you would leave us again," I said.

"I have no idea what she thinks." Maara gave me a cautious look. "What do you think?"

I met her eyes. "I trust you."

She sighed, as if she had been holding her breath.

"Why did we come out in the middle of the night?" I asked her. "Are we running away?"

"No," she said. "I wanted to get away from the household, to think things over."

I knew what she meant. Sometimes in Merin's house the thoughts of all the people there echoed in one's head, even when their voices were silent.

"And if Vintel plans on leaving early in the morning perhaps she won't bother looking for us."

"Then we did run away."

"I suppose we did. Just for a little while."

"They'll send someone to find us."

"Maybe."

"Vintel will be angry."

"She can't be angry with us for going fishing," said Maara.

"Fishing?"

"Let's hope we catch something." She smiled at me. "Don't be afraid."

I wasn't afraid for myself. I couldn't believe that in this house where I now had so many friends any harm could come to me. I was afraid for Maara.

"If we do go north with Vintel," she said, "I want you to leave your bow behind."

"Is that why you hid it?"

She nodded. "It will be safe enough where it is."

I was so used to having a bow in my hands that it felt strange to think of going anywhere, much less into danger, without it.

"Why can't I take it with me?" I asked her.

"You're an apprentice, not a warrior. I don't want anyone thinking otherwise."

"But I could hunt for us. And I need to practice."

"You'll have all winter to practice."

I would have argued with her a little longer, but she gave me a look that silenced me.

I woke before dawn. The fire was still burning. Maara was bent over it, holding something to the light.

I sat up to get a closer look. It was an arrow, but instead of a stone tip, the shaft was split into three parts and tied in such a way that they splayed out. The tips were sharp.

"What are you doing?" I asked.

"Getting ready to go fishing."

"With a bow?"

"Yes." She laid the arrow beside another like it and began working on a new one. "Did you bring your knife?"

She was speaking of the bronze knife she had given me to cut the leather thong that bound us together when we were hostages in Merin's house. I had made a habit of carrying it on my belt. I took it from its sheath.

"You might as well learn to do this," she said.

I took an arrow from my quiver and examined the stone tip. It was wedged into the split end of the shaft and stuck tight with a bit of pitch, then bound with a leather thong. I would have cut the whole tip off, but Maara stopped me.

"You may need that tip again. Take the time to remove it properly."

I undid the thong and held the arrow's tip to the fire to soften the pitch. Then I wiggled the stone tip off the shaft and stored it away in a leather pouch. Maara showed me how to split the end of the shaft and sharpen each tip, then splay the tips apart and bind them with a bit of thong. By the time I had prepared several arrows, the sun was peeking over the eastern hills.

"Let's go," she said. "We can leave the fire. We'll need it to cook our breakfast."

I admired her confidence. I couldn't imagine how we were going to hunt fish with bows and arrows, but it was easier than I thought it would be. We waited for the fish to rise, to feed on insects landing on the surface of the water. The splayed tips of our arrows went through their bodies and held them fast, although we had to be quick to pull them out of the water before they swam away to die where we couldn't reach them. A short time later we were roasting two fish in the coals of our fire, and we had more in our game bag to take home with us, to lend credence to our story that we had taken it into our heads to go fishing in the middle of the night.

After breakfast Maara slept for a while. Though she had been awake all night, she told me not to let her sleep too long. She wanted to time our return to the household so that we would be home before anyone came looking for us but late enough to miss the bands of warriors who would have made an early start on their journey north.

While Maara slept, I had some time to think. I wondered why Vintel would want us to go with her. In the spring, when we went with Laris to Greth's Tor, all had been well. Maara proved herself trustworthy then. And why would Vintel, who hated us both, want us to travel with her band unless she feared that Maara intended to leave us again?

Then I wondered why Vintel wouldn't be glad if Maara left us. Surely she would be delighted if Maara disappeared from Merin's house. Perhaps the Lady had charged her with keeping an eye on Maara. That made some sense to me. It was the only thing that made much sense, until it occurred to me that Vintel's hatred for Maara and for me might have prompted her to plan some mischief. That thought frightened me for a moment, until I convinced myself that Vintel would not take such a risk with so little reason.

We were almost home when Sparrow found us.

"Where have you been?" she said. "You were supposed to leave with us this morning. Vintel thinks you went with Laris against her wishes."

If Vintel thought we had gone with Laris, why did she send Sparrow out to find us? I thought I knew the answer.

"Vintel didn't send you after us, did she," I said to Sparrow.

Sparrow shook her head. "I volunteered," she said, in a way that told me Vintel knew nothing about it. She tossed her head back in a defiant gesture. "I don't suppose she'll leave without me."

For the first time I saw concern in Maara's face.

"She might," she said to Sparrow, and she set a fast pace for home.

As we trudged up the hill to Merin's house, we could see Vintel and her band of warriors standing outside the earthworks. Two dozen warriors waited there, armed and ready to travel. Their companions formed their own group that stood a little apart. They all looked restless, as if they had been waiting for some time.

When we reached the hilltop, Maara stopped a few paces from Vintel and wished her good morning.

"We thought you'd left us again," Vintel said.

The contempt in her voice made me angry, but Maara said nothing. As she stood looking at Vintel, a slow smile spread across her face. Vintel seemed unnerved by it.

"Do you intend to tell me where you've been hiding?" Vintel said.

"Hiding? We were fishing." Maara opened her game bag and showed its contents to Vintel. "I should get these to the kitchen."

Maara started to go inside, but Vintel stepped into her path.

"You haven't answered my question," Vintel said.

"I thought I had."

"You've kept us waiting. We should have left hours ago."

"If you had told me of your plans last night, we would have been ready," Maara replied, in a most reasonable tone of voice.

There was nothing Vintel could say to that, but she didn't move aside.

"May I go in?" Maara said.

"I have no more time to waste." Vintel folded her arms across her chest and stood her ground. "You've delayed us long enough."

"As you can see," said Maara, "I am unarmed. If you need a hunter, I'll come with you now, but if it's a warrior you want, you had best let me arm myself."

"I won't wait," said Vintel through clenched teeth. "You'll have to catch up to us."

She stood aside to let us pass. As I went by Vintel, she caught my arm.

"Bring your bow, little hunter," she said. "I fancy a bit of game now and then."

Vintel took hold of my bow and examined it. She ran her fingers over the smooth wood.

"Bring the other," she said.

"The other?"

"The pretty one."

Maara had stopped when she heard Vintel speak to me.

"Yes," she said to me. "Bring your war bow."

Maara sent me to get my bow while she went upstairs to arm herself and fetch the pack that we'd had ready for days. I returned to the great hall carrying my bow and a quiver of arrows just as Maara came down the stairs. Namet was with her.

"Go and bring the case," Maara said.

When I returned with it, she took it from me and slipped my bow into it. Made of thick cow's hide with the long, red hair still on it, it had an opening at one end covered by a flap. A carrying strap went over one shoulder, and there were loops of leather sewn into the sides. Maara used them to attach the quiver. Then she slipped the carrying strap over my head, pulled my left arm through it, and adjusted the strap so that the bow case and the quiver rested snugly against my back.

"How can I carry our pack?" I asked.

"You can't."

Maara unwrapped the pack we had folded with such care. Namet was holding my cloak, and Maara took it from her and spread it out on the floor. She put a bit less than half our things into it and rolled it into a long bundle. She closed it with a leather strap and fastened it across my back so that it lay alongside the bow case. She refolded our pack and shouldered it herself, and Namet helped her drape her cloak over it. Then Maara picked up her shield and slung it over her shoulder, adding its weight to the weight of the pack.

I was sorry to see her burdened with the things I should have carried.

"I could take more," I said, shrugging my shoulders under the weight of my own pack to show her that I found it light.

"We'll see." She gave me a stern look. "I want you to be aware every moment that you are the only apprentice going armed among this band of warriors. Even though it's just a bow, people will regard you differently."

Namet and I followed Maara out the front door of Merin's house and through the maze of earthworks. Vintel and her warriors were still waiting for us. When we appeared, the apprentices picked up their packs and the warriors slung their shields over their shoulders, ready to start their journey, but when they saw Namet, everyone stopped where they were, impatient to be gone, yet unwilling to show Namet any disrespect.

Namet approached Vintel. Her white curls fluttered in the breeze. Though a warm smile lit her plump and rosy face, her eyes glittered dark and powerful.

"I will look forward to your return," she said to Vintel. "Take good care to bring my child safely home to me."

Silence fell over the band of restless warriors. Vintel's face went white. I felt Maara become very still beside me. For a long, anxious moment, we all waited to see what Vintel would do.

At last Vintel yielded.

"Send us with your blessing, Mother," she said, "so that we may all come safely home again."

Namet placed the palm of her hand over Vintel's heart and smiled at her. Then she turned and looked at Maara. When their eyes met, I felt something pass between them like a ripple in the air before Namet turned and left us. All was well. With the usual noise and confusion, the band of warriors started down the hill.

35

VINTEL'S WAY

This journey could not have begun more differently than the journey we had made with Laris. As I joined the apprentices following our warriors down the hill, I hardly noticed the warriors' painted shields or their flowing cloaks, nor was I much aware of the beauty of the late-summer light that fell over Merin's land that morning. I was preoccupied with what Namet had done, astonished that she had spoken such a thing out loud in front of everyone. The last time she entrusted Vintel with a child of hers, that child had died, and everyone there knew it, but only Maara and Vintel and I remembered that the last time Maara had entrusted herself to Vintel's leadership, she had nearly lost her life. Then I wondered if Maara had told Namet about that.

I wished I could have spoken with my warrior. As we had done when we traveled with Laris's band, the warriors led the way, while the apprentices followed a little distance behind. I was unaware of Sparrow walking beside me until she whispered, "Did you know Namet was going to do that?"

"No," I said.

"Do you think she blames Vintel for Eramet's death?"

I'd never given it any thought, but it didn't seem like Namet to place blame without reason.

"No," I told her. "Eramet died in battle. Namet knows that."

Sparrow looked puzzled. "The elders never concern themselves with the affairs of warriors."

"Why not?" It seemed to me as though they should.

"The elders perform their rituals and consult the powers of life and death. They tell the Lady what they learn and give advice, but they never charge a warrior with a duty as Namet did. It's the Lady's place to do that."

Of all the elders, I thought Namet the least bound by custom. She would do what seemed right to her, whether or not it went against the way things had always been done before.

"I trust Namet's wisdom," I said to Sparrow. "She had reason to do what she did, even if we can't see it."

I did see it, but there was much that Sparrow didn't know.

I had no opportunity to speak with Maara that day or for many days afterwards. It was even more difficult to find any privacy in a traveling band of warriors than it was within the walls of Merin's house. At least when we were at home, we could go off by ourselves for a while. The members of a warrior band had to stay together, especially when we drew close to the frontier. Maara and I slept side by side, but we were always within earshot of the others.

Since I couldn't speak with Maara, I puzzled over everything that had happened in my own mind. I didn't understand Vintel's bullying attitude toward Maara when we came home, but Vintel certainly knew that she had been bested by Maara's calm and reasonable replies to her accusations. That must have made her angry, and it would have made Namet's charge to watch over Maara that much more difficult for Vintel to accept.

While it was sure to increase Vintel's resentment of Maara, it also cast a light on her intentions. Harm can come to warriors easily enough, but if any harm came to Maara now, and if it appeared that Vintel had failed in her duty as she had once before, she would be risking more than was prudent. At the very least she would lose face, but she stood to lose much more than that. She stood to lose the loyalty of the warriors who trusted her with their own safety. That was a price Vintel would never pay.

Once we set out, Vintel didn't concern herself with us. She treated Maara no differently than she treated anyone else. Because of our late start, we camped that first night well within our own borders, but still we set a watch, and Maara took her turn with the rest.

Although the apprentices weren't expected to stand watch, there was plenty for us to do. In addition to keeping our warriors' gear in order, we made and broke camp. We fetched water, gathered firewood, lit the fires, cooked the meals, and cleaned up afterwards.

Sparrow and I worked side by side. We had a few moments together when we could have talked privately, but I didn't take advantage of them to speak with her about Vintel. I never forgot that her loyalty was to her warrior, as my loyalty was to mine. I hoped that we would never come into conflict over it.

By the middle of the second day, we reached the northern boundary of Merin's land. The country there was hilly, its thin soil too poor for crops, though much of it was fine pastureland. As we traveled north, the grass became more sparse. Only gorse and bracken covered the ground, while a few trees tried to grow. The landscape that now stretched before us, drab in shades of grey and brown, seemed a different world from the one I knew. I might have imagined such a place from tales I'd heard, but never had I seen with my own eyes such a desolate land.

I felt uneasy when Sparrow told me that Vintel intended to take us into this wasteland. Claimed by no human tribe, this hostile place wanted no part of us. I could almost believe the tales of travelers who had been swallowed up by treacherous bogs or by the hidden mouths of caves that opened under their feet. If such places did exist, this was one, but in the folded hills Vintel hoped to find the hiding places of our enemies. On the morning of the third day, we ventured into the wilderness.

For several days we traveled without incident. As this strange landscape became familiar, I took pleasure in exploring it. What had appeared at first glance to be a barren place was full of life. Small furry creatures scurried about in the underbrush. Hawks drifted in the still air.

Sometimes we saw antelope nibbling at the tiny leaves of shrubs. They moved with the delicate grace of dancers, and I would have liked to sit quietly somewhere and watch them, but whenever we happened upon them, they bounded away.

Colors were subtle here. In boggy places small white flowers, star-shaped, lay strewn upon the ground. Bushes the color of smoke bore the most delicate of leaves. The morning mist blurred the boundaries of waking life and dreams.

Even in this crowd of people, I felt alone. The small band of warriors Laris had taken to Greth's Tor seemed more like a group of friends on an outing. Vintel's band felt very different. When we camped, there were few friendly conversations around the campfires. More often we heard boasting or heroic tales of warriors who had died in battle. Once, while we were listening to a particularly bloodthirsty tale, I heard Maara murmur, "Whistling in the dark." At the time I didn't know what she meant.

With two dozen warriors and almost as many apprentices in our band, it sometimes seemed that everyone was working at cross-purposes. People who had lived peacefully together in Merin's house became ill-tempered and contentious.

Vintel permitted the disorder to a point, but when a few sharp words became an argument, she would appear in the midst of the combatants and with a few words would end it. I had to admit, however grudgingly, that she had a knack for managing her unruly band. She spoke with the certainty that she would be obeyed, and everyone obeyed her.

Late one afternoon we found a deserted campsite nestled hidden in a dale. Vintel sent several warriors down to take a closer look at it. One man knelt by the fire pit and held his hand over the ashes, then sifted them through his fingers. Another examined the ground, while another searched through a dense thicket nearby, using his sword to move the branches aside. When they finished their inspection, they waved to the rest of us to join them.

"They were going north," said one. He pointed to the impression of a cart wheel in the soft earth.

"How does he know which direction they were going?" I whispered to Sparrow.

"From the depth of the track," she replied. "The cart was heavily laden. I've never known a raiding party to carry goods into Merin's land, so they must have been carrying grain, our grain, out of it."

"Will we go after them?"

She shook her head. "They're long gone now. No one has been here for several days."

I was about to ask her how she knew that when she pointed to the remains of the campfire.

"See how the surface of the ash is pitted?" she said. "A light rain fell after their fire went out, and we've had no rain for the last three days."

We made our own camp not far from the northerners' campsite. Although there was no sign that anyone but ourselves inhabited that corner of the world just then, I hardly slept at all. I was glad to see the sunrise so that we could move on.

It seemed to me at first that we were wandering about aimlessly, but after a while I saw that we were crisscrossing this empty land, going from one vantage point to another, steadily working our way west. After a week in the wilderness, we were running short of food, so we turned south again, toward one of our outposts, where we could rest and replenish our supplies.

The next afternoon it rained. We hurried on, hoping to reach our outpost by nightfall. We would find shelter there, and warm fires, and some hot supper. Wet and shivering, we arrived at last, only to find the camp deserted and the fires cold.

"Where is everyone?" I asked Sparrow.

"There must be trouble somewhere," she said.

Sparrow shook the rain out of her hair and drew her damp cloak close around her.

A few of the apprentices were already at work with their firestones. The shelters were nothing more than oiled hides stretched over flimsy poles, but they turned aside the rain, and the warriors huddled under them. All but Vintel. She stood out in the open, her head uncovered.

"Something isn't right," she said, as she looked around at the deserted campsite.

I saw nothing amiss. There were no signs of fighting. Tools and cooking pots were stacked neatly in their places. Everything seemed to be in good order.

"The stores are gone," said Sparrow.

Then I saw that in that whole camp, not one cooking pot or bowl had any food left in it, and the casks that should have held our stores of salted meat and flour were nowhere to be seen.

"We'll not stop here," Vintel said. "Laris and her warriors should have been here waiting for us. Until we know what's happened to them, we'll camp somewhere less conspicuous."

No one moved. The warriors gave no indication that they were willing to leave their shelters. The apprentices waited, to see what the warriors would do. Vintel paid no attention to them. She pulled the hood of her cloak over her head and strode out of the camp. She never so much as glanced back over her shoulder. After a moment, with only a little grumbling, her warriors followed her.

We walked until it was too dark to see where we were going. A light rain was still falling. Vintel allowed no fires, so we ate a cold supper of stale barley cakes and lay down to sleep wrapped in our soggy cloaks. We were all so tired that in spite of the damp we slept quite well.

In the morning Vintel sent out half her warriors in groups of two or three to look for Laris's band. She also sent two of the apprentices south to the nearest farm to replenish our supply of food. We would have to be careful of what little we had left, as they were unlikely to return before the evening of the following day.

Sparrow and I tried to make something edible out of the last of our barley and salted beef. Now that it was daylight, Vintel allowed us a small cooking fire. We soon had a watery soup simmering, and Sparrow found some wild onions to give it a little flavor. When it was ready, Vintel came over and squatted down by our campfire. She held out a bowl for me to fill.

"Do you hunt as well as you cook?" she asked me, when she had taken a sip of the broth.

"I'm not a hunter," I replied.

Vintel took another sip, then felt around in the bowl with her fingers to see if there might be any meat in it. There wasn't.

"Too bad," she said. "Hungry warriors can be unpleasant."

"Maara is a hunter."

Vintel pursed her lips. "Can't let her out of my sight, can I?"

"Why not?"

Vintel just looked at me, as if of all people I should know what she was thinking.

"She won't run away," I said. I tried not to sound as angry as I felt.

Vintel's lip curled. "And what would her mommy say if any harm should come to her?"

Then I knew that Vintel was trying to provoke me, for what reason other than her own amusement I couldn't imagine, and I refused to answer her.

Sparrow had fished a piece of meat out of the soup pot. She slipped it into Vintel's bowl. Vintel smiled at her, and I caught a glimpse of something I had never seen in her before. I saw genuine affection in Vintel's eyes. For a moment I thought a little better of her.

Then she said to me, "Take your bow, little hunter, and take any warrior you like to watch over you, but Maara stays here."

"Then Tamras stays here." Maara's voice came from behind us. Neither Vintel nor I had heard her approach. Together we turned and looked up at her.

Vintel set her bowl aside and stood up. "This is not the time to challenge my leadership."

"I am a warrior, yours to command," said Maara, "but Tamras is mine."

Vintel and Maara were beginning to draw a crowd.

"My warriors need meat," Vintel said.

"Then I'll do my best to bring them some."

"If you intend to run off again, it would suit me very well, but right this moment I dare not risk it. Until I know more about the situation here, you'll stay where I can keep an eye on you."

"Would I break my mother's heart?" said Maara.

It was well said. Those who heard her murmured their approval.

"Would you?" Vintel replied, and at once she knew she had made a mistake. Some things should never be called into question, and the love between mother and child is one of them.

Before the situation could go from bad to worse, Lorin stepped forward and said to Vintel, "I'll go along with Maara, if you like."

I was glad Lorin was with us. Ever since he had kept Maara and Vintel from fighting the day Vintel tried to take my brooch, he had been a friend to us. He was one of the warriors who sometimes sat with Maara in the great hall, and he always treated her with respect.

Vintel hesitated.

"As you say, we need meat," Lorin said. "This woman is a hunter, and right now we need her skill."

Vintel saw that she had no choice. "Take care she doesn't turn her bow on you," she said.

I would have liked to go with my warrior, but I knew better than to ask. Lorin waited while Maara took my bow out of its case and fastened my quiver to her belt, alongside her sword. Her shield was too cumbersome to carry. She set it down with the rest of our things.

As I draped her cloak around her shoulders, I whispered, "Take care."

She reached up to fasten it, and her hand brushed mine. It was trembling. I met her eyes. She didn't deny her fear or try to hide it from me.

"Why?" I whispered.

She shook her head. There was neither time nor opportunity for a private conversation.

"You take care too," she said.

As I watched them out of sight, cold fear lay in my chest like a stone.

Sparrow handed me a bowl of soup. "Vintel doesn't mean half of what she says."

"Why does she say it then?"

"It's just her way."

Her way. I knew other things that were Vintel's way. I knew of a prisoner, traveling under safe conduct, who had been taken from among his friends and murdered. If not for Namet's charge, would Vintel have tried to do the same to Maara? Or to me?

36

FEAR

Late that afternoon two of our scouts returned with the news that they had found Laris. They reported to Vintel privately. Then Vintel called everyone together.

"Laris and her warriors arrived at our outpost six days ago," Vintel told us. "They found it occupied. A band of northerners was encamped there. They had at least a dozen of our cattle with them and a cart heaped high with grain."

"That must be the cart that made the track we saw," Sparrow whispered in my ear.

"Laris thought it better not to challenge them until we joined her," Vintel said. "She sent one of her warriors to give us warning. Clearly he never found us."

"Who was it?" asked one of the men.

"Only one man alone?" said another.

"She had fewer than a dozen warriors in her party," said Vintel. "She could hardly spare the one. She sent Breda. He's young and strong, well able to take care of himself. We'll send scouts out after him tomorrow. Or maybe he'll have the sense to know he's missed us and come back."

"Where has Laris been?" Sparrow asked her.

"She took her band to the cliffs."

I hoped I would remember to ask Sparrow later where the cliffs were.

"Are the northerners gone home then?" someone asked.

"Some have," Vintel replied, "but Laris sent out scouts to watch them, and she says more have come. There may be as many as half a hundred altogether. They have separated into raiding parties, but before they take their booty home, they will all meet somewhere. We should deal with them now, before they gather their strength together."

It took me a moment to understand that Vintel intended to confront these northerners. I hoped that we might have the luck never to encounter them. Then I was ashamed of myself for being such a coward. What else were we doing there but trying to keep our enemies from taking what was ours? If their bands were camping in the open on our borders, and even in our outposts, they needed to be taught a lesson. Otherwise they would only become bolder.

Several murmured conversations had started among the warriors. Vintel hushed them. "We'll keep a watch on the approaches to our outpost, as well as on the trails leading north into the wilderness. Tomorrow Laris will join us here." She grinned. "When the northerners return from their raiding, they will find a surprise waiting for them."

It was past midnight when Lorin returned with Breda's body. Sparrow and the other apprentices had been long asleep. The warriors were sleeping too, all but the sentries. Sparrow had tried to get me to go to bed, but I insisted on waiting up for Maara. I was becoming more and more afraid for her.

I must have been dozing a little. I didn't hear the sentry's challenge or Lorin's answer. I looked up to see Lorin carrying something over his shoulder. At first I thought it was a deer.

Gently Lorin set Breda down.

"Where is he hurt?" I asked.

I reached for my pack, where I kept my remedies.

Lorin shook his head. "He's past healing."

I looked down at Breda's peaceful face. He wore his old tattered cloak. I wondered if he had ever found a new one. He wouldn't need it now.

Lorin sat down wearily and stretched his hands out to the fire. I peered into the darkness, looking for Maara.

Lorin saw my fear for her.

"She's right behind me," he said. "She'll be here in a few minutes."

When I heard her coming, I went to meet her. She was carrying the carcass of a small deer.

"Go and wake Vintel," she said.

When I returned with Vintel, Maara had joined Lorin by the fire and was busy butchering the deer.

Vintel knelt down beside Breda's body. "How did this happen?"

"We found him not far from here," said Lorin. "Maara thought we might have better luck in open country, where we could see the game, if there was any, so we went north, back into the wilderness. We finally found a small herd of deer, and Maara brought one down, as you can see."

Lorin rubbed his eyes. He looked exhausted.

Maara didn't look much better. I knelt down beside her and took the knife from her hand. She sat down across the fire from Lorin, while I cut thin strips of the tenderest meat and laid them on the hot coals.

My stomach began to rumble in anticipation.

"On our way back," said Lorin, "we followed the same trail we traveled yesterday. Soon after sunset we came across Breda's body. I can't imagine what he was doing there."

Vintel told again the story we had heard from Laris. Then she pulled Breda's cloak aside and examined his body for wounds.

"Someone put a knife in his back," Lorin said. He helped Vintel turn Breda over. Blood had soaked the back of Breda's tunic.

"Where are his weapons?" Vintel asked.

"Gone," said Lorin. "They're with whoever killed him."

"And where are they?"

Lorin shrugged. "We tried to read the signs, but it was too dark to make out much. Breda lay a dozen yards from the trail, and the bracken was trampled all around him. I'm of the opinion that those who killed him were going north, but Maara believes my judgment has been clouded by wishful thinking." He looked over at Maara and grinned.

"What is your opinion?" Vintel asked my warrior.

Maara looked up at her. "He was traveling south. So were his killers. They came upon him from behind. He knew they were there, and he was running from them. He ran for a long time, but at last they ran him down. All afternoon I had seen signs of many feet, running easily at a steady pace. Not long before we found Breda's body, they were running hard."

Vintel turned to Lorin. "Did you see these signs?"

"I wasn't paying much attention to the ground," Lorin said. "I was keeping an eye out for trouble."

The smell of food brought everyone out of their sound sleep. I fed Maara and Lorin first, then shared the rest of the meat out among the warriors. The apprentices waited until the warriors were fed before crowding around the fire.

While they waited for their turn to eat, Sparrow and a few others attended to Breda's body. They bound him up in his tattered cloak, a warrior's shroud, and set his body a little apart from the living. I wondered if we would bury Breda here on the frontier or if someone would take him home.

Sparrow knelt beside me and took the knife from my hand.

"Go and see to your warrior," she said. "I'll finish here."

I found Maara already sleeping. Now that their hunger was satisfied, many of the warriors had settled themselves around the rekindled campfires and were talking quietly together. While I was curious to hear what they were saying, I was too tired to stay up and listen. I lay down beside Maara, spoke a word of thanks to the Mother for her safe return, and slept.

Early the next afternoon, Laris and her band joined us. Donal and Kenit were among them, as well as Taia, Laris's apprentice. When Laris heard that yet another band of northerners had come, she tried to persuade Vintel to return to the safety of the cliffs, but Vintel was reluctant to camp so far from the trails the raiding parties would take when they came north again.

I had remembered to ask Sparrow where the cliffs were. Not far west of us, along an ancient streambed, they rose steeply on either side, and high in the cliff walls were caves. The narrow trails that led to them could be defended by a very few. It was a good refuge when such a thing was needed, but a poor place from which to launch an attack against a raiding party.

In the end we camped another night where we were, because the cart with our supplies didn't arrive until long after dark. I think Vintel would have let the oxen take the cart home by themselves and buried Breda where he lay, but Laris insisted that Breda's apprentice use the cart to bear Breda's body home to Merin's house before returning it to the farmer it had been borrowed from.

That night Laris sat up late by her campfire, mourning her dead warrior. Maara watched from a distance as others approached her and offered her their sympathy. When Laris was alone again, Maara went to sit with her. They talked together for a little while. Then Maara returned to our fire.

"What were you talking about?" I asked her.

"We talked about Vintel," she said in a low voice. "About what Vintel intends to do. Laris disagrees with her. She fears the northerners are too many for us and that we should send for help before we commit ourselves to a fight."

"Help from the farmers, or help from Merin's house?"

"A day's travel to the east there is another outpost. If we had time to send for them, we might add another two dozen warriors to our number, provided they aren't busy with troubles of their own. But if we wait for them, the northerners may again gather their strength together, so Vintel may be wise not to wait."

"You mean Vintel is right?"

"I think she's right about that. What concerns me is how she plans to deal with them. If there are as many as Laris thinks there are, we might consider them a war party. Laris says it's something they do in times of hardship, and it's something we will often overlook, because they're willing to fight for what they need. But this time is different."

"Because they killed Breda?"

She nodded. "Vintel won't take it lightly. She shouldn't take it lightly, but I fear she may go too far."

"Go too far? How?"

"Breda is dead. That is beyond changing. Others are alive tonight who will put their lives at risk tomorrow. If more are to die, we must be certain that their blood buys something worthy of them."

"What could be worthy of their lives?" I asked her.

"A time of peace," she said.

Maara took up a stick to prod the fire. Tonight her hand was steady. I remembered that the day before I had felt it tremble.

"Have we anything to fear?" I asked her.

"We have a great deal to fear."

"From Vintel?"

"No," she said. "Not now. Now Vintel needs us."

That night I had haunted dreams. I was walking in the wilderness when I heard the tramp of many feet behind me, and I ran, with the sound of my pursuers close on my heels. A tangle of deadfall ensnared my legs. I felt their hands take hold of me.

I started up out of my sleep, breathless and sweating. Maara lay awake beside me. When I spoke her name, she hushed me and turned over.

Once more I awoke that night. My face was wet with tears. Still half-dreaming, I saw Breda, his boyish face gazing with delight at the fox-skin bag my warrior made, pleased with the beauty of it and with himself for having acquired it. I wrapped close around me the cloak he gave for it. Was this cloak his mother's gift that kept me warm that night? I pulled it over my head and wept for his mother's grief.

The next day we moved our camp. Vintel chose a place that was a compromise, closer to the cliffs, but within striking distance of the trails the northerners must take when they returned. She sent no messengers to ask for help, only scouts to keep watch on the trails. That afternoon they brought us word that three raiding parties were returning north. Two carried wounded with them. Vintel chose to intercept those two. They would be burdened with their spoils, as well as with their wounded, and they were moving as fast as they were able, fearing pursuit more than what might lie ahead of them.

Our warriors formed into two groups of roughly equal size, armed and armored, ready for a skirmish. Almost a dozen warriors were to remain in camp, held in reserve so that, if things went badly, they would be ready to help the others or cover our retreat to the cliffs. Maara was one of them. Although the thought of coming face to face with the northerners still frightened me, I resented being left behind.

"Your turn will come," whispered Sparrow. Her eyes sparkled with excitement. With the other apprentices, she followed her warrior's band down the trail.

37

COURAGE

Late in the evening our warriors returned. We heard them coming long before they reached us.

"That's a good sign," Maara said. "Victory is loud. Defeat is silent."

Vintel's band arrived first. The warriors who had stayed behind joined them around the campfires to listen to their story. I was more interested in hearing what Sparrow had to say.

"The fight was over almost before it started," she told me. She sounded disappointed. "Most of them dropped what they were carrying and ran. A few stood and fought, but they didn't stand long against us."

"What happened to the wounded they were carrying?"

She shrugged. "I didn't see any wounded."

"What will they do now?"

"Go home, I hope."

A little later Laris's band arrived. They had much the same tale to tell. Laris's warriors joined Vintel's around the fires, and the boasting about the day's feats of arms went on long into the night. Maara sat up with them for hours, listening.

"Will the northerners go home now?" I asked her, when she finally came to bed.

She shook her head. "They won't go home empty-handed."

"What does Vintel think?"

"I think Vintel is encouraging her warriors to enjoy their victory."

Early the next morning, Vintel sent out scouts to see if any of our enemies remained nearby. In less than an hour two of them returned at a hard run, heedless of the noise they made. They didn't wait to speak to Vintel privately but blurted out their news as our warriors gathered around them.

"They're encamped," said one. "Not far. No more than a dozen, caring for their wounded."

"Breda's shield stands at the center of their camp," said the other.

An angry murmur ran through the crowd. I felt the warriors' outrage and their eagerness to vent it. After their easy victory the day before, they were ready for another. I saw on more than one face a determination to redeem Breda's shield and take revenge upon his killers.

Vintel stepped into their midst. "Are you all so determined to run head-long into the trap they've set for you?"

"Would you leave them unmolested to bind their wounds?" said Pol. Though no longer young, Pol had a reputation for being hotheaded.

"Rather than fall into their trap, I would prefer to set a trap for them," said Vintel. "Yesterday we had a victory, but yesterday is done. Today there is something new before us." She looked at the warriors gathered around her, at each one in turn, challenging them with her eyes. "Those who follow me today must do as I tell them or our plan will fail." She waited to see if anyone would challenge her leadership. No one did.

"Their display of Breda's shield is meant to goad us, and their small number is meant to make us careless. The rest of them are not far off. When we attack these few, they'll break and run, to lure us into giving chase. If we do, they'll lead us into the main body of their warriors. We will be among them before we know it, and they'll be prepared to meet us. They will be disciplined, and we will be no more so than a pack of dogs after a rabbit."

"What's the point of attacking them then, if we're not going to pursue them?" Pol complained.

Vintel ignored him and turned to the scouts. "How many able-bodied are there?"

"I counted eleven," said one.

"Twelve," said the other.

"And how many wounded?"

"Many," said the first with satisfaction.

Maara stepped forward. "There are no wounded in that camp."

Vintel regarded her with annoyance. "How would you know that?"

"Think," said Maara. "It makes no sense. Why would they leave their wounded in harm's way?"

Now Vintel was listening.

"When we attack their camp," Maara said, "their warriors will give ground, expecting us to ignore the wounded and pursue them."

I didn't see Maara's point, but Vintel did.

"And when we pursue their fleeing warriors," she said, "the wounded will be behind us."

Maara nodded.

"And if, as you say, they are not wounded but able-bodied, they will attack us from behind."

Maara nodded again.

"Clever," Vintel admitted. "Have you seen this trick before?"

"The northerners are full of tricks," said Maara.

"I think the northerners will find we're just as clever," Vintel said. Her eyes sparkled. She was enjoying this duel of wits as much as she was reputed to enjoy a duel of arms. "When their warriors fall back, those on the ground will be at a disadvantage, whether or not they're able-bodied."

"Would you put them to the sword?" said Pol, who for all his hotheadedness sounded a bit horrified at the idea.

"Not at all," Vintel said. "We'll take them alive before they know what's happening. Then we'll be the ones to fall back, and their warriors will have to pursue us. If there are more of them in hiding somewhere, we may draw them out. If they're foolish enough to chase us, we'll lead them into a trap of our own."

"It might work," said Pol.

"Will you lead the warriors who will lie in wait?" Vintel asked him.

Pol nodded. He looked pleased at being honored with command.

Laris bristled. "May I not lead my own band?"

Vintel turned to her. "I want your band to come with me, to attack the camp. I need cool heads for this. Will you and your warriors follow me?"

Laris nodded. She seemed well satisfied with that arrangement.

Vintel turned back to the assembled warriors. "Yesterday you had the pleasure of watching your enemies flee from you. If you believe that they are cowards, I assure you they are not. They fled because they were at a disadvantage. Today they will meet us on their own terms, and you will find them as courageous as any warriors you've ever faced. If they run today, it will be because they have a plan. If you pursue them, you will have handed them the victory."

This time no one would be left behind. Maara drew me aside.

"Stay with the apprentices," she told me. "Stay away from the fighting, and stay well hidden. If the day goes against us, get yourself to the cliffs."

Our scouts led us to the northerners' camp. We crept silently down a gully between lightly wooded hills. I was so busy trying to be quiet and keep my footing on the rocky hillside that I had no time to think about an encounter with the northerners. Then I smelled a whiff of smoke, and the first prickles of fear touched the back of my neck.

As we drew near their camp, I caught glimpses of it through the trees. We stopped in a clearing from which we had a partial view of it. We were still well hidden, out of sight and earshot. Everything was as our scouts had said. The camp had open ground around it, enough to give the northerners warning of attack. We had seen no sentries, and no one had sounded an alarm, but if this was a trap our enemies had set for us, there would be no sentries posted.

Vintel took Sparrow aside and spoke to her quietly, then gestured to the apprentices to stay where we were. We all understood that Vintel had left Sparrow in charge of us. Sparrow led us up the steep hillside to a place where a rocky ledge would conceal us from anyone coming up the hill.

Sparrow scrambled up onto the ledge. I followed her. The rest of the apprentices found hiding places for themselves, where they could see without being seen. Side by side Sparrow and I lay on our stomachs and peered over the edge. Directly below us our warriors were gathered. Farther down the hillside the trees grew close together, with undergrowth beneath them that would provide good cover.

From our vantage point we could see much of the northerners' camp, as well as the hillside rising steeply behind it, thickly wooded enough to conceal the warriors that Vintel believed were hiding there. Sparrow pointed it out to me, and I nodded that I understood.

"It would be hard fighting," she whispered.

"Yes." By now I knew enough about fighting to know that it was more difficult to fight going uphill than down.

I studied the northerners with curiosity, surprised to see that they looked just like us. I might easily have mistaken them for a band of our own warriors, guarding the frontier. They looked relaxed and confident, as if they belonged there.

Below us our warriors waited while Vintel and Pol put their heads together. Then Pol took his warriors farther down the hill. My warrior went with them, and I watched her out of sight. Her dark green cloak blended into the colors of the wood. I knew from my own experience that one might pass within a few feet of her and never know she was there.

Vintel's band waited for Pol's warriors to get into position and conceal themselves. Then they made their way down the hillside. Soon they too disappeared from sight among the trees.

The soft sounds of their passing faded. No bird sang. There was no wind. The northerners, unaware of danger, sat beside the smoking ashes of their fires. Sparrow lay still beside me. I wondered how she could remain so still. My own body was humming with excitement.

A cry rang out, and every hair on my head stood up. More voices joined in the battle cry. The northerners, too stunned to move, sat frozen beside their fires. A few heartbeats later they began to stir. They got to their feet and gazed about them in surprise, as if this attack were not something they expected.

Vintel burst into the clearing. Her sword raised high over her head, Laris and her band close on her heels, she ran at the man nearest her. Now the northerners found their voices. Shouting their own war cries, they drew their swords and took up their shields, but they had no time to brace themselves against the sudden force of the attack. For a few moments each one stood and fought. We heard no war cries then, only the clash of sword on shield. Suddenly the northern warriors broke and ran. Whether or not a retreat was part of their plan, there was nothing planned about their headlong flight from our warriors' swords.

Sparrow nudged me and pointed to the edge of the clearing, where a woman lay wrapped in her cloak. I looked in time to see her throw her cloak aside and spring to her feet, sword in hand. When she saw her comrades in full flight, she hesitated only a moment before she turned and followed them.

Now I understood the temptation to pursue a fleeing enemy. When I saw their backs, my legs began to twitch, and I could have dashed off after them myself. Vintel's warriors resisted the temptation. They fell upon the ones who still lay on the ground and quickly disarmed them. Some, like the woman we had seen, had already scrambled to their feet and run away, but our warriors captured at least four and withdrew with them into the shelter of the woods.

I watched the hillside opposite, waiting for the northerners to burst out of their cover and charge down the hill to rescue their comrades. Nothing happened.

Minutes passed more slowly than I had ever known time to pass. I saw no movement on the opposite hillside or on the hillside below us where our warriors waited. I heard only the thudding beat of my own heart.

Then Vintel stepped into the clearing. Carrying no shield, her sword sheathed at her side, she strode through the northerners' camp and vanished from our sight for a moment before returning with Breda's shield.

"What is she doing?" I whispered to Sparrow. "Are the northerners gone?"

"She's baiting the trap," Sparrow replied.

Vintel never glanced in the direction of the hillside where the northerners had fled. She looked around the camp for anything of value they had left behind, picking up a leather helmet and two swords the northerners had dropped in their hasty retreat. Then, with one final glance around her, she shouldered Breda's shield and walked with unhurried step back into the safety of the woods.

I didn't realize I had been holding my breath until my relief at Vintel's safe return allowed me to breathe again. I admired her courage very much, although I knew that, if they were needed, warriors stood ready to come to her defense. Vintel belonged to us, and for a little while I forgot she was my enemy.

More time passed.

"What's going on?" I asked Sparrow.

"We're waiting for them to attack," she said.

"What are they waiting for?"

"They must be waiting for us to attack them."

"How long will we wait?"

She shrugged.

After a time that felt like ages, Vintel stepped again into the clearing. Breda's shield hung from her shoulder, and she had one of the prisoners with her. His hands were tied behind his back. She pushed him ahead of her to the center of the clearing and forced him to his knees. Then she held Breda's shield high over her head, showing it to whoever might still be watching from the opposite hillside.

Vintel set the shield down and raised her right hand. A flash of sunlight glanced off the blade. She showed the knife to the unseen warriors of the northern tribes, then plunged it into the back of the prisoner who knelt before her. He made no sound, but only swayed a little before he fell. With the dead man lying at her feet, Vintel took up Breda's shield and drew her sword. Alone, she stood waiting for the northerners to answer her.

The silence lasted so long that I began to think the northerners had all vanished and left their comrade to die for nothing. Then a loud cry went up from the hillside opposite. Other voices joined it, and from our side, Laris and her warriors ran to join Vintel. Side by side, shouting their own war cries, they waited for the northerners' attack.

From the woods at last the northern warriors came. More than I could count, many more than we had seen at first, they rushed down upon Vintel's tiny band. Vintel and her warriors turned and fled.

So terrifying was the sight that I too might have leapt to my feet and run if I hadn't had the hillside at my back. It was now the enemy's turn to see our warriors flee, and they pursued Vintel and Laris and the others at full cry. Thinking they were chasing only a small band, they charged across the clearing and into the woods, where the rest of our warriors awaited them.

I could see nothing for the trees. At first we heard only the sounds of Vintel's flight through the thicket and the shouts of the pursuit. Then a roar went up as our hidden warriors showed themselves. Now we heard the clash of sword on shield, and many of the cries we heard were cries of pain.

For a time we listened to the sounds of a battle we couldn't see. Then the sounds receded, as our warriors pushed theirs back toward the clearing. Several of the northern warriors fled back across it into the trees. Behind me a cheer went up from the apprentices. I would have added my voice to theirs, but Sparrow turned and shouted at them to be quiet.

I thought that the northerners would soon be in full retreat. Instead the sounds of fighting continued. I was watching the woods below us, trying to catch a glimpse of the battle, when I saw something move out of the corner of my eye. I looked up at the opposite hillside. Warriors of the northern tribes poured out of the woods. There seemed to be no end to them.

Sparrow's attention was still on the fight below us. I nudged her and pointed at the clearing.

"The Mother keep us," she whispered.

"Are we outnumbered?"

"We are now."

She gestured to one of the apprentices closest to us.

"Get everyone ready to go to the cliffs," she told him. Then Sparrow turned to me. "Our warriors will try to cover our retreat, but you might get that bow ready, just in case."

38

DEATH

With shaking hands I loosened the strap of my bow case and slipped it off over my head. I drew my bow out of it and managed to string it by lying on my back, bracing it against my foot, and bending it around my thigh. Then I fastened the quiver to my belt and took an arrow from it.

"Listen," said Sparrow.

I heard nothing.

"It stopped," she said.

"What?"

"The fighting. It stopped."

We waited, listening.

Something moved on the hillside below me. I fitted the arrow to the bowstring.

"That's one of ours," Sparrow whispered.

Nothing was moving now in the woods below me, but I did see a patch of color in a thicket that seemed out of place. It might have been a bit of someone's cloak.

"They've retreated," Sparrow said.

"The northerners?"

"No, our warriors."

"Where are the northerners?"

"Still down there, somewhere."

"Why did they stop?"

"I don't know."

I thought about their first disastrous pursuit of Vintel's handful of warriors. "Perhaps they fear there may be more of us."

"Perhaps."

Another movement below us caught my eye.

"Our warriors are pulling back to where the gully narrows," Sparrow said.

Just as the narrow trails that led to the caves could be defended by a few against many, so too could the narrow neck of the gully, at least for a little while, and the northerners would have the added disadvantage of having to fight uphill.

I peered down into the woods. "Why can't I see them?"

"Most of them are still farther down the hill. Those below us here will cover the retreat of the rest, if it comes to that."

We waited. The anticipation of what would happen next was sending tingles up and down my spine. I was more excited than afraid. I had been too busy trying to understand what was happening to think about the danger we were in. I had yet to see the enemy close up or any of the fighting. But Maara was somewhere down on that hillside, and I did fear for her. I tried not to think about it.

A shout made me jump. Another answered it. Then the war cries of the northern tribes rose up through the trees. At once our warriors' cries rang out. Again the sound of battle filled the air. This time it was much closer.

A warrior burst out of the shelter of the trees, running toward us up the hill. She carried no shield, but from the color of her cloak I thought it must be Laris. Her sword was in her hand, and blood ran red down the arm that held it.

Taia cried out behind me. Before Sparrow could stop her, she slid down the steep hillside and started toward Laris. Laris saw her and shouted to her to go back. Taia stopped, but she didn't return to the safety of the rocks. She stood where she was, below the ledge where Sparrow and I lay. Laris turned then and stood between us and the enemy, as though she would hold them all back herself.

Sparrow gestured to the apprentices to begin the retreat. They slipped down the hillside, and some started back up the gully, but Taia still stood below the rock ledge, and many of them joined her, as if they were there on an outing, to watch the battle.

"They're going to get themselves killed," Sparrow said. "And they're going to get warriors killed trying to defend them." She backed away from the
edge of the rock. "Stay here and cover our retreat."

I nodded and turned back to the hillside below in time to see a warrior
of the northern tribes burst out of the woods and run at Laris. I forgot the
bow in my hands. I watched in horror as he raised his sword. I heard Taia
shout a warning, and Laris turned to face him.

More of our warriors ran out of the cover of the trees. Maara was among
them. She saw that Laris was in trouble and started toward her, but she
was too far away. The northerner struck at Laris. She had no shield, so she
raised her sword to deflect the blow. His blade descended, and Laris's blade
shattered.

Laris took a step backward and tripped. She fell to the ground, and it
was her fall that saved her. Before the northerner could reach her, Maara's
sword arced by his shoulder. He caught it on his shield, but the tip of it
drew blood.

The northerners had followed close on our warriors' heels. The open
ground below the rock where I lay was now filled with warriors. I lost sight
of Maara in the confusion. Our warriors could retreat no farther, and so
they turned and fought, some with fury, some with cold anger, some with
desperation, as they sought their last partner in a deadly dance.

When my eyes again found Maara, the man who had attacked Laris lay
unmoving at her feet. As I watched, another man ran at Maara with such
force that their shields crashed together and Maara was hurled backwards to
the ground. Her sword flew from her hand. The northerner stood over her,
his sword above his head. When the blow fell, Maara met it with her shield.
His blade sliced through the leather cover and bit deep into the wooden
frame. He struggled to free it.

By the time the northern warrior raised his sword again, I was on my
feet. I drew my bow and set the arrow's tip at the center of his chest. Then
I thought of Maara, lying on the ground between my arrow and its target,
and I raised the bow just a little before I let the arrow fly.

He stood still for a moment, his sword high above his head, his eyes open
wide and staring. Then he dropped his sword and with both hands clawed
at his throat, where only the fletching of my arrow protruded from below
his jaw. His mouth opened as if he meant to scream, but no sound came
out of it. Blood welled up out of his mouth, spilled down his beard and over

his hands. I watched him, fascinated, while his eyes searched for me. Just as they found me, the light died out of them. He fell to his knees, pitched forward, and lay still.

From below me a new cry rang out. Taia, brandishing a stick as if it were the finest blade, launched herself down the hill. The apprentices followed her, fists upraised, howling like a pack of wolves. None of them was armed, not even with sticks or stones, but the northern warriors didn't wait to see what their enemies had loosed against them. They fled. Many dropped their heavy shields, and some cast their swords aside. Terrified, they ran down the hill and across the clearing and disappeared into the thicket.

I watched our warriors fall upon the stragglers and bring them down. There was no stopping the pursuit. Warriors and apprentices together vanished into the woods.

Suddenly Maara was beside me, standing on the rock.

"I'm fine," I said.

"Good," she said. "Come down."

She held out her hand and backed away from me, away from the rock's edge. Out of habit, I followed her. She stepped aside and gestured for me to descend first, down the steep hillside. My feet skittered on loose rock as I slid down, but I arrived at the bottom still on my feet. She followed close behind me.

"Come with me," she said.

She walked away from me toward the open ground. Toward his body.

I didn't move. She turned to face me. I felt my face crumple like the face of a child about to cry, but the place around my heart was ice.

Maara came back for me. Her fingers closed tight around my upper arm. She pulled me along with her, as a mother pulls a reluctant child, until we stood beside his body.

I refused to look.

"You dishonor a brave man," she said.

Her voice was colder than the ice around my heart.

Dishonor?

"Look at him," said Maara.

I looked down at the ground beside him. Blood dappled the leaves around his head. Maara turned him over. I looked away and closed my eyes.

"Take his shield."

At last I found the courage to look at him, although I couldn't bring myself to look directly at his face. His shield lay beside him, still strapped securely to his forearm.

I bent to pick it up, but even in death, he held on to it with a grip I couldn't break. I drew my knife and cut the strap that bound it to his arm. Then I was able to wrest it from him.

"Tamras."

I turned to her. Her face was so close to mine that I couldn't avoid her eyes.

"Your enemy lies at your feet," she said. "He was a brave man, a strong man who was made to yield to someone stronger. His power is now yours, if you will take it."

"His power?"

She spoke a word I didn't understand. It had a sharp edge to it. She saw that I didn't understand it. She let go of me and knelt beside the northern warrior's body.

"I don't know the name for it in your language," she said. "Your language may not have a name for it. It encompasses many things. Among them is the part of him that may yet prove stronger than you are." She dipped two fingers of her right hand into the blood that had pooled around his wound and stood up. "Are you strong enough to add his power to your own?"

Although I didn't understand what she was asking, I knew what she expected of me. I nodded.

"Well done," she said.

She touched her fingers to my temple and drew them across my brow and down both cheeks. The blood, warm at first, chilled my skin as it dried. Maara went to the body of the warrior she had killed and marked herself with his blood, as she had marked me.

Someone behind me said, "I would wear war honors too, if I could."

It was Laris. She approached Maara and, drawing her a little away from me, said something to her I couldn't hear. Her wound still bled.

Our warriors were returning. Elated by their victory, they showed off to one another their spoils — swords and shields, knives, bits of armor, helmets. One woman wore a necklace of boar's teeth taken from the dead. I had seen her in the melee. Only minutes earlier hatred had twisted her face into a contorted mask, and I thought I saw it smoldering still behind her self-satisfied smile.

Sparrow touched my arm. "I'm fine," I said.

She murmured something in my ear and went to join Vintel.

I watched the activity around me. Several of our warriors sat on the ground while their apprentices washed and bound their wounds. One of the apprentices cut two saplings and tied her cloak between them to make a litter for her wounded warrior. We stayed where we were only long enough to gather everyone together. Then we retreated to the cliffs, where our wounded would be safe until we could bring a wagon to take them home.

Sparrow had been right about the trails that led up to the caves. They were so steep and so narrow that I couldn't imagine how anyone could reach the caves if there were even one person to oppose them. In single file we straggled up the cliff face, taking the hand of the person in front for help over the difficult places and then extending our own hand to the person behind.

Halfway up the cliff we arrived at the mouth of an immense cave. The narrow ledge in front of it was large enough to accommodate all of us and more. Fires were laid, ready to light. One of the apprentices took out her firestones.

"Won't the northerners see our fires?" I asked Sparrow.

"Let them," she said. She chuckled. "Although I doubt they're anywhere within sight of this place. They won't stop running now until they're safe at home."

"Won't they come back for their wounded?"

"Oh, I suppose so," she said, "but they won't trouble us anymore."

"How can you be sure?"

"Their hearts are defeated," she said.

While the other apprentices set up our camp, I helped tend the wounded. One of Laris's warriors had a bad cut on her thigh. It was she for whom they had made the litter. I stitched her wound as I had seen the healer do for Maara. Laris's wound didn't require stitching, but I bound it up with herbs, to speed the healing. The only other injuries were a few blows to the head and some deep cuts that could prove dangerous if not well cleaned and cared for, but none of our warriors had taken a mortal wound, and none had died.

The northerners had not been so fortunate. I learned from Sparrow that at least a dozen of their warriors lay dead upon the hillside, and many more had wounds so dreadful that they must surely die.

While I had so much to do, I had no time to think about the battle or about my part in it. I was glad for the distraction, but at last I had done all I could for the wounded. As I put my medicines away, Taia came to me and put her arm around my shoulders.

"Tamras of the Bow," she said, "you did well today."

"As did you," I told her. "You showed great courage on the battlefield."

A common phrase, it was what one said to a warrior who had fought well, and I meant every word of it. I'd never had much of an opinion of Taia as a warrior. That day she surprised me. She smiled with pleasure at my praise. I think she had surprised herself.

I went with Taia to join the other apprentices. They had all gathered around one of the fires, while the warriors were gathered around another. Food had been prepared and the warriors fed. Sparrow handed me a bowl of soup. Although it was our first meal since breakfast, I could swallow only a few mouthfuls of it. I looked out over the treetops and watched the darkness fall.

Someone was watching me. I turned and met Maara's eyes. She was sitting next to Laris at the warriors' fire. I wondered why her face was dirty. Then I remembered. I put my hand to my own face, and a bit of dried blood crumbled into my palm.

Now the time had come for the warriors to relive their victory. One of the men leaped to his feet and praised the courage of another who had fought beside him before telling of his own exploits that day. He waved his arm above his head and danced back and forth to demonstrate his skillful swordplay.

When he sat down, another man stood up and told of his fierce combat with a much bigger man than he, a man so large that by the end of the story he had become a giant.

As the warriors spoke, their eyes gleamed with more than firelight. Then I saw the smudges on one warrior's face. He had marked himself with blood, as Maara had marked herself and me. When I looked around at the others, I saw several more.

I nudged Sparrow, who was sitting beside me. "Is it the custom here for warriors to mark themselves like that?"

She shook her head. "It never has been before. Perhaps they didn't want to be outdone by Maara."

"I think your warrior has set a fashion," said Taia, who sat next to Sparrow.

I laughed at that. It felt good to laugh, but at the same time, I felt as if the laughter had come from someone else.

Now more warriors stood up to tell their stories. Soon almost all of them were on their feet, congratulating themselves, encouraging one another, adding something to someone's story or correcting someone who had made a mistake. A good-natured squabble broke out over who had drawn first blood. In the shadows, Laris and Maara watched them from a distance.

Then Vintel took up her shield and beat her sword upon it until everyone was quiet. Once she had their attention, she didn't speak right away, but gazed at them with pride, until I could feel in the air their anticipation of her praise.

"Today victory is ours," she said at last. "The retelling of these tales will warm our hearts through the coming winter. Great feats of arms were done today. I expected no less from the warriors of Merin's house."

She looked around at them, and her warriors grinned back at her, well pleased with themselves.

"Before you take all the glory to yourselves," she said, "let us praise the one who turned the tide of battle."

While the warriors were glancing at one another, wondering who she meant, Vintel approached our fire. She went directly to Taia and extended her hand. Taia took it, and Vintel drew her to her feet and led her to the warriors' fire.

"Now it's your turn," Vintel said to her. "Tell us of your own brave deeds."

"I have no brave deeds to boast of," Taia said.

Vintel turned to Laris. "You have neglected to teach your apprentice the greatest of the arts of war. This young woman doesn't seem to know how to make much of herself."

The warriors laughed.

"If she can't do her own boasting, I'll have to do it for her, just this once." Vintel put her arm around Taia's shoulders. "Today this young woman showed as much courage as I've ever seen upon the battlefield. With no sword, no dagger, no weapon but a frail twig, she led a band armed with nothing more than brave hearts against the enemy. If she had not, I think we would be telling grimmer stories of the fighting this day."

"I didn't——" Taia said.

"This is not a day for modesty," Vintel told her. "In a few months' time you would have received your shield in any case, but today you proved yourself a warrior."

Vintel gestured to Laris, who approached her, carrying a sword.

"This sword was captured from one of the enemy that you helped put to flight," said Vintel. "Let it be the token of your part in this victory."

Laris fastened the sword to Taia's belt.

Sparrow took my hand and squeezed it.

"Now she'll honor you," she whispered.

But Vintel sat down beside the warriors' fire and made a place for Taia beside her, and the warriors resumed their celebration.

I was relieved that Vintel wasn't going to call attention to me, but Sparrow was disappointed.

"It isn't fair," she said. "She should have honored you too. It isn't fair for Taia to get all the glory."

"She's welcome to it," I said.

But Sparrow was indignant. "How can she disregard what you did?"

"I did very little."

"You killed a warrior of the northern tribes. Vintel should have honored you for the kill, if for nothing else. And it was your kill that put the heart into Taia in the first place."

"Maybe Vintel doesn't know."

"She knows."

"She does?"

"Your skill hasn't gone unnoticed," Sparrow said. "I heard several of the warriors speak to her about it. Laris made a point of speaking to her about it. Vintel can't be overjoyed that your warrior was right about something, but that doesn't excuse her from giving praise where praise is due."

"I don't want Vintel's praise."

Sparrow gave me a puzzled look. "I don't understand. Why are you so at odds with her?"

"Because she and my warrior are at odds."

"That's all?" Her voice told me she thought there must be more.

"Vintel hasn't had much use for me since she asked for me as an apprentice and I chose someone else."

"Well," said Sparrow, smiling her sweetest smile at me. "I can't blame her for being angry about that."

While the warriors sat at their fire recounting to one another their feats of arms, the apprentices had a celebration of their own. At first they were all elated, swept up in the excitement. They chattered on about their wild charge and the thrill of seeing the enemy flee from them in confusion. What they had done that day made them feel powerful, more powerful than they had ever felt before, and as they had every right to do, they indulged their pride in themselves.

But as the night wore on, they grew quiet and thoughtful. They must have seen some dreadful things that day. I wondered if the killing bothered them. Since I was one of the killers myself, I didn't ask.

Maara waited until I was alone. All evening she had been sitting with Laris in the shadows. All evening I had known exactly where she was. Even while I was talking with Sparrow and listening to the others tell their stories, I was waiting for her. When the last of the apprentices had gone to bed, she came and sat beside me.

I don't know what I expected. I felt hollow, as if the ice around my heart had melted and left nothing in its place. I wanted her to make me feel like myself again.

"Only a few weeks ago," she said softly, "you told me you were reluctant to take the lives of birds, but you found your power, and you learned to take no harm from exercising it."

It felt to me like a very long time since I had been hunting birds.

"You will master this new power too," she said.

She started to stand up. Fearful that she was going to leave me, I clutched at her sleeve, like a child grasping at her mother's skirts. At once I was ashamed of myself, and I let go.

"I'll be right back," she said.

She disappeared into the shadows of the cave. When she returned, she was carrying a shield. I remembered that her shield had been damaged in the fighting, and I thought she had brought it to the fire to repair it, but when she sat down beside me, I saw that it was the shield I had taken from the northerner.

"Vintel should have honored you too," she said.

"I'm glad she didn't."

"So am I, but you deserve the honors of war no less than Taia."

Maara set the shield down in front of me. "This is yours." She lifted the edge, so that I could see the sword that lay beneath it. "So is this."

When I started to say I didn't want them, she put a finger to my lips.

"When you told me you didn't want the bow, I said nothing, because you weren't ready to accept it, but I believe it was a gift for you. However it came to be where we found it, it was meant to find you. Now it has brought you glory and the spoils of war. I think it would have been better if this had not happened so soon, but nothing can change what's done, and now you must be worthy of the man you killed."

The man I killed.

Maara leaned close to me and peered into my eyes. "Do you regret what you did?"

I saw in my mind's eye my warrior lying on the ground, sheltering under her shield, and the northern warrior standing over her. I shook my head.

"That's good," she said, "because your regret would do him a great wrong. It would be as if he died for nothing."

She said no more, but she made no move to leave me, and I took comfort from having her nearby. I tried to think of something to ask her, so that she would talk to me some more.

"Some of the men marked themselves with blood," I said.

"Yes."

"Why?"

"You must ask them that."

"Why did you mark me?"

She sighed. "It's the custom among my people. Laris told me it hasn't been done here in many years. I should have thought before I did it, but it has a meaning I would have you understand."

"What does it mean?"

"When you butchered animals at home," she said, "did you not make an offering of blood to the Mother?"

"Of course we did."

"Why did you do that?"

"Because all life comes from her."

"That's right," she said. "We offer her the first blood of everything — the first blood of the animals we kill, the first blood of the maiden, the first blood of childbirth. All life is hers, and when a warrior marks herself with blood, she offers back the life she took."

"I thought it was a kind of boasting."

"Not at all," she said. "Not at all."

In spite of myself, I yawned.

Maara stood up and spread her cloak on the ground there beside the fire. The others had made their beds in the shelter of the cave, but Maara made ours out in the open air. She waited for me to lie down. Then she lay down beside me and pulled my cloak over us.

Although I was exhausted, I was in no hurry to sleep. I lay open-eyed, gazing up at the stars.

"Yes," she said. "He will come to you in dreams."

That she understood my fears was a comfort to me. "What shall I do?"

"Sleep," she said, "and when you meet him face to face, don't be afraid to speak to him. Tell him that though you are young and small of body, your spirit is large and powerful. Tell him it was no disgrace to be defeated by someone so powerful. Then tell him to go on to the place of new beginnings and leave you in peace."

In spite of my fear, I had to laugh. Surely this was boasting so absurd, so grandiose, that his spirit would only laugh at me.

"But my spirit isn't large and powerful," I said.

"You think not?"

"I think not."

"Look back over this day and tell me what you did."

All evening I had been trying to forget what I did that day, but she made me look at it again.

"You shot an arrow," she said. "And you killed a man."

I nodded.

"Don't you see? That act was the pivot around which everything changed. The world changed, because of what you did. Because of you we celebrated a victory tonight, and because of you the man who would have killed me died, while I went on living. Now tell me how powerless you are."

She didn't wait for a reply. She turned away from me, onto her side. I lay beside her, gazing up at the stars, while my heart grew warm again and tears gathered in my eyes.

At last I turned to her and laid my face against her back. For a long time I listened to the life in her, until I slept, untroubled by dreams.

39

P OWER

I woke to angry voices.

"—not my doing," said Vintel. "It's as well for you she brought the thing with her."

My warrior spat out a few words in a language I didn't understand. It sounded like a curse.

"Take her home, then," Vintel replied. "I'm sick to death of looking after the both of you."

Before I could gather my thoughts together, Vintel was gone.

It was still dark. Not even the first hint of dawn lightened the eastern sky.

"Let's go," said Maara.

"Now?"

"Now. Before she changes her mind."

As quickly as we could, we got our things together. Maara bound the northerner's sword alongside my pack and slung his shield over my shoulder. By the light of a quarter moon, we picked our way down the steep trail and headed south, toward home.

By midmorning I was tired and hungry and out of sorts. The heavy shield chafed my shoulder and bumped against my back at every step. I could have done without the spoils of war, I thought to myself. I was so preoccupied with the burden of the man's shield on my body that I scarcely felt upon my heart the burden of his death. I didn't think of him at all until we stopped at last, early in the afternoon.

Maara took the shield from me and leaned it against a tree. It was old and battered, its colors faded, but still visible around the rim was a border in blue, dark and light entwined, and in the center a magical animal of some kind. The golden eyes of a ghostly figure in grey and white, all legs and tail, stared back at me from a face half hidden by a leafy branch.

"It's beautiful," said Maara.

"Yes."

"He was a chieftain."

"How do you know?"

"The chieftain's shield bears the image of the guardian of his clan."

"What kind of animal is it?"

"Perhaps a wolf. Perhaps no animal anyone has ever seen. It may have come to one of his ancestors in a dream."

I stepped outside myself and listened to the two of us talk about this man, who the day before had awakened to his last day of life. Though the image of his face in agony remained vivid in my mind, I began to see another face, the face of an ordinary man.

I thought we had stopped only to rest and to have something to eat, but Maara intended for us to camp there. She had found us a sheltered place by a sheer rock wall, in a clearing hidden at the heart of a wood. A stream meandered through the clearing. The soft sounds of running water and the wind in the trees made me sleepy. While we ate our meal of salted meat and barley cakes, I could hardly keep my eyes open.

"Sleep a little," Maara said.

I didn't argue with her. I was asleep almost before I lay down.

He was sitting by his hearth.

His house was not made of stone like the one I lived in as a child, nor of wood like Merin's house. His house was round, with walls of wattle daubed with mud and a roof of hides stretched over a pole framework like a tent. The fire burning on the hearth at its center lit his face but left the edges of the room in darkness. He made a gesture to me to sit down, and I took the place across the fire from him. There was a bearskin on the floor, soft to sit upon.

I heard the sounds of grief outside the house.

"My wife," he said. "My child."

In his voice I heard his love for them, the love that brought him into Merin's land, where his death awaited him.

"You too, someday," he whispered.

"Whether it was his spirit or your own heart that spoke to you in your dream," said Maara, "take it as a warning."

"Of course it was his spirit," I said.

"It may have been."

"It was." A stubborn anger began to burn in my chest.

"Whether it was or not, it was still a warning."

"A warning? Of what?"

"When strangers come into Merin's land to steal food for their children, will you let the children of your own people starve to feed them?"

"The children of Merin's land have plenty," I said. "We've never starved."

"Has not even old Gnith known a time of hunger? If she has not, you are a fortunate people. Isn't it possible that you owe your good fortune to the power Merin has gathered around her?"

I had to admit that it was true.

"And when your enemy stands before you," she said, "will you think of the grief of those who love him? Will you stop to weigh their grief against the grief of those who love you before you take another life? If you do, it will not be his loved ones who will grieve."

I felt she was scolding me for something I had not yet done.

"That's unfair," I said. "When I killed the man who would have killed you, I doubt I was thinking of anything, but if I was, it was of my own grief."

She smiled at me. "I thank you for that, but I'm not thinking of him. I'm thinking of the next time."

"Why would I do differently the next time?"

"Yesterday you stepped into the unknown. In that new place, you had no expectations. You had no doubts. Now you know what awaits you there. You know, or think you know, what to expect."

I struggled with myself a little before I could open my heart to what she was trying to tell me.

"Why do you so want to believe it was his spirit that came to you?" she asked me.

In my dream I had felt from him no anger, no malice, only his sadness. He seemed to bear me no ill will.

"If it was his spirit," I said, "then he has forgiven me."

"Listen to me," she said. "You have no need for his forgiveness. You have no use for it. Wanting it will weaken you, and needing it may be your downfall."

I didn't understand.

"When you take up a weapon," she said, "you take up the power of life and death. This power resides, not in your weapon, but in yourself. Part of that power is your willingness to take a life, and part of it is the willingness to sacrifice your own. Every warrior offers herself willingly, and nothing done on the battlefield need be forgiven."

My mind understood, but my heart protested.

"All the same," I said, "his forgiveness would make me feel better."

She looked at me closely. "What do you feel?"

"Sorrow," I replied. "I'm not sorry that I killed him, but sorry that he had to die, that anyone had to die."

We were sitting in a patch of sunlight on the soft leaves of the forest floor. Just then the sun slid down behind the rock. I shivered. Maara got to her feet, cleared the leaves from a place against the rock wall, and made a fire. While I gathered enough firewood for the night, she prepared our supper. Soon our fire was burning brightly and barley cakes were baking on a hot stone.

"Are we going home tomorrow?" I asked.

She nodded.

"Why?"

"Did you want to stay with Vintel's band?"

"No." I had been reluctant to leave Sparrow, but I had also been relieved to get away from that noisy crowd of people. "Wasn't Vintel angry at our leaving?"

"Vintel was delighted to be rid of us."

We ate our meal in silence. In the wood the dark came quickly. The pale twilight sky still shone down on us through the branches overhead, while night gathered under the trees. Firelight flickered on the rock. I watched the play of shadows over its rough face.

Maara broke the silence. "Do you understand now why Vintel's warriors follow her?"

As much as I hated to praise Vintel for anything, I answered honestly, "I believe so."

"Why?"

"When she walked alone into the northerners' camp, I was so proud of her courage that I would have followed her into battle without a second thought."

Maara nodded. "Vintel is powerful. Her warriors trust her power. They understand it. Her power comes from her hatred of the enemy and from her love of war. That's why it will never mislead her."

Something uncomfortable prickled at the back of my mind.

"Vintel will never make the mistake of feeling pity or compassion for her enemies," Maara said. "Deciding who is her enemy and who is not will never give her a moment's pause. To Vintel, the stranger is always the enemy. She will never doubt herself, and so she will never hesitate to act."

Now I thought I understood what she was getting at.

"Are you afraid I will?"

"I know you will."

"Yesterday I didn't hesitate."

Maara brushed my words aside. "Your power is nothing like Vintel's. Her desire is to match herself against the power of her enemies. Her power comes from that desire and from her determination to prevail. Your power comes from something very different."

I was a little relieved that she thought I had a power of my own, but the suspicion that she found me wanting in some way unsettled me.

"Tell me," she said. "If you had been our war leader yesterday, what would you have done when the scouts told us about the northerners' camp? Would you have led your warriors against them?"

"I don't know," I said. "I suppose so."

"So you think Vintel did the right thing when she decided to attack them?"

It had never occurred to me to question Vintel's decision. "What else could we have done?"

"We could have done nothing. It was clear that they had laid a trap for us, but we didn't have to fall into it."

"We didn't fall into it," I said.

"Didn't we?"

Then I remembered, and a chill ran down my spine. Though in the end we put the northerners to rout, they had very nearly routed us.

"Vintel took a risk," she said. "It may have been too great a risk. But for you and Taia, I believe the day would have gone against us."

"Then Vintel made a mistake?"

Maara shrugged. "The day didn't go against us, did it? And there's something else to consider. What if Vintel had decided against the attack? Could she have kept control of her warriors once they knew of the northerners' arrogant display of Breda's shield?"

I hadn't thought of that. I doubted that even Vintel could have held her warriors back from answering such a provocation. Surely it was better for them to fight together under Vintel's leadership than as an angry rabble.

"Then Vintel did the right thing after all?"

"Whether by cleverness or luck," she said, "Vintel led her warriors to victory."

I nodded, but something in her voice made me doubt that she was agreeing with me. I gave up trying to decide if Vintel had been right or wrong.

"Is all now well?" she asked me.

"Sparrow said the northerners will go home. She said their hearts are defeated. If she's right, then all is well."

"I believe she is right," Maara said. "The northerners will go home. But of course that's not the end of it."

"It's not?"

"What about next year?"

"Next year we'll fight with them again. Next year it will be the same as it is every year."

"Will it?" said Maara. "The northerners have gone home empty-handed and with hearts filled with grief. All winter, along with their empty bellies they will nurse their grievances, and in the spring, not only their hunger, but their hatred will drive them when they make war on us again."

Her words frightened me. For all our speculation about what we could have done differently, what had happened seemed inevitable. Until then I had believed that everything had happened for the best. Now I began to doubt.

"What should we have done?" I asked her.

A gust of wind stirred the branches of the trees. I looked up and caught a glimpse of the night sky, splendid with stars, through the canopy of leaves over our heads. When I looked at Maara again, I saw that she wasn't going to answer me, not because she wanted me to find the answer for myself, but because she didn't know the answer. I felt the earth shift under me, leaving me off balance.

"I sometimes think I'm not the best teacher for you," she whispered. "I ought to be teaching you to be more like Vintel."

"I don't want to be like Vintel."

"I've known only one other person who had the kind of power I feel in you," she said. "She was very old, a great leader in her time, not a war leader, but a woman of great wisdom. I wish you had someone like her to teach you, because yours will be a difficult power to master, and if you fail to master it, it will be a dangerous power."

Another gust of wind rattled the leaves overhead, and a scattering of rain pattered down around us. I shivered, chilled not by wind or rain, but by fear awakened by her doubts. It took me a few moments to recover my courage and to remember how I had felt when I asked her to apprentice me. I had been so certain of her then, that she should be my teacher, that she already was my teacher, and the power of the oak grove had agreed with me.

"When I chose you, I chose well," I said.

She said nothing.

Once my fear had subsided a little, I began to resent her for having caused it.

"You frightened me," I said.

"Good." She turned suddenly to face me and gripped my shoulder hard and shook it. "You ought to be afraid."

At first her fierceness startled me. Then I saw her fear.

That night I lay awake for a long time. A hard wind was blowing, sending leaves down upon us in showers until we were all but covered by them. Before morning the rain would come.

Maara's sleep was restless. As she always did, she lay with her back to me, and I snuggled against her for both warmth and comfort. Once or twice I drifted into a half-sleep in which it seemed that Maara and I were having a conversation that went round and round in circles, never making sense and never reaching a conclusion.

At last I slept.

I fell into a dark dream. I was lost, alone in a wood. A raw wind drove the rain through my cloak until I shivered with cold. I looked for shelter, but there was none. Then my warrior stood before me. She lifted a corner of my cloak, and as if she had lifted a veil from a lamp, a light shone out from under it. I felt its warmth envelop me.

When I woke, I found I was wet through.

"We might as well go home," Maara said when she saw I was awake.

"Now?"

"Would you rather lie here in the rain? We can be home in a few hours."

"Let's go," I said.

As cold as I was, my dream had left a warm glow around my heart.

40

Spoils of War

We arrived at Merin's house not long after sunrise. If it hadn't been raining, I would have suggested that we bathe in the river. We were both filthy with the dirt of camp life, our hair too tangled even to be finger-combed. Maara's clothes were bloody from the battle. So were mine, from nursing the wounded. Both of us still had on our faces traces of the blood of dead men, but I had begun to shiver, and all I wanted was a bath in warm water, dry clothing, and a seat by the fire.

Before we went inside the earthworks, Maara stopped.

"We will enter Merin's house through the front door," she said. "The household will be at breakfast. Go directly to the Lady and offer her the northerner's shield."

"What if she's not there?"

"Then find her."

"What shall I say?"

"You'll know what to say."

I followed her through the maze of earthworks and through the yard, until we stood before the door of Merin's house. Maara stepped back and gestured to me to go ahead. The heavy door was closed against the rain. I had to throw my whole weight against it before it yielded and swung open.

The Lady was still at table, and it seemed that all the women of the council were breakfasting with her. I almost asked Maara if I might wait a while before I approached her, but she gave me a gentle push in the direction of the high table. I had to walk from one end of the great hall to the other.

Heads turned as I passed. The shield weighed heavy on my shoulder. I could hardly wait to put it down.

Before I was halfway across the hall, the Lady saw me. Our eyes met, and she never took her eyes from me as I approached her. When I stood before her, I set the shield down in front of me and turned it so that she could see the design painted on its face.

Before I could think of anything to say, the Lady asked me, "What is this?"

"Your enemy's shield," I said.

She looked displeased. "If your warrior wished to present me with this gift, why didn't she offer it herself?"

"It's not her gift," I said.

"Then whose gift is it?"

"Mine."

A woman cried out. It sounded like the cry of a woman who sees her child in danger, and that's exactly what it was. It was the voice of the woman seated at the Lady's right hand. It took me a moment to recognize my mother.

In spite of my bedraggled appearance, my mother recognized her child. She opened her mouth to speak, then closed it again when Merin put a hand on her arm.

"This is your gift?" the Lady said.

I nodded.

"How did you come by it?"

Before I could answer her, my warrior spoke. She was standing right behind me.

"Tamras offers you the spoils of war," she said.

The Lady's eyes went from my face to hers. "Have you any idea what you've done?"

I started to protest, but Maara spoke first.

"I think you had better listen to what we have to say before you lay blame," she said.

In the silence that followed I heard my own heartbeat. Then there was a commotion at the far end of the table. Suddenly, all by herself, Namet created a bustle of activity. She got up from her seat, hurried over to me, and swept me away, calling to one of the servants to attend to me. Together she and a very strong, very stout kitchen servant hustled me toward the warmth of the kitchen.

When my mother would have followed, Namet let go of me and took her arm. She drew it through her own and led her back into the great hall.

"First let's get her warm and dry," I heard Namet say as I was led away. "Time enough later for a nice long talk."

"Maara did the right thing," said Namet, "although her timing could have been better."

"Is my mother angry?" I asked her.

"No, not angry. Worried. In a little while we'll all sit down together and try to put her mind at rest. Are you tired? Would you like to sleep a little?"

"I want to see my mother," I said.

We were in Namet's room, where I had been taken after the servant gave me a thorough bath. I was sitting up on the foot of Namet's bed wearing nothing but a blanket. Maara had gone to find some clean clothes for me.

Someone pulled aside the curtain covering the doorway. I looked up, expecting to see Maara, but it was my mother who came into the room.

"I'd like to greet my child, Mother," she said to Namet.

Namet sighed. "And I must go and give my child a bath."

When we were alone, my mother sat down beside me. "Are you too big now for a hug?"

I shook my head and fell into her arms. Nothing could have pleased her more.

"Have you missed me?" she asked.

I nodded. Seeing her was like finding a part of myself that I had misplaced without noticing its absence until I discovered it again.

"I've missed you so much," she said. "I came with the wool wagons. I couldn't wait until springtime to see you."

"How long can you stay?"

"Not long. We would have left today if the weather had been better. We'll be on our way once the roads are dry enough for the wagons."

It had been worth my getting soaked if the rain had kept my mother in Merin's house until I arrived.

"It's a good thing we came home then," I said.

My mother frowned. "Why did your warrior bring you home? None of the others have come home yet. Are you hurt?"

"I'm fine," I said. "See?"

I opened the blanket so she could see for herself that I was unscathed.

"Then it must have something to do with the shield you brought to Merin."

It was not a question, but I knew she was waiting for me to explain to her why we had left Vintel's band and come home alone. It was such a long story, I hardly knew where to begin.

Just then Maara appeared in the doorway with my clean clothes. She handed them to me, nodded to my mother, and left.

"I see you insisted on making your own choice," my mother said.

"I made the right choice," I told her, ready to defend it.

But my mother was smiling. "Merin has let me know her feelings about your apprenticeship. I wondered why she was so surprised that you insisted on having your own way, but of course she doesn't know you as I do."

"Then you don't disapprove?"

"I don't know her yet," my mother said. "It will take a while for me to make up my mind whether I disapprove of her or not."

"What did the Lady say?"

"Merin has told me a great deal," she said, "but I want to hear your side of the story before we speak of that."

"There's so much to tell."

"And plenty of time later to tell it. Let's get you dressed."

For the first time in years, my mother helped to dress me. I was surprised to find I didn't mind at all. We talked about ordinary things. My mother told me what had been happening at home, and I told her a bit about what life was like for me in Merin's house. Neither of us was ready to talk about the important things. How does a child tell her mother that she has gone into battle and killed someone?

We heard footsteps in the hallway, and Namet's voice said, "Get yourself dressed while I find a comb."

Then Namet came into the room, a broad grin on her face.

"She's as bad as Eramet ever was," she chuckled. "Fussed at everything. Now she thinks she's not going to let me comb her hair."

Namet opened the chest by her bed and rummaged through it until she found a comb. Still grinning, she went next door to Maara's room. Soon I heard their voices in amiable argument.

I was surprised that Maara had given Namet so much trouble. When I bathed her, she never fussed at all.

By the time our mothers had made us presentable, it was time for the midday meal. I was desperately hungry, and the smell of stew drifting up from the kitchen had my stomach grumbling. We all went down together to the great hall. The northerner's shield was leaning against a post near Merin's chair. No one had moved it from where Namet set it down when she whisked me away. The four of us sat at a table by ourselves. The Lady didn't show herself.

"She'll send for us sometime this afternoon, I imagine," said Namet.

"All of us?" I asked her.

She nodded. "All of us. I intend to speak for Maara. That was very nearly a disaster this morning."

"It was?"

Maara looked annoyed but said nothing.

"My darling child as good as commanded the Lady to hold her tongue."

"I wouldn't have," said Maara, "if she hadn't accused me."

"Hush," said Namet.

Maara hushed.

The four of us spent the afternoon sitting together by the fire. Although the rain had stopped, it threatened to start up again at any moment. A cold wind was blowing, and the sky was dark. I hoped the rain would go on for days. I was in no hurry to bid my mother good-bye again.

Every once in a while someone would join us for a few minutes, but mostly the folk of Merin's house left us to ourselves. No one asked us what was happening on the frontier. Namet said that the Lady should hear our news before we spoke with the others.

Maara let me tell the story of our adventures. When I came to the part about Maara going hunting, my mother asked her, "How did you happen to have a bow with you?"

"She took my bow," I said.

"Your bow?"

"My warrior has been teaching me the bow."

"I see."

I watched her think over which question to ask me next.

"Why did you take your weapon with you?" she said at last.

"Vintel told me to bring it."

"Vintel did?"

"Yes."

"Why?"

"For hunting game," said Maara. "Or so she said."

My mother turned to her. "You didn't believe her?"

Maara shook her head. "It was her way of trying to hold Tamras up to ridicule. She spoke of the bow as if it were a child's weapon, good only for hunting birds." Then she grinned. "She'll not make that mistake again."

My mother was troubled. "Why should Vintel wish to hold my daughter up to ridicule?" She turned to me. "Have you made an enemy already?"

"I'm Vintel's enemy, not Tamras," said Maara. "Vintel would strike at me any way she can, and sometimes Tamras has had to bear the brunt of her malice."

"That's not entirely true," I protested. "Vintel holds a grudge against me as well. She would have apprenticed me if I had been willing, but I refused her."

"So Merin told me," my mother said. "Why did you disregard her wishes?"

"My heart was set on someone else."

I had the satisfaction of seeing Maara's ears turn red.

"I knew Vintel when she was a child," my mother said, "and I admired her even then. She was a natural leader and clever about many things."

"And so she is still," said Namet. "Still a leader, and clever too, but not yet wise. She is blind to things she ought to pay attention to."

I was glad Namet had spoken. I had seen my mother glance at Maara with a question in her eyes.

"Perhaps this is the time to tell your mother about the cause of your quarrel with Vintel," I suggested to Maara.

Maara started to reply, but Namet spoke first. "I imagine there's little she can tell me that I don't already know."

Maara looked at her, surprised.

"She would have left you for dead, wouldn't she?"

Maara nodded. "How did you know about that?"

"I've had my suspicions for some time that there was more to the story of your wounding than we learned from Vintel." Namet's voice was soft. Only her eyes revealed her anger. "The night before you and Tamras left with Vintel's band, Laris confirmed my suspicions. She came to speak to me, hoping that I could do something to protect you, because she feared Vintel meant you harm. When I asked her why, she told me that once before, Vintel had failed to protect you as she should have."

"To do her justice," Maara replied, "Vintel would have had to risk lives to do it. She chose not to risk the lives of her friends for the life of a stranger. Her decision may have been understandable, but it didn't endear her to me." She chuckled. "Nor did it endear me to her that I failed to die."

"I imagine not," said Namet. "Laris also told me that Vintel didn't want to take the trouble to bring you home. Laris insisted on it, though they all believed your wounds were mortal. She and Vintel had a serious disagreement about it."

"I didn't know that," whispered Maara. "I've done no more than repay a debt."

Namet and my mother looked puzzled.

"Yesterday Maara saved Laris's life," I told them. "During the battle with the northerners, Laris's sword broke, and she fell. Maara killed the man who would have killed her."

"As Tamras killed the man who would have killed me," said Maara.

Namet said, very softly, "Oh," and reached for Maara's hand.

"Was it his shield you offered to the Lady?" my mother asked me.

I nodded.

Namet's face was grim. "Tell me if I have cause to take Vintel to task about this."

"Not about this," said Maara. "Not unless you would accuse her of being too bold, and this time her boldness endangered everyone."

"Tell me how it happened," Namet said.

So Maara told them about the battle, about the trap the northerners had laid for us and the trap we devised for them in turn, about our retreat, and how she had killed one man only to be knocked down and disarmed by another.

"He was standing over me," she said, "and I thought his face would be the last thing I would see in this world, but an arrow pierced his throat, and he fell."

She looked at me with so much pride that now it was my turn to blush.

It was difficult to tell which mother was more troubled by what she'd heard. Namet grasped Maara's hand so hard that I thought Maara must find it painful, and worry lines furrowed my mother's brow.

Then Namet smiled. "You say it was Vintel's doing that Tamras had the bow?"

Maara nodded.

"How the wicked frustrate themselves!" she said. "Do you think she knows that she thwarted her own designs?"

I remembered the few words I heard Vintel say just before we left her band.

"I believe she does," I said. "Maara was angry with her, and Vintel said it was as well for Maara that I had brought the bow."

My mother turned to Maara. "Why were you angry?"

Maara hesitated. She glanced at me, then replied, "I was angry because what I feared had happened."

"What did you fear?"

"I feared that Tamras would be drawn into something before she was ready to bear the consequences."

My mother looked at me. "And how has she borne them?"

"Very well so far," Maara said, "but it's early yet. We'll have to see."

All of this was news to me.

"I'm fine," I said.

At that moment, sitting in the great hall of Merin's house with these three people who were so dear to me, I felt safe and happy and unburdened.

Maara ignored me.

"I thought you could do a healing for her, Mother," she said to Namet.

My mother looked alarmed. "A healing?"

"Where I come from," Maara told her, "Tamras would now be under-going her initiation as a warrior. I'm glad that's not the custom here, because she still has much to learn, but among my people, there are rituals done for warriors, to remove the blood from their hands so that they can become part of the family of humankind again. Are there such rituals here?"

"Not that I know of," my mother said. "There should be."

"A healing would accomplish much the same thing," said Namet.

Maara saw that the worry hadn't left my mother's eyes.

"It may not be necessary," she said. "Tamras has already begun her own healing."

I thought she must be talking about my dream.

"Still, it can't hurt," said Namet. "After we speak to the Lady, I'll see what I can do." Then she turned to Maara. "How long are you going to keep us in suspense?"

Maara gave her a blank look.

"You haven't yet told us the outcome of the battle."

Then Maara told how Taia had led the unarmed apprentices against the enemy and how the northerners had fled before them. That story lightened the mood a little.

"At what cost did we gain this victory?" Namet asked her.

"None of our warriors were killed," Maara replied, "and only a few were wounded. Tamras tended them with great skill."

My mother turned to me, a pleased smile on her face. "So my daughter practices what I taught her?"

"She does," said Maara. "I owe my life to her skill twice over, both as a healer and an archer."

My mother's eyes were on me still. "An archer," she murmured.

"Are you disappointed?" I asked.

"Disappointed? Why would I be disappointed?"

Out of the corner of my eye, I saw Maara hide a smile.

"I thought you would want me to learn to use a sword," I said. "Like you did."

"I wish someone had had the sense to put a bow into my hands," my mother said.

I could hardly have been more surprised. "But you handled a sword well. The Lady told me so."

"Evidently not well enough for her to allow me to go into battle," she said bitterly.

"But you were not yet a warrior."

"Many who were not yet warriors fought in battle then, as did Merin herself."

Namet took my mother's hand. "You were the last of your line, Tamnet," she said, "and she loved you too well to risk losing you too."

It was midafternoon when the Lady sent for me. Namet and Maara got up from their seats by the fire only to be told to stay where they were. Namet started to protest, then thought better of it, so I went alone to the Lady's chamber, where I found her seated by the hearth. She gestured to me to sit down on the hearthstone.

"Are you well?" she asked me.

"Yes, Lady," I said.

"You weren't injured?"

"No."

"I'm glad to hear it. It wouldn't have done for your mother to find you unwell. It wouldn't have done at all." Suddenly she smiled. "Have you had a good visit with her?"

I nodded.

"Good."

She said nothing more for a time, but she didn't seem to be waiting for me to speak. She sat gazing into the fire. Then she said, "I knew the man you killed."

"You knew him? How?"

"He was one of the chieftains who came to seal the peace between our people and the northern tribes."

I was puzzled. The man I killed wasn't old enough to have been a chieftain before I was born. Perhaps she was thinking of his father.

"Tell me what happened," she said.

When I started to tell her about the battle, she stopped me.

"Tell me everything from the beginning," she said. "From the moment you left this house."

And so I told her everything. If it surprised her to hear that it was Vintel who told me to bring my bow, she gave no sign. She listened patiently, gazing into the fire, a faint smile on her face, as if she were listening to a made-up tale. As uncomfortable as her keen eyes often made me, her apparent indifference now made me more uncomfortable. Even the story of Breda's death seemed not to move her.

I told her of the trap the northerners had set for us, of how Vintel had seen it was a trap and warned her warriors of the danger, and of how my warrior had warned Vintel of a danger she hadn't seen. I described the battle as well as I could remember it. I told her about Maara saving Laris's life. Then I came to my part in it.

"The man who bore the wolf shield would have killed Maara if I hadn't killed him first," I said.

"Were you in the fighting?"

"No, Lady. I was still hiding among the rocks, ready to guard the apprentices' retreat."

"I see," she said. "And did the apprentices retreat safely?"

"They didn't retreat at all. Taia led them in a charge down the hill, and the northerners fled."

For the first time since I began to speak, the Lady looked at me. "Taia led them in a charge?"

"Yes. It was a brave thing to do. None of the apprentices was armed."

"None but you."

"Yes."

"Where are the northerners now?"

"Gone home," I said. "At least we believe so. They lost many killed and many more wounded."

"When are our people coming home?"

"I don't know. Soon, I think."

She nodded. "Go now," she said, "and send your warrior to me."

Maara was with the Lady for a long time. It was suppertime when they entered the great hall together. While the warriors took their places, the Lady stood behind her chair, waiting for everyone to be quiet.

"We have had good news from the frontier," she said. "Our warriors defeated a large band of northerners and sent them running for home, leaving many dead behind them. Vintel believes we have seen the last of them this year."

Then the Lady turned to Maara, who stood behind her.

"Show them the shield," she said.

Maara picked up the northerner's shield and held it above her head, so that everyone in the hall could see it.

"This shield was taken by Tamras, Tamnet's daughter," the Lady said. "With her bow she killed the man who bore it. It is her first prize won in battle, and she has offered it to me. Let it be hung here in the great hall as a reminder that a warrior's strength and courage are not measured by her size."

My warrior hung the northerner's shield on the wall with the others, all taken in war, a sign to everyone who saw them of the power of Merin's house.

My mother reached for my hand under the table and squeezed it. When I looked at her, I saw that her eyes were still on the Lady. She watched as the Lady took her seat at the high table. Then she turned to me.

"Merin has kept a place for me beside her," she said. "I had better join her for a while."

And she went to take her seat at the Lady's right hand.

Maara soon joined Namet and me, a satisfied smile on her face.

"How in the world did you accomplish that?" Namet asked her.

"I told her Tamnet would be pleased," said Maara.

41

A Choice of Evils

I was dozing by the fire when Namet came for me. She led me through the kitchen and out the back door. A slender moon was rising.

We descended into the place of ritual. A fire had been laid in the center of the chamber, but it had not yet been lit. The only light came from an oil lamp on the stone altar. I peered into the shadows, expecting to see Maara.

"I sent my child to bed," said Namet. "She was worn out, though she wouldn't admit it."

I was a little disappointed that my warrior would have no part in my healing. As much as I trusted Namet, Maara understood as no one else did how I felt about what I'd done.

"Will my mother be here?" I asked.

Namet shook her head. "A warrior's healing is no place for a mother's worry."

Namet knelt and lit the fire. Then she settled herself next to it and patted the place beside her, and I sat down.

"There's a touch of chill in the air tonight," said Namet, holding her hands out to the flame.

I waited for her to begin the ritual. I was a little afraid that she would change, as she had done the night I first set foot upon the warrior's path, but she only smiled and hummed to herself as she encouraged the fire to grow into a cheerful blaze.

"Let's talk a little, shall we?" she said.

"Before you do the healing?"

My anxiety about it made me want to have it over with.

"Oh, I don't think a healing is really necessary. You seem fine to me."

"I do?"

She turned to look at me. "You killed someone. He was an enemy, but he was also a man. I see that you have uneasy feelings about it, and so you should have. I would be worried if you didn't, but it's nothing that requires the power of a healing."

"Why are we here then?"

"To put your mother's mind to rest. And your warrior's too, for that matter. And I thought you might be glad not to have the two of them hovering over you for a little while."

Ordinarily I didn't care to be hovered over, but ever since the battle, I had taken comfort from the presence of the people who loved me. Now only Namet stood between me and the dark.

"Maara told me of your dream," she said.

I remembered how much my dream had disturbed her.

"She didn't believe it was his spirit that came to me," I said. "She said it was a warning from my own heart."

"So it may have been," said Namet, "but if it was his spirit, I fear he meant you no good."

A chill went down my spine.

"If he came to you, it was for the good of those he left behind. He may have come to you to put a human face upon a faceless enemy."

He certainly had never been faceless to me, I thought, as the image of his dying came again into my mind's eye.

"It's difficult to hate someone you know," she said. "Now you know him a little, and through him you also know his people."

"Not as I know my own," I replied, and remembering Maara's fears, I added, "I would never endanger our people for a stranger's sake."

Namet turned to me and smiled. "You have done that already."

She waited for me to understand her. I had no idea what she meant.

"For whom did you stand before the council? For whom did you offer your life as a guarantee? In whom have you put all your trust?"

I didn't know how to answer her. Maara hadn't been a stranger to me from the time I'd been her healer.

"Why were you so sure of her?" Namet asked me.

"My heart was sure of her from the beginning. I don't know why."

"And were you proved wrong?"

"No."

"But she ran away."

"Not to do us harm," I said. "She ran away to save her life."

"And she returned to save yours."

"Yes."

"So you were right to trust her."

"Yes."

"And the man who came to you in your dream? Did you trust him?"

"I trusted my dreaming self to him," I said, "but I was careful of him."

"Then you know the difference."

Before I could question her, she took my hand and closed her eyes.

"Think of him," she said.

As soon as I closed my eyes, I saw his image.

"Now look into the fire."

I did as she told me, and in the flames, I saw his face.

Namet reached into the pocket of her gown and took out a handful of dried leaves. When she crumbled them into the fire, a column of sweet-smelling smoke drifted up and found its way through the hole in the roof. It seemed as if a presence took shape within the smoke, then drifted away, out into the night air.

"Is he gone?" she asked me.

I looked again into the fire. This time I saw only the dancing flame.

"He's gone," I told her.

"Good." She let go of my hand. "Now we can go to bed."

We left the fire to burn itself out. When we had climbed the ladder and stood once again under the night sky, Namet turned to me and put her hand on my shoulder.

"I have yet to thank you," she said. "I hardly know how, except to say that I could not have borne the loss of another child."

She slipped her arm around my shoulders, pulled me close to her, and kissed my brow. Before I could think of anything to say, she let go of me and changed the subject.

"How did you feel when Merin ordered the shield hung in the great hall?" she said. "Did it make you proud?"

"It did, a little," I admitted.

"Why?"

"It pleased my mother."

"And you were proud of having pleased her?"

"Yes."

"What will you feel, do you think, in the days to come when you see that shield hanging on the wall?"

"I suppose I'll get used to it," I said, "and after a while I won't see it anymore."

"You'll see it," she said. "You'll see it every day you spend in Merin's house. Just remember that your heart knew the right thing to do and that you did it."

We had three days of blustery weather. I was grateful, because the rain kept my mother from going home. We spent most of the time sitting by the hearth with Maara and Namet. All through the first day, warriors and their apprentices joined us, eager to hear about our adventures on the frontier, but after everyone's curiosity was satisfied, we were left to ourselves.

On the fourth day, the sun came out. My mother took me aside and said, "Let's go for a walk, shall we? Just the two of us."

It was a beautiful autumn afternoon, too beautiful to waste indoors, and I was glad of the chance to spend some time alone with her.

"Bring your bow," she said. "I'd like to see for myself what your warrior has been teaching you."

I took her down to the place where I used to practice shooting at targets. It had been a long time since I had shot at things that didn't move, and I put arrows through the targets so easily that I amazed myself. I was looking for something more difficult to shoot at when a songbird flew up out of a bush. I followed it with the bow until it was out of sight, but I didn't loose the arrow.

"Could you have hit that tiny bird?" my mother asked me.

"Maara taught me to hunt birds," I said, "but only ones that were big enough to eat. I doubt I would have come anywhere near it."

"All the same, I'm glad you didn't try." She took the bow from me and examined it. "Where did you get this?"

I saw no reason to conceal the truth from her. I told her the story of the men who came across the river, of the death of Eramet, and of finding the body of the man who killed her.

"This bow was with his body," I said. "Maara took it and kept it for me. She believed it was meant to find me. She believed it was a gift."

"A gift," she murmured. "Your warrior has an odd way of looking at things."

"She speaks of things a little differently than we do. That's all."

"I'm not finding fault," my mother said. "If anything is a gift to you, she is." She saw that she'd surprised me. She smiled. "Your warrior has taught you well, and I can see that she cares for you. I couldn't ask for more than that." She gave me back the bow. "Come with me now. There's something we must talk about."

She started down the hill. Since the afternoon had become quite warm, I thought she might take me down to the river, but she turned aside toward the oak grove. The cool air under the trees was heavy with damp, and the wet earth smelled of dying things. We sat down in the center of the grove.

I prepared myself to be patient, expecting to hear the usual motherly advice. Instead she said, "Who killed the man whose body you found?"

I blinked in surprise. "I don't know for certain."

"Was it Vintel?"

"Maara believes so. I can't imagine who else could have done it."

"Does Vintel know you found his body?"

I was going to say no when I thought about what Vintel had said to me when she told me to bring my bow to the frontier. She told me to bring "the pretty one." At the time I was preoccupied with other things, and it didn't occur to me that she might have recognized the bow that killed Eramet.

"I don't know," I said. "It's possible."

"Does anyone else know?"

"Only the Lady. She told us not to speak of it to anyone else."

"That was wise." My mother frowned. "You must be very careful of Vintel."

"I am," I assured her.

"You must be more careful now," she insisted. "For the reasons you have told me and for reasons you know nothing about." She glanced around us, as if she suspected that even the sacred trees might hide an adversary. "I believe you stand between Vintel and her ambitions."

I didn't see how I could stand between Vintel and anything.

"Before you came home," she said, "Merin spoke to me of something we used to talk about when we were young women together. It was almost a joke between us then, because when we were young the future we spoke about seemed to lie so far ahead of us that we thought we might never reach it. I always wanted children, but Merin never did. She used to tell me that I must have two at least, one to be my heir, and one to be hers. She has chosen you, Tamras."

"Chosen me? Chosen me for what?"

"Chosen you to be her heir," my mother said. "She wants to adopt you as her daughter on midwinter's day."

I forgot that we had been talking about Vintel.

"Adopt me?" I could hardly understand what those words meant.

"Merin needs an heir," my mother said.

"Not for many years yet," I protested.

"Who can tell? And if she were to name someone on her deathbed, what good would that do? She needs a child now, so that when the time comes, no one will remember that once her heir was not her child."

I still didn't understand how Merin could adopt me, who had a living mother.

"It's the motherless who are adopted," I said.

"Adoptions such as this are not unheard of."

I couldn't hear her. I felt as if I were losing her, as if she were giving me away, and my eyes filled with tears.

"Tamras," said my mother, with exaggerated patience, "you are no longer a child. You have no more need of me, but Merin has great need of you." She took my hand. "She has need of you in ways she hardly knows."

In spite of myself, I was curious to know what she meant.

"What ways?" I asked her through my tears.

"Motherhood is a great teacher," she said. "I wouldn't recommend it to every woman, but a woman who has the care of many, as Merin does, could learn a great deal from caring for just one child of her own." She lifted my chin so that she could look me in the eye. "Will you at least think about it?"

All the thinking in the world, I knew, would not change my mind. "I already have a mother. I don't want another, and if I had to choose one, it would not be the Lady Merin."

"Why not?"

"I've been a great disappointment to her. Surely she must have told you. She hasn't approved of anything I've done since I arrived here."

My mother chuckled. "Merin may command warriors, but I defy her to command my daughter. She complained to me that you would never avail yourself of her advice. She was furious when I laughed at her."

My mother seemed amused, but I was serious. "How could she become my mother then? We would always be at odds."

"As are many mothers and daughters."

"I wouldn't change a good mother for a bad one."

Although she tried to hide her smile, my words pleased her.

Suddenly I had an idea.

"Let her take my sister for her heir," I said. "Tamar would be delighted to inherit Merin's place."

"She would, and that's why you are Merin's choice. And mine." The smile left her eyes. "No one can compel you in this. I ask only that you think of all the good that could be done and all the evil avoided if you were Merin's heir."

I found it difficult to believe that any good could come from doing something that felt so wrong to me.

"There's another thing to consider," she said. "If you were Merin's acknowledged heir, you would be protected from Vintel."

I had forgotten about Vintel.

"Vintel isn't blind, and she isn't stupid. Through me, your tie to Merin is almost as close as a tie of blood. Vintel can't help but see you as a rival."

If Vintel saw me as a rival, she must see herself as Merin's heir. Though I now understood her value as a war leader, I could not imagine her in the Lady's place.

"Why would Vintel expect the Lady to choose her?" I said.

"I doubt she would," my mother replied, "but if anything were to happen to Merin," and she touched the earth beneath her so that her words would not come true, "the strongest woman here would take her place, because there would be no one to stand against her. Whoever would succeed Merin must be strong enough to hold the power she inherits."

"What good would it do then for the Lady to name me? Vintel is much stronger than I am."

"Tradition and custom are even stronger than Vintel. If Merin adopts you, the elders will nod and say, 'This was spoken of long ago.' It will seem right to them, and so it will come to seem right to everyone else. If everyone believes you are Merin's child, their belief will give you Merin's power, and when the time comes for you to take her place, you will also have power of your own."

"I still don't see how becoming Merin's heir would protect me. Wouldn't it make Vintel more my enemy?"

"It might," she said, "but she would find it much more difficult to do you harm. If anyone suspected that harm had come to you through her, she would never be allowed to profit from her betrayal. She would lose the place she has, and possibly her life as well. But as long as you are only one apprentice among many in Merin's house, you will be vulnerable. It's much easier to drown the kitten than the cat."

Still I couldn't see myself as Merin's child.

"Why in the world would Merin want me for her daughter?"

My mother sighed. "Although she may not show it, Merin cares for you. She loved you at first for my sake. Now she has come to know you, and I believe she sees in you something she will hardly acknowledge, even to herself." She smiled mysteriously. "It is the very thing that puts the two of you at odds."

"What's that?"

"You two are so much alike. You are both so certain that your view of the world is the right one, and you both hold so stubbornly to your own opinions."

She set a finger against my lips, to silence my denial.

"Part of Merin's greatness as a leader is that she cannot be swayed easily by contradictory advice," she went on. "Merin sees the same strength in you, and it annoys her only because your opinions don't coincide with hers."

The daylight was fading, and it was growing chilly under the trees. My mother shivered and stood up.

"Let's go in," she said. She helped me to my feet and put her hands on my shoulders. "All I ask, Tamras, is that you not close your mind to the possibility that you were meant for greater things than to sit in judgment over the disputes of a tiny village in the hill country."

That much I could agree to.

Early the next morning, my mother left for home. I walked with her until midday, when she insisted I turn back. We said no more about my becoming Merin's heir. She knew me well enough to know that I would be more likely to come around to her way of thinking if she left me alone to make my own decision.

She had, however, one thing more to say to me about the Lady. When she took her leave of me, she said, "Take care of Merin for me. Will you?"

"Take care of her?" I replied. "How can I take care of her?"

I had thought it Merin's duty to take care of me.

"I'm not at all sure," my mother said. "I'm uneasy about her. I suspect she may be unwell, although she has assured me otherwise. There may be nothing wrong, but it would ease my mind if I knew you were keeping an eye on her. Will you?"

"Of course I will. I'll do whatever I can for her."

"Thank you." She smiled and kissed my brow.

"If she'll let me," I added.

"Remember," she replied, "that Merin may appear hard on the outside, but hard things are brittle, and when they break, they shatter."

I had all afternoon to think as I walked back to Merin's house, and the more I thought, the more uncertain I became. My mother had said nothing to the Lady about my unwillingness to become her heir. I think she hoped that by the time the Lady mentioned it to me, I might have changed my mind.

The day before I had been certain that would never happen. Now I had begun to doubt. Perhaps I was being selfish. Perhaps I should be thinking more of the good of others and less of my own feelings. My sister would not hesitate to seize the opportunity if such an important place were offered to her. Although she loved our mother no less than I, she would think it sentimental of me to be so reluctant to give her up.

After supper I asked Maara to come with me to the oak grove. The first stars were just twinkling out. In the grove it was almost dark. Neither of us spoke until we were safe among the trees.

"My mother told me that the Lady wants to name me her heir," I said.

"I thought as much," said Maara.

"What?"

"You're the obvious choice."

Why was it that so many things were obvious to everyone but me?

"And it explains a great deal," she said.

"It does?"

"It explains why Merin didn't want to entrust you to a stranger, and why she was so determined to apprentice you to Vintel, who would have been to you a powerful ally, instead of the adversary she is now. And it explains why Vintel was so eager to apprentice you, because through you she would increase her own importance. For a long time I thought Vintel was your enemy because of me. I'm glad it isn't altogether true."

"My mother is afraid that I stand between Vintel and her ambitions," I said. "That means Vintel must see herself as Merin's heir."

Maara nodded.

"She also says that becoming Merin's heir will protect me from Vintel."

"I believe your mother is right. This has come not a moment too soon."

"I have no intention of becoming Merin's heir," I protested.

"Why not?"

"I have a mother. How can I let go of her?"

I was already missing her, and the thought of losing her brought tears into my eyes.

"Your mother will never let go of you," said Maara, "whether or not you become Merin's child."

"Even if that were true, how could I be Merin's child? It's been difficult enough trying to do what seems right to me when everything I do she disapproves of. If I were her child, how could I resist her?"

"It would be difficult," Maara conceded.

"And I could never love her as a child should love her mother."

"You might learn to love her."

"Every time I called her my mother, it would feel like a lie."

"Perhaps."

"It would be wrong," I insisted.

She shrugged.

"Why don't you believe me?"

"Why are you trying so hard to convince yourself?"

Then I had to face my fears.

"I'm afraid I'm being selfish," I said. "What if it's the best thing for everyone?"

"The best thing for everyone but you?"

"Yes."

"Then it would be a difficult decision."

"What do you think I should do?"

"You should do what feels right to you," she said. "Always."

And always before I had done just that. Now I found myself caught in a dilemma. Neither path felt right to me.

"What would you do?" I asked her.

She smiled. "What I would do makes no difference. Life hasn't asked me that question."

But life had asked it of me and was waiting for my answer.

"I don't know what to do," I said.

"Then wait."

There was a reason I couldn't wait. It took me a moment to remember what it was.

"My mother fears the Lady is unwell," I said.

Maara grasped in a moment what it had taken me all day to understand. "If your mother is right, Merin will need to name an heir as soon as possible."

"Then I have no choice."

"You always have a choice," she said.

"A choice of evils," I replied.

"That may be, but if that's all you see, now is not the time to choose."

Three days passed before the Lady appeared in the great hall, and when she did, she was pale and listless, as if she had been ill. Mindful of my mother's wish, I had inquired of the healer if the Lady was in good health, and the healer had assured me that she was. Now I wished I had insisted on seeing her myself.

To my surprise, the Lady gave no indication that she intended to speak with me. At mealtimes I sometimes caught her watching me from the high table, but when I met her eyes, she looked away. Perhaps she was waiting for me to approach her.

Maara said nothing more to me about my decision. I thought I would wait before speaking to Namet about it. I wanted to come to a clearer understanding of my own feelings before anyone told me how I ought to feel. Maara hadn't done that, and I had trusted that she wouldn't, but I was unsure about Namet. If I was in danger from Vintel, Maara was in danger too, and if my becoming Merin's heir would protect me, it would protect her as well. That was almost enough to make my decision for me.

It was another week before Vintel brought her warriors home. They arrived unheralded at suppertime. Vintel barged through the front door of Merin's house with such force that several of the warriors sitting near the door leapt to their feet and drew their swords. She had, of course, meant to call attention to herself, but something caught her eye, and she stopped abruptly to stare at the wall above my head. The man behind her walked into her, knocking her off balance. The warriors she had startled laughed, enjoying her embarrassment all the more because she had given them a scare. It was an inauspicious homecoming.

The warriors of Vintel's band sat down to eat. Their unwashed faces, tangled hair, and filthy clothing showed me what I must have looked like when I walked through the great hall to offer the Lady the spoils of war. When I remembered the shield, I knew what Vintel had been looking at.

Taia and Sparrow came in together. I was delighted to see them both. They joined me at the companions' table, and I listened eagerly to their account of what had happened after we left them. Vintel had followed the northerners' retreat, to drive them out of Merin's land for good. She had pursued them so relentlessly that they left behind unburied the bodies of their wounded who had died.

Sparrow told me that the apprentices now spoke of the battle as Taia's day. Taia blushed with embarrassment and pride.

"I wish your warrior had let you stay with us," Taia said. "I made sure everyone knew the part that Tamras of the Bow played in our victory. They would have made much of you too, but now it's old news."

Although I didn't say so, I was glad I had avoided being made much of. Maara had been wise to bring me home.

42

A JOURNEY OF THE HEART

W inter came early that year. Almost before the trees had changed their colors, the first snowfall dusted them with white. A few weeks later a heavy snow fell, and as we had done the year before, Maara and I went out into the countryside to set our snares. Sparrow and a few of the other girls had asked me if I would make fur leggings for them.

The first animal we caught was a hare, its fur pure white and very thick.

"This winter will be long and bitter," Maara said.

For those who'd had a meager harvest, it would be a time of hunger. Again I was reminded how fortunate we were.

Only a few weeks remained until midwinter's day, and the Lady still hadn't spoken to me about my adoption. I began to wonder if I should speak with her about it. Although I had given the matter a great deal of thought, I had come to no conclusion. It still felt wrong to abandon the mother I loved, but it felt just as wrong to refuse the place the Lady offered me. When I tried to think of someone else she might choose to be her heir, it seemed that not only was I the obvious choice, but that there was no one else.

At last I spoke to Namet about it. She had no advice to give me.

"You must follow your own heart," she said.

A few days before midwinter's night, in the early morning before anyone was up, the healer came to the companions' loft. She woke me and gestured to me to come with her. She didn't speak until we were in the kitchen.

"I'm sorry to wake you so early," she said. "The Lady wants you."

The day I dreaded had come, I thought, but when I turned to go up to the Lady's chamber, the healer said, "Wait a minute. I want to brew something for her fever."

"Is she unwell?" I asked.

The healer's brow furrowed with worry.

"Out of her head all night," she told me. "Full of wild talk. She finally slept an hour or two this morning. She's a bit better now, but she refused the medicine I gave her. She may be willing to take something from your hand."

"Does she have winter sickness?"

"It's a fever of some kind, but worse than any winter sickness I've seen."

I waited while the healer brewed an evil-smelling tea of goldenroot.

"How long has she been ill?" I asked.

"Her servant called me at midnight," she said. "Merin complained all day yesterday of headache, but last night she was feeling better. Then in the middle of the night the fever came on her. She called out for someone in her sleep." The healer gave me a strange look. "Your name, her servant thought."

"My name?"

"Yours or your mother's, but this morning it was you she asked for."

I took the tea upstairs and knocked on the Lady's door. No one answered. I went in and found her sleeping. Before I could decide which would do her the most good, medicine or sleep, she opened her eyes. When she saw me, a light came into them for a moment. Then it died, and she turned her face away.

"You sent for me, Lady," I said.

She moved her hand a little, as if to wave me away.

"I've brought something for your fever."

She gave no indication that she'd heard me. I sat down beside her on the bed and felt her forehead. It was dry and hot. I think she would have pushed my hand away if she'd had the strength. In her eyes I saw a weariness that frightened me.

"Drink this," I said.

I slipped my hand behind her head, to raise it enough for her to drink from the bowl. She was too weak to resist me, and she drank a few sips of the tea. After a while she began to doze. I went downstairs and brought a basin of cold water and a cloth back to her room. I bathed her face and hands and left the cool cloth on her forehead. I believe it made her feel a little better.

Most of that day I stayed beside her. I brewed her a remedy I had learned from my mother. She seemed to like it better than what the healer had given her. I also got her to take some bread soaked in broth, though it was difficult for her to swallow.

All day her servant kept up a good fire. The room was stuffy, but it was much too cold outside to take the shutter down, and even the dim lamplight in the room seemed to hurt the Lady's eyes. While she slept, I dozed in the chair by the hearth. In the evening the healer sent me downstairs to eat my supper.

"Tell them it's winter sickness," she told me. "Let's not frighten anyone."

I nodded, but when I spoke with Maara after supper, I told her the truth.

"Will she recover?" Maara asked me.

I knew what she was thinking. "I can't believe it's the Lady's time to die. So many people need her."

And none more than Maara and I, I thought to myself.

Maara frowned. "The gods never stop to think that someone may be needed," she said.

That evening the healer told me she would sit up with the Lady, so I went to bed, but only a few hours later, she sent for me again. When I entered the Lady's chamber, the healer was sitting on the edge of the bed, her hands on the Lady's shoulders, to keep her still.

I heard the Lady say, "Where is she?"

"She's coming," the healer told her. Then she saw me come in. "Here she is now."

The healer beckoned to me. When I approached the bed, she got up and had me sit down beside the Lady. She took the Lady's hand and placed it in mine.

"Is it you?" the Lady asked me.

The healer bobbed her head at me.

"Yes," I said. "It's me."

The Lady sighed and closed her eyes. "Don't leave me."

"I won't," I said. "I'm here."

After a few minutes she fell asleep.

"She insisted on getting up to go after your mother," the healer whispered, when she was sure the Lady was sleeping soundly. "I didn't know what else to do. It was all I could do to keep her in bed."

The healer looked worn out.

"I'll sit with her now," I told her.

"Don't let her get out of bed."

"I won't."

"She's very strong, as ill as she is."

"I've nursed people with fevers before," I said. "I'll keep her quiet."

"All right," she said. "Send for me if you need me."

Although there was a good fire burning, I was cold. I made sure the Lady was well covered. Then I wrapped myself in a blanket and sat down again beside her.

She slept peacefully for half an hour. I had begun to doze. Her restlessness woke me. She struggled against the bedclothes, trying to push them aside, as if she would get out of bed. I covered her again and took her hand.

"Hush," I said.

She quieted a little. "You're here."

"Yes, I'm here."

Her grip on my hand tightened. She drew it to her lips and kissed it. Then she held the back of my hand against her cheek and closed her eyes.

"I'm sorry," she said.

"It's all right."

She turned onto her side, facing me, and settled herself to sleep, her cheek pillowed on my hand clasped in hers.

"Beloved," she said.

"I hoped time had healed that wound," said Namet.

"They were more than friends," I said.

Namet nodded. "Much more."

"I didn't know."

"It was over and done with before you first drew breath."

"Evidently not," I told her.

"No," she conceded. "Evidently not."

It was still early morning. As soon as the healer had released me from my charge, I went to Namet's room. The Lady had slept peacefully through the night, although she still burned with fever.

"Why did my mother never tell me?" I asked Namet.

"You must ask her that," she said.

"Did my mother love her too?"

"Very much."

"But she went home."

"Yes."

"Why?"

"That is something you shouldn't hear from me."

"Who else can tell me?"

"Only Merin and Tamnet know the truth of it."

"No one else?"

Namet took my hand. "Let it be. What good can come of awakening the dead past?"

"The past is awake in Merin," I said.

And in my mother too? I wondered.

"That may be," said Namet, "but the sooner it sleeps again, the better off she'll be."

"And if it doesn't sleep?"

Namet sighed and shook her head.

"You awakened the past for Maara," I reminded her.

"Yes," she said. "Because I had a remedy for it. I awakened a longing in her for something she once knew long ago, and had forgotten, because wanting it hurt too much. And the remembering did hurt her, but when the hurt had passed, she was no longer motherless."

Namet's eyes grew fierce. "There is no remedy for Merin's pain."

As I tried to make some sense of what I'd heard, my mind discovered all the questions I had never asked because I didn't know enough to ask them. As a child I had been surrounded by mysteries of which I was ignorant. Now my heart was telling me that ignorance would shelter me no longer.

"It isn't fair," I said. "So many things happened in the world before I came into it. I can't know any of them unless someone will tell me. It's like walking into a room where everyone is keeping a secret. I hear the whispers and see the sidelong glances, and I know the secret must have something to do with me, but no one will tell me anything."

"This secret has nothing to do with you," said Namet.

"Of course it does," I said.

Namet sighed. "I believe they had a falling-out. Their hearts didn't change, but something came between them."

"My father?"

"No."

"What was it then?"

"Let me begin at the beginning," she said. "When I came here to find my husband, I saw the love between them. It hurt me very much, because it reminded me of what I had lost. It hurt so much that I avoided them.

"But I couldn't avoid Merin's mother, and one day she insisted on telling me how delighted she was that her daughter and Tamnet had found each other. She told me that Merin had been a difficult child, and I could well believe it. She was disobedient and disrespectful, impossible to discipline, and her mother had little confidence that she would ever be able to bear the responsibility that would one day be hers. But when she loved Tamnet, she began to care about herself, and she also began to care about other people."

Namet gave me a wry smile. "While my love for my husband made me think only of myself, Merin's love for Tamnet made her think about other people when she had never cared anything about them before. Love sometimes does that.

"After the war, Tamnet went home, but there was something wrong about her leaving. She would have gone home in any case. There was never any question about that. Her mother had lost every child she had but one. How could Tamnet have deprived her mother of her only living child? And of course she had to take her place as her mother's heir.

"But she left suddenly one morning, and for days afterward, Merin was in a rage. She was every bit the spoiled child in a tantrum that she had been before. No one had any sympathy for her. After all, her beloved still lived, while all around her people grieved loved ones lost forever.

"Merin cared nothing for what anyone thought of her, but in time the storm blew over. What saved her, I think, was that there was so much to do. She was so young, with responsibilities that a much older woman would have found daunting. Her mother's health was failing, and this place was a shambles. To Merin fell the task of setting everything to rights. She put the breach with Tamnet behind her and went on."

"But they remained friends," I said, remembering the times Merin had come to help us when I was a child. "How did they heal their hearts?"

"I don't know," she said. "I know nothing about their relationship since Tamnet left. Merin has never spoken to me about it. After the war our positions were reversed. I had my beloved with me, and she had lost hers. I knew what that felt like. And I bore such a responsibility for what had happened that to speak to her about it could only have caused more pain."

"Did my mother go home alone?"

Namet nodded. "As far as I know, she did."

"Where was my father?"

"He was here. A few months after she went home, he followed her."

"Did she love him?"

"I don't know," she said. "He certainly loved her. In time she could have come to care for him too."

Not as she had cared for Merin, I thought. While I had no way of knowing, I was sure that it was true.

All day Merin's fever burned. She was too weak now to try to get out of bed, too weak to do anything but sleep, and when she woke, she was not herself. Sometimes she babbled nonsense. Sometimes she gazed past me at something in the distance. Sometimes she wept quietly into her pillow.

"I don't know where her fever has taken her," the healer said, "but I think it's a place she never visits unless she can't help herself."

I wondered if the healer knew as much as I did about the Lady's sorrows.

"Have you seen her like this before?" I asked her.

"Only once," she said. "Not long after I joined this household. It must be almost ten years now. She called for your mother then too." The healer gave me a sidelong glance. "Why do you think she did that?"

I didn't distrust the healer, but the Lady's secrets weren't mine to tell.

"My mother is her closest friend," I said. "Who else would she call for when she has no family of her own?"

The healer made a sound like "humph" that told me she knew that I knew more than I was telling.

"When she's better perhaps she will confide in you," I said.

"Confide in me? I don't think so." The healer shook her head. "But I wouldn't be surprised if she were to confide in you, and if she does, you must listen to her carefully. This illness of the body both masks and reveals a disorder of the spirit. When her fever cools, another healing must begin, if she'll allow it."

The healer regarded me appraisingly. "Have you any experience with that kind of healing?"

I shook my head.

"I think that in any case there is no one else," the healer said.

"There is Namet."

"Not for Merin. There's no love lost between those two."

"Perhaps Namet can advise me then."

"Perhaps." The healer gazed at me for so long that I began to feel uncomfortable. Then she said, "Do you understand how serious this is?"

I nodded. I thought she meant to impress upon me how ill Merin was, both in body and in spirit. That wasn't what she meant at all. She was thinking of what would become of us, of what would become of all of Merin's people, if Merin could no longer care for us.

The healer lifted my chin and gazed into my eyes.

"Old eyes," she said. Her thumb lightly stroked my cheek. "Such old eyes in such a young face." She let go of me. "Are you willing?"

"Yes."

"Then go get some rest while you can. I expect she'll have a bad night."

It was the third night of the Lady's fever, and the third night of a fever is usually the worst. If I could get her safely through this night, there was a good chance she would recover.

The Lady slept fitfully for several hours. Then around midnight she woke and asked for water. Her lips were chapped and painful, so I dampened a cloth and squeezed the water into her mouth. She mumbled a few words I didn't understand.

"Sleep now," I said.

"Soon you'll be gone," she whispered.

"I'll be here when you wake."

"You might wait for midsummer's day."

"Hush."

"One more night," she said.

She closed her eyes and was quiet for a while, but her breathing told me she wasn't sleeping. Suddenly her eyes flew open. They glittered in the lamplight, dark and angry.

"I should have hated you," she said.

Although the Lady was so weak that she could barely raise her head, the force of her anger struck me like a blow. Her eyes demanded an answer. I couldn't give her one. I didn't know if she was talking to my mother or to me.

"You were a two-edged sword," she said, and at last she closed her eyes.

Sparrow had once said almost the same thing to me, that love is a sword with two edges.

The Lady struggled to draw breath. It didn't seem as if her illness was the cause. She sounded more like a child trying not to cry. I laid my hand over her heart, and then I felt what she was feeling, as I had felt her grief when I stood beside her at her window searching the night for ghosts. The ache of her longing seized my heart and brought tears into my eyes.

She fought to pull air into her body, but there was no room in her breast for anything but grief. She must have seen her own pain mirrored in my eyes. She freed one hand from the blankets and caressed my cheek.

"Lie with me," she whispered. "For the last time."

She slipped her hand around my neck and drew me down beside her. I didn't resist her. It seemed to me that in her arms I too would find relief from pain. I laid my forehead against her cheek, while her fingers stroked my neck and found the place that I thought only Sparrow knew. My body responded, and I blushed to know my mother's secret.

I understood what Merin was asking of me. When I became for Maara the child she sought along the misty riverbank, I wasn't aware until afterwards that I had gone with her on her journey back through time, and that I had not only stood in the place of the child that she had been, but that I had become that child, so that in me she could find a lost part of herself.

Now Merin was asking much the same thing of me. I didn't know if I could go with her as I had gone with Maara, not only because I didn't love her as I loved Maara, but because I would be standing in my mother's place, and this was a journey the two of them should make together.

Even so, I felt nothing strange as I lay in Merin's arms, nothing alien in her touch, nothing disturbing in her caress. Maara's arms had made me the child she needed me to be, and when that happened, I lost myself for a little while. In Merin's arms I remained myself, but though I couldn't become my mother for her sake, I thought I might serve as a mirror, reflecting back to her the woman she had loved before I existed. My heart was certain then that I had found the answer. Wearing Tamnet's face, I would have gone with Merin wherever she needed me to go, even into the most intimate embrace of love, but although she asked it of me, she didn't take me there. Perhaps she found my willingness enough. Or perhaps her journey swept her past the act of love into the abyss.

For a long time I lay in Merin's arms while her spirit traveled the paths of memory. She had wandered into some dark corner of her heart where she had hidden her agony even from herself. Sometimes she wept silently. From time to time she spoke to me. I never answered her. She seemed not to need an answer. All the while she held me to her heart. I listened to her heartbeat, and to words only my mother should have heard. I heard the story of her rage and her regret. I heard her curse love for changing her, so that she couldn't leave the ones who needed her, not even to follow love. I heard her beg my mother not to leave her. I heard words of love and longing that broke my heart.

At last sleep took us both. Dreams touched me in passing, leaving me weightless with joy, then heavy with grief. These dreams brought no images, only the rainbow of the heart that people said love was. The colors of love wound themselves around me, bright and dark.

I woke to the familiar sounds of activity in the kitchen below. The servants were up, lighting the fires, drawing water, kneading the day's bread. I shivered. The fire had gone out.

I got up and bundled Merin's blankets around her. She didn't wake. Her sleep was deep and peaceful, and when I touched her cheek, I felt only the slightest trace of fever. The worst was over.

I made a new fire. Then I wrapped myself in a blanket and sat down on the bed beside her. My breath made little white clouds in the chilly air. For a long time I watched her sleep. She was beautiful.

Suddenly she opened her eyes. She looked up at me and smiled. Her eyes drew mine and held them. I wanted to blink or look away, but her eyes wouldn't let me go. A look came into them as if a light had kindled within her. I had never seen a look like that. Love had never looked at me like that. Not even my mother's love had looked at me like that, because a mother's love would someday have to let me go, but the love in Merin's eyes would have held me until time ended, if I had been the object of it. When she closed her eyes again, it took me some time to grow accustomed to the dark.

I got up from the bed and slipped out the door. Soon she would wake. I hoped she would be hungry, and I wanted to have something ready for her to eat. In the kitchen I found a basket of fresh eggs. I put two in a bowl and filled the bowl with boiling water. To measure the time, I sang a song quietly to myself. When the eggs were cooked, but still soft, I broke the shells and mixed the soft egg with a handful of breadcrumbs. I was about to go back upstairs when the healer came into the kitchen.

"She must be better," said the healer, when she saw the contents of the bowl.

"She's much better," I said.

"Is she awake?"

"She soon will be."

"I can feed her if you'd like to get some rest."

"No," I said. "I'll feed her."

When I returned to Merin's room, I found her awake and struggling to sit up. She looked at me, surprised. I realized that I had neglected to knock.

"You've been very ill," I told her.

"Nonsense," she said. "Yesterday I had a touch of headache, that's all."

"That was three days ago," I said.

"Three days?"

I nodded.

She tried again to sit up, but her arms were too weak to hold her. I helped her prop herself up on a pillow. Then I fed her her breakfast. She didn't speak to me. She was confused and trying to gather her thoughts together. She had just finished her breakfast when the healer came in, bringing a steaming bowl of tea.

"Ah," said the healer. "I see she's quite herself again."

"I've always been myself," the Lady muttered.

The healer smiled with relief and pleasure.

"Yes, yes," she said. "Quite herself. Very much herself."

Although I had slept, I was exhausted. The healer took over the Lady's care so that I could rest. Before I went to the companions' loft, I stopped by Namet's room to tell her Merin would recover. Namet took one look at me and made me sit down on her bed. She peered anxiously into my eyes. Then she held her hand over my heart and cocked her head to listen.

"How do you feel?" she asked me.

"I'm all right."

"There's something odd about you. I can't put my finger on it."

"I've been up with Merin all night. I'm just tired."

Of course she knew I wasn't telling her the whole truth. She waited to hear the rest.

"Merin's fever took her into the past," I said, "and I went with her."

"Ah," she said. "You joined Merin on a journey of the heart, just as you did for Maara."

"This time was different."

"Every time is different," she said, and sent me off to bed.

I woke early in the afternoon feeling much better. When I looked in on the Lady, she was sleeping, so I sat down on the chair by the hearth to wait for her to wake.

As much as Namet had told me about Merin's love for my mother, nothing could have prepared me for my encounter with it. I thought about the one whose love she'd lost. Then I wondered if she had lost it. Did my mother's heart too have this grief locked away in it? If she had loved no less than she was loved, grief must lie buried in her heart still.

The Lady murmured in her sleep. She looked so young. Was it her fever or her journey that had changed her? Or was I the one who changed? I had seen Merin through the eyes of love. She would never look the same to me again.

43

MERIN

I knew your answer when you didn't come to me right away," the Lady said. "If you intended to accept my offer, you would have come to speak with me about it."

"I should have spoken to you either way," I said, "if only to thank you for the honor. I'm sorry now I didn't."

She made a gesture as if to brush my apology aside. "I don't blame you. I'd be a dreadful mother. My own mother used to accuse me of selfishness, because I didn't care to bring children of my own into the world. I told her that I was only sparing them my many faults."

She was making light of my refusal, but I was ashamed now to remember my own words, that I wouldn't change a good mother for a bad one. I could, however, tell the Lady the truth about one thing.

"I wasn't thinking of what kind of mother you would make," I said. "I didn't want to lose the one I had."

"Ah," she said. "I can understand that."

We were silent for a while. Then she asked me, "What time of day is it?"

"It must be almost evening."

"Will you take the shutter down?"

"It's very cold."

She pulled a blanket around her shoulders. "Just for a minute. Please."

I took the shutter down. The sun hovered just above the western hills. Faint stars glowed against the darkening sky. The night would be clear and cold.

When the sun touched the horizon, a wordless cry rang out. It didn't come from within the house. It sounded like a cry of lamentation. *All is lost, all is lost,* it seemed to say. Although it had no words, the song was eloquent. It spoke of endless darkness, the loss of hope, the death of the heart.

"Who is that?" I whispered.

"The elders," she replied. "They're in the place of ritual, mourning the death of the sun."

I had forgotten. It must be midwinter's night.

When the last remnant of the sun vanished, the lamentation ended and another song began. This time it was a song I knew, and this time the voices came from within the house, from the great hall, where everyone had gathered to watch through the longest night. The voices of women and men blended together in a song of hope.

The room was growing cold. I put the shutter up.

"Go down and join them," she said. "I'll be all right."

"I'd rather stay with you. May I?"

"Of course." She looked pleased.

I sat down again on the chair by the hearth, and for a long time we listened to the singing.

"When I was a child, I used to love midwinter's night," the Lady said.

"All children love midwinter's night."

"Why is that?"

I thought back to the midwinter's nights of my own childhood.

"I got to stay up late," I said, "and everyone I loved gathered around the fire. We ate sweet cakes and roasted nuts dipped in honey. My mother held me on her lap while we sang songs and told stories. When I fell asleep in her arms, I had good dreams. In the morning there were gifts."

The Lady smiled. "I too loved midwinter's night, but for a different reason. Just as you did, I sat with my family by the fire. I only half-remember the songs and stories. I was always listening for something else. Outside the circle of firelight, a mystery surrounded us. I thought that if only I could remain within it long enough, I would learn its secrets. For me, the dawn always came too soon."

I had never felt anything like that.

"Sometimes I think we long for all the wrong things," the Lady said. "This world we see can seem so dark, even on a bright midsummer's day. What if our heart's desire can be found only in the dark?"

"But in the dark is death."

"Yes."

Her words made the skin prickle on the back of my neck. Of all nights, midwinter's night was not the time to call things out of the dark.

"I've always felt just the opposite," I told her. "That the light that shows the world to us conceals a brighter one."

"It does," she said. "I looked upon it once. It blinded me."

A new song began downstairs. We listened for a while. I must have dozed a little. When I opened my eyes, the Lady was watching me.

"I could almost believe you were your mother sitting there," she said.

"Am I so like her?"

"Not so like her as she is today, but you are the image of Tamnet when she was your age. The first time you entered my hall, I could hardly believe my eyes. As if a door had opened into the past, I thought I saw your mother, as I saw her all those years ago, coming to be fostered in my mother's house. Then I saw her standing next to you."

Although her tone was wistful, in her words I heard no more than a nostalgic longing for an absent friend. The night before she had been in agony. What could account for the difference, I wondered, between the woman she was then and the woman she was now? As soon as I asked the question, I knew the answer. Even in her agony, the woman who had held me through the night had hope. This woman had none.

The fire was now just a bed of coals. I reached for a few sticks of wood to build it up again.

"Let it burn down," the Lady said.

"It will be too cold."

"I'm well wrapped up. Come and sit here beside me. There are blankets enough for both of us." She patted the bed beside her. "Please."

I tucked her blankets more closely around her and wrapped another around her shoulders. Then I sat down on the edge of the bed. A cold draft blew across the floor. I drew my legs up onto the bed and sat cross-legged.

The Lady handed me a heavy blanket, and I snuggled into it.

"Are you warm enough?" she asked me.

I nodded.

"Put out the lamp," she said.

Only one lamp burned on the chest beside her bed. I pinched it out.

"What is the lesson of midwinter's night?" she said.

I smiled. While she lived, my grandmother had asked me the same question every midwinter's night of my life.

"It teaches us never to lose hope," I said.

"What is it that we hope for?"

"The return of light."

"What else does it teach us?"

This time her question puzzled me. My grandmother had never asked it. I didn't know the answer she wanted.

"Does this night teach us nothing about the dark?"

Then I remembered. My grandmother had sometimes asked me, what does the dark teach us?

"The dark teaches us to trust," I said.

"And what is it that we trust?"

"Life."

"And death?"

I was afraid to agree with her. Of course we trusted death. We trusted death to spare us the infirmities of age or the pains of an illness or an injury that is past healing. We trusted death to comfort us with forgetfulness of life's sorrows. We trusted that death was a passageway from life to life, and that the spirit, freed of the body it had outworn, would again clothe itself in flesh and time. In that way I trusted death, but Merin was speaking of something else.

She began to sing.

In the darkness of the womb, we are made.

It was the first line of a chant I had heard the grown-ups sing when I was a child. I had never heard it sung at midwinter. It was sung when someone died, or on a day of remembrance for the dead. It was meant to go from voice to voice, and now Merin waited for my response. I was afraid to sing it.

"Don't you know it?" she asked me.

I nodded.

"Sing it with me then."

Reluctantly I sang.

In the darkness of the womb, we are unmade.

Her voice answered mine.

In the darkness of the Mother's womb,
we are made and unmade and made again,
and so it will be until the world grows old.

She waited for me to begin the chant again.

In the darkness of the womb, we are made.
In the darkness of the womb, we are unmade.
In the darkness of the Mother's womb,
we are made and unmade and made again,
and so it will be until the world grows old.

We handed the words back and forth between us, and every time we began the chant anew, the melody changed, just a few notes every time, until what had been a lament became a song of joy.

"Listen," the Lady said.

I listened. No sound came now from the great hall. The winter world outside was silent too. From the corners of the room the dark crept closer.

"Feel how soft it is," she whispered.

I closed my eyes. The dark was soft and deep, and I could have fallen back into it and kept falling forever.

"There is no wanting here," she said.

It was true. I wanted nothing. Wherever I now found myself, neither cold nor hunger could afflict me. No pain could touch me here. Nothing to want. Nothing to fear. Nothing to hope.

I opened my eyes. By the last glimmer of firelight I saw a shadow fall over Merin's face. Then I saw the danger. She had been so close to death. Perhaps it lingered still, just out of reach.

But Merin had reached for it.

I touched her cheek. She gave a start, as if I had awakened her from sleep, and opened her eyes. On this darkest of nights I wanted to bring the light of truth into the darkness of this woman's heart.

"I know how much you loved her," I whispered.

Anger flashed in Merin's eyes. "I doubt that very much. I doubt that even she has any idea how much I loved her."

"I can't answer for my mother, but when you were ill, you mistook me for her. Without intending to, you revealed yourself."

Warily Merin waited to hear the rest.

"The light that blinded you still shines," I said. "I've seen you standing in the light."

"Who are you?" she whispered.

"I'm not the one you loved," I said, "but I am her gift to you."

The cold breath of that long night blew upon the dying embers of the fire, and by a light so dim I hardly knew if it showed me the world of light or the world of shadows, I saw her eyes bright with tears.

"You must live," I said, "so that you can share with her what you shared with me last night."

"And what was that?"

"The truth."

"The truth? What is the truth?"

"You love her still, as she no doubt loves you."

"How do you know your mother's heart?" she asked me. "Did she too reveal herself to you?" She knew my mother had done no such thing.

"I know she never loved another."

Merin was silent for a long time. At last she said, "It's a cruel thing you've done this night."

"Cruel?" I asked her. "Why?"

"You've taught me hope, and it has taken me half a lifetime to unlearn it."

I smiled. Hope is the first lesson of midwinter's night. It was this night that taught her hope even as she tried to redeem its promise of forgetfulness.

"It seems to me," I said, "that the cruelest thing would be to leave this world without the love you've found here."

"Little enough it's been," she said.

Although her bitter words made my heart ache, I chided her. "If you think my mother's love a small thing, you were never worthy of it. And surely hers is not the only love you've known."

"I know of no other."

"For what it's worth," I told her, "you have mine."

"I would never have guessed it."

In her voice I heard her disappointment that we had not been to each other what she had once hoped. Yet beneath her disappointment I heard something else. In my mind's eye I saw a child peering out at me from behind a door. If something frightened her, she would quickly pull it shut again.

"I never knew you," I said. "Until last night you never let me see you as you are. Now I understand a great many things I didn't understand before."

"Tell me," she said. "Just what is it you believe you understand?"

"I understand that you must have thought me very selfish. I have insisted on having my own way in everything, while you sacrificed the only thing you wanted."

"I don't suppose that means you'll do any differently in future."

"Probably not," I admitted. "I'm not capable of being that unselfish."

I felt her hand search for mine. When she found it, she held it tight.

"I wish your mother had been more like you," she said.

She didn't need to explain herself to me. I understood. If my mother had been more selfish, she might never have gone home.

I wished I could have known the young woman Merin loved. As much as I loved my mother, and as close as I had been to her all my life, the girl Merin loved was someone I had never met.

"Tell me about her," I said. "What was she like when she was my age?"

The Lady sighed. "She was just a country girl. There was nothing unusual about her. At first I thought I disliked her very much. I didn't understand why I couldn't keep my eyes from following her whenever she was in my sight."

"Why did you think you disliked her?"

"She was so simple, so innocent. The world seemed a drab place to me, but she found it fascinating. I must have been quite dour in those days. Your mother was the only one who dared to tease me. She used to laugh at me and call me silly names. She called me things like Dismal and Frown Face. She took me by the hand and led me into the light of a world no one else had ever shown me."

"She loved you."

"Yes. Much to my amazement, she did."

A cold draft blew under the door. It scattered the ash in the fireplace and brightened the embers for a moment. The light fell upon the Lady's face. She looked very tired.

"Sleep now," I said. "Sleep and grow strong again."

"Build up the fire," she said.

By the time I had a bright blaze burning on the hearth, she was asleep. I wrapped myself in a blanket, lay down beside her, and closed my eyes.

44

A Wicked Lie

All through midwinter's day, while the feasting went on downstairs, I stayed beside the Lady. In her fever she had hardly eaten anything. Now she had no appetite, and a few spoonfuls of soup would satisfy her. I had to encourage her to eat, as one encourages a fussing child to take just one more mouthful. Sometimes I saw a flicker of amusement in her eyes. I think she made a game of it. I enjoyed her playful spirit, and I made tut-tut noises in pretended disapproval when she refused to open her mouth to take another bite.

When the room was warm enough, I helped the Lady move to the chair by the hearth. I bathed her, while her servant changed her bedding. Then we put her back to bed. Her servant offered to sit with her a while so that I could rest, but I sent her back downstairs to enjoy the holiday with the others. I felt such tenderness for the woman in my care that I couldn't bring myself to leave her side.

That evening, when she found me dozing by the fire, the healer woke me and insisted I go to my own bed for a good night's rest. When I awoke, it was midmorning, and everyone else was up and gone.

I wanted to talk with Namet, but when I went to her room, I found her napping. I was about to go downstairs to look for Maara when I heard a noise in her room. I lifted the curtain and looked in. She was sitting on her bed doing a bit of mending.

"I thought you'd be downstairs with the others," I said.

Although the holiday was over, there was still a good deal of feasting and merrymaking going on in the great hall.

Maara rolled her eyes. "One day of it was enough for me."

Her mock distaste for our boisterous holidays warmed my heart. I smiled. "I've missed you," I said.

"Oh." She looked puzzled, as she tried to think of an appropriate reply.

Then I realized that midwinter's day had gone by and I hadn't given her her gift.

"Wait here a minute," I said, and went to get it from the companions' loft.

I had traded several of my best rabbit skins for a plain wooden brooch. I stayed up late every night for weeks carving an intricate design into it. When I gave it to her, she said nothing, but her smile and the way she ran her fingers over the design told me that it pleased her.

Then she gave me the gift she had made for me. It was a bow case made of goatskin, beautifully tanned and very soft. Unlike the stiff and heavy cowhide case I took to the frontier, this one was light and flexible. When I wasn't using it to carry the unstrung bow, it could be folded and put into a tunic pocket, while the other one had to be carried over the shoulder, where it was in the way.

We were admiring our gifts when Namet looked in the door.

"Aha," she said when she saw me. "Merin must be better."

"Yes," I said. "She's mending. She's in no danger."

Namet came in and sat down beside me on the foot of Maara's bed. She took my hand and gazed into my eyes. "And how are you?"

"I'm fine," I said.

"Truly?"

I nodded. "I've made my decision."

Namet showed no curiosity, as if she knew what it would be, but I could feel Maara hold her breath, waiting for my answer.

"If she still counts me worthy of the honor, I will become Merin's child."

Maara breathed again.

"What changed your mind?" Namet asked me.

"I didn't understand at first how my mother could let go of me so easily," I said. "Now I know what was in her heart." I turned to Maara. "You were right when you said my mother would never let me go."

Namet glanced at Maara and raised her eyebrows. "Is my child already so wise in the ways of motherhood?"

Maara looked down at her hands, to hide her smile and the color that came into her cheeks.

Namet turned back to me. "Tell me how your mother can give you away without letting you go."

"A gift of love never goes from one hand to another without binding the two together," I told her.

Namet nodded, as if that was the reply she had expected. "Have you given Merin your answer?"

"Not yet."

"Then let me counsel you to wait a while," she said.

"Why?"

"Tell Merin your intentions, but ask her to make no announcement until she's well again. Then let your adoption take place as soon as possible. I hope it's not too late even to do that."

Fear prickled the back of my neck.

Namet turned to Maara. "I should have spoken to you sooner about this. I hoped it would prove to be no more than idle gossip."

She turned back to me, and in a soft voice, she said, "Whispers have come to me that certain people here have begun to question Merin's strength, if not yet her leadership."

"She was ill," I protested. "She was very ill, but there's no reason to believe she won't recover. Soon she'll be as good as new."

"It's not her strength of body that's in question. They question whether Merin's power will return to her."

"Do they think her power left her just because she fell ill?"

"Had you noticed no change in Merin?"

Dread stole into my heart. I felt that Namet was going to tell me something I knew already but hadn't dared to look at.

"She had a way of paying close attention," Namet said. "She was aware of everything, of what went on inside a person, of what was behind the things a person said and the things she left unsaid. Ever since Tamnet's visit, Merin seems to pay little attention to what goes on around her. I think she pays attention to something else."

"That may be true," I said.

"Others have noticed. They have become unsure of her, and her illness has frightened them."

"What does that mean? Would someone try to take Merin's place?"

"No," she said. "This house and its land belong to her. No one can replace her simply by saying so, but while she will keep her position, her right to command may be in doubt. Although people will always treat her with the greatest respect, they will follow whoever is strong enough to lead them."

"Vintel?"

She nodded.

"Would no one charge Vintel with disloyalty?"

"Only if she puts herself forward," said Namet, "and she's too clever to do that. She will wait for others to come to her."

"Why would anyone come to her?"

Namet heard the contempt in my voice, and she gave me a sharp answer.

"Don't underestimate Vintel," she said. "Vintel knows better than to plot against Merin openly. She has begun to change people's minds without their being aware of it. She has said no more than that she hopes Merin will recover, but in a way that says she doubts Merin will recover her power, even if she recovers her health."

"They will soon learn differently," I said.

"Are you so confident of Merin's healing?" Namet's eyes held mine. I felt an echo of her power ripple through my mind. I could never be less than completely honest with Namet, nor could I, when she looked at me like that, be less than completely honest with myself.

"Merin has changed," I told her. "I don't know what that will mean for her strength of leadership, but I don't believe it is a bad thing for Merin."

"You may be right," she said. "Perhaps in the long run, she will have changed for the better. It's the immediate danger that worries me. The question of your adoption has come at a bad time."

"Wouldn't it strengthen Merin's position to name an heir?"

"It would, if she were to name anyone but you."

I was too surprised speak, even to ask her why.

"Vintel's cunning has caught me unprepared," said Namet. "She knew you would be Merin's choice, and she has found a way to cause Merin's choice to weaken her."

"What is Vintel saying?" Maara asked.

"Nothing she could be challenged for. She hints. She suggests. She makes seemingly innocuous statements of fact. Tamnet is a healer. She has taught the healing arts to Tamras, and in healing there is always a bit of sorcery."

"That's ridiculous," Maara said.

"Of course it is."

"What sorcery could she accuse Tamras of?"

"As I said, she never speaks directly. She says things that work on people's minds in the dark. How did Tamras the Small defeat a warrior of the northern tribes? How is it that Merin listens to this child as she has never listened to even the wisest of her counselors? How did a child attain such influence? Merin grants her every wish. Is it not possible that Merin has fallen under an enchantment? What dark magic do we harbor here in Merin's house?"

"And does Vintel suggest where this dark magic comes from?"

Namet looked long into Maara's eyes. "Your wounds were seen by many who believed them mortal, yet you survived them. You lay under the sword of a chieftain of the northern tribes, yet it was he who fell. What power must be yours, that Death herself fears you? Vintel certainly fears you, and her fear lends power to her words. Tamras may have power of her own, but Tamras is just a child, and a child is easily led."

Namet's words terrified me. I saw the dark come into Maara's eyes.

"For some time Merin has not been herself," said Namet. "Now she has fallen ill, and she has sent the healer from her side in favor of this child."

"That's not what happened at all," I said.

"Who will deny it?"

"Merin will."

"Of course she will, if she is enchanted."

"The healer knows the truth."

"The healer would deny that Merin sent her away, even if it were true. Would she allow people to believe that Merin has lost confidence in her?"

"Merin's servant also knows the truth," I said.

"Does she?" said Namet. "Why then does she whisper that Tamras has taken her mother's place in Merin's bed?"

I felt my skin grow cold. Nothing Vintel had said seemed as wicked to me as that lie. It made of my love for Merin something unholy.

"I have not," I whispered.

"Is the woman a liar then?"

I paused to think. "She may have seen something she misunderstood."

"And Vintel may have prepared the woman's mind to believe what would best suit Vintel."

Vintel had been more clever than I would ever have suspected. She had used the issue of my adoption to weaken Merin while at the same time making it impossible.

"In my heart I may be Merin's child already," I said, "but I can never now be her child in fact."

"Why not?" said Namet. "Would you let the lie stand?"

"How can I disprove it?"

"Perhaps you can't. People will believe what they believe. Why would that stop you from claiming your inheritance?"

Namet was testing my understanding.

"If people believe the lie," I said, "they will believe that I used Merin's heartache for my advantage, and they will never see me as her child, whether she adopts me or not."

"So evil, from the simple truth, fashions a great and hideous lie," said Namet, "and so Vintel poisons the minds of innocents, until they begin to see as she would have them see."

"What can I do?"

"You can begin by refusing to behave as if these lies were true," said Namet. "They're only whispers now. They float upon the air like gossamer, waiting for something substantial to settle on. Give them nothing, and they'll float away."

"It's easier said than done," Maara murmured, as we trudged through the snow on our way to check our snares.

I had been lost in my own thoughts. For a moment I didn't know what she was talking about.

"You must behave as if you know nothing of these rumors," she said, "yet you must be constantly aware of them."

"I defy anyone to see something wrong in what I've done."

"Don't fall into the trap of taking offense at what is said behind your back," said Maara. "If any whisper of it comes to your ears, you must laugh and make light of it. Anger will only convince them that you have done something wrong and been found out."

"But I *am* angry."

"Of course you are. Namet has shown you a picture of what Vintel hopes to make everyone believe. She sees the pattern Vintel weaves as if it were whole cloth. But so far others have seen only scraps of it."

"They will soon piece the scraps together."

"Perhaps," she said, "but we may yet prove more clever than Vintel."

⌒○

Maara and I returned to Merin's house late that afternoon. Before we went out, I had looked in on the Lady and found her sleeping. Now I was anxious about her, and I went to see how she was feeling. I found her sitting in her chair by the hearth, well wrapped up in blankets, her feet on a flat stone that had been warmed in the fire. The window was tightly shuttered against the cold.

"I thought I might not see you today," she said reproachfully.

"My warrior needed me," I told her. "I trust the healer has taken good care of you in the meantime."

She shrugged.

Although she was determined to be difficult, I found her pout more charming than annoying.

"I'm glad to find you better," I said. "Can I bring you something?"

She shook her head. "Sit down."

I sat down on the hearth.

"Will your mother come in the spring?" she asked.

"I expect she will."

"With your sister?"

"Yes."

"Tell me about her. Is she like you?"

"She's not like me at all," I said. "She's cheerful and light-hearted. She's also full of mischief, and her playfulness will wear you out, but everyone adores her."

"Has she no serious side?"

"She hides her serious side."

"Is she clever?"

"Yes."

"And quick to learn?"

"She is."

"Does she aspire to leadership?"

"I believe so."

"Yet your mother seems to think she would mishandle power."

A memory stirred in a corner of my mind, of Tamar's eyes when she had challenged me to a trial of strength or skill, and of the anger in them when she failed to win. Sometimes I had seen in her a glimpse of something dark, a wanting, a desire for something that could only bring bad feelings with it, bad feelings that some mistake for happiness.

"She's young," I said. "She may outgrow her faults."

The Lady gave me a thoughtful look. "Does power never tempt *you?*"

"Perhaps I've never understood it. Why is it worth having?"

"People believe that power will give them everything they want."

I said nothing. She knew what I was thinking, that Merin's power had cost her the only thing she wanted.

"With power one may enforce one's will," she said.

"On others?"

"Of course on others."

"Why?"

She smiled. "Why does power make you so wary? Have I been such a tyrant?"

"Not at all," I protested.

"Perhaps your suspicion of power blinds you to its rightful use."

"What is its rightful use?"

"With power one may exercise wisdom on behalf of the unwise. I see no harm in that. Do you?"

I shook my head.

"There is satisfaction in doing for others what they lack the ability to do for themselves."

"I don't doubt it," I replied.

Still, she wanted something more from me, something I couldn't give her. When she spoke again, her words had an edge.

"I have kept this land at peace for twenty years," she said.

I nodded. I agreed with her. Maara had taught me to appreciate what I had taken for granted all my life, that our safety and prosperity came from Merin's power. But was it enough to justify a life?

"You paid too great a price," I said.

"A price you would not have paid?"

Even though life had not asked me that question, I knew my answer to it.

"No," I said.

Her eyes grew sad. "Have I nothing then to tempt you?"

"There's no need for you to tempt me," I told her. "Now I understand my mother's wish, and I am willing to become the child she promised you."

I had surprised her. She smiled with pleasure.

Before she could reply, I said, "I think you should first be certain that you've made the wisest choice."

"Haven't I?"

"Some people in this house hold the opinion that I have had too great an influence on you already."

"And why would anyone fear your influence?"

"They fear who may have influenced me."

Merin knit her brows in thought. "Your mother warned me that Vintel might be unhappy with my choice. Not that Vintel should have any say in the matter. But I'll bear it in mind that she has an opinion about it."

"She has more than an opinion. She has already whispered it about that Maara's magic has enchanted you."

Merin laughed. "Has she indeed?"

"You don't take her seriously?"

"I take everyone seriously, but Vintel plays a dangerous game. Has she the subtlety to play it well, do you think?"

"I think she's powerful enough that she may not need subtlety."

"Nevertheless," said Merin, "together I'm sure we can overcome Vintel's objections." She gave me an ironic smile. "I don't suppose it will do any good to point out that if you had heeded my advice, Vintel would have nothing to complain of."

I smiled back at her. "If it gives you some satisfaction, you may point out anything you like. I don't regret my choice. If someday your power comes to me, I will wield it well because of what Maara taught me."

"Well," said Merin, "what do you suggest we do?"

"About Vintel?"

"About your adoption."

"I think we should wait. By the time you're well and strong again, things may be different."

"I think you will make a wise leader, Tamras," she said.

Her praise made me blush. "Why do you say that?"

"When there's trouble, people are always impatient to be doing something, but sometimes the wisest course is to do nothing. Many problems will solve themselves."

45

A Warrior's Burial

Six weeks after midwinter's night, a child was born in Merin's house. Reni, one of the kitchen servants, had conceived on the night of the spring festival, and all through the long, tedious winter, everyone in Merin's house had been looking forward to the baby's birth.

Reni's labor began just after supper. Almost the entire household sat up all night in the great hall, waiting to greet the new arrival. The few who went to bed couldn't have slept much. Warriors who had heard the screams of the dying on the battlefield grew pale when they heard the noise that Reni made.

In a household of warriors, a midwife is seldom needed, and the healer protested that she was out of practice delivering babies. I had helped my mother deliver lots of babies, so I took charge of Reni's labor. Fortunately Reni needed little help. Although it was her first child, all went well. At dawn she gave birth to a little girl.

When they heard the baby's cry, the people waiting in the great hall gathered in the kitchen doorway. The healer let them come in for a few minutes, to see the child and say a few words of praise to the mother. Then she chased them all out again.

The servants slept in a tiny room at the back of the house. It was too cold there for the baby, so we made a bed for mother and child in a corner of the kitchen. For days the kitchen work was constantly disrupted by people coming to visit them. No child ever had so many aunts and uncles. In the spring Reni would take her baby home to her mother's household. A fortress is no place to raise a child. In the meantime we were all delighted to have a new life among us.

A few days after the birth of Reni's child, something woke me in the middle of the night. I heard a man's voice call my name. It came from below me, from the great hall. I peered over the edge of the companions' loft to see Kenit looking up at me.

"Tamras," he called again. "Come quickly."

"Wait there," I said.

"Dress warmly. Bring your cloak."

When I joined him in the great hall, he clutched at my arm. His eyes were wide with fear. "You must come with me."

"Where?"

"It isn't far. She needs your help." He began to pull me toward the door.

I tried to free my arm from his grasp. "Wait. What is it? What's the matter?"

"Please come quickly," he said. "She's giving birth."

"Who?"

"It isn't far, but we must hurry."

"I need to bring some things with me," I told him. "Medicines."

At last he understood and let me go. I left him pacing back and forth while I went into the kitchen. Because of Reni's pregnancy, the healer had collected herbs not usually kept in Merin's house, and I found everything I needed—herbs to ease a woman's pains, to strengthen her labor, to give a gentle sleep, to help her grow strong again after her delivery. I had no idea what to expect, so I took some of everything. Then I went with Kenit out into the night.

I was glad for my warm cloak. The light of the crescent moon, reflecting off the snow, was enough to light our way. We walked for half an hour before we came to a farmstead. The house was small. When I stepped through the doorway, the lintel brushed the top of my head, and Kenit had to stoop to enter. Inside there was only firelight. I wished I had thought to bring a lamp with me. On a pallet by the hearth a young woman lay unmoving. Beside her sat an older woman who I took to be her mother.

When Kenit saw the girl lying so still, he gave a soft cry.

The woman put her finger to her lips. "Asleep," she whispered.

"How long has she been in labor?" I asked her.

"Since early yesterday," she replied.

I knelt down by the girl. Her black hair lay in a tangle on the pillow. There were dark circles around her eyes, and her lips were pale, but she was still a beauty. She was the girl Kenit had danced for.

There was little I could do for her. She was small and delicate, with narrow hips. By the time she delivered late the next morning, she was exhausted. As soon as she was satisfied that her baby lived, she fell into a deep sleep. Kenit wrapped his son in blankets and cradled him in his arms. Even when I would have laid him down beside his mother, Kenit wouldn't let him go.

"When she wakes, she must feed him," I said.

Kenit nodded. He too looked exhausted.

In the meantime I wet a cloth in warm water and gave it to the baby to suck. Then I handed a packet of herbs to the girl's mother.

"This will help to make her strong again," I told her.

I returned to Merin's house alone and slept the afternoon away. At bedtime I wasn't sleepy, so I sat up a while by the hearth. Around midnight I began to yawn. As I was getting up to go to bed, Kenit came in. He had the baby with him. I didn't ask him why. His eyes told me that the dark-haired girl had died.

We took the child into the kitchen. Reni was kind enough to nurse him. In a few days Kenit would have looked for a nurse among the country people, but Reni, who had plenty of both milk and mother love, took the boy to her heart.

The next morning, when the Lady heard the cries of two infants downstairs, she left her room for the first time since her illness. I had heard them too, and I got up to see if Reni needed anything. I met the Lady on the stairs, and together we went down to the kitchen.

Kenit had slept that night in the great hall. We found him in the kitchen with Reni, holding her baby while she nursed his. Before the Lady could scold him for trespassing where only women were allowed, he explained that the child at Reni's breast was his son.

"Has his mother not enough milk?" asked the Lady cautiously.

"His mother died," said Kenit.

The Lady slipped her arm around his shoulders. "I'm sorry," she said.

Kenit looked surprised at her show of sympathy, but he was bold enough to ask her, "Will we give her a warrior's burial?"

"Of course," said the Lady. "I'll see to it."

I was puzzled. I didn't like to ask Kenit for an explanation, so when I dropped by the Lady's room later that afternoon, I asked her how we could give a country girl a warrior's burial.

"Few households keep such ancient customs anymore," she said. "We still keep it here, and I hope we always will. When a woman gives her life for others, whether in battle or in childbirth, she should be honored for her sacrifice."

"But it's not the same thing," I said. "Is it?"

Merin smiled. "I fought in battle and your mother bore two children. Of the two of us, I think she was the courageous one."

46

TAMAR

At first we heard only rumors of trouble. Though people seldom traveled any distance in wintertime, a few souls came to us cold and starving. They were herding people who lived in the mountains to the east of us. They weren't our allies, but we had always been on good terms with them. They told disturbing tales of raiders so desperate that they traveled in the most dreadful weather, willing to exchange the lives of many to feed the rest. Those who couldn't stand against them took what food they could carry and fled.

We took the travelers in, as the laws of hospitality demanded. Some went to farms where help was needed. Those who stayed in Merin's house slept on the floor of the great hall and did their best to be both grateful and inconspicuous. Many of the older warriors remembered other times of hunger when Merin's house had become a place of refuge. They told tales around the hearth that hadn't been told for years, cautionary tales of the misfortunes of others that reminded us how fortunate we were.

But it seemed that our good fortune might not last. Spring came late that year. The elders counted and recounted the days, but the time for planting came and went before the last of the snow melted. Although the elders felt the spring sowing shouldn't wait, the earth was still cold and heavy with damp, and the first sowing rotted in the ground. A second sowing sprouted. We watched with cautious hope as it grew and prayed to the goddess of the grain that there would be time and warmth enough to ripen it.

⟨∕⟩

Even before the snow had melted, the cattle raids began. Vintel took a band of warriors north to the frontier. Maara and I stayed at home. While they had succeeded in postponing my adoption, Vintel's malicious rumors had found nothing substantial to settle on, and as Namet said they would, people soon lost interest in repeating them. I think Namet used them as an excuse to keep Vintel from taking Maara with her to the frontier. In any case, we assumed that Laris would ask us to join her band, as she had done the year before.

One evening after supper, Laris approached Maara and drew her aside, into the shadows at the back of the great hall, far away from any who might overhear. When I would have followed them, Laris gave me a fierce look, and I stayed where I was.

Maara and Laris talked quietly together for a long time. Then Laris went upstairs, and Maara beckoned to me to join her. I expected her to tell me to get our things ready. Instead she said, "In the morning Laris is going home."

"She is? Why?"

"Her mother sent for her. There's trouble there."

"There's trouble here too," I protested. "What does the Lady say?"

"Laris hasn't spoken to the Lady. She doesn't intend to ask permission. Her first duty is to her family."

Maara was right, of course.

"Laris asked me to go with her."

A strange fear gripped my heart. "Why?" I whispered.

"She believes I'll be safer there."

That was certainly true. I couldn't speak.

"I'm not going," she said.

Whatever had gripped my heart let go.

Maara knit her brows. "Would you —," she said.

"Would I what?"

"Would you consider going with me?"

Once I had begged Maara to take me with her if she ever left Merin's house. Now everything had changed. Now I was to be the daughter of the house, the Lady's heir. Even if I were in danger, my duty to the Lady would keep me in Merin's house for as long as she needed me.

"I can't," I told her.

"No," said Maara softly. "Of course not."

That springtime Merin needed me. She had made a good recovery, though her fever had left her with a little weakness, a shortness of breath when she climbed the stairs, and she tired easily, but she would have all summer to grow strong again.

Rumors notwithstanding, I made myself her healer. I looked in on her every morning and insisted she lie down for a few hours every afternoon. She would seldom sleep during the day, so I sat with her while she rested, and we talked together like old friends.

One morning I found her standing at the window. The sun was just rising, its golden light burning the mist off the river.

"There's a warm breeze this morning," she said.

"Perhaps spring has come at last."

"Perhaps." She turned away from the window and sat down heavily on her bed. Lines of worry creased her brow. "Isn't it past time she should have been here?" She was speaking of my mother.

"There may still be snow on the ground in the hill country," I said, although I too had begun to wonder what could be keeping her.

"Ah," said Merin. "I had forgotten."

Another week passed. I was beginning to be anxious.

Early one morning, before the sun was up, Merin's servant came to the companions' loft and roughly shook me awake.

"The Lady wants you," she said. She waited while I dressed and went with me to Merin's room. She stopped outside the door and whispered, "Don't upset her." Then she left me there and went downstairs.

Merin was sitting up in bed. She looked as if she hadn't slept all night.

"She isn't coming," she said.

I thought she must have had a message from my mother. "Why not? Is there some kind of trouble?"

"How should I know?"

"You haven't heard from her?"

"Of course not. Why would I have heard from her? When has she ever told me anything?"

I sat down beside her on the bed and tried to think of something I could say to comfort her.

"I should have known better than to get my hopes up," she said.

I didn't like to worry her unnecessarily, but a little worry, I thought, would be better for Merin than self-pity.

"There may be trouble in the hill country too. It seems there's trouble everywhere these days."

Merin looked more hopeful. "Do you think so? Do you think something's keeping her?"

"I wouldn't be surprised."

"She would send for help, wouldn't she?" Merin's brows furrowed with worry. "Wouldn't she send to me for help if she needed it?"

"Of course she would," I said. "Of course she would."

Although I did my best not to let the Lady see my anxiety for my mother, I couldn't keep Maara from seeing it.

"We could go see what's keeping her," Maara suggested.

I had already thought of that. I doubted the Lady would object to my going, but before I could ask her for permission, a messenger arrived. He and a companion had brought my sister Tamar to Merin's house. He had run on ahead to let us know that she would arrive that evening. My mother wasn't with them. As I suspected, there was trouble, even in the peaceful place where I grew up, and my mother had to stay at home.

Merin took the news more calmly than I expected. I think she had resigned herself to being disappointed.

I went to greet my sister and walk with her the last few miles. She had changed so much I doubt I would have recognized her if I had run across her unexpectedly. When I left home, she was a child. Now she was a woman, taller than I by several inches and less lighthearted than I remembered her.

When we arrived at Merin's house, it was suppertime. I stood with Tamar in the doorway, as my mother had stood with me two years before. The Lady was in her place, waiting for us, and she beckoned to me to bring my sister forward. As she had done with me, she drew her sword and laid its point against Tamar's breastbone. Tamar simply smiled at her. I wondered if she saw, as I had seen, a vision of the battlefield. My memory of that

vision came back to me, as clear and vivid as it was the first time I looked into the Lady's eyes.

I spent the evening with Tamar, introducing her to the other companions and helping her make a place for herself in the companions' loft. I wanted to get used to this young woman who had replaced my baby sister, and I wanted to hear about what was happening at home, but I worried about Merin. Late that night, although she should have been in bed, I tapped lightly on her door.

"Come in," she said.

I found her sitting by the window, looking out at the night.

"Is she settled in?" Merin asked me.

I nodded. "My sister has never been the least bit shy. She has already made several lifelong friends."

Merin smiled.

"She brings news of our mother."

The briefest shadow crossed Merin's face. Then she shrugged. "I'm sure she has had plenty to keep her busy."

"My mother kept Tamar at home until she nearly burst with impatience," I said. "She very much wanted to come with her, but she was afraid to be away from home for even a few days."

Merin looked alarmed. "Is she in danger?"

"There are travelers in the hills, living on whatever they can forage—wild game and birds' eggs, and whatever they can dig up out of the ground. Sometimes they approach our people, to trade wild food for meat or grain, and when they leave, a sheep or two may disappear. Other than stealing food, they haven't been a trouble to us, but my mother was afraid that if she left, they might be tempted to take advantage of her absence."

"I understand," said Merin.

I don't believe she did.

Laris had taken her band of warriors home with her, all but Kenit. Even if he could have found a wet nurse, the baby was too young to travel such a distance, and Kenit wouldn't leave him. At night the baby stayed in the kitchen with Reni. During the day, when he wasn't at Reni's breast, he slept in the folds of Kenit's cloak. Everyone had gotten over being startled by the sudden thrust of a tiny fist or the strange wails and gurgles that emerged from Kenit's clothing.

One evening I found Kenit sitting outside the earthworks, his baby in his lap. He beckoned to me, and I sat down beside him.

"I never thanked you for the help you gave his mother," he said.

"I wish I'd had more help to give her," I replied.

The baby reached out and clutched at my sleeve.

"Would you like to hold him?" Kenit asked.

I nodded, and he handed the boy to me. I laid him down in my lap and offered him a finger, which he grasped and drew into his mouth. Though he was only two months old, he was quite heavy, fat and strong and very healthy.

"Will his grandmother raise him?"

Kenit shook his head. "His grandmother isn't well. She depended on her daughter to care for her. Now she has no one left. Another family took her in, but they have no place for a child."

"What will you do with him?"

Kenit set his jaw. "I'm going to keep him, if I have to bribe every servant in Merin's house to help me care for him."

I doubted he would have to do any such thing. Every woman in the household had been drawn to the babies like bears to honey.

"Who will nurse him when Reni leaves?" I asked.

"Reni isn't leaving. She changed her mind about going home. She feels safer here."

The boy began to fuss, and Kenit took him from me. "He favors her. Don't you think he favors her?"

"He does," I said.

In truth I thought I saw more of Kenit in him. The child's black hair was curly like Kenit's, while his mother's had been straight, and he had Kenit's strong jaw. I did see his mother's beauty in his eyes. Knowing he would find her nowhere else, Kenit gazed upon his sweetheart in his baby's face.

For the first few weeks that Tamar was in Merin's house, I tried to spend as much time with her as I could. I had little time to spare. My first duty was to the Lady. While her body was growing stronger, I had to work hard to keep her in good spirits. I was still an apprentice too, of course, and Maara had me practice with the bow every day, so that I wouldn't lose the strength I needed for it.

When I did find time for her, it seemed that Tamar had little time for me. She was quickly becoming popular with the other companions, and they were all glad to teach her. I was a little disappointed that she didn't look to me for help and guidance, although I understood that perhaps she preferred not to stand in the shadow of her older sister. I tried not to mind too much.

One thing I did mind was the way she treated Maara. On her first evening in Merin's house, right after supper, I brought Tamar to where Maara was sitting by the hearth and introduced her to my warrior. Tamar said the proper words, but her eyes slid away from Maara's face, and I caught a look in them I didn't like, as if Maara were beneath her notice. The next day I took her to task about it.

"She's funny-looking," Tamar said.

"She's my teacher and my friend," I told her. "I have the greatest respect for her. You would do well to look more deeply into people, and to judge them, not by what they look like, but by their hearts."

Tamar pouted. "I couldn't see her heart."

"When did my sister become so foolish?"

Tamar laughed at me. "You haven't changed a bit," she said. "Always frowning, always serious." She took my face in both her hands and, as she had done when we were children, tried to turn my frown into a smile. For the first time I was not charmed by it. I took her hands and held them.

"You're not at home anymore," I said. "You can't be the baby here."

She paid no attention to me.

47

A TIME OF TROUBLE

The spring festival was only a few days away, and at last we were enjoying pleasant weather. Not even on the warmest nights did anyone suggest building a bower out of doors. This year no one wanted to linger long outside the fortress walls.

From the frontier came nothing but bad news. The cattle raids had not yet ended. Our outlying farms had been attacked and lives were lost. This time last year the house had been full of people. This year most of our warriors were still at the frontier. This time last year the people of Merin's house were giddy with springtime. This year fear clouded our sight, so that the sky was not as blue as a springtime sky should be.

What frightened me the most was how often the elders went down into the place of ritual or to the oak grove, where I had more than once found the blood of sacrifice poured out upon the ground. Even the elders — whose tranquil faces always reassured me that they had seen everything that could happen under the sun — even the elders were afraid.

We dreaded the sight of an oxcart coming from the north, bringing us our wounded or our dead. We dreaded the sight of a messenger, though we hurried to the great hall to hear the news he brought. We were careful not to speak about our fear. We kept it to ourselves. To speak of it would make it real.

One morning when I looked in on the Lady, her haggard look told me she hadn't slept well. Many nights her sleep was troubled. Although she denied it, I suspected that some nights she never slept at all. I made her a tea of chamomile, and into it I put a drop of something stronger, distilled from oil of poppyseed, to ensure that she would get the rest she needed. Then I made her go back to bed.

Early in the afternoon she woke and asked for me. She was weak and a little groggy, from sleep and from the drug I'd given her, but she insisted on getting out of bed. I helped her dress. Then I took the shutter down and set a chair by the window for her.

A fragrant breeze was blowing. The clear spring light fell over Merin's arm where it rested in her lap. Her skin was pale against her gown of meadow green, and in its loose folds her body appeared frail and insubstantial. She could have been a queen of the fairy folk, who at any moment might shimmer and vanish into the air.

I sat down on the foot of her bed.

"Why haven't you been sleeping well?" I asked her.

"Dreams," she said. "Cruel dreams."

She gazed unseeing out the window.

"Are you having nightmares?"

"Nightmares? No, not nightmares. Beautiful dreams."

"If your dreams are so beautiful, why can't you sleep?"

She turned and looked at me. "If I could sleep and never wake, I would."

By now I was used to hearing remarks like that from her, and I didn't dignify it with an answer.

"Tell me about these dreams," I said.

She shook her head. "I dream what should have been."

"You can't live there."

"No," she said. "Not yet."

I did not intend to allow her to resume a courtship with her death.

"Not for a long time yet," I told her. "My mother gave you into my care before she left for home, and I refuse to let you break her heart."

"She left me in your care?"

I nodded.

A sly look came into Merin's eyes. "Is that the only reason you take such good care of me?"

"You know better," I replied.

A faint blush crept into her cheek. "Still," she said, "it's nice to hear."

The door flew open. We turned and saw Vintel standing in the doorway.

Merin got slowly to her feet. "You presume too much," she told Vintel.

The ice in Merin's voice sent a shiver down my backbone, but Vintel ignored it, nor did she so much as glance in my direction.

"There is a matter that requires your attention," Vintel said.

Merin waited. She appeared to rest her hand lightly on the windowsill, but she was using it to steady herself.

"It should be plain enough by now that the northern tribes have given up hope of a crop this year," Vintel said. "That means the fighting will go on all summer. It's time we sent for help."

She paused, but she had more to say, and Merin waited for her to say it.

"A small band of warriors has arrived from my sister's house," Vintel said. "They tell me more can be spared. With your permission, I will send for them."

"Your sister may keep her warriors," Merin replied. "I sent to Arnet's house for help a week ago."

The look of surprise on Vintel's face gave Merin a great deal of satisfaction. One corner of her mouth lifted. "Did you think I wasn't paying attention?"

Vintel was bolder than Merin expected her to be. "I did," she admitted. "You were mistaken."

Vintel came into the room and closed the door behind her.

"You have been very ill," she said. "You should let others lift the burden of responsibility from your shoulders for a little while, until you're stronger."

"The burden of responsibility always rests upon my shoulders," Merin said. Then, in a soft voice, she added, "When I'm no longer able to bear it, you may try to take it from me, if you can."

Vintel looked confused. "I meant no disrespect."

She sounded petulant, like a child whose clumsy efforts to help are unappreciated.

Merin's hand on the windowsill trembled, and she sat down. "Was there something else you wished to speak to me about?"

Vintel shook her head. "No. Nothing else." She turned to go.

"Perhaps we should call a meeting of the council," Merin said, "so that we can hear the wisdom of those who have lived through other times of trouble."

Vintel didn't care much for that idea, but she dared not refuse. "Let them meet soon," she said. "I have no time to waste here."

"We'll meet first thing tomorrow morning then."

Vintel nodded her assent and left us.

"Well," said Merin. "That was interesting."

"It was?"

I had found the encounter rather frightening, but Merin's dark eyes sparkled, as if she had taken pleasure in sparring with Vintel.

"She overstepped a bit," said Merin, "and she knew it." She settled back into her chair. "What will Vintel tell me, do you suppose, when a large band of warriors arrives from her sister's house?"

"Will she send for them anyway?"

"She has already sent for them."

"How do you know?"

"Vintel is clumsy. There's only one reason for her to send to her sister's house for help. Her sister's warriors will be loyal to her, not to me. She sought my permission because she knew that without it, it would appear that she was preparing to challenge my authority. And of course that's exactly what she's doing. That's why I sent to Arnet's house. Arnet's warriors will be loyal to Namet, and through Namet, to me."

I was surprised to hear her show such confidence in Namet.

"I thought you and Namet didn't get along," I said.

"She and I have had our differences, but I trust her loyalty. Don't you?"

"Of course."

For a few minutes we were silent. Merin stared out the window, a thoughtful look on her face, while I tried to understand what had just happened between Merin and Vintel.

"Why did you decide to call a meeting of the council?" I asked her.

"I want the council to know what Vintel suggested and that I refused her offer."

"So that when her sister's warriors arrive, the elders will see there's treachery in it?"

"Something like that," said Merin.

"Why do you tolerate Vintel?"

Merin leaned forward in her chair and took my hand. She squeezed it hard enough to make me wince. "I need Vintel." She spoke softly, but a cold fire burned deep in her eyes. "We all need Vintel. In troubled times, warriors like Vintel come into their own. When this troubled time is over, wisdom and cooler heads will prevail, and Vintel will have to step back into her proper place. The danger now is that Vintel's power will grow so great that she cannot be made to step back. It is in times like these that great houses fall."

"What can we do?"

"Power always rests in a delicate balance," said Merin, "and power comes from many things, not from strength of arms alone, but from wisdom and experience. We need only hold the balance."

I was reassured by the strength of purpose I saw in Merin's eyes. "How can Vintel believe that she could challenge your power?"

"She may not need to. I think Vintel believes I'm going to die."

"Vintel is wrong."

"Perhaps." She shrugged and smiled at me, as if it didn't matter.

"You're not going to die. I'm not going to let you die."

Merin looked amused. "Has Tamras power over life and death?"

"No," I said, "but you do."

"If the Dark Mother should reach for me," she said gently, "how can I resist her?"

I had meant to scold her, but my eyes filled with tears. "Please," I said. "Don't speak of death as if she is your friend."

"Friend or not, no one escapes her."

"But you invite her," I said. "You court her. You challenge her. Someday she may hear you."

Merin looked long into my eyes. "What would you have me do?"

"Love your life a little longer."

I watched her struggle with herself. Then she said, "I'll make a bargain with you. I will love my life for as long as Tamnet lives."

I would have liked to sit in on the council meeting, but since nothing that would be discussed concerned me, at least officially, I waited in the great hall with Maara and worried about it. The meeting was a long one, and I grew impatient.

"The elders are long-winded," Maara reminded me.

At last Namet emerged from the kitchen. Fodla was with her. They spoke together for a few minutes. Then Namet came over to where we were waiting and sat down beside Maara.

"In a little while, let's go for a walk," she said calmly.

Maara nodded. We sat silent for a time. I studied Namet's face. It was untroubled, and some of my impatience left me.

After half an hour, Namet stood up. "Let's go," she said.

Maara and I followed her out of the great hall. Trying to look like we were only out for a stroll in the spring air, we walked in silence down the hill. Namet took us to the river, where she sat down on the mossy bank. She slipped her shoes off and dangled her feet in the water. Maara and I sat down on either side of her.

"Merin held her own," said Namet. "She seemed almost her old self today." Namet turned to me. "Is she doing as well as she appears to be?"

"I believe she is," I said. "She has more good days now than bad ones."

"How bad are her bad days?"

"She's often very tired. She doesn't sleep well."

"Why not? Is something troubling her?"

"She complains of dreams," I said.

"I don't wonder."

I must have looked surprised.

"Merin keeps a tight grip on her demons," Namet said, "but surely there must be a few of them still lurking under the bed or perched in the rafters out of reach."

Namet's words drew a picture in my mind of vague, malevolent shapes hovering in the shadows of Merin's room.

"Are you sure it's only dreams that trouble her?" asked Namet.

"She tries to hide her disappointment, but I believe she was counting on seeing my mother again this spring."

Namet made an impatient gesture. "She needs to get that nonsense out of her head."

"I disagree with you," I said quietly.

Namet gave me a stern look. "Merin has work to do. She needs to pay attention."

"She is paying attention," I told her. "I had a long talk with Merin yesterday. She spoke to me about keeping the balance between her power and Vintel's. She understands what Vintel intends, and she has already taken steps to forestall her."

"But still Vintel's power grows," murmured Namet. "Vintel doesn't have Merin's depth of understanding, but one thing she does understand. She knows what fear does to people."

Maara made a noise deep in her throat.

"Vintel will use their fear," Namet said. "She will stand between them and their fear, so that challenging her power will be too terrible for them to contemplate."

"And when the troubled times are over?" I asked her, remembering what Merin had told me.

"When will that be?" said Namet. "Vintel's power depends on troubled times."

We had waited so long for mild weather that Maara and I made a point of going outdoors every evening to enjoy it. Sitting together on the hillside, watching the changing light, we sometimes talked of things that didn't matter, but we seldom felt the need to talk. In silence we took pleasure in the twilight and in each other's company, until the mist, rising from the river, chilled the night air.

That evening the tranquillity around us couldn't calm our troubled thoughts. Although Maara had said nothing to me about our talk with Namet, I knew she was worrying about it. I thought about how different this year had been from the year before. When had things changed, and why? The weather, of course, had been against us, but I also remembered what Maara told me after the battle on Taia's day. Her prediction had come true. The northerners had returned, both for food to ease their hunger and for blood to ease their hearts, and Vintel had made the most of it.

A thought popped into my head, and I blurted it out before I took time to think about it. "Did Vintel pursue the northerners last year on purpose?"

Maara stared at me for a moment, as if she didn't understand my meaning. Then her eyes changed. "You think she intended to provoke them?"

"Namet said that Vintel's power depends on troubled times."

Maara lightly brushed my forehead with her fingertips. "What god kissed your brow," she whispered, "to give you such understanding?"

I smiled with pleasure at her praise, although I wasn't sure I understood it. "It was your words I remembered."

Maara frowned. "What I don't understand is why. What prompted her to challenge Merin now?"

That was something that made no sense to me. For years Vintel had been Merin's right hand, a respected leader of warriors, and she had seemed content with her position. When had she first aspired to something more?

"We know what Vintel doesn't want," said Maara. "She doesn't want you to be the Lady's heir, not because she always wanted that place for herself, but for another reason." Maara put her elbows on her knees and rested her chin on her clasped hands. "There is a malice in what Vintel does that baffles me."

I counted up all the reasons why Vintel hated me. I had refused her, and made a fool of her, though that much was her own fault. And I had chosen for my teacher someone she regarded as an adversary. Vintel's hatred for Maara was easier to understand, because Maara was a threat to her, while I was merely an annoyance. Perhaps she hated me because through me Maara might someday hold a power even greater than Vintel's.

As if her thoughts had mirrored mine, Maara said, "It's not enough. There's something else. Something we haven't thought of."

I would have liked to sit longer with Maara, but in the morning Sparrow would leave with Vintel for the frontier, and tonight would be my last opportunity to spend a little time with her. Vintel kept her so busy that I hardly had a chance to exchange a word with her. The night before, she had come to the companions' loft after I had been long asleep. In the middle of the night I awakened to find her arms around me. Remembering how comforting it was to lie in someone's arms, I missed her at that moment more than I had missed her when she was gone.

After I said good night to Maara, I brewed Merin a bowl of chamomile and took it up to her room. She was in bed, already dozing, so I pinched out her lamp and left her.

I found Sparrow waiting for me in the companions' loft.

"Where have you been?" she said impatiently. Before I could answer her, she took me by the hand and led me downstairs and out the back door.

"Where are we going?"

"I need to talk to you."

"Why?"

"Wait," she said.

She took me to a favorite place of ours by the river, where a little meadow led down to a strip of sand along the shore. We sat down and leaned back against the water-smoothed trunk of a great tree that lay half buried in the warm sand. The moon was low in the sky behind us, and Sparrow's face was in shadow. I turned to her and tried to make out her expression.

"What?" I said.

"Are you ever afraid?" she whispered.

I felt my heartbeat quicken at her words. "Of course," I replied. I wondered what she had seen on the frontier, to make her say such a thing. "Are we in danger?"

"In danger?"

"From the northerners?"

"Oh," she said. "The northerners are everywhere this year, and they're not going to go home until the snow falls, but that's not what frightens me."

"What is it then?"

"Things here are different."

"Different? How?"

"Don't you feel it too?"

"I suppose so," I admitted. "A little."

"And you're different," she whispered.

"I am?"

She turned and met my eyes. "Are you still my friend?"

"Of course I am." Her strange talk was making me more afraid. "What's the matter?" I said. "What's wrong?"

Sparrow turned her gaze back to the river. "They say the Lady is unwell."

"She's mending," I told her.

"They say you still spend hours with her every day. They say you go to her every afternoon, that you enter her chamber without knocking, that you come and go as you please. I thought you were afraid of her. I thought you disliked her and distrusted her. Now it seems you've become her familiar."

I sighed. There was so much Sparrow didn't know about what had changed between Merin and me.

"I'm her healer," I said, thinking that was the simplest explanation.

"I hear you're more than that."

"What have you heard?"

"I hear you're to be named her heir."

"Who told you that?"

She turned and looked at me. "Is it true?"

I nodded, and she looked away.

"When did you learn the Lady had these plans for you?"

"Last fall. My mother told me."

"You never said anything to me." There was more sadness than accusation in Sparrow's voice. "You might have told me that my friend would some-day inherit a position of great importance." She gave me a sidelong glance. "Unless my friend found our friendship inconvenient."

I was too astonished to speak. Sparrow misunderstood my silence. She started to get up.

"Wait," I said, and took hold of her wrist.

She sat back down, but she wouldn't look at me.

"In the first place," I told her, "I didn't decide until midwinter's day that I would accept the Lady's offer. And in the second place, it didn't seem wise to speak about it to anyone, even to my friends, while there were unpleasant rumors going around."

"Rumors?" said Sparrow. "What rumors?"

I had never mentioned the rumors to Sparrow. If she had heard them, she should have come to me as a friend and told me about them. If she hadn't, I hesitated to repeat them. I understood why she might not have heard them. The companions, knowing she was my friend, would have been careful not to speak ill of me in her hearing. For the same reason, Vintel would not have spoken to Sparrow about her suspicions, and she would also have been careful to conceal from any friend of mine that the rumors came from her.

"When it began to occur to people that I would be the Lady's choice," I said, "some people spoke against me because of Maara. They feared a stranger having so much influence."

Sparrow gestured with her hand as if she were brushing the idea aside. "That's the silliest thing I ever heard. Maara has nothing to gain by treachery and much to lose. Besides, who would pay attention to a few whispers?"

"They were more than whispers. They frightened people enough that they prevented my adoption. Now we'll have to wait, until this time of trouble is over, and until Merin is strong again."

Sparrow thought that over.

"How did you hear about my becoming Merin's heir?" I asked her.

"Vintel mentioned it to me. She seemed to think I knew all about it."

"What did she say?"

"Only that she wondered why there had been no announcement."

"What did you tell her?"

"I told her the truth," she said. "I told her I knew less than she did." Sparrow scooped up a handful of sand and let it drift through her fingers. "I thought you must not want my friendship anymore, if you forgot to tell me something so important."

I knew I should be cautious about what I said to her, but I had hurt her feelings, and I wanted her to understand.

"I didn't like to put you in a difficult position," I said. "I think Vintel would prevent me from becoming Merin's heir, if she could."

I held my breath, waiting for Sparrow's answer.

"Why would Vintel do that?"

"I think she wants Merin's place for herself."

"What?" Sparrow stared at me in disbelief.

"Hasn't she ever suggested such a thing to you?"

"No," she said. "I don't believe it."

"Nevertheless, I think it's true."

Sparrow shook her head. "You're wrong." She got to her knees and turned so that she was facing me. "Vintel has taken more responsibility upon herself since the Lady's illness, but she only means to free her from care while she recovers."

The moonlight shone on Sparrow's face, and I saw that she believed what she was saying. She believed so completely in Vintel's good intentions that for a moment I could almost believe I had misjudged her.

"If I were in Merin's place," I said, "do you think Vintel would submit to my authority?"

"That time is a long way off."

"I hope so, but in the meantime, I would be the daughter of the house. Is Vintel prepared to treat me with the respect due to Merin's child and to respect Maara as my counselor?"

Now Sparrow was listening, although doubt still lingered in her eyes.

"And could Vintel believe that when I stand in Merin's place, she will be my right hand?"

Sparrow slowly shook her head.

"She may not always have been so ambitious," I said, "but now I think she would prefer to succeed Merin herself."

Sparrow stared at me. "Are you accusing Vintel of treachery?"

"No," I said. "So far she's done nothing treacherous. I believe she bides her time. She waits, to see if Merin will recover, to see if I will prove strong enough to claim the place that Merin offers me. Vintel's best chance is to allow events to take their course, until they present her with an opportunity."

Sparrow stared at me as if I were a stranger. Suddenly I was afraid. Had I spoken too openly? Had I trusted her too much?

"Please," I said. "Say nothing to Vintel about this."

I saw that once again I'd hurt her feelings.

"Don't worry," she said. "I won't betray your trust."

"Forgive me. I had to ask."

She nodded.

"You said things here are different. They are. The Lady is unwell. The harvest is in doubt. The fighting on our borders never stops. People are afraid, and Vintel is their shield."

"I can't believe she would betray the Lady," Sparrow whispered.

"Vintel may believe that the Lady will never again be strong enough to lead. Or that she may die." I touched the ground, to keep my words from coming true. "If she did, who would the council choose to lead us?"

There was no need for Sparrow to answer me.

"Be careful," I told her.

Sparrow turned and sat down again beside me. The night was mild, and the river made a pleasant chuckling sound as it flowed around the tumbled rocks by the shore. I remembered better times, when Sparrow and I had sat shoulder to shoulder, hand in hand, innocent of intrigue and treachery, safe and free of care.

I took her hand. Her fingers curled tight around mine. When I turned to look at her, I saw that her face was wet with tears.

"You be careful too," she whispered.

48

HEARTS

Before dawn the next morning Sparrow left with Vintel for the frontier. Although it was the first day of the spring festival, Vintel refused to stay home for the holiday. Only a handful of warriors and their companions remained in Merin's house. This year the country people would have to celebrate without us.

When I went into the kitchen to brew some tea for Merin, I felt Gnith's eyes. More often than not when I went to the kitchen in the mornings, Gnith was sleeping. This morning I felt her waiting for me. Her eyes followed me as I made the tea and set it to steep. I went to greet her.

"Has Tamras come for her blessing?" she said.

I shook my head and sat down beside her on the hearth. "I've come to wish you good morning."

Gnith looked disappointed. "Has Tamras nothing left to wish for?"

"I have much to wish for," I told her. "I wish for an end to these troubled times. I wish for a good harvest, for us and for our enemies too, so that they will leave us alone. I wish the Lady's body well and her heart whole."

"Is that all?"

It seemed like a great deal to me.

"It would be more than enough," I said.

Gnith peered up at me. "Does Tamras want nothing for herself?"

I remembered how lonely I had been the year before and that Gnith had known what I wanted before I knew enough to ask for it.

"What should I want?" I asked her.

She shrugged. "Last year, was it what you wanted?"

I thought of Sparrow, who ever since had shielded me from loneliness. "Yes and no," I told her.

Gnith chuckled. "Tamras speaks in riddles like an old woman. Did she think I wouldn't understand her?" She took my hand. "There is time for love, Tamras, even in times of trouble."

This time I had an answer for her.

"I have made time for love," I said.

Gnith waited to hear more.

"The Lady," I said.

"Merin?"

"She loves my mother still. Even after so many years."

I thought I might have taken Gnith by surprise. Was it possible for anything to take Gnith by surprise? Her next words told me otherwise.

"You've taken it upon yourself to guard her heart," she said.

I nodded.

"Guard it well today."

I had already thought of that. Namet, I knew, would stay close to Maara, and I meant to sit up with Merin, to keep her safe from the power of the night.

"Guard your own heart too," said Gnith.

At midmorning it began to rain. The Lady came downstairs for breakfast, but as soon as the meal was over, she complained of headache and went back to bed.

A few of the companions went down to the river. Despite the rain the country people were gathering there. Merin's house would provide the feast, and the bonfire had been laid on the meeting ground outside the earthworks.

While Merin rested, I sat with Maara in her room. A tune, played on a single pipe, drifted in the window. The sky was dark with angry clouds, and thunder rumbled in the distance.

Maara was restless. She rummaged in the chest by her bed, trying to find something that needed doing—a shirt to mend or a scrap of leather to work into a scabbard piece.

"Are you all right?" I asked her.

"Fine," she said. She gave up her search and went to the window to look out at the troubled sky.

"I need to stay with the Lady tonight," I told her.

She gave no indication that she'd heard me.

"Will you be all right?"

No answer.

"Maara?"

She turned to me. "What?"

"I'm sitting up with Merin tonight."

"You told me that already."

Her strange mood was making me uneasy. "If you sit down, I'll tell you a story."

She smiled. It was the first time I'd seen her smile all day.

"All right," she said.

In ancient days, when only women were warriors, lived three sisters and their mother in a village in the hill country. The oldest sister hunted game in the woodlands and fished the streams for salmon. The middle sister herded sheep, traveling afar in search of pasture. The youngest sister stayed at home, tending her garden and caring for her aged mother.

In the wintertime the whole family sat around the hearth and listened to the two older sisters tell of their adventures. The hunter told of taming wolves to serve her in the hunt and of tracking the wild boar deep into the heart of the forest, where the hunter might find herself the hunted. The shepherd told of following her sheep up steep mountainsides, guarding them from wild beasts, sleeping in the open in all weather. The youngest said little. She listened to her sisters' tales and kept them in her heart.

One morning in springtime, when the two older sisters were away, as they so often were, from home, the youngest sister was tending her garden when she heard her mother calling her. She went into the cottage and, finding her mother unwell, helped her into bed.

"My child," her mother said, "this is my dying day, and I have little to leave with you but my advice. Let the old women tend my death. You belong to life. Go out and weave a wreath of hawthorn for your hair and join the dancing this spring night."

That afternoon the old woman died, and her neighbors came to the cottage to prepare her for burial. The youngest daughter did as her mother had told her. She set her grief aside and wove a hawthorn wreath, and that fine spring night she went out into the hills, where the bonfires burned.

Too shy to step into the circle of firelight, the young girl stood alone in the dark, while the young men, enchanted by the promise of her beauty, tried to draw her out of the shadows. She turned them all away, until her eyes fell upon a young man she had never seen before. Around him shone a golden light. The moment her glance touched him, he came to her and drew her into the dance. That night he lay with her on the hillside and loved her, and in his arms she slept.

At dawn the girl awoke alone. She went home to find her sisters there. She told them of the young man and said that she meant to have him for her husband.

"That was no ordinary man," her oldest sister warned her. "You'll be lucky if you don't give birth to a monster. If it's a husband you want, there are plenty of fine young men right here in this village. Choose one of them."

"What do you want with a husband at all?" said the middle sister. "A husband is a nuisance."

But the girl would not let her sisters change her mind, and that night she went again out into the hills. As they had done the night before, the young men courted her. She saw none of them, until her own young man appeared. She danced with him in the firelight and lay with him on the hillside. This time she was determined to stay awake until the dawn, but as soon as she laid her head upon his chest, the sound of his heartbeat lulled her into sleep, and in the morning, he was gone.

When she went home, once again her sisters tried to make her see sense and take a young man from the village, but she refused to listen, and that night she went again to join the dancing.

Everything happened as before. Her young man came to her, danced with her, lay with her on the hillside, but this time she had the presence of mind to speak to him.

"Will you leave me in the morning?" she asked him.

"If you would keep me," he replied, "you must follow me."

"How will I know where to find you?"

"Let your heart lead you," he told her, and before she could ask him anything more, he embraced her, and she slept.

In the morning, the young girl again awoke alone. She remembered her young man's words, but she had no idea how to follow him or where to look for him. She knew she would no longer find him waiting for her on the hillside, so that night she slept in her own bed. All through the night, her young man came to her in dreams so sweet that she awoke feeling more bereft than she had felt awakening alone on the hillside after a night of love.

For days she wandered the hills in search of him, but she found the whole world empty, and at last she gave up her search and stayed at home. Whenever a traveler came to her door, she asked for news of her young man. None could tell her anything about him. Whenever a young man came to court her, she asked him the same question. None remembered seeing her young man at all.

She forgot to tend her garden. Briars grew up around the doorway and thistles choked the path, and no one came to see her anymore. Her dreams made her love the night and hate the dawn. Only hope carried her from one day to the next. Her beauty faded. Her sisters chided her and worried over her, but she seemed not to hear them. She lived in a dream of love that was strange to everyone around her, and more and more they left her alone.

A year and a day went by. Then one night she heard her beloved's voice. Not knowing if she woke or slept, she rose from her bed and walked out into the night. The moon was dark, and soon she lost her way, but she kept on, and for a much longer time than nighttime should have lasted, she walked in darkness.

When dawn came at last, dark clouds filled the sky. The girl walked in a twilight world until she came to a forest, dense with ancient trees and tangled thickets, where she could find no path. In despair she sank to the ground and began to cry. When she had cried all her tears, she dried her eyes and thought of her sister, the hunter, who had pursued the wild boar into the heart of the forest.

"My sister loves to hunt wild things in the wood," she thought to herself, "and she never let a thicket hold her back. No more will I."

She slipped between two trees and stumbled through the thicket, where she came across a path that wound between the trees. She followed it until she was too tired to go on. She found a nest among the brambles, where once a family of deer had made its bed. There she lay down and slept. She awoke in darkness to the howling of wolves and the fearful beating of her own heart. Terrified, she cowered in her bramble bed till morning.

At first light she wandered deeper into the forest. Its canopy shut out the sky. Her eyes forgot the light of day. She drank from streams, bitter with the taste of rotting leaves. She ate what wild food she could find and slept where animals had sheltered. The path she followed turned and twisted, leading her in circles. Whenever she felt she could not go on, she thought of her beloved and found within her heart the courage to take one more step.

After a timeless time, the air grew light around her. She emerged from the forest to find herself standing at the foot of the tallest mountain she could imagine. In despair she sank to the ground and began to cry. When she had cried all her tears, she dried her eyes and thought of her sister, the shepherd, whose flocks had led her over mountains as tall as this one.

"My sister loves to follow her sheep into the wild places," she thought to herself, "and she never let a mountain stand in her way. No more will I."

She began to climb. She climbed and climbed until her legs were trembling and her heartbeat thundered in her ears, and still she didn't stop. She climbed until the clouds drifted beneath her and the sun shone down on her from a clear sky of brilliant blue. The air was cold, and the mountain wore an icy mantle. In peril of falling, still she climbed, until she reached the top. Far above the treetops, far above the clouds, far above the darkness that awaited her below, she stood enraptured in the light, with the whole world spread out before her. She might have stood there until time ended, if she had not remembered her beloved. Turning from the light and from the wonders that dazzled her eyes, she began her descent.

After a timeless time, she stood on the far side of the mountain, only to find before her a river so wide and turbulent that she couldn't see what might await her on the far shore. The water tumbled down from icy places in the mountains, running fast and cold, with a roar louder than anything she'd ever heard. It would be death to try to cross it. In despair she sank to the ground and began to cry. When she had cried all her tears, she dried her eyes and remembered the words of her beloved.

"If I must cross this river to find my love," she thought to herself, "my own heart must lead me, for there is no one to teach me how to cross."

She stood up and leapt into the water. She let the river carry her. The icy water numbed her. The tumbling water dragged her down. Black water closed over her head, taking her into a dark and silent place, a place so cold she lost all feeling in her body and all power to move her limbs. Then, deep within her heart, love began to burn. Its fire warmed her body and surrounded her with light. The river treated her more gently. It bore her up and carried her until it laid her down on its far shore.

The young girl sat up and looked around her at a world more beautiful than any she had ever seen. Most beautiful of all was the face of her beloved, who awaited her. In his eyes she recognized the wildness of the forest and the rapture of the mountaintop, and his arms, like the river, bore her home.

"It's been ages since I've heard that story," said a voice behind me.

I turned and saw Namet standing in the doorway. I made a place for her to sit next to me, at the foot of Maara's bed.

"It's been ages since I've told it," I said.

The story had disturbed me. As many times as I had told it and heard it told, at that moment I couldn't make up my mind if it was a love story or a cautionary tale.

Maara looked puzzled.

"What do you suppose it means?" Namet asked her.

Maara met Namet's eyes for a moment. Then she turned to me and put her hand over her heart.

"You once told me that stories are meant to make you feel something here," she said.

I nodded.

"What did that story make you feel?" asked Namet gently.

"Sad," she said, her eyes still on my face. "Was it supposed to?"

I shook my head.

Namet turned to me. "What do you think it means?"

"I'm not sure," I said. "How can such a love exist? And even if it does, who would dare to reach for it?"

Namet smiled a knowing smile. I remembered then that she had dared. She had walked away from everything she knew, was willing to walk away from life itself, to find it.

"I can assure you that it does exist," said Namet, "but you're right that few dare reach for it. They sense the peril in it, and it frightens them. Merin was frightened by it, though it always seemed to me that, whether a person reaches for love or turns it away, either choice demands a price."

Merin paid a heavy price, I thought, but it had never occurred to me that she might have been afraid of love.

"Go to her now," said Namet. "It's time."

I got up to go, but I was still uneasy about Maara, and I stopped in the doorway and looked back at her.

Namet chuckled. "Don't worry. I intend to sit up all night and bore my poor child silly with stories of my youth. I have no intention of letting her out of my sight. I'm too old to go chasing her around the countryside."

I saw a little color come into Maara's cheeks.

"If there's any chasing to be done," I said to Namet, "call me."

"I'm fine," said Maara.

"I know." I smiled at her and held her eyes until she smiled back.

The Lady was in bed. When she saw me poke my head in the door, she gestured to me to come in. Someone had brought her a plate of food. It didn't look as if she'd touched it.

"Are you feeling better?" I asked her.

She nodded.

"You need to eat something." I picked up the plate and sat down beside her on the bed.

Merin sighed. "Are you going to insist on feeding me?"

"Yes," I said, "unless you'll feed yourself."

She sat up and took the plate from me. After she had taken a few bites, she set it aside. I shook my head at her in disapproval, and she picked up the plate again.

While she ate, I went to the window and looked out. The rain had stopped. On the meeting ground people were gathering for the feast. Their voices murmured on the warm spring breeze. Laughter and music, joyful sounds, the sounds of springtime, of innocence, reached us as if from a great distance.

"You'd better go," said Merin. "You'll miss the feasting."

"I thought I'd sit with you a while."

Merin's eyes challenged me. "Are you worried I'll do something foolish?"

"It wouldn't be the first time."

My bluntness surprised her.

"Well," she said. "I hadn't intended to."

"I don't think anyone intends to. On days of power, strange things may happen. People may do things they don't intend."

Merin regarded me thoughtfully for a moment. Then she said, "It was on the morning of the spring festival that she left me."

I didn't need to ask her who she meant. More than the pain in Merin's eyes, my own experience told me how much that must have hurt. On a day when the power of life draws lovers together, how could either of them have borne such a parting?

"I've survived many spring festivals since," she said. "I'll survive this one too. Go get yourself something to eat. I'd like to spend the afternoon alone. You may come to me this evening, if you like. I wouldn't mind some company tonight."

The feasting had begun. Trestle tables set out on the meeting ground held platters of lamb and beef, garnished with spring greens, along with loaves of fresh bread, rounds of cheese, whole onions and mushrooms roasted with the meat, all the delicacies of springtime, as if there were no fear of want in Merin's house.

I helped myself to a plateful of food and a beaker of ale and made my way through the crowd of country people, looking for someone I knew. Tamar and a few of her new friends were sitting together on the grass. I hesitated to intrude upon my sister without an invitation. I stood still for a moment, undecided.

"Tamras!" someone called out behind me.

When I turned around, I was astonished to see Taia. She was carrying a plate heaped high with food. Her hair shone like copper in the sunlight, and she seemed taller than I remembered her.

"What are you doing here?" I asked her. Taia had gone home with Laris. I wondered why she had come back to Merin's house so soon.

Taia smiled mysteriously. "It's nice to see you too," she said. "Come sit with us."

She led me to a shady place a little distance from the meeting ground. Kenit was waiting there. On his cloak, spread out in the cool shade, his baby lay sleeping. Taia sat down next to him and set the plate between them.

"What are you doing here?" I asked again. "Has Laris come back?"

Taia shook her head. "I came alone. I only just arrived an hour ago. I'm famished."

She picked up a slice of lamb and took an enormous bite out of it.

"You came back alone? Why?"

Taia's mouth was full of lamb. She gestured with her head at something that lay a little distance away in the grass. It was a shield, bearing as its device a boar's head, freshly painted.

"I've heard that Merin's house is in need of warriors," said Taia shyly.

"Wonderful!" I said. "Congratulations!"

"My foolishness won me a sword," she said. "Now I've a shield to go with it."

Kenit's baby woke and began to cry. Kenit picked him up.

"He's hungry," he said.

As Kenit strode across the meeting ground on his way back to Merin's house, Taia's eyes followed him. When she saw that I was watching her, she blushed.

"I know what you're thinking," she whispered. "It isn't true."

"What in the world are you talking about?"

"I was sorry when his sweetheart died. I wouldn't wish such grief on anyone I care for."

"Of course not," I replied.

She smiled at me for understanding.

I had eaten and drunk more than was good for me. I was so sleepy that I napped for an hour in the warm afternoon sun. Taia was tired from her journey, and she too slept for a little while. Then we went for a swim in the river. When we came out of the water, Tamar and her friends were sitting a little distance away on the riverbank. Taia and I sat down in the grass to dry off. Tamar came over and sat down beside me.

"Are you coming to the bonfire tonight?" she asked me.

I shook my head. "Merin has asked me to sit with her this evening."

"But it's a holiday. You're not supposed to have to work today."

"It isn't work," I said.

A suspicious look came into Tamar's eyes. "What's going on?"

"What do you mean?"

"Are the rumors true then?"

"What rumors?"

"That you're going to be adopted."

Out of the corner of my eye, I saw Taia's head turn toward us.

Tamar studied me through narrowed eyes. "It must be true. You never could bring yourself to tell a lie."

The mock disapproval in her voice reminded me how often my inability to make up excuses had gotten us both into trouble.

"Nothing is decided," I told her.

Tamar ignored me. "I should have known." Her eyes glittered with excitement at her discovery. "You call her by her given name. You go to see her in her chamber whenever the mood strikes you. You sit with her for hours. She's chosen you to be her heir." She made a gesture with her arm meant to encompass all of Merin's land. "Someday this will belong to you."

Tamar would have chattered on about what she imagined life would be like when her sister, and therefore by extension she herself, became a person of great importance, but I took hold of her hand and gave it a little shake to get her attention.

"The only thing that will belong to me will be a responsibility that I hope I'll be strong enough to bear," I said. "I'd be just as happy if it never came to me at all. But don't count ducklings when the duck hasn't yet laid her eggs. This is not the right time for the Lady to name an heir."

"Why not? Hasn't she made up her mind?"

I knew Tamar wouldn't stop until she had the whole truth out of me. "She's asked me and I've accepted, but this isn't a good time to speak of it, and I don't want you to talk about it with anyone."

"Why not?"

"Because it's dangerous."

Tamar rolled her eyes.

"I'm serious," I said, more sharply than I meant to. "There are people here who might try to prevent such a thing from happening, if they knew about it."

"Why would anyone do that?"

Although I hesitated to cast a shadow over the innocent world Tamar still lived in, I felt I had no choice.

"There are others who believe Merin's power should come to them," I said. "There may be a few who would try to take Merin's power from her while she still lives. These are troubled times."

Tamar frowned. "I can't imagine how anyone could take the Lady's power," she said, but she sounded less sure of herself.

"Tamras is telling you the truth," said Taia. "If people knew the Lady had made her choice, Tamras would be in danger. So would you."

Tamar turned to Taia. "What do you know about it? Who are you anyway?"

"Forgive my sister's rudeness," I said to Taia. "No one has yet taught her the respect due to warriors." I turned back to Tamar. "This is Taia, a warrior, and heir to a powerful house."

"Oh," said Tamar. A blush colored her cheeks.

"Tamar," I said, "please do what I ask. Don't say a word to anyone."

Tamar nodded meekly.

"And you should know that Vintel is no friend of ours," I said. "I'd keep away from her, if I were you."

Having thoroughly embarrassed herself, Tamar didn't question me.

"I hope you know I'll keep your secret," said Taia, when Tamar had rejoined her friends. "Laris guessed that you would be Merin's choice. She'll be glad to hear this news. She has always feared Vintel's power."

"I thank you for your loyalty," I replied. "Merin is stronger than people think, but she won't challenge Vintel until we're no longer in danger from the northern tribes."

Taia moved closer and whispered, "If you need a place of refuge, Laris will welcome you. Although she hasn't said so, I believe she would help you lay claim to your inheritance. I had more than one reason for returning to Merin's house. I'm here to give you whatever help I can. Will you count me as your friend?"

I took Taia's hand and squeezed it. "Of course. We *are* friends."

Taia lifted my hand to her lips and kissed the back of it. Then I understood that Taia was speaking of a different kind of friendship. Taia was a warrior, and her gesture was a pledge, not only of her own loyalty, but of the loyalty of the house she now represented.

I withdrew my hand from hers. "You should make your pledge to Merin, not to me. I'm not her child. I'm not even a warrior."

Taia smiled. "Can you deny that, if not for Vintel, you would be Merin's child already?"

I shook my head.

Taia looked into my eyes. "You have taken your rightful place, Tamras of the Bow, even if no one knows it."

49

DEMONS

The sun had set when I went to Merin's room that evening. I found her standing by the window in the last of the dying light. The glow in the western sky lent her pale face a blush that made her look quite young. When she turned to me and smiled, her beauty made me catch my breath.

"Come and look," she said.

I went to stand beside her at the window. The sky was dark, all but a band of deep red that burned like flame on the western hills and spilled the color of blood over the silvery surface of the river. Pale stars twinkled out, mirrored by the flickering light of bonfires on the hillsides.

Merin slipped her arm around my shoulders. Her touch struck a spark that sent a warm glow through my body and a blush like fire to my face. I fidgeted a little in embarrassment.

Merin caressed my shoulder.

"It's only the power of the night," she whispered.

Her words reassured me, and my body relaxed against her. It was not her arm around me that pulled me close to her, but the bond between us that grew stronger as the darkness deepened and desire faded into tenderness.

"Thank you," Merin whispered.

"What for?"

"For giving me someone to love," she said. "I had forgotten how much joy there is in loving. More than in being loved."

For a long time we stood together in silence, until we could no longer see the outline of the hills. The shrill music of the pipes and the heartbeat rhythm of a drum drifted up from the meeting ground where, in the flickering firelight, long shadows of the dancers cavorted on the hillside.

Merin leaned more heavily against me.

"I think I need to sit down," she said.

I brought her chair over by the window and settled her into it before I took my usual place on the edge of her bed. A single lamp cast a little pool of light around us, leaving the corners of the room in darkness.

"How was your holiday?" Merin asked me.

"Fine," I replied. As an afterthought, I added, "Taia came back."

"Did she?" Merin sounded neither surprised nor very interested. I had intended to tell her about my conversation with Taia. Before I could speak, she said, "I spent the afternoon remembering."

Wisely I held my tongue and waited for her to go on.

"The young make such terrible mistakes," she said. She gazed up through the window at the sky. "When we're young, we feel things so intensely, and our elders never think to teach us how to contend with our feelings, because they have forgotten their own."

She spoke as if she and I were of an age, and that night perhaps we were, as she returned in memory to a time that was more real to her than yesterday.

"You haven't forgotten," I said.

"No." She sighed. "I knew better even then. I knew she had to go. I knew that nothing I could say would keep her here. In time we might have found a way not to lose each other altogether, but I made that impossible. I said things that couldn't be unsaid and did things that couldn't be undone. And I paid the price for it."

My mother too, I thought, had paid that price. "What did you do or say that was more than someone who loved you could forgive?"

"I couldn't let her go," she said. "I knew how her mother's grief weighed on her heart, but still I kept her here. I found one excuse after another. The weather was unsettled. It threatened rain. Traveling alone was dangerous. Then the weather turned fine, and a band of warriors stopped by on their way south and asked to stay the night. Tamnet arranged to travel with them in the morning. Before dawn I sent them on their way, telling them that she had changed her mind.

"She didn't discover what I'd done for several days. Then, on the morning of the spring festival, she accused me. I denied it at first. When she got the truth out of me at last, she was furious. She insisted on leaving right away, even if she had to go alone. I was desperate. I used every argument I could think of. Nothing moved her, so I told her that if she left me, on that day of all days, how could I believe she'd ever loved me? She never said another word to me that day. She closed her heart and walked away. I watched her go from this window. I didn't understand what I had done until long afterward."

"What had you done?"

"I called her love a lie."

"You spoke in anger."

She nodded. "I did, but I should have taken those words back. I couldn't do it." Merin frowned. An echo of her anger burned in her dark eyes. "She was the air I breathed. How could I have failed to fight for my last breath of life? I would have done anything to keep her here. I knew it was wrong, but I couldn't help myself."

"Why couldn't you have told her that?"

"I didn't understand it myself then. I fought to put her out of my heart, to close my heart against her. She who once made my life worth living had made it unbearable. She became my enemy. I'll never understand how love can turn so quickly into something else. It was bad enough to call her love for me a lie. It was unforgivable that I denied my love for her, even to myself."

"I can't imagine the pain of such a parting," I said. "I don't know how either of you could have borne it, but I see no blame in what you did. My mother used to tell me that the mind will play tricks on itself, in order to bear the unbearable."

Now I understood where my mother's words had come from.

Merin too understood. "What tricks did she play, I wonder?" She leaned her head back and closed her eyes. "Why is it that wisdom comes to us too late to do us any good?"

"It's not too late."

She opened her eyes and looked at me.

"You're both still living," I said. "And you're still friends."

"Friends," echoed Merin. "Friends, and nothing more."

"Have you asked for more?"

"I meant to once," she said. "Time went by, and it didn't hurt so much to think about her. I thought about her more and more, and at last I went to see her. I don't know what I had in mind. I might have asked her for reason to hope. I found her married and big with child. That was my answer."

"You never asked the question?"

She shook her head.

"You need to," I told her.

I don't think she heard me.

The bonfire had burned down. Only the moon brightened the world outside the window. Its pale light fell on Merin's face. She looked frail, and very tired.

"You should rest now," I said. "Come get into bed."

For a few moments more, Merin didn't move. Then she stood up and turned toward the window.

"I used to believe that if she had stayed just one more night, I could have let her go," she said. "Now I know better. Your mother was wise to leave me when she did. Once we had joined together under the moon, I would never have let her go."

Merin untied the ribbon that fastened the bodice of her gown. She shrugged her shoulders, and the gown fell to the floor around her feet. Her small breasts were as shapely as a maiden's. It was plain to see that her slender waist and narrow hips had never cradled a child. As I watched her standing in the moonlight, untouched by time, her terrible beauty a sign that life had never used her, a wave of sadness swept over me.

Merin shivered in the night air. Her sleeping gown lay folded on her pillow. I took it to her and slipped it over her head. Then I turned down the bedclothes for her and helped her into bed.

"Don't leave me," she whispered.

I sat down on the edge of the bed beside her.

She took my hand. "You'll tell her, won't you?"

"Someday you'll tell her yourself."

"Promise," she demanded.

"I'll tell her."

Merin gave me a shy smile. "I used to make her tell me all the time. I lived in fear that she would stop loving me. I used to make her tell me, over and over again. She never seemed to mind, but she must have found it tiresome. It was different, though, when I saw her this time. This time it didn't matter whether she loved me back or not. I only wanted her to hold still for a little while, and not to mind that I loved her."

Merin closed her eyes. After a few minutes I thought she had fallen asleep. When I started to get up, to go to my own bed, her fingers tightened around mine.

"She took me by surprise this time," she whispered. "You were away at the frontier. I told her you weren't expected back anytime soon. I thought she would go home, but she decided to wait a while. She waited more than a week. She didn't seem at all impatient.

"It was wonderful to have her here. She had been changed so little by the years. She still delighted in doing the things we used to do together. We took long walks around the countryside. I've never been fond of walking, but while I was with her, I didn't mind it. Every day she was here, I woke with a light heart. I could almost believe that the years of loneliness had been no more than a cruel dream. She stayed just long enough to bring it all back to me."

I thought that might be what my mother had intended, but I didn't presume to say so to Merin.

Merin's eyes grew sad. "What an unkind thing for her to do."

"But you said she made you happy."

"She did," said Merin. "I had forgotten what happiness felt like. I wish I'd never remembered."

Merin's brow furrowed with pain. Her eyes met mine for a moment. Then she looked past my shoulder, into the dark. "Something always interferes. Our heart's desire comes within our grasp for just a moment, only to be snatched away again."

Merin's gaze was fixed on something in the shadows. I remembered what Namet had said about Merin's demons. The hair on the back of my neck stood up, and I resisted the urge to glance over my shoulder. What demons lurked here still?

Now I understood that it was my mother's visit that sent Merin on her journey of the heart. Merin had opened the door to some dark and secret place, and all her demons had flown out of it at once. Many she had come to terms with, but there were others she had yet to face.

Merin reached up and with her fingertips lightly touched my brow. For a moment her palm cradled my cheek. Then her fingers fluttered across my temple and down the side of my face.

"Love's wings," she murmured.

Her gentle touch made me smile, and her words warmed my heart.

"Love is a bird of prey," she said. "While her feathers caress your face, her talons tear at your heart."

When I woke at dawn, I was lying across the foot of Merin's bed. Merin was still asleep. I got up carefully so as not to wake her and managed to slip out the door without making the hinges creak.

I had intended to go to the companions' loft, but when I passed the hallway that led to the warriors' rooms, I thought of Maara. I had no fear for her. I knew that Namet would have kept her safe. Nevertheless, something drew me down the hallway to her room. Outside her door I stopped to listen. I heard no voices. Thinking she must be asleep, I turned to go, but my feet refused to move until I had looked in, to make sure she was still there.

When I lifted the curtain, I saw Namet, sleeping sitting up at the head of Maara's bed. Maara lay beside her, her head nestled against Namet's side, her arm lying across Namet's lap.

I should have let the curtain fall. I should have found nothing disturbing in the sight of them together. Instead I stood looking at Maara, at the exposed curve of her neck and shoulder, and at Namet's fingers, tangled in her hair. For a moment all I felt was jealousy, that she could show herself to Namet in a way she had never shown herself to me.

Namet opened her eyes and looked at me. Slowly she brought one finger to her lips. I nodded and closed the curtain. Then I tiptoed back to the companions' loft.

50

THE SPIRAL PATH

The bright, warm days of spring had their effect on Merin, making her more cheerful and less apt to brood about the past. I still sat with her for hours every day, and I was growing restless with inactivity. Maara and I would go outside the earthworks in the evening to watch the sunset, and sometimes we would take a short walk along the riverbank. I wished I had an excuse to go out with her into the countryside, as we used to do.

One morning I found Namet and Maara in the kitchen, packing food into a basket.

"We're going to the council stones," said Namet. "Would you like to come along?"

I had not yet looked in on Merin. "Can you wait a few minutes? I'll ask the Lady if she can spare me today."

"Of course," Namet replied.

Merin saw my eagerness to go.

"I'm doing very well," she said. "Go and enjoy the day."

I had forgotten what a strenuous hike it was. My legs would be sore in the morning, but it was delightful to be out of doors. Namet led us a little out of our way, taking a shady path through a wood where birdsong filled the air. From time to time Namet stopped to listen. I was glad to have a chance to catch my breath.

Namet regarded me with amusement. "Tamras is panting so loudly I can hardly hear the birds," she said.

I felt the blood rush to my face, and I wiped my brow with my sleeve, to hide my embarrassment.

"You have no reason to be ashamed," said Namet kindly. "Your care of Merin has taken up your time. Now that she's so much better, your warrior should reassert her claim to you. It's time you resumed your training."

I was grateful to Namet for saying so. I had found it difficult to ask Maara to spend time with me. As her apprentice I had gone to her as a matter of course, but after I became Merin's healer, Maara let go of me. I was surprised to realize that I resented her for it.

"Tomorrow morning we could go hunting," Maara suggested.

My resentment vanished.

Now that I knew where to find the council stones, I wouldn't have bothered treading the spiral path, but Namet insisted.

"Just because you know the way doesn't excuse you from approaching the place properly," said Namet.

"Properly?"

"One cannot approach a mystery directly," she said.

Perhaps the council stones were something more than a place to picnic.

"Let Maara lead us this time," I said.

Namet nodded, and Maara studied the ground until she found the way. This time the path felt different. The first time I walked it, I was paying close attention, watching for the small stones that marked the winding path. Now, following in Maara's footsteps, I had nothing to think about, and my mind wandered. Disconnected thoughts came into my head, but before I could take hold of them, they faded and were gone.

We ate our lunch in silence. I had thought that we might take advantage of the opportunity to talk over our situation, but neither Namet nor Maara seemed to be concerned about anything but enjoyment of the present moment.

The people of Merin's house were more at ease. The lovely weather calmed our fears about the harvest. In any case, there was nothing we could do now but wait and see. The news from the frontier was good. The northerners had found our warriors more formidable than they expected and had taken to raiding farther west, among tribes little known to us. Even so, our warriors weren't yet confident enough to come home.

Best of all Merin grew stronger every day. When the time came for her to match her strength against Vintel's, I was certain she would prove as capable as ever. Then my adoption could be spoken of.

In the meantime it seemed like borrowing trouble to talk of all the bad things that might happen. I lay back in the grass and listened to the songs of insects and the sighing of the breeze. When I dozed a little, images came into my mind of something that had happened when I was a child.

My mother used to take me out among our sheep when I was barely tall enough to see over their backs. They frightened me, and I would cry and reach out my arms to her, begging to be carried. As I grew, my mother more often left me to find my own way.

One day we came across a lamb lying in the grass asleep. I sat down beside it and stroked its wool, soft as thistledown and warm with sunshine. I laid my head down on its wooly back, and there I fell asleep. I woke not knowing where I was and cried out for my mother. She didn't answer me. I got to my feet and looked for her. She wasn't there. She wasn't anywhere.

People were sitting on the hillside not far away. Perhaps they knew where she was. I made my way toward them through the jostling sheep. When I reached them, there was my mother, sitting and talking with the others. I was so relieved to see her that I ran into her arms. As I sat in her lap and listened to the grown-up talk I didn't understand, I realized that she had been there all along. She had been there, and I hadn't seen her.

For the first time I understood that she was someone else, someone who was not a part of me. With the memory of that moment long ago vivid in my mind, I woke among the council stones.

That evening Maara went to see the Lady, to speak with her about my training.

"Your warrior is right," Merin told me, when I went to bid her good night. "I have taken advantage of your kind heart. It's time I let you go."

The next morning my warrior took me hunting. I wanted to do well. I wanted it so much that my arrows refused to find their target until doing well no longer mattered. Then I was able to bring down a fine, fat bird. We made a fire on the riverbank and set the bird on a spit to roast. It was still early morning. Tendrils of mist uncoiled themselves over the surface of the water, and dewdrops beaded Maara's hair. I smiled to myself with happiness.

Maara caught me watching her and raised her eyebrows in a silent question.

"I've missed this," I told her.

It was not what I had meant to say. I had meant to say that I had missed her, but at the last moment, shyness stopped me.

Maara grinned back at me. "You may change your mind before this day is over. You have a lot of catching up to do."

51

THE HARVEST

The summer was so uneventful that it was easy to forget the dangers that lurked just out of sight. Our warriors remained at the frontier. Although they saw very little of the northerners, Vintel continued to make a show of guarding our borders.

Midsummer's day came and went. Most of those who had completed their time of service to the Lady stayed on. The warriors she had sent for from Arnet's house had formed their own band, independent of Vintel. While everyone assumed that they too were guarding our frontier, sometimes Maara and I saw them camped not far from Merin's house, up in the hills.

We tended to stay close to home. When we did go out into the countryside, we stayed away no longer than overnight. My concern for Merin kept me near her, and both Maara and I felt safer in Merin's house.

Every day I practiced with the bow. Maara taught me how to make new arrows. We split shafts from billets of hazelwood, shaved them down with draw-knives, and smoothed them with sand from the river. We made flint arrowheads and fletching of goose feather. While we worked, Maara told me about battles she had heard of or witnessed herself. Before I had gone into battle, her accounts would have meant no more to me than all the other battle stories I'd ever heard. Now that I had experienced the battlefield myself, I listened with greater understanding.

One day Maara took me to the practice ground, where in more peaceful times the apprentices would have been sparring with one another. She handed me one of the wicker shields and waited until I had a good grip on it. Then she took up a wooden sword and without warning brought it down hard on my shield. The shock of the blow went up my arm to the shoulder and hot pain followed it.

"Fighting with swords is a trial of strength," she said. "Those who lack strength must make up for it with cleverness."

My arm still hurt, and I was too angry to pay attention to what she was saying. She ignored my anger.

"When the blow falls, don't try to stop it with the shield," she said. "Turn it aside. So."

Slowly she brought her sword down again, to show me. When the blow was about to land, she reached out with her other hand and tipped my shield, so that the sword glanced off it.

"Try again," she said.

She brought her sword down, a little harder. I turned the blow aside.

"Good," she said.

We practiced until I became bored and my mind wandered. The flat of her sword stung my thigh.

"Pay attention," she said.

Tears came to my eyes.

"I want your body to remember," she said. "Do you remember this?" She ran her hand down her thigh, over the scar she bore from the wound that almost killed her. "I was distracted for a moment, wondering where the others were. Before I knew it, the damage was done. I want your body to remember the sting of the blade, and to fear it."

For the next few weeks, we sparred a little every day, but Maara never put a wooden sword into my hand. Pain had made me cautious, and as I had no sword to strike back with, I concentrated on keeping her sword away from me.

"When will you teach me how to use a sword?" I asked her at last.

"Not for a while yet," she replied.

"Why not?"

"When people fight with swords, what are they trying to accomplish?"

The answer seemed so obvious to me that I knew it must be a trick question.

"Each one is trying to kill the other?" I replied cautiously.

As I expected, Maara shook her head. "Each one is trying to keep from being killed. Each one is trying to keep from being hurt. As long as you remain unhurt, you can keep on fighting, or you can run away. If you ever find yourself in a situation where you must fight with your sword, the most important thing will be to keep yourself in one piece."

She was teaching me, not how to win, but how to survive. While I was thinking that over, she lifted her sword. Without my having to think about it, my arm raised the shield to counter it, but while my attention was on her sword, she gave me a powerful shove with her shoulder, and I went down. In a moment the point of her sword was at my throat.

"Next we'll work on balance," she said.

Maara made a slight motion of her head toward one of the upstairs windows that overlooked the practice ground.

"Don't look now," she said, "but someone is watching us."

Of course I looked. Before I could make out who it was, the watcher stepped back into the shadows.

"Merin takes great pride in you," said Maara.

It could have been anyone. It could have been Namet or Tamar or one of the servants, but I believed Maara was right. When I asked the Lady that evening if she had been watching us, she didn't deny it.

"Why did you hide?" I asked her. "I wouldn't have minded."

"I didn't want you to think that I intended to interfere," she said, "although I do find her teaching methods unusual."

"She's teaching me how not to get myself killed," I said.

Merin nodded. "Very wise of her."

Harvest time came at last. Because of the late planting, little of the grain had ripened, but if the good weather held for another few weeks, we might not go hungry that winter. Just as we had begun to hope that we would be left in peace to bring in the harvest, the raids began again, and fear returned to Merin's house.

Reports reached us from the frontier of constant fighting. No sooner had our warriors driven one band of northerners away than more came to challenge them. While some of the raiders confronted our warriors, the others slipped past them and attacked our farms. They paid in blood for what they took. Our warriors bled too. The raids continued until all the grain had been brought in. Then the northerners went home.

It was a poor harvest, and the northerners had made off with a large share of it, but if we were careful, we would have enough, and we were grateful. That year at the harvest festival, when the Lady burned the Mother-sheaf, it felt more like a sacrifice than a celebration. In good years we offered the Mother a share of our bounty, because she was the source of it. This year I wondered if someone would starve to death who might have lived but for the sheaf of grain we'd given back.

On the last day of the harvest festival, Vintel and her warriors returned from the frontier. That evening Sparrow and I slipped away from the celebration and went down to sit by the river. Her safe return was the only thing I felt like celebrating.

When I first saw her, her appearance shocked me. Her face was gaunt, and there were dark circles under her eyes.

"What was it like?" I asked her.

"Relentless," she replied.

"You look exhausted."

She nodded. "I could sleep away the winter."

I felt guilty that I hadn't done my part. "I wish I'd been there."

"Me too," she said. "I've missed you."

Gently, almost shyly, she took my hand.

"I've missed you too," I said. "And I've been afraid for you."

"Have you?"

I nodded.

Sparrow smiled at me. Then she lay down and put her head in my lap. "If I weren't so tired, I'd show you how much I missed you."

Before I could think of a reply, Sparrow was asleep.

A quarter of an hour went by. I heard no footfall, but I felt someone behind me. She knelt down and touched my shoulder.

When I turned to see who it was, my face was inches from Vintel's.

"May I have my apprentice back?" she whispered.

I nodded, too surprised to speak.

Vintel took Sparrow up in her arms, lifting her as she would have lifted a sleeping child, and carried her back to Merin's house.

Namet saw the difference right away.

"She has the confidence of undisputed command," she said.

Vintel's bullying ways were gone. She no longer had to call attention to herself. When she appeared in the great hall, heads turned and voices fell silent. Warriors who had led their own small bands the year before and who would have considered themselves her equals then, now deferred to her.

"All summer she has commanded them," said Namet. "She has had all that time to instill in them the habit of obedience. And she has had no opposition. Laris and her band are gone, and Arnet's warriors are too few to matter."

I had noticed too that many of the warriors who stayed closest to Vintel were new to Merin's house. They were the warriors she had sent for from her sister's house. They had joined her at the frontier, and no one now objected to their presence. Our warriors had fought beside them, and those whose safety had depended on them made them welcome.

"It may be just as well," said Namet. "If she feels her place here is secure, she may be more inclined to ignore you. Do nothing to provoke her, and she may leave you alone."

I had forgotten how noisy a houseful of warriors could be. There was hardly space in Merin's house for all of them. The great hall was always full. At night those who couldn't find room enough upstairs slept there.

When they were safe at home, our warriors usually showed their softer side. This year, after their long summer spent in harm's way, they were slow to shed their belligerence and gentle into the people I had come to know.

Both the warriors and their companions talked endlessly of the fighting they'd seen. Those who had lost friends kept their grievances fresh by telling them endlessly to anyone who would listen. No evening passed without threats made against the warriors of the northern tribes. The air itself had a bitter taste, poisoned by their hatred.

I wasn't looking forward to spending the winter cooped up with them in Merin's house. For as long as the good weather lasted, I was determined to stay out of doors, where I could feel some space around me and breathe clean air and hear only the quiet sounds of the countryside, where I could forget that I had seen the ugly side of people I cared for.

One evening I was late coming home. I was sitting on the riverbank, watching the golden light of the autumn afternoon fade into twilight, until my mind forgot to think of anything at all and I lost track of time.

Maara's voice startled me. "I was beginning to worry," she said.

She looked so troubled that I tried to make a joke. "Did you think I'd fallen into the river?"

"No," she said.

My unstrung bow and a quiver of arrows lay beside me.

"Do you always bring your bow with you?"

I nodded.

"Good," she said, "but keep it strung and ready."

A chill went down my spine. "Why? Is something going to happen?"

Her eyes avoided mine. "I don't know."

"Please," I said. "Tell me. I'd rather know the truth, even if it scares me."

"I know no more than you do, but I feel uneasy."

I patted the ground beside me, hoping she would sit with me a while.

"We should go home soon," she said. "Namet will worry."

But she sat down.

I gazed up at stars that had begun to show themselves against the darkening sky. With my friend beside me, I was content, and I didn't want to go anywhere.

"I don't like it there," I whispered.

Maara waited for me to explain.

"It's too loud and too crowded, and everyone seems so strange."

"They'll change," she said. "In a little while they'll let the wildness go."

The wildness.

"Has Vintel spoken to you?" she asked.

I shook my head.

"How is Merin?"

"She's fine. She says she's going to start taking her meals in the great hall, although the noise gives her a headache."

"That's good," said Maara.

There was no moon. The dark gathered around us. As the world vanished from my sight, night sounds filled my ears. I heard the river, flowing by on its way to places I would never see. Something splashed into the water, perhaps a fish, leaping at a star. In the grass a cricket made its scratching sound. I had my friend beside me. All was well.

52

An Undivided Heart

A fortnight had gone by since our warriors' return, and I still hadn't had a chance to spend any time with Sparrow. Most nights she slept beside me in the companions' loft, but during the day Vintel seemed to have a great deal to do out in the countryside, and she always took Sparrow with her. Soon enough winter weather would keep us all indoors. Then perhaps Sparrow would have some time for me.

It was a fine autumn day. Maara took me to the practice ground and put a wooden sword into my hand. I felt awkward, and I was glad I had spent so much time working with the shield alone. Making both arms work together was more difficult than it looked.

An hour later we were both covered in sweat and dust. When Maara suggested we go for a swim in the river, I was more than ready to put my weapons down. After our swim, we lay in the soft grass of the riverbank to dry off. I was looking forward to a lazy afternoon and hoping I could persuade Maara to spend it with me.

Warmed by the sun, I fell asleep.

Someone whispered something in my ear. The echo of a dream faded before I could bring it into memory, but my body remembered it. The touch of love on my skin had warmed me in a way the sun could not. The touch returned, but now I was awake. I opened my eyes. Sparrow lay beside me.

"What a lovely thing to find lying about on a riverbank," she said. She caressed the side of my breast lightly with one finger.

I was about to take Sparrow into my arms when I wondered where Maara was. I sat up and looked around. Her clothes no longer lay with mine on the riverbank.

Sparrow stood up and pulled me to my feet.

"Come on," she said, and drew me in the direction of the willow tree.

"Wait."

I wanted to pick up my clothing and my bow, but Sparrow wouldn't release my hand.

"They'll be fine where they are," she said.

She took me in her arms and kissed me, and desire made me forget everything else.

Under the willow tree, we lay down. I was impatient. I tried to help Sparrow unfasten the ties of her shirt, but my hands were shaking, and she pushed them away.

"What's gotten into you?" she said. She was laughing at me a little, but beneath the laughter I heard her own excitement. She slipped off her boots and trousers. "Have you missed me that much?"

I reached for her. If I had been honest with myself, I would have known that it was not Sparrow I had missed. I had missed being touched. I had missed feeling cared for, as I always felt cared for after we made love. I knew that others cared for me. My heart knew how much others cared for me, but my body needed to be told, in a language it could understand, that someone loved all of me, enough to create this need in me and satisfy it.

Sparrow had always been gentle with me. Now I was impatient with her gentleness. Tenderness had been so much a part of the way we touched each other, but this time my body demanded something else. This time we grappled with each other like adversaries. My body spoke to hers in a language that was strange to me, but she knew it well. She knew that I was angry with her, because she couldn't give me what I wanted.

She satisfied my body. That was easy. When I lay quiet in her arms, she kissed my tears away.

"I'm not crying," I told her.

"Hush," she whispered. "Of course you are."

We spent a long afternoon together under the willow tree. Sparrow told me about a few of her adventures that summer. I think she left out the parts that would have frightened me. She never mentioned Vintel.

"Where is your warrior today?" I asked her.

"Visiting some farm or other, I suppose."

"I'm surprised she didn't take you with her."

"She did. I complained that I wasn't feeling well, and she let me come home."

I opened my mouth to ask her if she truly was unwell, but Sparrow chuckled.

"Silly," she said. "I wanted to see you."

"Oh." Then I worried that Vintel would come back to Merin's house and discover that Sparrow wasn't there.

Sparrow touched the frown line that had appeared on my brow. "Don't worry," she said. "She won't be angry with me."

We arrived home in time for dinner. As I took my place at the companions' table, I caught a glimpse of Vintel out of the corner of my eye. She was deep in conversation with several of her sister's warriors, but I was certain she had seen us come in, and I hoped Sparrow wouldn't have to pay too great a price for our stolen afternoon.

Sparrow went over to Vintel and whispered something in her ear. Vintel smiled. I was relieved for Sparrow's sake. They spoke with each other for a few minutes. When Sparrow turned away and came back to the companions' table, Vintel's eyes followed her until Sparrow sat down beside me. Then Vintel's eyes found mine. A scowl replaced the half-smile on her face, and I quickly looked away.

"What did you tell her?" I asked Sparrow.

"I told her I was feeling better."

"That's all?"

"And that I'd come to her this evening, if she needed anything."

I had no illusions about what Vintel might need from Sparrow. I frowned my disapproval.

Sparrow put her hand on my arm. "She's my friend, Tamras. I don't mind."

Taia sat down across the table from me. Although she was now a warrior, entitled to sit with the other warriors as their equal, she preferred the company of friends. I admired her for it.

"I think your sister has picked out her teacher," Taia whispered, giving Sparrow a sly glance.

"Tamar?" I asked.

"Do you have another sister I don't know about?"

I shook my head.

"She's been pestering me all day, asking questions about a certain someone."

"I won't be a warrior for at least another year," said Sparrow, "so she had better look elsewhere."

"I think she'll wait," Taia replied. "I think she might have a little case of hero worship."

Sparrow frowned. "She'll soon grow out of it."

"Maybe." Taia chuckled to herself. "But in the meantime, don't be surprised if you catch sight of her every time you turn around."

Sparrow sighed. "That's happening already. She followed us a few days ago. When we discovered her, it was too late to send her back alone, so Vintel let her tag along."

That news made me uneasy. I had no objection to Tamar being close to Sparrow, but much of the time being close to Sparrow meant being close to Vintel too.

It was several days before I could get Tamar alone to talk to her. Whenever I approached her, she always had something urgent that had to be attended to. I knew she was avoiding me, and I finally cornered her. She was sitting by herself in the shadow of the earthworks near the practice ground, watching the apprentices spar from a discreet distance.

While she was trying to think up yet another reason that she had to be somewhere else, I sat down beside her, and because I was annoyed with her, I spoke more harshly than I meant to.

"Why do you always do just the thing I ask you not to do?" I said.

She gave me a blank look. It seemed genuine, not her usual expression of mock innocence when she had done something she knew I would object to. I tried to be more patient with her. "I told you to stay away from Vintel."

"I do stay away from her."

"You followed her."

"Not Vintel."

"You didn't follow Vintel's band the other day?"

Tamar's cheeks were tinged with pink. "It wasn't Vintel I was following," she said. On her face was the beginning of a stubborn pout.

"You can't follow Sparrow and stay away from Vintel at the same time."

Now her cheeks burned red. "I wasn't."

I looked over at the practice ground, where Sparrow and Taia were sparring with each other.

Tamar saw that I had found her out.

"She's wonderful," Tamar whispered. "Look."

As I watched my friend spar with Taia, who had begun to show much more interest in becoming an accomplished swordswoman, I realized that what I saw and what Tamar saw were two very different things. I tried to remember how the apprentices had appeared to me before I became one of them. I had certainly felt the warmth of hero worship around my heart, but in Tamar's eyes there was something more. Her face shone with a pride that had something of possession in it, as if Sparrow were perfect, and as if that perfection were Tamar's own discovery.

"She's head over heels," I said to Maara, as we sat together that evening on the hillside outside the earthworks.

The sky shone red and gold. Towering thunderheads lost their black hearts in a blaze of color. I watched their eerie light reflected in Maara's eyes.

Frown lines appeared on Maara's brow. "Does that worry you?"

"I've been trying to keep her away from Vintel. I don't think she takes my warnings seriously, and if she insists on being with Sparrow every waking moment—"

"Ah." Maara's eyes searched mine. My heart heard the question she didn't ask. Did I see my own sister as a rival?

"Sparrow is my friend," I said. "I trust her to keep the balance between her loyalty to her warrior and her loyalty to me. But Tamar is too young to have a divided heart, and I fear Vintel's influence over her."

Maara nodded. "Tamar is at the age where one knows everything." A sly twinkle appeared in her eye. "At that age her older and much wiser sister was no different."

A cloud of doubt settled around my heart. Maara saw that I had misunderstood her.

"Don't you remember, Tamras?" she said gently. "You insisted that you knew what was best for you, and you were right. Your undivided heart showed you the path you were meant to take."

I looked away from her at the darkening sky.

"The path I chose has brought trouble to people I care for," I told her. "It has brought trouble to Sparrow, to Merin, to Namet." I met her eyes. "To you."

"Not to me," she whispered. "Not to me."

The words, *not yet,* echoed in my head. I couldn't say them aloud. While my mind considered the trouble that might still come to Maara through me, my heart grew light with hope.

Late that night as I lay in my bed in the companions' loft, I thought over what Maara had said. In a way she had accused me of standing between my sister and her heart's desire. Something was drawing Tamar in a direction that she couldn't help but take, no matter how much I might disapprove of it.

I remembered what that felt like and how, against all opposition, I had been determined to take the path my heart chose for me. Tamar too was following her heart. She would find her own path, and I could either help or hinder her.

At dawn the next morning I got Tamar out of bed. She was too sleepy to complain. She stumbled after me down the stairs and out the kitchen door. We were sitting together on the damp earth under the ancient trees of the oak grove before she found her tongue.

"If you're going to kidnap me every morning to keep me from going where I please, I'll find another place to sleep," she said.

"Hush," I said. "I'll do no such thing. I brought you here because I owe you an apology."

I had to smile a little at the look of surprise on her face.

"I had no right to tell you what to do," I said. "I trust you to find your own way. Even if the path you choose seems dangerous to me, I promise I won't interfere."

I watched Tamar's expression change. She smiled at me with a shy openness that touched my heart.

"Just keep in mind the dangers I've told you about," I said.

"I haven't forgotten," she replied. "I hardly speak to Vintel."

"I'd rather you didn't speak to her at all," I said, a bit too sharply, and watched the good my words had done undo itself.

Tamar bristled. "I must speak if I'm spoken to. To do otherwise would be rude and would do nothing but call attention to me."

I sighed and thought of all the times my warrior had spoken to me as I was now trying to speak to Tamar. Even when Maara said things that hurt my feelings, I knew she spoke the painful words because she cared for me.

"Forgive me," I said. "I only meant to give you good advice. I can't tell you what to do and what not to do. I must leave that to your own good judgment."

Tamar's bristling resentment subsided. "My own good judgment?"

I nodded.

Her smile returned. "Perhaps it was my own good judgment that kept me quiet long enough to notice what was happening around me. Did you know that Vintel has warriors quartered on the farms along our eastern border?"

It was now Tamar's turn to enjoy my look of surprise.

"How do you know that?" I asked her.

Tamar gave an exaggerated shrug. "I'm nobody," she said. "I'm not even anyone's companion yet. I'm as insignificant as a worm, and no one minds if the worms hear what they say."

"Have you heard Vintel speak of this?"

She shook her head. "I've only heard the warriors speak of it, and there are many things they don't say in Vintel's hearing."

I knew that to be true. What warriors spoke of among themselves generally took the form of a complaint, or criticism of whatever authority they were subject to. It used to bother me, until I realized that it was traditional and was done whether they had anything to complain about or not.

"How many warriors are there at each farm, do you think?" I asked.

"Not many. Three or four at most. If they become a burden to the farmers, they'll find themselves unwelcome."

"But why?" I wondered aloud. "We'll be in no danger from the northern tribes once the snow falls."

"I couldn't tell you why," she said. "I don't think the warriors themselves know why. They're just glad to be in a warm place with plenty to eat and friends to swap stories with. And more than one young man has his eye out for a country girl."

I gave my little sister a look of genuine admiration.

"You surprise me, Tamar," I said.

Although Tamar tried to hide her smile, she enjoyed my praise. Then I wondered if she would show me her heart.

"Is that why you followed Sparrow?" I asked her. "To spy on Vintel?"

Tamar turned red to the tips of her ears.

"I suppose not." I smiled at her. "Sparrow is my friend, Tamar. She is worthy of your admiration. You've chosen well."

53

A Different Light

It unsettled me that Sparrow hadn't said anything about Vintel quartering her warriors on the farms, but I didn't voice my doubts aloud to Tamar. First I had to talk to Sparrow.

"Where else can we put them all?" Sparrow asked me, when I spoke to her that evening. "Merin's house is bursting at the seams."

"Is that the only reason?"

"What other reason could there be?"

I shrugged. Although I couldn't think of one, the news still bothered me.

We were sitting by ourselves in a dark corner of the great hall, where we wouldn't be noticed or overheard. Maara was upstairs with Namet. Vintel had gone to bed.

Sparrow frowned at me. "You're so suspicious. Can't you believe in her good intentions just a little?"

I made a noise with my tongue that told her I believed in Vintel's good intentions not at all.

That made Sparrow angry.

"I know she's not your favorite person in the world," she said, "but you do her an injustice. Hasn't it occurred to you that if you treated her with some respect, she might have more respect for you?"

It was the first time Sparrow had sided with Vintel against me, and it hurt my feelings. When Sparrow saw that her words had stung, she slipped her arm around me.

"I'm sorry," she said. "I know you're in a difficult position."

Sparrow felt me pull myself into a tight knot around my wounded heart.

"Oh dear," she said. "I didn't mean to scold."

She took my hand in hers and kissed it. She would have gone on holding it, but I withdrew it from her grasp.

"Please don't be angry with me," she said. She brushed my hair away from my face and caressed my cheek. Her tenderness brought me closer to tears than her sharp words had done.

"I need your friendship," I whispered. "More now than ever."

Sparrow's hand cupped my chin and lifted my face up so that she could look me in the eye. "I'll always be your friend," she said. "Never doubt it." She leaned toward me and kissed me gently on the mouth.

Something disturbed the air. At the far end of the great hall someone was standing in the shadows. I felt her eyes.

"You don't know Vintel as I do," said Sparrow.

I wished then that I had told Sparrow what Vintel had done to Maara, what Vintel had done to the man who killed Eramet. Then she would see her warrior in a different light.

"I know you suspect her motives," Sparrow said, "but she does what she believes she must, to protect us all, to keep us safe. If you knew what I know about her, you'd understand."

Across the hall the figure in the shadows stood very still.

"Tell me then," I challenged her. "Tell me what you know about Vintel that you believe could change my mind."

"Her mother brought her here when she was only eight years old," she said. "When she was ten, she saw her mother killed in the fighting with the northern tribes."

I opened my mouth to say that, while I understood Vintel's grief, it didn't justify the things she'd done. Sparrow put her finger on my lips to stop me.

"There's more," she said. "That same evening Vintel took her mother's sword. She slipped away from Merin's house and went to the northerners' camp. The northerners were sitting around their campfires eating their evening meal. Vintel walked in among them. She was just a little girl, dragging a sword she could barely lift. No one tried to stop her. They thought it was funny. They watched her, and they laughed. She went from group to group until she found the warrior who had killed her mother. Then she lifted that heavy sword and nearly took the woman's arm off."

I had forgotten we were being watched. My eyes were on Sparrow's face, while my mind formed a vivid picture of that courageous child.

"What happened then?" I asked.

"She wouldn't tell me, but I've seen the scars she bears."

"Many have grievances against the northerners, just as the northerners must have many grievances against us. What does that have to do with her hatred for Maara, or for me?"

"Before the fighting started," Sparrow said, "the northerners had feasted day after day with our warriors right here in this hall. They passed Vintel from lap to lap and fed her the tenderest bits of meat and bread dipped in honey. Those who could speak as we do told her stories, and the others sang to her in their strange tongue. When she fell asleep at last, one or another of them would carry her up to bed. They were strangers, and she trusted them. It was a mistake she'll never make again."

Although I didn't want to see Vintel as Sparrow saw her, I understood the feelings of the child Vintel had been. The northerners' betrayal must have been incomprehensible to her, and the loss of her mother impossible to bear.

In the back of my mind a warning sounded. Maara had taught me not to let compassion blind me to the malice of an enemy. Understanding Vintel made her no less dangerous. It was time to show Sparrow the side of Vintel I had seen.

"I've always understood why Vintel distrusted Maara," I said. "Everyone distrusted her a little, but it was Vintel who put her in harm's way."

"Whatever do you mean?"

"Maara was wounded almost to death because Vintel failed to stand by her."

I expected Sparrow to be shocked. Instead she said, "That wasn't Vintel's fault. Warriors are wounded all the time."

"When a warrior is wounded because her comrades refuse to help her," I said, "that is someone's fault."

Sparrow frowned. "I don't think Maara can be a fair judge of what happened."

It took me a moment to understand that Sparrow already knew what Vintel had done. "What did Vintel have to say about it?"

"She said that Maara got herself into trouble. Vintel had to make a choice, and she chose the people she cared about."

"Vintel was their leader. She was responsible for them all."

Sparrow considered her words before she spoke. Then she said, "Would you leave Maara's side to help a stranger?"

I didn't want to admit, to her or to myself, that I would not.

"The others understood. They didn't blame Vintel."

"I do," I said.

"Of course you do. But with you it's personal. You cared for Maara."

Sparrow's words woke my memory of a time that seemed very long ago. Sparrow was mistaken. I hadn't cared for Maara then, and because I didn't care for her, I might have let her die. When I threw the healer's sleeping potion out, it was the impulse of a moment. I could just as easily have done what I was told. The thought terrified me. I almost lost my warrior before I knew what I was losing. That was Vintel's doing, and I could not forgive her for it.

I believed that it was I, not Sparrow, who was seeing Vintel clearly, but I couldn't make Sparrow see what she didn't want to see. I rubbed my eyes.

"I think it's time for bed," I said.

Sparrow nodded and stood up. She took my hand and drew me to my feet, but when I turned to go upstairs, she held me there.

"Are you still angry with me?" she asked.

I shook my head.

Sparrow pulled me gently into her arms and held me for a little while, so that I would feel her love for me. Then she stepped away and took both my hands in hers. "Friends?" she asked.

I nodded. "Friends," I told her. "Always."

Someone laid a pine bough on the fire. It smoldered a little, sending its fragrance out into the great hall. Then the dry needles burst into flame. In the sudden light I saw Vintel, who had been standing in the shadows all this time. On her face I saw a look of pain as if her heart would break.

The light lasted only for a moment. Vintel vanished into the dark.

I began to doubt what I had seen. Anger I would have understood. Even jealousy, that Sparrow was as much my friend as hers. Perhaps that was what I saw.

I watched the place where Vintel had been, but I sensed no presence there. I watched until another bough caught fire and drove the shadows back again. Vintel was gone.

Sparrow turned to see what I was looking at.

"Vintel was watching us," I whispered.

Sparrow gave me a teasing smile. "What an imagination you have. You see enemies lurking everywhere."

"No," I insisted. "She was there." I gripped Sparrow's hands more tightly and looked into her eyes. "Do you love Vintel?"

Sparrow hesitated. "Yes and no," she said.

I waited, hoping she would tell me more.

"I have an affection for her," Sparrow said, more softly, "but I don't love her the way—" She looked away from me. I waited. I thought she was going to say that she didn't love Vintel the way she had loved Eramet. Instead she said, so softly I could barely hear her, "—the way Vintel loves me."

I stood outside my warrior's door. Her lamp was out. She must already be asleep. I hardly knew what I was going to say to her. The world had changed, and no one had noticed it but me.

I lifted the curtain and went in. The room was filled with moonlight. I stood in the doorway and gazed at Maara's face. No one would have said she was a beauty, but I found her beautiful, and I wondered how anyone could look at her and fail to see her as she was, as someone of great value, as someone just like us. But Vintel and others like her would see only what was on the surface. They would see the color of her skin, the shape of her eyes and mouth, the texture of her hair, and they would see no further.

Though I wouldn't have admitted it to Sparrow, in my heart I had found a little compassion for Vintel. Knowledge of her sorrows made understandable the way she dealt with strangers. Was it possible for someone who had learned to hate in childhood to unlearn it later in life? If it was not, the world would never change.

Maara murmured in her sleep. I hesitated to disturb her dreams. I waited until she was quiet before I approached the bed and sat down beside her. She woke and looked at me.

"I think I'm in trouble," I said.

Maara sat up. "What is it?"

When I opened my mouth to speak, I didn't know where to begin.

"What happened?"

I thought for a minute she was going to take me by the shoulders and shake me.

"Tonight —" I said.

"What?"

"Tonight I saw Vintel —"

I took a breath. There was no way to describe that look.

"Vintel loves Sparrow," I whispered.

"Oh," she said. She didn't sound surprised. "I don't think you have anything to worry about."

"Of course I do."

I was thinking that any humiliation I had caused Vintel or any resentment she felt that I might someday be in a position of authority over her was nothing compared to the pain of wounded love.

Maara looked puzzled. "Does Sparrow love Vintel?"

"Sparrow?"

I didn't understand. This had nothing to do with Sparrow.

"Are you afraid you're going to lose her?"

I stared at Maara for a moment before I realized that she thought I'd come to her to talk about Sparrow and me.

"No," I said. "I'm afraid of Vintel's jealousy."

Maara frowned. "Why does Vintel's jealousy surprise you?"

She had reason to be impatient with me.

"When you warned me about this," I said, "I didn't take it to heart. It meant nothing to me then, because Sparrow and I weren't —"

Maara waited for me to find the word.

"— what you thought."

"But you are now."

"Yes," I whispered. "No. Not really."

"I don't understand you."

"Sparrow is my friend," I said. "More than my friend."

Once again I couldn't find the words for what Sparrow was to me. I had never been so tongue-tied.

"Hush," said Maara. "You don't have to explain."

"Yes," I said. "I do." I wanted to tell her the whole truth, so that there would be no more misunderstandings.

"Sparrow loved Eramet," I said. "She may never again love anyone the way she loved Eramet. She and I are friends, and we love each other, but not like that." I took a deep breath and met Maara's eyes. "Vintel loves Sparrow like that."

"Oh," said Maara. She had a strange expression on her face. Her eyes looked worried, while at the same time her mouth trembled, then softened into almost a smile.

I smiled too, from relief that the most difficult part of our conversation was over.

"How did you find out?" she asked. "Did Sparrow tell you?"

I told Maara what had happened that evening, and for the first time I saw the irony in it. While Sparrow was trying to make me see Vintel as she did, with understanding and compassion, Vintel must have felt betrayed.

Maara pulled her legs up, rested her chin on her knees, and gazed past my shoulder into the dark. She was silent for a long time.

I waited while she thought over what I'd told her. There were other things I would have liked to tell her, but until we dealt with the problem of Vintel they would have to wait. I wanted to make her understand why I had ignored her warning. I wanted to explain why I had never told her that my friendship with Sparrow wasn't what she thought. I wanted her to understand how it had become something more than friendship, and that by the time I remembered her advice it was too late to take it. Most of all I wanted to tell her I was sorry that I hadn't told her all these things before.

"What do you think Vintel will do?" she said at last.

"I have no idea."

"Be very careful. Don't let her catch you alone."

I nodded.

"I never thought about love," said Maara.

Her words sent a prickle of fear into my heart. "What?"

"It never entered my head that Vintel was capable of love. Did it ever occur to you?"

"Oh," I said. "No, I suppose not."

"Hatred can be just as blind as love," she said.

I had, of course, heard it said that love is blind. I knew what people meant by that. They meant that we never see the imperfections or the faults of our beloved. That night those words meant something else to me. Perhaps it was the moonlight. Perhaps it was the look I'd seen on Vintel's face. That night I saw that I had been blind to something in myself, and that my heart's desire, so looked for and so longed for, was at that moment before my eyes.

54

THE MOST
IMPORTANT THING

I heard a sound behind me. I turned to see Tamar standing in the doorway, rubbing the sleep out of her eyes.

"Someone woke me up," she said. She sounded grumpy. "I told her to deliver her own message, but she insisted that I had to do it." Tamar turned to Maara. "She said to tell you that Laris wants to speak with you. She's waiting for you by the river."

"Now?" asked Maara.

"I suppose." Tamar turned to me. "Who is Laris?"

"Laris is a friend," I said.

"Where is the messenger?" Maara asked her.

"Gone," said Tamar. "May I go back to bed?"

Maara nodded, and Tamar left us.

"Laris's timing is impeccable," said Maara, as she got out of bed.

"Why didn't she come in?"

"She may want to know how things are before she enters Merin's house."

I remembered how cautious Laris was.

Maara pulled on her trousers and tucked the long tails of her sleeping shirt into them. Then she sat down beside me to put on her boots.

"Do you think she's come back to stay?" I asked her.

"I hope so."

Maara finished tying the laces of her boots. "If Laris does stay, her presence may be enough to keep Vintel from doing something foolish, but if she doesn't—" Maara turned and looked at me. "If she's here to renew her offer of refuge, I think we should go with her. I need to know before I speak with her. Will you go with me?"

I nodded.

Maara looked relieved. She got up and turned to go.

"Wait." I stood up to follow her. "I'm going too."

Maara turned in the doorway and put her hand on my shoulder to stop me.

"No," she said. "Wait for me here."

When I started to protest, she frowned and shook her head.

"All right," I said. I put my hand over hers. "Take care."

I turned her hand over and kissed her palm. Then I let her go.

I sat down on Maara's bed. Although the news of Laris's return was more than welcome, I could hardly spare a thought for Laris. I picked up Maara's blanket and pressed it against my chest, to ease the sweet ache around my heart. Maara's scent rose up around me. I breathed it in.

I waited for my mind to make sense of what I was feeling. Of course I loved her. I had known that for a long time. But this feeling was new and unexpected. Like a child who hides in a dark corner, waiting with mischievous anticipation for someone to discover her, my love for Maara had hidden in a dark corner of my heart, and like a child, suddenly leapt out of hiding, leaving me breathless with delight.

After a time I gave up trying to understand. I lay down on Maara's bed, still warm from her body, and brought her image into my mind's eye. Only a short while ago I had watched her face lit by moonlight. I had filled my eyes with her, and now I wondered if she had seen, even before I knew it was there, my heart in my eyes.

When I woke, it was still dark. My first thought was for Maara. She should have been back by now. I got up and went downstairs to look for her. I was about to go into the kitchen when I heard muffled voices in the great hall. Two people were sitting side by side near the cold hearth. It was too dark to make out who they were. It might be Maara and Laris. I waited in the hallway, hoping to overhear a scrap of their conversation, to make sure.

Someone took me roughly by the arm and pulled me backwards. Before I could cry out, she put a hand over my nose and mouth so that I couldn't breathe. She dragged me past the kitchen door and down the narrow hallway to the armory.

I struggled, but her strength was so much greater than mine that I couldn't free myself. She shoved me through the armory door and stood blocking the doorway. Although the light was behind her, I knew who it was.

"Quiet," Vintel said. "Not a word."

I was determined to yell for help as loudly as I could, but before I could draw breath, she said, "Hold your tongue and save your warrior's life."

I held my tongue.

"You and I need to talk things over," she said. "I'm going to get a light. You're going to be quiet until I get back. Do you understand?"

"Yes," I whispered.

She left the armory and shut and barred the door. Soon she was back, carrying a lamp. She closed the door behind her and set the lamp down.

"Where is Maara?" I demanded.

"Where she won't cause me any more trouble," Vintel replied.

She reached into the pocket of her tunic and drew out a long cord that had something dangling from it. She held it up so that I could see it. It was the token Maara always wore, Namet's midsummer gift.

I made a noise then that betrayed my fear.

Vintel smiled a cruel smile. "Don't worry. As long as you do as you're told, I'll take good care of her. If you're very good, I'll let her go to Laris."

"But Laris is here."

"Laris? Here? I don't think so."

Vintel sat down on a crate. "Oh," she said. "You must have misunderstood my message. Didn't Tamar get it right?"

Tamar had said exactly what she was told to say. Now I understood, and at that moment I so hated Vintel that if I'd had the power, I would have struck her dead and paid the penalty.

"Sit down."

Vintel gestured to one of the crates. I perched on the edge of it. She looked me up and down, then knit her brow as she thought something over. All the while I watched her, trying to set aside my anger and my fear, so that I could think clearly about what to do.

After what felt like a long time, Vintel said, "What shall I do with you?"

"You have no right to do anything with me."

"Little thief!" she hissed. "I have every right to keep you from taking what belongs to me."

She could have been speaking of her position in Merin's house, and perhaps she was, but she must also have been thinking of Sparrow. It was on the tip of my tongue to say that Sparrow was neither hers nor mine. Just in time I bit the words back. I would gain nothing by provoking her or by revealing how much I knew about the secrets of her heart.

"What do you want?" I asked her.

"Go home," she said.

"If Maara and I leave this place, the Lady will know who drove us out of it."

"Then we'll have to think of a good reason for your leaving Merin's house."

"At least you admit this is her house."

"Of course it is. What did you think? Did you believe I would betray her?"

My expression told her that was exactly what I believed.

"You do me an injustice," she said. "I'll be happy to leave things in Merin's house just as they are, as long as you're not in it."

I lowered my gaze in what I hoped she would interpret as submission.

"All right," I said. "I'll go home, but only if Maara comes with me."

"No."

"Then let me go with her to Laris."

"Not a good idea." Vintel slowly shook her head. "The two of you together are troublesome."

"No one will believe that Maara and I suddenly took it into our heads to leave Merin's house the same night and go in opposite directions."

Vintel pretended to think the problem over. "Of course we don't need to explain Maara's disappearance. Let people think what they will about that. But we do need to explain yours." She folded her arms across her chest and tapped one finger on her chin. "Responsibilities at home?" She grinned. "An illness? If your mother were taken ill, wouldn't she call you home?"

Now, along with my fear for Maara, I began to be afraid for Merin.

"The Lady will be alarmed if she thinks my mother is so unwell that she needs me with her."

"I imagine she will."

"She won't rest until she hears that my mother has recovered. Then she'll begin to look for my return."

"That's true," Vintel said. "Maybe we can think of something else."

"Something that won't frighten her," I said.

"Something that won't frighten her," Vintel agreed. She studied my face for a moment. "You'll go of your own will then?"

I nodded. It was the best bargain I could make, but I knew it to be a poor one. While I had no intention of going meekly home if I could help it, I didn't doubt that Vintel would provide an escort charged with preventing me from doing anything else. If I could get away from them, perhaps I could find Maara, and then we could decide together what to do.

Vintel stood up. "You'll have to stay here for a little while," she said.

In a moment she would be gone, and I would lose what might be my last chance to change her mind.

"It's not too late," I said.

"Too late for what?"

"Let me go. Bring Maara home. I swear to you, nothing will be said about it."

Vintel chuckled softly. "Why would I do that when I can be rid of the both of you so easily and no one the wiser?"

"This kind of secret is hard to keep."

"My warriors can hold their tongues," said Vintel.

An idea came into my head. I didn't have time to think over whether it was a good idea or not. I took a chance.

"How will you explain this to Sparrow?"

Vintel's eyes met mine, and I thought I saw in them the beginning of a doubt.

"She's as close to you as your own shadow," I said. "Do you think she won't find out what you've done? She will, and when she does, she'll see you as you really are."

Anger flashed in Vintel's eyes.

"I told her you might do something like this, but she wouldn't listen to me. She was angry with me, that I didn't share her high opinion of you. Now she'll see that I was right about you."

Vintel moved so quickly that I had no time to back away from her, even if there had been room. She closed the fingers of one hand around my throat and squeezed. Her face was close to mine, but it looked small and far away. I could hardly hear her voice above the roaring in my ears.

"No," she said. "I'll make Sparrow see that she was wrong about you."

When Vintel let go, my legs refused to hold me. I fell in a heap on the floor. She took the lamp and left me in the dark.

I lay on the floor of the armory for what seemed like hours and tried to anticipate what Vintel would do next. How would she get me out of the house? What would she tell Merin? And where was Maara? Vintel had threatened to harm her if I cried out, so Maara must not be far away. When I dozed, dreams troubled me, and I awoke feeling as helpless as I truly was.

I heard a noise outside the door. It opened a crack, and an arm appeared holding a lamp. I shielded my eyes against the light.

"Get up," said Vintel.

I got to my feet. She came into the armory and shut the door behind her.

"We're going to talk to Merin," she said. "You speak first. Tell her your mother has sent for you."

"What shall I tell her when she asks me why?"

"I'll take care of that," Vintel said.

She opened the door and stood aside to let me pass. As I went by her, she grasped my arm so hard that it bore the marks of her fingers for days afterward. "Behave yourself," she whispered in my ear.

She didn't need to renew her threat. As long as Maara's life was in her hands, I would give Vintel anything she wanted.

We went upstairs. From the light that found its way into the house, I judged it must be about midday. Merin was surprised to see the two of us together.

"I've come to take my leave of you," I told her. "I have to go home."

Merin's eyes went from my face to Vintel's. "What does this mean?"

"Tamras has had bad news," said Vintel.

She looked at me, as if she expected me to supply the reason why I had been called home. I didn't know what to say.

"Tell her," Vintel said to me.

"Tell me what?" said Merin.

What did Vintel expect me to say? I tried to think of an excuse that wouldn't alarm Merin.

"My mother needs my help," I told her. "There's illness in our village. She needs me there, to help her nurse the sick."

Vintel made a sound of disapproval.

"Tamras," she said. "You must tell her the truth."

"That is the truth."

Merin met my eyes and knew it for a lie. She turned to Vintel. "What is it that Tamras wants to keep from me?"

Vintel hesitated, as if she were truly reluctant to be the bearer of bad news.

"Tamras has lost her mother," she said.

"Lost?" Merin sounded lost.

"She died."

I stared at Vintel. "It's a lie."

Vintel kept her eyes on Merin's face. "She didn't want to tell you. I thought it would be better if you heard of it from her, but Tamras was afraid that you were still too frail to hear such sad news."

"It isn't true," I cried out to Merin. "Don't believe her. It isn't true."

But when Merin looked at me, I saw what she believed. I remembered her promise, that she would love her life for as long as Tamnet lived. She knew I had every reason to keep the knowledge of my mother's death from her.

As Vintel drew me away, Merin turned to the window and gazed out of it, as if she were watching her beloved leave her for the last time.

Vintel took me back downstairs. Tears were running down my face. I couldn't hold them back, even though they appeared to confirm Vintel's story. She must already have told it to others in the household. The few people we encountered regarded me with sympathy. Some offered words of condolence. Vintel hurried me past them. She took me back to the armory and shut us both in.

"You lied to me," I said.

Vintel smiled. "No, I didn't."

"You said you wouldn't frighten her."

"She isn't frightened."

"No," I said. "She's worse than frightened."

I was furious with Vintel for what she had done to Merin, although she couldn't know what I knew, that Merin's life might depend on whether or not my mother was still in this world.

"And while she's grieving, I'll look after things for her," Vintel said. "The way it used to be."

I had a sick feeling in my stomach. The lives of two people who were dear to me hung by a slender thread, and I was helpless.

"In the morning," Vintel said, "my warriors will see you on your way. They'll make sure you reach home safely."

"What about Maara?"

"As soon as you're well away from here, she'll be sent to Laris."

"Why would I trust you?"

"Because you have no choice. For all you know your warrior may be dead already. But if you refuse to leave here as you promised, I assure you, she will be dead before anything you say or do can save her."

I should have slept. I was exhausted, but hunger and my own restless thoughts kept me awake. My heart ached for Merin. I knew that she would not believe my mother wasn't dead until she saw her living. Once I found Maara, I would have to go home anyway, to bring my mother back to Merin's house. Would Merin wait that long?

And how would I escape my escort? I couldn't begin to imagine how I would accomplish all I had to do. The more I thought about my situation, the more my heart gave way to hopelessness.

I found nothing to comfort me. When I thought of Maara, I understood what Merin must be feeling. Maara's death was an impossibility. How could someone so real vanish from the earth? How empty the world would be without her. How empty my heart would be.

No light could penetrate the armory. My eyes beheld a darkness so complete that my mind began to make pictures of its own. A young woman with Namet's face peered out at me from a thicket in the wilderness. Merin's body, like an empty shell, sat gazing out her window, while her heart followed my mother home. In an oxcart, Sparrow lay with Eramet in her arms.

I remembered something I'd heard long ago, that love is the most important thing, but the only ones who know that are those who've lost it.

55

A STRONG FRIEND

There was a noise, a light. I opened my eyes and saw Sparrow's face. "Are you all right?" She knelt beside me. "What's going on?"

"Sparrow?"

"Yes," she said. "Are you all right?"

"I'm hungry."

"Wait here." She started to get up. I caught hold of her shirtsleeve, to keep her from leaving me. "I'll be right back," she said.

Gently she freed herself from my grasp and slipped out the door, leaving it ajar. The hallway outside the armory was lit only by the lamplight that spilled through the kitchen doorway. It must be nighttime.

Sparrow returned, bringing a small oil lamp, a bowl of soup, and a piece of bread. She set everything down. Then she shut the door and sat down beside me on the floor. She waited until I had taken the first edge off my hunger. Then she said, "Will you please tell me what's going on? Why are you hiding?"

"How did you know I was here?" I thought Vintel might have sent her.

"I didn't," she said. "I've been looking for you all evening. No one had seen you. I was in bed and almost asleep when I remembered this place. I thought you might have come here to get away from everybody."

"Why were you looking for me?"

"To comfort you, of course. I didn't hear about your mother until this afternoon. Vintel sent me out this morning with Tamar on some stupid errand, but Tamar must have had an inkling. She said she felt uneasy and insisted on coming home. When we arrived, we heard the news. Tamar is inconsolable." She put her hand awkwardly on my shoulder. "Tamras, I'm so sorry."

"My mother isn't dead," I told her.

"What?"

"It was an excuse."

"An excuse?"

"It was the excuse Vintel gave Merin, to explain why I'm going home." Sparrow looked confused.

"Vintel has Maara," I said. "She says she won't harm her as long as I do what she wants. She wants me to go home."

"Vintel has Maara?"

I nodded.

"What do you mean she has Maara? I don't understand."

Then I told her how Vintel had used my sister to lure Maara out of the house, out into the night, where she would be at Vintel's mercy.

Sparrow stared at me as if I'd lost my reason.

"You don't believe me," I said.

"I don't know what to believe."

"Why do you think I've been shut in here?"

She shook her head in puzzlement. "I can't imagine."

There was nothing more I could say that would convince her. I could only let Sparrow think things over for herself. I watched her face as her mind struggled to reconcile what I had told her with her vision of Vintel. She couldn't do it. I sensed her reluctance to believe the worst about her warrior.

"Vintel wants you to go home?" she said at last.

I nodded.

"Forever?"

"Yes."

"Because of me?"

I didn't answer.

"This is my fault," she whispered.

"No, it isn't. This is Vintel's fault."

Sparrow's face grew thoughtful. "Vintel said the strangest thing to me tonight. She asked me if I would miss you, and I told her, yes, I would. She said I might think differently if I knew about you and Merin."

"Me and Merin?" My heart grew cold. "What did Vintel say?"

"She says you're Merin's lover."

"It isn't true."

"I know that." Sparrow met my eyes. "I couldn't imagine why Vintel would say such a thing. Now I understand."

"You do?"

"She wants me not to care what happens to you."

My parting words to Vintel may have done me some good after all.

"Is Maara going with you?" she asked.

"No," I said. "If Vintel keeps her word, she'll be sent to Laris."

If Vintel keeps her word.

I saw in my mind's eye a dead man's body lying in a snowbank.

"I don't believe she will," I said. "I think Vintel intends to kill her."

I half expected Sparrow to protest, but this time she didn't argue with me. She got to her feet, then held her hand out to help me up. She had a determined look in her eye.

"I'll come back as soon as I can," she said.

"Where are you going?"

"To get the things you'll need." She opened the door of the armory a crack and peered out of it. "I don't want to leave you in here, in case someone prevents me from coming back. Go out the kitchen door and wait for me. But don't wait too long."

She gestured to me to follow her. We slipped out of the armory, and I closed and barred the door behind me. Sparrow tiptoed down the hallway and started up the stairs. I went into the kitchen and paused to listen. I wasn't sure what time of night it was. Some of the servants might still be up.

I heard my name, as if Gnith's voice had whispered it inside my head. I couldn't refuse to answer her.

"I must hurry, Mother," I said, as I knelt down beside her. "I am in danger here."

"Yes," she whispered. "Life is very dangerous."

She beckoned to me with one finger, and I leaned closer. When my face was inches from her own, she touched my brow with her fingertips.

"No time to ask a blessing now," she said, "but you need no more gifts from me. It's time to try your wings, little bird."

By the time Sparrow returned, I had been standing in the shadows outside the back door for what felt like ages, although it couldn't have been much above half an hour.

"I kept running into people," Sparrow told me. "I had to bring everything downstairs bit by bit."

She had two bundles, one wrapped in my cloak and one wrapped in Maara's. She laid the two side by side and bound them together, so that I could carry them both over my shoulder. Then she went back inside and returned a minute later with my bow in its case and my quiver of arrows. When I reached out to take them from her, she refused to let go of them until I met her eyes. "You be careful with these," she said.

"I will."

I knew what she meant—that there's a difference between war and murder.

"I'll tell your sister she has no cause to grieve," said Sparrow.

"You must speak with the Lady too," I said. "You must convince her that my mother is alive."

"I'll try."

"You must do more than try. If Merin believes my mother has left this world, she'll let go of the thread of life to follow her."

"Why would she do that?"

"My mother is to Merin what Eramet was to you."

Then Sparrow understood. "I remember," she said. "If you hadn't held on to me, I might have followed Eramet."

I smiled at her. "It was you who held on to me," I reminded her.

Even in the moonlight, I saw her blush.

"Once I find Maara," I said, "I'll go home and bring my mother here. Nothing but the sight of her will convince Merin that she's alive. Tell Merin anything you like. Just don't let her give up hope."

"Wait," said Sparrow. "I have a better idea. Let Tamar go to fetch your mother. If I send her off tonight, she can be back again within the week."

"But she'd have to go alone."

"Of course."

"She's too young."

"She's young," said Sparrow, "but she has her sister's courage. She approached Vintel at dinnertime and demanded that Vintel allow her to go home with you. Vintel refused, and Tamar stamped her foot and let loose a stream of language that turned even Vintel's ears red."

If she had been there, I would have scolded my little sister for doing something so foolhardy, but I couldn't help chuckling a little at the picture of Tamar berating someone as powerful as Vintel.

"After she put on a show like that," Sparrow said, "no one will question her disappearance. They'll think she ran off home anyway, with or without Vintel's permission."

I didn't like the idea of risking my sister's life until I wondered how safe she would be in Merin's house.

"All right," I said. "Tell her I'm confident that she'll do well."

"I will."

"When my mother arrives, you'll have to find a way to take her to Merin without Vintel seeing her."

"Let me worry about that," said Sparrow. "I'll speak with Namet. She'll know what to do."

Of course Namet would know, I thought. Namet might cast her cloak of invisibility over my mother and bring her unseen into Merin's chamber, even under the noses of Vintel and all her warriors.

"Give Namet my solemn promise," I said. "Tell her I'll bring her daughter home to her."

I bent to pick up my pack. Sparrow helped me lift it to my shoulders. It was bulky, but not too heavy for me. Then I slipped my bow out of its case and strung it.

It was near midnight. The moon, waxing almost full, shone brightly overhead. Sparrow took hold of my bow and turned it to the light.

"So beautiful," she said. "And so deadly."

The last secret I had kept from her lay upon my tongue. I would have loved to spit it out.

"I knew Vintel killed him," Sparrow whispered, "but I didn't know this was his until a few weeks ago."

When I opened my mouth to tell her I had withheld the truth from her only to spare her pain, she put her fingertips against my lips.

"It doesn't matter," she said. "Vintel thought it would, but it doesn't. If I were to break this bow into a thousand pieces and throw them in the river, Eramet would still be dead." She put her arms around me. "May it serve you well, Tamras of the Bow. There's no one in the world I love more than you."

56

BLOOD DEBT

I feared the moonlight would reveal me to someone in the household, so I left Merin's house by an unused way that wound through a thicket to the east, away from the river. I took cover in a grove of alders that grew along the banks of a stream. There I sat down, to consider what to do next.

My words to Sparrow had been echoing in my head ever since I spoke them. *I think Vintel intends to kill her.* I had no reason to believe that Vintel would keep her word to me. Why would she send Maara to Laris, someone who had opposed her in the past? Maara's death was what Vintel wanted. She had wanted it for a long time. She would never have a better opportunity.

I had thought and thought about where Vintel's warriors might be holding Maara. There was no place within Merin's house to hide her. She must be out in the countryside. I doubted that Vintel would keep her at one of the farms. What Vintel was doing was best done in secret, with as few witnesses as possible.

My first idea was to travel south, toward Laris's house, but if Vintel's warriors were taking her to Laris, they didn't mean to kill her. If they did mean to kill her, where would they go? They wouldn't travel south, where someone might see them commit their treachery, where someone might find her body. They would go the other way. They would go north and kill her close to our northern border, and if someone chanced to find her, her death could be blamed on our enemies.

And Vintel would claim that Maara had been returning to her own people, as Vintel always suspected she would.

Two roads went north, the one that followed the river and the one that wound through the hills to the northeast, the road we took with Laris to Greth's Tor. The river road was the easier one. A day's travel would take them beyond our borders, and then they could do anything they wanted.

Keeping out of sight of Merin's house, I made my way north and west until I reached the river road. Soon I discovered that my choice had been the right one. A band of warriors had passed along that road not long before. I found a place just out of sight of the household where they had camped. The ashes of the fire were cold. Farther on I saw places where they had rested or where someone had left the trail to relieve herself. They were traveling at an easy pace. I pushed myself, to close the distance.

By the time the sky began to lighten in the east, I was far from Merin's house. Although I hadn't slept more than a few hours in the last two days, I dared not stop to rest. As the light grew, I saw signs all around me of their passage. The grass, wet with dew, showed me every footprint, the trodden blades still bent.

The winding trail followed the river. Tall rushes grew on either side of it, making it impossible to see very far ahead. I tried to listen, but there was a roaring in my ears. The gentle ground offered itself as a soft bed. I stumbled. Had my eyes closed? I had seen tired warriors walk along beside their comrades fast asleep. Had I slept?

They were resting, sitting by the side of the road. I never heard them, although I heard them fall silent when they saw me. I came around a bend and blundered into them. Were there only half a dozen? There seemed so many.

I stopped. For a long time no one moved. Then we all moved.

The closest was several yards away. Before she reached me, I buried an arrow to the feathers in her chest. The others stopped.

I nocked another arrow in the bow but didn't draw it. I waited. The woman who lay dead at my feet must have been their captain. The rest were uncertain what to do.

"Disarm yourselves," someone said. It was Maara's voice.

One of them started to lay down her sword. Another said, "She can't stop all of us."

I drew the bow and sighted the tip of my arrow on the woman who had spoken. She dropped her sword. The rest let their swords fall. I lowered the bow, keeping the arrow nocked.

"Step back," said Maara. "Stay close together. Tamras, kill anyone standing alone."

The warriors quickly bunched together. When they stepped away from their weapons, Maara collected them. All but one she hurled into the river where it ran swiftest through tumbled rocks. The last she kept. Then she came to stand beside me.

"Go home," she told them.

"We need to make a litter," said one, "to take our friend home."

"Come back for her," said Maara, "or carry her as best you can."

Two of them picked up their fallen comrade and followed the others back the way they had just come. As soon as they were out of sight, Maara drew me off the trail into a stand of trees that gave us a little cover.

"How far behind is the pursuit?" she asked me.

"The pursuit?" I hadn't thought about that.

Maara could see that I wasn't thinking clearly. She took the pack from my shoulders, to carry it herself.

"I can take mine," I told her.

"No time now," she said. She reached out her hand. It took me a moment to understand that she wanted my bow. I gave it to her. "And the quiver." I gave her that too. She turned and walked away from me. I was confused again, until I saw that she meant for me to follow her. Then I knew how tired I was.

After we had traveled for several hours, Maara found a place for us to rest in a thicket on the side of a low hill where we had a clear view to the south, so that we would see anyone coming after us in time to elude them. The moment we stopped, my legs collapsed under me. A litter of dry leaves and twigs barely covered the stony ground, as comfortable to me as a featherbed.

Maara sat down beside me.

"Before you sleep," she said, "tell me what's happened."

How she made any sense of what I told her I don't know, but she seemed satisfied.

"We'll talk more later," she said. "Go to sleep."

I awoke in the dark. Maara's hand was on my shoulder.

"I know you're tired, but it will be safer if we travel at night."

I could just make out the silhouette of the hills against the last of the twilight. The moon was rising. We had the whole night before us.

I started to get up.

"Wait," said Maara. "Eat first." She handed me a piece of bread and a thick slice of meat. "It was good thinking, to bring food with you."

"I never would have thought of it," I told her. "Sparrow did. She made up our packs."

"Sparrow did?"

I nodded.

"You better tell me again what happened in Merin's house."

This time I had my wits about me. I told her what she already knew, that it was Vintel who sent the messenger to Tamar, to lure Maara away from the household. I told her about my conversations with Vintel, about the bargain I had made, about what Vintel had done to Merin, about Sparrow finding me in the armory and helping me escape.

"Why didn't you keep your part of the bargain?" Maara asked me.

It was the last thing I expected her to say. "Because I doubted that Vintel would keep her part of it. Where did you think her warriors were taking you? They certainly weren't taking you to Laris."

"They were taking me to my death," she said, "as they would also have taken you to yours."

That had never once occurred to me. I had been so concerned for Maara that I hadn't spared a moment to wonder what Vintel meant to do with me. Now I saw that by saving Maara's life I had saved my own, and Vintel had once again defeated her own designs. If she had persuaded me to trust her, I might have kept our pact, but her cruelty to Merin destroyed the last shred of trust I might have had in her.

A chill breeze blew, rustling the branches overhead. Clouds drifted across the moon's bright face. I shivered. Maara reached for my cloak and settled it around my shoulders.

"What are we going to do?" I asked her.

"First," she said, "we're going to keep from being caught. The minute Vintel discovered you were gone, she would have sent her people out after you. She can't afford to let you get away from her now. You have too much power to cause her serious trouble."

"Me?" I had never felt so powerless.

"Vintel has done something now that she can't undo. As long as you're alive, you are a witness to her treachery."

"Can we go to Laris?" I asked. "Will she help us, do you think?"

Maara shook her head. "We can't go south now. It's too dangerous. We can't travel through Merin's land. We'd have to go around it, through the mountains, and it's too far on to wintertime to go that way."

"Where can we go then?"

"We have no choice but to go north and find someplace to winter there."

In the north? In stories the north was a place of mystery and danger. Our enemies dwelt there, and other things I knew of from tales meant to frighten children. They frightened me, until I remembered that the north was not unknown to Maara.

We walked all night, keeping away from the well-traveled trails. At first light we made camp in a forest of young trees. The night had been chilly, and now a thick mist rose up around us. Maara chanced making a small fire. Fires were hard to see in daylight as long as they didn't smoke. The little bit of smoke our campfire made hung like the mist, invisible.

We huddled close to the small blaze and had a bite to eat. Maara was preoccupied. She stared into the fire but her eyes looked inward. I watched her as the pale daylight burned through the mist. I wasn't thinking of our situation. I was thinking how beautiful she was.

"If you hadn't come after me," she said at last, "you could have brought your mother back to Merin's house and exposed Vintel's lie."

"What good would that have done? Vintel has a household full of warriors loyal to her."

"It would have been a risk, but I think one worth taking."

"Then let's go back," I said. "When Tamar brings my mother—"

"No." She shook her head. "Don't you understand? The warrior you killed belonged to Vintel, and she will claim her right to take your blood for the blood you spilled. You can't go back now, not until you have the power to challenge Vintel with arms."

My heart fell. "When will that be? I have no warriors to command. I'm not even a warrior yet myself."

"I would dispute you about both those things," she said, "but your situation is much worse now than it might have been."

Was she scolding me? I felt the first touch of anger.

"Are you saying I should have let them kill you?"

"In all honesty, I'm glad that I still have my life, but I hate the price you paid for it."

I would have paid any price, I thought to myself. I couldn't say the words aloud. I didn't know how to speak to her, to tell her what was in my heart, that I could never have made Merin's choice. Of what use to me was my inheritance if keeping it meant losing love.

Maara took the first watch. When she woke me, the mist had burned away, and I caught a glimpse of deep blue sky through the golden canopy of leaves overhead.

I was afraid that if I sat still I would fall asleep, so I reorganized our packs, just to have something to do. Sparrow had thought of everything. She had packed a change of warm clothing for each of us, an awl and several needles, scraps of cloth for mending, bits of thick leather to make new boot soles, firestones, even a copper pot. She must have taken everything of value we owned that was light enough to carry. She had also found my knife, the one Maara gave me. I fastened it to my belt.

There was food enough to last us several weeks if we were careful — dried meat and fruit, barley, oat flour, salt — as well as the packages of herbs I always carried with me. The one thing I regretted was Maara's token, her mother's gift. She had a habit of playing with it when she was thinking, and more than once that morning I'd seen her reach for it.

I was doing up Maara's pack when I discovered, tucked away among her clothing, the thong that Gnith had told me was a binding spell. A love spell, Namet called it. I smiled at Gnith's cunning, but I knew no leather thong had created the feeling that now filled my heart. At best it had only encouraged it to grow, by drawing close to me the one who had been the center of my world from the moment I first saw her.

I wished I could see Maara's face, but it was covered by a fold of her cloak, to keep the daylight out of her eyes. A thought tickled the back of my mind and made me smile. When I looked at it more closely, I nearly laughed out loud. I had lost everything, my home, my family, my friends, my inheritance, my safety, almost my life, and I had never in my life been happier.

57

Outlaws

After another night's travel we were far from Merin's land. No pursuit would find us now. Now we faced new dangers, from strangers and from the weather. So far we had seen no one. It wasn't likely that we would meet other travelers as long as we traveled at night, and during the day Maara kept us well hidden. We'd had good weather too, though the early morning air had a bite that made me shiver.

We had traveled all night through open country until, just before dawn, Maara took us into a forest where we made our camp. Again we took turns watching through the day. I woke, late in the afternoon, to the smell of oat cakes. Maara had a small fire burning, and she had set the cakes to bake on a flat rock. I would have eaten them half-cooked, but she warned me away with her eyes.

"I'm starving," I protested.

"Do you want to walk all night with a stomach ache?"

I laughed. "I don't get stomach aches."

"No?"

"Never."

Maara looked up at me and smiled. Now that we weren't in danger of being caught by Vintel's warriors, worry lines no longer creased her brow, but the dark smudges under eyes blurred with weariness made me anxious for her. She had slept too little because she had let me sleep too long.

"Must we travel tonight?" I asked.

"Are you too tired?"

"No," I told her. "You are."

She sat an arm's length from me across the fire. I reached out and touched her cheek with my fingertips. "You look worn out."

She closed her eyes. "I wish you hadn't reminded me."

"Then let's both sleep through the night and go on in the morning."

She considered the idea for a moment, then nodded. "That would be wise. We have a long way to go, and we'll travel faster by daylight."

In Merin's house we had filled oat cakes with bits of dried fruit and nuts and drizzled honey over them, but none had ever tasted as good to me as those plain, unsweetened cakes roasted by the fire. We washed them down with icy water from a stream. When our hunger was satisfied, Maara built up the small cooking fire into a blaze big enough to ward off the chill of the night air.

"Do you have any idea where we're going?" I asked her.

"If the good weather lasts, I think we can reach a forest I know of," she said. "It marks the boundary between the lands of the northern tribes and the place where I lived before I came to Merin's house. Because it's a boundary, people seldom go there."

"We're going to live in a forest?"

She nodded.

"How will we find enough to eat?"

"We'll hunt and fish and set snares. There are edible roots to dig. And nuts and acorns. Not even the squirrels can carry them all away."

I still had my doubts. "Where will we find shelter in a forest?"

"Where the people sheltered who used to live there."

People who lived in a forest? Those who lived by farming didn't live in forests. There was only one people I knew of who lived in forests. A shiver of excitement went through me.

"The old ones," I whispered.

"The old ones, yes. And people who have nowhere else to go. Outlaws."

"Outlaws?"

Maara heard the fear in my voice. "Yes," she said. She didn't try to hide her smile. "Like us."

"Oh."

Maara was quietly laughing. I didn't see the humor in it. Outlaws were people to be feared. They belonged to no one. No one could take them to task about their misbehavior. They could do anything they pleased.

When I lived at home, we never traveled alone in the wild places, for fear of outlaws. Were we now the people to be feared?

Maara saw that I didn't share her amusement. "Did it never occur to you that it is possible to change places with anyone?"

Her question baffled me.

"With me?" she said.

"You were an outlaw?"

I saw the answer in her eyes.

"And you lived in the forest?"

"Yes, and I could have lived there very well, if I had not been hunted."

She meant to reassure me that we would be able to survive in the forest, but I felt her loneliness and fear as if they were my own, though the danger was long past.

"Hunted?" I said. "Why were you hunted?"

Maara shook her head. "I lived another life then, a life I've almost forgotten."

Was she asking me to allow her to forget? I didn't want her to forget. That life had led to this one, and I wanted to know her as she had been then. I wanted her to give me the gift of her past, so that I would no longer be shut out from any part of her life.

Then I saw that I was jealous — of the time she had spent apart from me, of the people who had shared that time with her, of any time or place or person that had known her in a way I had not.

"I would like to hear about the life you lived then," I told her.

"Someday," she said, "but not tonight. Tonight we need to sleep."

We made a bed of leaves. With her cloak beneath us and mine tucked close around us, I snuggled against her back and listened for her breathing to tell me she was asleep.

I wasn't sleepy. I had too much to think about. In all the time I'd known her, Maara had told me very little of her life before she came to Merin's house. At first I didn't like to trespass on something she kept private. Later, out of habit, I never thought to ask her. Now my curiosity was mixed with the desire to know each hurt she'd ever suffered and to comfort it.

I thought about the things she had told me, about losing her mother and living for years as best she could among people who didn't care for her. Then she had been taken into a household of warriors. Sold or given, she had said. Either way, she had been someone's possession.

How old was she then? How long had she lived there before she came to Merin's house? If that's where she was made a warrior, she must have been there for many years. About that time I knew nothing.

A strange forest at nighttime isn't the best place for clear thinking, and my imagination began to supply images of what that time might have been like for her. My imagination may have been too pessimistic. My heart ached as I thought of all the painful things she must have endured. That she said so little about it was proof enough that it had been a difficult time.

She murmured in her sleep. I stroked her back to quiet her, touching her more tenderly than I had ever touched her, as if I could give her now what she had needed then, as if mine could be the touch she had once longed for, a touch that never came. I wanted to take into my own heart all the pain, the loneliness, the heartache she had known, not to take it from her, but to bear it with her.

My eyes filled with tears. I wiped them away. More fell. I felt her wake.

"What is it?" she murmured.

She sat up and turned to look at me. Although it was too dark for her to see my face, I tried to cover it anyway. Gently she pulled my hands away.

"We're going to be all right," she said. "Don't worry. We'll be fine."

"I know."

"What is it then?"

I had thought to comfort her. Now I was the one in need of comfort.

"Tamras," she said, "I don't know what to do."

She still held my hand. I drew hers to my lips and kissed it.

"Lie down," I said. "Go back to sleep. I'm all right."

I felt her hesitate.

"I wish I'd known you then," I whispered.

"I'm glad you didn't."

"Why?"

"It was a dreadful time," she said. "I wouldn't share that time with some-one I care for."

Someone I care for.

"Will you share it with someone who cares for you?" I asked her.

Her grip on my fingers tightened.

"Yes," she said. "Someday I will."

I woke first, still wrapped around her, my face against her back, as we had fallen asleep the night before. I kept myself from moving, so that I wouldn't awaken her. Half an hour went by, but when she woke, it was still too soon.

That day we traveled through the hill country to the northeast of Merin's house. We were approaching the wilderness, where we had traveled with Vintel's band. Although we would find no cover there, by now that country would be deserted. The northerners had gone home.

The day was cold. Late in the afternoon the cloudy sky scattered a few snowflakes around us. As the daylight faded, Maara took us deeper into the woods and built a shelter of pine boughs, just big enough for the two of us to lie down in, with a thick bed of pine needles to keep us from the cold ground. She lit a fire in the doorway, so close I was afraid she would burn the shelter down, but the heat found its way inside without the fire doing any harm. A few snowflakes drifted through the trees and dusted the ground around us, while we stayed warm and dry.

After we had eaten, I reminded Maara of her promise to tell me the story of her past. We had been sitting side by side in the tiny shelter. Now I lay down and leaned up on one elbow so that I could see her face.

She peered at me in the dim light. "Why do you want to know these things?"

I had no answer for her. That I loved her she knew without my saying so, but the love that wanted all her secrets, of that love she knew nothing. I would have told her of it then if I'd known how. I could not have found a better way to reveal myself than to ask her to share her pain with me.

"I want to know," was all I said.

Maara sighed. I knew she was reluctant, but I was patient, and at last she settled herself and gazed into the fire, as she had seen me do a hundred times when I was about to tell a story.

"You know all I know of my early childhood already," she said. "I don't remember much of it, although I used to. When I lay down to sleep at night, I called back the memory of my mother's house. I lay in the dark and imagined my home all around me. It was both a comfort and a hope. I believed that as long as I remembered, someday it would become real again, and I would wake one morning in my own bed.

"When I grew older, I came to understand that my home was gone forever. Then the memories became too painful, and I made myself forget.

Now those memories are only shadows. I don't know if they're real or if I made them up."

She laid a few twigs on the fire. She said no more.

"Do you remember the villages where you lived after you were captured?" I asked her.

She shook her head. "I had nothing to remember by. Your people are always telling stories. That's how you remember. You tell one another the stories of your lives, but I had no one to tell. All I remember is that there were times when I had enough to eat and a warm place to sleep, and there were times when I had neither."

My heart was beginning to hurt. "How long did you have to live like that?"

"I don't know. Nothing measured out that time for me. Every day was the same as any other."

"But you were taken into a warrior household. Surely you must remember that. How old were you then?"

She shrugged.

"Had you begun to bleed?"

"No," she said. "That happened afterwards. I remember, because one of the servants there showed me what to do."

If she had been taken into that household when she was still a child, I thought, it could not have been with the intention of making her a warrior.

"Why did they take you in, when you were still so young?"

She smiled. "I knew something about the working of metal."

"You did?" I was impressed. A smith's skill was precious, and smiths were notorious for keeping their secrets to themselves. "Who taught you?"

"No one taught me," she said. "I watched. There was a smith who needed someone to work the bellows and fetch charcoal for the forge. He thought I was stupid, no more intelligent than an animal. I never gave him reason to think differently. I never spoke. I never gave a sign that I understood more than a few simple words, but I watched everything he did.

"While he was away, I practiced what I had seen him do. One day a young woman came in and caught me at it. She was looking for the smith, and when he came home, she sat with him in his house and spoke with him for a long time.

"When she came out, she made signs to me to come with her. I refused to obey her until the smith came out and chased me away. I thought he was

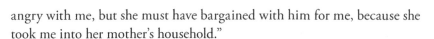

angry with me, but she must have bargained with him for me, because she took me into her mother's household."

"What did you do there?"

"A little of everything. When I could, I worked with their smith. It spared me from doing kitchen work or being someone's personal servant."

"Did they treat you well?"

"Very well," she said. "They fed me, every day, almost more than I could eat. I slept indoors. They gave me clothing, shoes, everything I needed."

"But you were still a servant."

Maara met my eyes. "I may have been a servant, or I may have been a slave. It made no difference, because my life was so much better there than it had been before. I was grateful to be there at all, and to be useful."

"Did you have friends there?"

"Friends." She gazed into the fire, considering her answer. "I suppose so. There was a group of us, all about the same age. We slept together, ate together, worked together."

"But was there no one special, no one who cared for you more than for the others?"

She turned her face away from me. "No."

"No one you cared for?"

She didn't answer me. I had blundered into a painful place, and I tried to think of something to ask her that might not hurt so much.

"Who apprenticed you?" I said. "How did you become a warrior?"

"No one apprenticed me. The girl who took me from the smith was the daughter of the house. She was an apprentice herself then. When she became a warrior, she took me to be one of her companions."

"Not her apprentice?"

Maara shook her head.

"Then how did you become a warrior?"

She smiled at me. "Tell me, am I a warrior now?"

"Of course."

"Then at some time I must have become one, apprenticed or not."

"But someone must have taught you. Surely they didn't send you into battle untrained."

"Even slaves were taught the use of arms," she said. "When the daughter of the house went into battle, it was my duty to protect her. For that I was trained."

"What was her name?"

"Elen."

I felt a twinge of jealousy. I looked away from Maara, out into the forest where, beyond the circle of firelight, darkness gathered.

"What?" said Maara.

I answered her honestly. "I'm jealous of Elen."

"Why?" she asked, surprised.

"Because she knew you then. I wish I'd known you then."

"Why?" she said, more softly.

"Because I would have loved you."

She made no sound. Had she heard me? I turned to look at her. She had been playing with a sprig of pine, rubbing the needles between her fingers to release their scent into the air. Now her hands were still. Her expression was unreadable. Not surprise, not gladness. More than anything, I thought she looked wistful, like a starving person gazing at a fairy banquet spread out before her in the grass, seeing there her heart's desire and knowing it will vanish the moment she reaches for it.

I would not vanish.

I sat up. Still she didn't speak. It was her eyes that questioned me.

My love for her filled my heart. Everything was there all at once—the sweet warmth of tenderness, the ache of longing, a joy that bubbled up inside me and made me want to laugh, a piercing pain that brought tears into my eyes, and a deep glow that would, with the slightest breath, burst into the flame of desire.

Some hearts break from love, Namet said. Mine was about to break.

"Why?" Maara whispered.

The world was silent, waiting for my answer.

"I don't know why," I told her. "I don't think love ever asks the question."

The last flame of our campfire flickered out. The glowing bed of coals warmed us but gave little light. Her face was in shadow, and I couldn't see her eyes. I began to wonder if I had been mistaken, if I had misunderstood her, if the kind of love I'd offered her wasn't what she wanted.

"Are you glad," I asked, "or sorry?"

I waited a long time for her answer. As if my life were hanging in the balance, my heart held its breath.

"Both," she said at last.

It was the one answer I had not expected.

"I don't understand," I said. "What does that mean?"

Too dark. Too dark to look for her heart in her eyes.

"I don't know how to say these things," she said.

I waited for her. Perhaps she could say them in the dark.

"No one taught me about love," said Maara. "It comes to me like a visitor. It sits like a guest at my fire for a little while, but it never stays."

"Am I guest? Am I a visitor?"

I felt for her hand. When I found it, I took it between both of mine and held it tight.

"I'll give you all I can," she said. Her fingers entwined themselves with mine. "I'll teach you what I know. I'll fight for you. I'll fight beside you. I would give my life for you, but I don't know if I can give you what you want."

"What I want? What do you think I want?"

She didn't answer.

"Beloved," I said, "my heart is full to bursting with things it doesn't understand. If they stay there, locked away, they'll die there, or they'll break my heart to pieces trying to get out. All I want is for you to want those things. Touch the door. One touch from you and it will spring open."

She pulled her hand from between my hands and left them empty. What had I done wrong? Tears stung my eyes, and for a moment I glimpsed the future, a life as barren as the wilderness through which we soon must pass. Then I felt her fingers touch my breast, over my heart.

The world turned on that touch. I felt my heart break open, and a brilliant light spilled out of it. As blinding as the darkness, the light surrounded us. I had to close my eyes against it, but I felt it on my skin, as warm as sunshine.

I covered Maara's hand with mine and held it there. She was the one familiar thing in this strange world where I now found myself. I laid my head on her shoulder. Her breath warmed my cheek. She was real. She would not vanish. The light faded. I opened my eyes.

"Sleep in my arms tonight," I whispered.

I lay down and waited for her. She found my cloak and with a mother's tenderness tucked it around me. Then she lay down and took me into her arms. For a long time we held each other, until we could resist sleep no longer. While snow fell all around us, I dreamed of summertime.

58

WILDERNESS

When I woke, Maara's arms tightened around me. I hid my face in the rough wool of her tunic and slipped my arm around her waist, wishing I could drift for another hour on the edge of sleep, forgetful of everything but that I was in her arms.

She moved a little, as if she had lain too long in one position.

"How long have you been awake?" I asked her.

"A while," she said.

I opened my eyes. Bright daylight glanced off the snow outside and spilled into our shelter. It was past time we should have been on our way.

"Why didn't you wake me up?"

In a voice soft with sleep, she said, "I didn't want to let go."

Sweet words. My head lay in the hollow of her shoulder. I pulled aside the collar of her tunic and kissed her, just above the collarbone.

"I don't want to let go either," I said, "but we have a long way to go today."

"Yes."

Still, neither of us moved.

"I wish we were home," I whispered, "lying in a warm bed."

"With Namet about to come in to wish me good morning."

I chuckled. "I think Namet would understand."

Then I thought about where we were and why, and I wondered if Maara would ever see Namet again.

Maara must have been thinking the same thing.

"I miss her," she whispered.

"I made a promise I intend to keep. I promised your mother I would bring you back to her."

"You did?"

"I did," I told her. "And I will."

Maara sighed. "I hope it's possible."

"We have a home to return to. We both have family there. We can't be outlaws all our lives. In the springtime, we'll go back."

Maara pulled away and looked at me. "Is that what you want?"

"What else can we do?"

She rolled over onto her back and gazed up at the roof of pine boughs that sheltered us. "I hadn't thought that far ahead. Anything could happen to us between now and then."

"Just as anything could happen in Merin's house between now and then."

She met my eyes. "That's true," she said.

I may have meant to say something more, but her gaze distracted me. In her eyes I saw a look I had never seen before, a soft look that caught at my heart. I touched her cheek with the backs of my fingers.

I would have kissed her if I hadn't heard a noise outside. Maara heard it too, the crunching sound of footsteps in the snow. She listened for a moment, then gestured to me to stay where I was. She sat up and peered out the doorway of the shelter. I tried to see past her, but her body blocked my view. She turned and pointed at my bow. I had already reached for it. I had just room enough in the tiny shelter to string it. Then I handed it to her, and an arrow with it.

Maara nocked the arrow and sat very still. After a long silence I heard another cautious footstep. A pause. Two more. Maara drew the bow and let the arrow fly. Something ran crashing through the thicket. Maara leaped after it, and I scrambled after her. We followed the crisp tracks of cloven hooves until, not far away, we found the body of the deer.

Maara handed me the bow. "Do you have your knife?"

I had left it in the shelter. I ran back to fetch it, and she gutted the deer where it lay and carried it back to our campsite. She set me to skinning it while she built a fire. Then she cooked some of the deer's liver, the first fresh food we'd had in days.

After we had eaten, Maara scraped and trimmed the hide while I cut some hazel wands and made a frame to stretch it on. We set it by the fire, where the heat would dry it and the smoke would help preserve it. Then we began cutting up the meat.

We had always worked well together. By now we were so used to each other that we were able to anticipate almost every move the other made. Vintel had taken Maara's knife, so we shared mine, and she would often reach for it at the same moment I held it out to her. That morning I took pleasure in the harmony between us, surprised that until then I had taken it for granted.

It was midday before we were ready to travel. The meat added considerable weight to our packs, a weight we were glad to bear. The deer would feed us for many days.

In spite of our late start we covered a lot of ground that day. The snow was no more than ankle deep, and the trail we followed wound gently downhill. Soon we would leave the hill country behind. As always we spoke little, keeping our attention on our surroundings, but the memory of what had passed between us the night before tempted my thoughts away from the world around us. For most of that day I walked as through a mist that hid everything but the woman who walked beside me.

By late afternoon we were in the wilderness. It was a very different place than I remembered. No animals scurried in the bracken. They snuggled in their burrows now, lost in winter sleep. Snow had not fallen here, but the air was cold, and the north wind cut through our clothing.

Darkness fell before we found a sheltered place to camp. Maara built a fire by a rocky outcrop that blocked the wind and reflected the fire's heat back to us. Although there were few trees here, I managed to gather enough deadfall to feed our fire through the night. Then I cut soft heather for our bed and laid it out between the fire and the rock.

We made a good meal of venison and oat cakes. While we ate, we talked a little, of the country we had passed through that day, of where we would be traveling tomorrow, of the weather. While we talked together as we always did, I found myself listening for something else, although I couldn't have told either Maara or myself what I was waiting for.

After supper Maara cut more strips of venison and hung them over the fire to smoke. Then she looked around her for a moment, as if she had forgotten what she meant to do, before she reached for the deerskin. She began to work on it, to make it supple.

I could have found some work to do. Instead I sat and watched her. The fire lit her hands and face as she leaned close to it. As I watched, it seemed that she grew smaller, as if she were moving away from me. I rubbed my eyes, and the world looked right to me again, but fear sent prickles down my spine.

Fear of what? Nothing was amiss. We sat across the fire from each other as we did every night. This night was no different.

But it should have been.

I began to doubt myself. Had I misunderstood or misremembered? Had I indulged in wishful thinking? What had happened between us the night before? When I asked her to share her past with me, I hadn't intended to reveal myself, but in spite of my intentions, my love had sprung out at her like a lion springing at its prey. I was surprised I hadn't frightened her to death. Then I remembered waking in her arms, the look she'd given me. Although I may indeed have frightened her, I knew my love for her was not unwelcome.

While I watched her hands, my own were tightly clasped together. They were trying not to reach for her. Last night my heart ached with unspoken love. Tonight it burned in the palms of my hands.

"Must we waste this time apart?" I whispered.

She looked up at me, on her face a look of confusion mixed with shy delight. She had been waiting for me. I stood up and went to sit beside her. The deerskin lay in her lap. Her hands were still. I took both of them in mine.

"I need to touch you," I said.

Now that I was close to her, I longed to close even the small distance that remained between us. I leaned toward her and laid my head on her shoulder.

"I need your arms around me," I said.

She opened her arms to me, and I settled into her embrace. At first stiff and awkward, her body soon relaxed and welcomed me. Beside my ear her heart beat, strong and steady.

"What do you need from me?" I asked her. I gave her time to answer.

"I hardly know," she said at last.

"This?"

She held me closer. "Yes."

"What else?"

No answer.

"When you think of something, will you ask me?"

Her heart beat a little faster. "If I can."

"Of course you can. Why not?"

The rhythm of her heartbeat changed, became uncertain. "I wish I could speak as you do."

"Why? What did I say?"

"Beloved," she whispered. "That word has been in my ears all day."

Now I was the one who had no words. What a gift it was that she would tell me such an intimate thing.

"You are eloquent," I told her.

Her lips touched my brow. I felt her smile. I closed my eyes and took a deep breath against the fullness in my chest. Beloved, I had said, and now she had said it back to me, not as an endearment, but as a revelation. Her words lit a flame that filled my heart with light. Warm and golden, it flowed between us, between her heart and mine. It drew my arms around her, stopped my words, my thoughts, so that for a time I felt as if we had stepped out of this world altogether. Then my heart began to ache, and I remembered Namet's words. *Hearts break because they are too small to contain the gifts life gives us.* My heart felt much too small. Perhaps both our hearts together might be able to contain this gift.

"Come to bed," I whispered.

When she let go of me, I caught both her hands in mine and kissed each one. Then I took her cloak from around her shoulders and spread it over the soft bed I had made for her. The fire's heat had warmed the rock, and our bed lay close against it. Although I could hear the wind moaning through this empty land, I didn't feel it here. In the shelter of the rock the air was still.

Maara lay down. The fragrance of the heather rose up around us. When I lay down beside her, she reached for me. I resisted the temptation to fall into her arms. The palms of my hands still ached with the need to touch her.

"Not yet," I said. "Turn over."

She gave me a puzzled look, but she turned over and pillowed her head on her arms. I leaned up on one elbow and brushed her hair back, so that I could see her face. My fingers caught in the tangles.

"I don't suppose Sparrow thought to pack a comb," I said.

As gently as I could, I began to finger-comb her hair.

Maara smiled. "Perhaps we shouldn't make ourselves too presentable. If we chance to meet someone, they might mistake us for trolls or goblins and run the other way."

"They would mistake us for forest wights, more likely," I replied, as I picked bits of leaf and twig out of her hair.

"What are forest wights?"

"You've never heard of forest wights?"

"No," she said.

"Well, they're a bit like fairies, except they're only found in forests, of course."

"Where are fairies found?"

"The fairy folk live underground."

"They live in burrows?"

I laughed. "They live in the hollow hills, in vast caverns lit by a thousand lamps, where feasting and merrymaking go on for days on end."

"Do they never come out?"

"Only at night," I said. "They come out to dance in the meadows under the moon, but they seldom stay past daybreak." I had the worst of the tangles out of her hair now, and I began to run my fingers through it, to get it all going in one direction. "Did no one ever tell you about the fairy folk?"

"Will you tell me?"

I tried to remember the stories I had heard about fairies. One came to mind, but I wanted to go over it, to make sure I had it all by heart.

"I'll tell you about the fairy folk tomorrow," I replied. "Now it's time to sleep."

I slipped my hand under her tunic and began to rub her back. She still wore the old sleeping shirt that she'd had on when she left Merin's house. It was soft with wear, warm with the warmth of her body, and so thin that through it I could feel the texture of her skin.

With my fingertips I kneaded the muscles along her spine. As she relaxed, her breathing slowed, and I began to touch her with my open hand, making slow circles across her shoulders, across the small of her back. Her eyes closed, and my touch became a caress, meant to give her pleasure without arousing desire. Her breathing deepened. Soon she was asleep.

"Beloved," I whispered, into her dreams.

59

A Fairy Tale

The cold woke me. I shivered and snuggled closer to Maara's warmth. She put her arms around me.

"The fire's out," she said.

"Did we burn all the wood already?"

"No, there's plenty of wood. The rain put it out."

"Rain?"

Then I noticed the soft sound of rain falling all around us. Sheltered by the rock, we were still dry, but water was beginning to run in rivulets down the rock face.

"It's almost morning," said Maara. "We might as well be on our way."

It rained all day. Cold droplets ran down my brow, dripped off my nose, found their way under the hood of my cloak and trickled down my neck. I wondered how it was possible to be so happy and so miserable all at once.

We didn't stop to rest, not even to eat. As we walked, we nibbled on stale oat cakes and smoked venison. By late afternoon, I was beginning to feel the cold, and I worried that we wouldn't find a place to shelter from the rain in this open country. While spending a damp night out in the open wouldn't kill us, I wasn't looking forward to shivering through a sleepless night.

When it began to grow dark, Maara looked for a hillock that might serve as a vantage point. We scrambled up the nearest one, and from its top we had a view of the surrounding country.

Through veils of rain and mist, it all looked the same to me, but Maara peered intently into the distance, as if she knew what she was looking for.

We were exposed to the wind here, and now that I was standing still I began to shiver. I moved close against Maara's side for warmth. When she felt me touch her, she put her arm around my shoulders and drew me closer. The gesture took me by surprise, and the sudden rush of pleasure it gave me drove everything else out of my head.

"Look there," said Maara. She pointed at something in the distance.

"What is it?" I couldn't see a thing.

"It can't be above half a mile," she said.

I thought I saw what she was pointing at, a dark smudge against the lighter grey of fern and heather. It could have been anything.

"Come on," she said.

As we approached it, the smudge became first a jumble of stones, then the ruins of a cottage. I didn't stop to wonder who could have built a stone cottage in such a lonely place. However it had come to be there, I was delighted to see it.

The walls were tumbling down and part of the roof had caved in. Fallen timbers blocked the doorway. We squeezed through a gap in the wall and stumbled through the wreckage until we found a corner where the roof only leaked a little and we were sheltered from the wind.

While Maara used some of the old thatch to start a fire, I pulled from the rubble a few timbers still sound enough to burn. Soon our little corner was surprisingly warm, so warm that we took off our damp cloaks and tunics and hung them up to dry.

Maara filled our copper pot with water and set it on the fire. When the water began to boil, she dropped chunks of meat into it, along with a handful of barley and some wild onions we had dug several days before. I added a pinch of herbs for flavor.

"Are there any oat cakes left?" I asked.

I was ravenous, and the stew would take some time to cook.

Maara shook her head. "Don't spoil your appetite. We need a good hot meal tonight."

I resigned myself to wait, staring glumly into the stew pot as if watching it would speed the cooking. I could feel Maara's eyes on me. I didn't need to look at her to know that if I did, I would see laughter in them.

After a few minutes she stood up and came to sit behind me, and as I had done for her the night before, she began to finger-comb my hair. Her touch made me forget my hunger. When she had the tangles out, she ran her fingers through it rather longer than she needed to. I closed my eyes while pleasure rippled over the surface of my skin, until even my toes and fingers tingled with it.

At last Maara stopped and moved away a bit, so that she could lean back against the wall of the cottage. She tugged at my shirt, and when I too moved back, she slipped her arm around my waist and pulled me close, until I was sitting between her outstretched legs, leaning back against her body, with her arms around me.

"Is this all right?" she asked me.

I nodded, breathless with surprise and pleasure.

"It won't be long," she said.

"What?"

"Supper."

"Oh."

"In the meantime," she said, "you could tell me a story."

In ancient days, the fairy folk were not, as they are now, estranged from humankind. It was not uncommon then for mortal children to see the fairies dancing in a field as they passed by. Even older folk, attending to their work, might look up and catch a glimpse of them, and some, returning home past the time they were expected, might give as their excuse that they had been invited to a fairy banquet and dared not refuse.

Still, in the ordinary course of things, the two peoples had little to do with one another. While humankind tilled their fields and tended their flocks, the fairy folk lived in the wild places, nourished by the Mother's bounty. She satisfied their thirst with water from her springs that sparkled like gemstones and gladdened the heart like wine. She provided for them food of every kind. Forest and meadow bore fruit for them, and the animals came to offer themselves, the forest deer, the trout and salmon, birds and their eggs, each in its season. For the fairy folk, each day was a day of ease, and the nights were given to music and the dance.

There was in those days a queen of the fairy folk whose heart chose a mortal man. Such things were not unheard of then. The hearts of fairies love as do the hearts of humankind, although their bodies neither join together nor bring forth new life, but for those who take a mortal lover, joy is brief, while grief is long, for mortal men must die, while the fairy folk do not.

For many years, years that for the fairies seemed to pass as swiftly as a summer afternoon, the fairy queen and her beloved lived together as one soul, but as it must happen, one day time overtook him, and he died.

Deeply the fairy queen mourned him, and no one could comfort her, for none of her own people understood her grief. The fairies' life of ease and pleasure went on unchanged, while her own happiness was now lost forever.

At last the fairy queen could bear her grief no longer. She left her home and wandered out into the wider world, where her path soon crossed that of an old woman, who knew her at once for a queen of the fairy folk.

"You are far from your home under the hill, o queen of fairies," the old woman said. "What brings you out among humankind?"

"Grief," the fairy queen replied. "I loved a mortal man, and he died."

"Ah," the old woman said. "I too loved a mortal man. He died, and has been dead these many years."

"How do you bear your grief?" the fairy queen asked her, and the old woman answered, "I found my grief impossible to bear until I remembered that I too will die, and when I do, my grief will end. Anything can be borne if one can see an end to it."

The fairy queen could not hope for death to release her. "Is there no other remedy for grief?" she asked.

"Perhaps there is," the old woman said. "If you would try it, come with me."

The old woman led the fairy queen to a cottage in a meadow a little distance from a village. By the window was a chair, and the old woman bade the fairy queen sit down. Then she took her own cloak from around her shoulders and laid it upon the shoulders of the fairy queen. She drew the hood over the fairy queen's golden hair, until all that could be seen of her was her lovely, ageless face and her shining, golden eyes.

"Stay and watch," said the old woman as she left her, "and learn that all bright things cast a shadow."

It was then high summer. The village children came to bathe in the stream that ran through the meadow. Their laughter reminded the fairy queen of the laughter that echoed through her own great hall. Farmers too passed by her cottage on their way to till their fields, and she heard them singing at their work. All around her in the meadow, birds taught their fledglings how to fly, squirrels gathered seeds and acorns, flowers bloomed and died. Then came the harvest, and the farmers sang new songs as they carried the sheaves home to the threshing floor.

The heart of the fairy queen grew sad when she saw the bright summer days begin to fade, but soon she was enchanted by the golden light of autumn, the bright colors of the trees, frost on the meadow. Leaves of red and gold rained down, and the children came again, to play in the fallen leaves.

One morning the fairy queen awoke to silence. She looked outside and saw the whole world white with snow. She who had never seen the winter wondered that anything still lived in that dark and silent world. The nights were longer than any she had ever known. The days were cold. Few of the villagers ventured out. She sometimes heard the children playing, although their mothers kept them close to home. Every day she watched at the window, and it seemed to her that nothing changed but the lacy patterns of the shadows of bare trees against the snow.

As the world slept, so too did the fairy queen fall into a sleep in which she dreamed back the past. When she awakened, she cried bitter tears for all that she had lost, until the fragrance of apple blossom and new grass drew her to the window, to look out at the springtime.

The meadow bloomed with crocuses and bluebells. Children came to pick the flowers. The farmers went out to sow their fields. A doe came to the stream to drink, her fawn beside her, and a young mother sat down in a patch of sunlight and bared her breast to nurse her child.

For the first time since she entered it, the fairy queen left the cottage. She breathed deep the air of springtime and sat down on her front step. All bright things cast a shadow, the old woman had said, and the fairy queen whispered to herself, the shadow too is beautiful. She was content, and those who passed by saw only an old woman sitting in the sunshine before her cottage door.

Winter's early dark had fallen. Inside the ruined cottage we were snug and safe. Both of us were in our shirtsleeves, and against my back I felt the warmth of Maara's body, the rise and fall of her breathing. Her arms held me as if nothing would persuade her to let me go. It was a long time before either of us spoke.

"Don't die," she said at last, and a tremor went through her body, as if a cold wind had blown through her bones.

I didn't know how to answer her. If she had been someone else, I might have made a joke of it, but I couldn't speak lightly of my own death to Maara, because she loved me.

"Supper's ready," she said.

We ate in silence, sitting side by side. Although I couldn't see her face, I felt her discontent. When we finished, she set the empty pot aside and sat staring into the fire. I waited for her to talk to me, but I didn't question her. I knew from experience that she would think about a story that puzzled her, sometimes for days, before asking me about it.

I smiled, remembering the question I had asked when I first heard that story. "Are the fairies real?" I asked my mother, and she replied, "Of course they are. As real as moonbeams."

"How did the fairy queen overcome her grief?" said Maara.

I thought for a minute before I said, "I think she learned to accept it."

"I can't." I heard in Maara's voice both desperation and defiance. I wondered if the story had taken her into the past and made her feel again some loss long forgotten, until she said, "I would like to keep this for a while."

Though my heart was glad to hear it, her words cast a dark shadow. It was the shadow of her own grief, which even now intruded on our happiness, as if loss always follows closely on the heels of love.

"For as long as I'm living, this is yours," I told her, "and I intend to live for a very long time."

She turned to me and smiled. "I believe you will."

My heart heard what she had left unsaid, that she believed she would not, or that something else would separate us.

I took her hand. "I don't intend to grow old without you."

Maara looked down at her hand in mine. She seemed puzzled, as if she wasn't quite sure what I wanted with it. Then she opened my fingers and brushed her fingertips across the palm of my hand. Her touch sent a shiver of pleasure through my body. My hand would have answered her in kind, but she let it go.

Before I could reach for her again, Maara stood up.

"I think these are dry," she said.

She took our cloaks down from where they hung and looked about her for the driest place to make our bed.

I needed to use the privy.

"I'll be right back," I said.

She nodded. "Don't go far."

The rain had stopped, and the moon was just rising. Its light, caught in the mist, hung around the cottage like a veil. I shivered a little in the cold air, although I found it pleasant after the stuffy warmth indoors. I took care not to stray too far from the cottage to relieve myself. The mist was treacherous.

Before I went back inside, I stood for a while by the tumbled wall. I wanted a few minutes to myself, to think about Maara and about the story I had told her. I had always accepted without question the lesson it taught, that things are as they are and as they should be, and that there is beauty in all of life, both the bright and the dark. But Maara had taken another lesson from it. Though I couldn't put it into words, acceptance of life as it is certainly had no part in it.

Suddenly Maara was behind me. Before I could turn around, she rested her hands lightly on my shoulders.

"I was worried," she said. She was so close to me that her breath tickled the back of my neck. I shivered.

"You're cold," she said.

I was a little, though the shiver that went through my body had nothing to do with the weather. As if to warm me, Maara's hands caressed my shoulders, and her touch did warm me, but it was desire that kept me from the cold. I wondered if she had intended to provoke it. Then she turned me around to face her. In the misty moonlight, her face seemed lit from within. I saw her desire in her eyes. I felt it in her touch. Her fingers brushed my cheek, but they didn't have to lift my mouth to hers. We met in an embrace that shattered the last barrier between us.

Her first kiss was fierce. After the shock of it, I felt her draw back. I waited for her, and she returned to me, more gently this time. Her kiss was a caress, but it tasted bittersweet. She tried to make me understand. Her meaning slipped into the darkest places in my heart and showed me my own fear. I clung to her, as if she could be my shield against it. It would be a long time before I understood that fear is only the dark face of love.

It was too late to go back, too late to undo the bonds I had made to hold her, when I knit my life to hers. Those bonds held me as well. Now I had no choice but to go forward. I might have locked my fear away in some dark corner of my heart, and by doing so I would have locked her out of it. Instead I forced the door and let her in. She met me there. She understood. Love turned again and showed me her bright face. We stood on the threshold of our cottage and kissed each other as if this were a homecoming.

She drew back and took my hand. "Come inside," she said.

We ducked through a ragged hole in the fallen thatch and picked our way through the ruins. This time our fire lit the way. She had already made our bed. I sat down, expecting her to join me, but first she knelt to build up the fire into a bright blaze.

I was impatient. "It's warm enough," I said.

She smiled at me. "I want the light."

Thinking she wanted to see my body, I loosened the ties of my shirt and began to pull it off over my head.

"Don't," she said. "You'll be too cold."

She came to the bed and sat down beside me. It was my face she wanted to see. With a touch of her fingertips on my cheek, she turned me to the light. I searched her eyes to discover her intentions. My desire for her had coiled into a tight knot in my belly. I thought that her desire might have faded, until she touched me. Her fingers trembled with it as they caressed my face. When her thumb brushed my lips, my own desire made me tremble, and the knot in my belly began to loosen. I closed my eyes. Her lips touched mine, but before I could return her kiss, they moved away. It was just enough. She wanted what I wanted. I smiled.

"What?" she whispered.

I opened my eyes. "What do you need from me?" I asked her.

"Lie down," she said.

I obeyed her, and she lay down beside me, taking care not to shield me from the light. She leaned up on one elbow and looked down at me, brushed my hair away from my face, let her fingertips drift over my brow and across my cheek. Her eyes moved from my face to the ties of my shirt, as her fingers loosened them a little more. She bent and kissed the exposed skin between my breasts. Then she laid her head down over my heart and was still.

For several minutes she lay like that, lost in her own dream, gone where I couldn't follow. I tangled my fingers in her hair, to bring her back to me. Her warm hand rested on my stomach, just above my belt, and under it the blood began to beat stronger in my belly. Surely she could feel it. She slipped her hand under my shirt, to caress the tender skin beneath my breast.

I had never felt a more intimate touch, because it was she who touched me.

She stretched her body out beside me and laid her head down next to mine. When I turned to her, she put her arms around me. With one arm she held me close, while her other hand caressed the bare skin of my back.

I lost myself for a time in the pleasure of her touch, but soon I understood that giving pleasure wasn't her intention. She touched me as if she had set herself the task of learning my body's secrets, not to find what gave me pleasure, but to discover things I might wish to conceal, to explore my boundaries and my defenses.

Perhaps she felt me hesitate, because her hold on my body loosened, and she drew away from me. Then I was glad for the firelight. In her face I saw a tenderness that reassured me. Whatever her intentions, she was the woman I knew and trusted.

Her thumb circled the orbit of my eye, pressed the skin below it, feeling for the bone beneath, traced the outline of my mouth, the line of my jaw, touching me more with curiosity than with desire. Again she slipped her hand under my shirt, to caress my belly and my breasts. Sometimes a certain touch would draw a response from me — a sound, a change of breath, a movement of my body against hers — and she would return there, again and again.

I knew what she was doing. Each touch was a question. She was asking me what I would give and what I would withhold, what I would reveal, what I would hide. I had told her that I loved her. Perhaps she was unsure of what I meant, and now she was asking me the questions she couldn't frame in words. How much of myself would I give her? How much was hers?

I hid nothing from her. I had no wish to. And if she believed that only I revealed myself in that exchange, she was mistaken. Her every touch revealed her. Each one told me that she doubted me, doubted herself, doubted her own perceptions, that she needed to see, again and again, what I could have told her in a word, if she would have believed me.

But if this was how she chose to question me, I was glad to answer her. The pleasure of her touch on my skin gave way to a deeper pleasure. She had explored the boundaries, and now she easily slipped past them, to take my heart into her hand and teach it to beat to the rhythm of her own heart. When her lips touched mine, they made me tell her all my secrets, in a language more ancient, more eloquent, than speech.

She undid my belt and loosened the waistband of my trousers, slipped her hand inside them and began to touch me. Her fingers opened me, explored me, caressed me, and this time her intent was to give me what I wanted. I hid my face against her shoulder, inhaled the sweet fragrance of her skin, listened to her breathing quicken with mine. She was as gentle as I wanted her to be.

If she could have held me in that place forever, I would have been content to stay there. The purest pleasure flowed from the secret place between my legs over the surface of my skin and through my blood and bones. The taste of it lay on my tongue. The sweetness of it filled my heart. It was enough. It needed nothing more, it had no destination, but it was more than my body could contain. It burst through my skin, ran through me like fire, burned itself to ash, and left me breathless in her arms.

I needed her arms around me then. I needed her to gather me up and hold me, until all the scattered parts of me came back together. She understood, and she stayed with me. She pulled me into a tight embrace and soothed me with whispered words I didn't understand and with a touch so tender it made me want to weep. I felt as if I were returning to her after a long journey, yet she had been with me all the time.

I became aware of her in a way I hadn't been before. Against my body hers was soft and yielding. I felt the heat of her skin even through her clothing. I turned my head to kiss her, and my lips touched the base of her throat. Her desire still beat there. My hand found her breast, and her body responded to my touch, but she took my hand in hers to stop me.

"The fire," she whispered.

I hadn't noticed that the fire had burned down to a bed of glowing coals. I almost let her go, but when she began to leave me, I felt a sudden shock of fear, as if something precious that had been within my grasp was about to slip away.

"Leave it," I said. I tangled my fingers in her shirt front.

For a moment I thought she would resist me. Before she could make up her mind to free herself, I pushed her gently onto her back and lay half on top of her. She lay still, although she could easily have moved me aside. Even if her body did not resist me, her heart was already searching for a hiding place.

"Don't," I whispered.

"What?"

"Don't leave me."

"I'm right here."

I leaned up on my elbow and looked down at her. Even in the dim light, I saw her confusion in her eyes. She didn't know what she was doing.

"Do you want me?" I asked her.

When she opened her mouth to reply, her lower lip trembled. She said nothing, but she had answered me. I took her lower lip between my lips and loved it, because it had trembled, because it had given her away. She returned my kiss. Her lips were full and soft, and they caressed mine with tenderness and longing.

I closed my eyes and let my mouth explore her, and although I didn't think about it at the time, I questioned her as she had questioned me. I had never listened as intently as I listened to that wordless conversation. Again and again I asked her permission. May I? Here? And here? Is this too much? Too little? Can you hear me? This is my heart.

She made a sound deep in her throat, and her body moved under me. I slipped my leg between hers. Then her arms were around me, holding my body tight against her, as her hips rose and she pressed herself against my thigh. I was afraid she would satisfy the desire of her body before I found her heart. It was her heart I wanted.

"No," I whispered.

She stopped. Her body stiffened, and she let go of me. I thought she might push me away, but she didn't move. She waited.

"Let me touch you," I said.

I didn't wait for her answer. I undid her trousers and opened them, slipping them down as far as I could, to expose the soft skin of her belly. I slid down to kiss her there. She recoiled a little, more from surprise, I think, than from displeasure. I laid my cheek against that tender place. Just beneath the softness of her skin, the muscles tightened, as if to shield her. I gave her a little time to grow used to my touch before I began to kiss her again.

Slowly she relaxed, and the way she moved told me that my kisses gave her pleasure. I slipped her trousers down a little more, until I could see the dark curls between her legs. I brushed my fingertips across them. I longed to touch her more intimately, but I knew it was too soon. I pushed her shirt up and laid my head down on her breast. Her skin was hot against my cheek. I cupped her breast in my hand and held it, stroking it gently with my fingertips for a little while before taking her nipple into my mouth.

She responded differently to each new touch. She was easily surprised. I learned to wait for her body to catch up with me. Touching her gave me so much pleasure that I might have become impatient, but this was for her pleasure. I listened to her body, not my own, and although her movements were subtle, they were revealing. She held herself still for as long as possible, until her pleasure took control away from her and her body responded to my touch.

I brushed my fingers through the curls between her legs, then pressed the heel of my hand against her, until her hips rose in response. Her legs opened when I touched her. She was swollen and slippery with desire. I was careful with her, careful not to hurt her and careful not to hurry her. I let her body tell me where she wanted me to touch her, what kind of touch she wanted.

I began to learn the rhythm of her desire. It flowed through her in waves, building until her body was rigid with it, then fading as she softened and coiled back into herself. And little by little, I coaxed her heart out of hiding. I felt first a shy touch on my back. Then her fingers clutched at my shirt as her desire grew. Her hips rose to my touch. My own desire was intense. Her body joined mine in a dance of love and pleasure.

Then she stopped.

I waited for her to tell me what she needed.

"I can't," she said.

She put her hand over mine, to hold me still. Her desire still beat against my fingertips, but Maara was gone.

I lay quiet next to her and hid my face against her shoulder, so that she wouldn't see how much she'd hurt me. For a time the pain was so great that I couldn't think of her at all, but in a little while it lessened, and then I began to wonder. What was it she didn't want me to see? Was she hiding her own pain?

"Why?" I asked her.

She didn't answer.

When I tried to look at her, she turned her head away. In the soft glow of what remained of our fire, I caught a glimpse of her expression. It looked like shame.

"Who hurt you?" I asked her.

She was silent.

"Who else has touched you like this?"

"No one," she whispered.

"Then why?"

I knew she wouldn't answer me. Her heart was a fortress. Was she waiting for love to breach the walls?

"Touch me," I said.

She didn't move.

"Please." I shifted my hips back a bit, so that she could reach me more easily, and she slipped her hand between my legs and held me.

"Caress me."

My desire had waited for her. She could feel it. She was hesitant at first, but now she knew my body. Soon she had me on the edge. I leaned over her.

"Look at me," I said.

She turned her face toward me, but she wouldn't meet my eyes. I bent and kissed her, and at the same time I began to caress her. Her desire had waited for me too.

When I raised my head, she looked up at me. I let her see my pleasure. I held it in my body and waited for her. She was watching me so intently I doubt she was aware that I was watching her. I watched her face change, as mine must have been changing. Then her touch grew stronger, more demanding, until I could hold back no longer. The pleasure was so powerful that I cried out. Still I held myself above her, so that she could see me, but at last my arm began to tremble, and she pulled me down into her embrace. I was close to tears, but they were not tears of pleasure. She hadn't made the journey with me.

Again her hand covered mine, but this time she pressed my fingers hard against her, and I felt her desire uncoil between her legs as her body shuddered under me. She too cried out, a cry of pleasure mixed with pain, as if something within her had broken, so that her heart could find me.

60

WINTER

We lay breast to breast, heart to heart. Maara held me there, and there I was content to stay. The walls that had held her heart captive lay in ruins. Of course she would rebuild them. The heart needs its walls. But for the moment she was unguarded.

It was enough then to let our hearts rest side by side. It was the most perfect moment of my life.

At last her hold loosened, and she shifted a little. I moved the weight of my body off of her, but she didn't let me go far. When I lay next to her, she tucked me close against her side. I knew better than to speak. Words would only have put distance between us. I spoke to her with my hands. She touched me too and kissed my brow in answer. Then we wrapped our arms around each other and lay still.

We lay like that for a long time. I thought she was asleep.

"You chose me," she whispered.

"I chose you," I said.

I waited for her to ask me why. Instead she drew back, so that she could look at me, and smiled. "Are we cold?"

In her arms I had been warm enough, but she was right. We were cold. I let her go this time, to tend the fire. When she came back to bed, she pulled my cloak around us and took me into her arms.

That night I dreamed. Several times I woke with my heart full of feeling from what had happened in a dream, but the dream itself I never could remember. Once I woke thinking that Maara had been trying to awaken me, only to find her deeply asleep. Her face was bathed in light, not the warm light of our fire, but the cold blue moonlight shining through the broken roof. Even in that hard light, she was more beautiful than I had ever seen her.

Toward morning I woke with a start from the sensation of falling, and that brought pieces of a dream back to me. In the dream it was not I who had fallen. It was Maara. As she fell, her cry was the cry I remembered from the night before.

I understood the dream at once, in a flash of insight that reached my heart before my mind could make much sense of it. It took some time before I could put it into words, and the words never did justice to what I had seen, but I knew that what I had done so easily when I revealed my heart to Maara was for her so difficult that I wondered how she had found the courage to do it at all.

My dream left me with a vague uneasiness, an apprehension that I might have, as my dream suggested, pushed her off a cliff, that I might have pushed her farther than she was prepared to go. She had balked at the cliff's edge. Perhaps I had done wrong by forcing her to fly before she knew she had wings.

Her kiss on my brow brought back my happiness, and for the moment I put the memory of my dream away.

"We should get up," she whispered.

I wrapped my arms around her and snuggled closer. "Please. Not yet."

Her arms settled around me, and her fingertips traced a gentle pattern between my shoulder blades. We had begun to learn how our bodies fit together. Without realizing what I was doing, I began to rock against her.

"If you keep that up," she said, "we'll get no traveling done today."

I would have liked nothing better.

"Can't we stay here, just for one day?" I said.

"It's going to snow," she said. "We need to move on before we're trapped here."

"I wouldn't mind being trapped here."

"There's nothing to eat here," she said gently. "There's no game here, no streams to fish, no animals to snare. We need to reach the forest."

"How far is it?"

"Not far now."

I sighed. "All right. I suppose we should get started."

It was almost as difficult to leave the warmth of our bed as it was to leave the comfort of Maara's arms. In the cold air my skin broke out in goose-bumps. I hurried into my tunic and handed Maara hers. Then I knelt to rekindle the fire.

After a hasty breakfast of porridge, Maara refolded our packs. She helped me shoulder mine, then moved to stand in front of me to adjust my cloak, frowning a little in concentration as she tugged the hood into place. It was all I could do not to step forward into her arms. Instead I studied her, seeing with new eyes the face I thought I knew better than any other. She felt my eyes on her and raised her eyebrows in question.

"You look—" I was suddenly too shy to tell her she was beautiful. "Different," I said.

"I am different," she replied.

Her frown deepened, and her tone alarmed me. While I helped her with her pack, I thought again about my dream.

"Last night—" I said.

"What?"

I finished adjusting the straps of her pack before I answered her. Even then, I didn't meet her eyes. "Did I ask too much?"

"Tamras," she said.

The way she spoke my name made me look up at her.

"You told me to ask for what I wanted," she said.

I nodded.

"You too."

I opened my mouth to speak, but words wouldn't come.

"Hush," she said. "I know what you meant. We'll talk tonight."

At midmorning it began to snow. By midafternoon the world around us wore a veil of white. As we had done the day before, we traveled all day without stopping. By evening I was tired and cold and hungry. For several hours the north wind had been blowing, and my fingers were stiff from clutching my cloak tight around me.

Even after dark Maara didn't seem to be looking for a place to camp. There was no moon. I stumbled as the ground grew rough underfoot. When I was so tired I didn't think I could take another step, Maara stopped.

"We'll rest here a while," she said.

"A while?"

"The forest isn't far."

"Shouldn't we keep going then?"

"We'll go on when the moon rises."

Although she said nothing about the weather, I understood that if it grew much worse, we would be in danger as long as we were in open country. Once we reached the forest, we could find some kind of shelter and fuel for a fire. Until then we were at the mercy of the storm.

Maara lifted my pack from my shoulders and shrugged out of hers before I thought to help her with it. She cut some bracken and shook it free of snow to give us something dry to sit on. When I sat down, I found that we were in a little hollow in the landscape that gave us shelter from the wind, though I could hear it whistling by inches above my head.

"Are you sleepy?" she asked me.

My legs were tired, and I was glad to be off my feet, but I didn't feel like sleeping.

"No," I said. "Are you?"

She shook her head. "Better not to sleep."

Even in that dreadful weather, she got a fire started. While she collected enough twiggy shrubs to feed it for a few hours, I threaded strips of venison onto sticks and propped them over the flames. Maara sat down and leaned back against our packs, which she had arranged to serve as a backrest. Then she opened her cloak and beckoned to me to come sit between her legs, as I had sat the night before when I told her the story of the fairy queen. I took my own cloak off and pulled it around us like a blanket. After a little while, I was almost warm enough, and by then, our supper was ready.

It would be several hours until moonrise. A full stomach and the warmth of Maara's body made me sleepy. Although I hadn't intended to fall asleep, I must have slept soundly for at least an hour. When I awoke, I found that I had half turned to her in my sleep and now lay with my head on her breast, my legs tucked under me. I was so comfortable, I didn't want to move, but it was Maara's turn to sleep, and one of us had to stay awake. When I started to sit up, Maara's arms held me where I was.

"Don't move," she said. "I'm finally warm."

"You should sleep a while."

"I'm all right," she said.

She must have been as tired as I was, but I didn't argue with her. The burden of keeping us alive in that hostile place lay entirely upon her shoulders. As long as she kept watch, nothing would surprise us. I depended on her so completely that I forgot to worry about the dangers that surrounded us. I thought of other things, of what had passed between us the night before.

"I didn't tell you everything," she said.

I caught my breath and waited, knowing that what she was about to say would be hard to hear.

"I didn't tell you about Elen."

She hadn't told me in so many words, but she had told me more than she realized. "I know you loved her," I said, and before she could accuse me of jealousy, I added, "I'm glad you had someone then, even if it wasn't me."

"I was only her companion."

The ghost of a memory sat just out of reach in the back of my head.

"I was her property." A pause. "Her slave."

The ghost whispered, *I was there for her pleasure, not my own.* They were Sparrow's words about Arnet, the old woman who had taken a child to bed.

"I counted myself lucky," Maara said. "She had changed my life. She probably saved my life. I was grateful, glad to repay her in any way I could. I had nothing to offer her but myself. I never expected her to love me back."

"Did she?"

"No."

I reached for Maara's hand and held it against my heart. She had told me that no one in that household cared for her, but I never imagined that anyone could have used her as Elen did.

"She did a shameful thing," I said.

"Shameful? Why?"

"She hurt you," I said. "She used you."

"And I used her."

"It's not the same thing."

"Listen," she said. "I needed to love her. I needed to love someone."

As do we all, I thought, but at what cost.

"I would have died for her," she said.

"And she would have let you." I began to dislike Elen very much.

"Are you angry with me?"

I brought her fingers to my lips. "Of course not."

She brushed her fingertips over my mouth. When she cradled my cheek in the palm of her hand, she felt my tears.

"Why?" she said.

"You deserved so much more than that."

She wrapped her arms around me and held me tight. "And now I have you," she said.

We spoke no more about it. Nothing more needed to be said. While we waited for the moon, I tried to imagine how it would feel to love someone as Maara had loved Elen, without hope of a return. The more I thought about it, the more I believed that it was impossible not to hope, and few things could be more painful than to hope for love only to be constantly disappointed.

61

The Forest

A half moon rose at midnight. The air was still, and the sky began to clear. Maara whispered to me that it was time to go. When I stood up, I shivered in the bitter cold.

We walked for hours, through wind-blown drifts that barred our way. Where we could we went around them. Maara kept our direction true by following the stars.

At dawn we saw the distant hills. By midday we had reached them. We passed a scattering of trees, their trunks wind-twisted into fantastic shapes. On the hill's crest, their silhouette against the pale sky looked like a line of dancers waving long ribbons that curled above their heads. It seemed as if they danced us on our way, as they swayed back and forth. The silence thundered in my ears. I fell.

When I woke, I was lying on a bed of leaves, wrapped in my cloak, with Maara's cloak beneath me. Close by a fire was burning. Our packs lay beside it. I was alone.

The smell of food awakened my hunger. Steam rose from our cooking pot. In it was a rich soup, made from the deer's marrow bones. I wanted to wait for Maara, but I couldn't resist eating my share of it. I set the pot down a little more than half full.

"Finish it." Maara's voice came from behind me. Even in snow that crunched and squeaked underfoot, I hadn't heard her approach.

"That's for you," I said.

"I've had mine."

I doubted that. "Then have some more."

She frowned and held the pot out to me. I refused to take it until she had swallowed a few mouthfuls.

"I'm not the one who made a faceprint in the snow," she said.

"I'm all right."

"You should have said something."

She was trying to scold me, but I heard the worry behind her words.

"Next time I will," I said, although I doubted I could keep my promise. I hadn't known I was so tired.

"Can you go on?"

"I'm fine," I insisted.

"From the top of this hill, you can see the forest."

A shiver of anticipation went through me. "Then let's go," I said.

What we called forests were really only groves or woodlands. I had never seen one of the ancient forests, although I had heard tales about them. The old forests had many names — abode of wolves and of the old ones, outlaws' haven, hunters' home. It was said that once all the world had been covered by the forests and that humankind had lived in them like creatures of the night, always in darkness under the trees.

When we reached the hilltop, I thought I would never be able to look long enough. The forest was immense, covering the hills as far as I could see. As my own breath hung in the cold air, mist hung in the treetops as if it were the forest's breath, as if the forest were not only made up of living things, but as if it were a living thing itself, a being of mystery and power.

Maara was patient with me. She let me stand there looking. When I began to shiver, she took me under her cloak.

"What will it be like to live there?" I asked her.

"The forest once felt like home to me," she said.

It took us the rest of the day to reach the forest's edge. As we grew near, I felt it waiting for us. When we were safe among the trees, I gathered firewood, while Maara hurried to make a shelter before we lost the light. She wove together twigs and branches to make three walls and a roof. One end she left open to the fire. It looked a little like the pens we made for our sheep at lambing time. It was all I could do to stay awake long enough to eat my supper. That night we were both too tired to do anything but sleep.

We slept through the long night and well into the next day. It was mid-morning before we continued our journey into the heart of the forest. I had expected that we would have to make our way through a tangle of under-growth, but only bracken and a few creepers grew on the forest floor. The evergreen yew and pine blocked out the sky, and even the bare branches of the oaks had grown so thickly intertwined that they let in little light.

The still air was warmer here than in the treeless wilderness. A breeze stirred the treetops, but made only the softest sound. The rustling of our footsteps in dry leaves was muted by the forest's stillness. In the silence and the gloom, I found I couldn't speak above a whisper.

The trunks of the ancient trees were as big around as a shepherd's hut, and their limbs were thicker than my body. They sometimes sprawled their lower branches across the forest floor, and we had either to go around them or to clamber over. I preferred to go around. As I would have been reluctant to disturb the sleep of giants, I feared to wake the spirits of these great trees.

We rested for half an hour in the afternoon. Perched on the rotting trunk of a fallen oak, we made a cold meal of smoked venison. Maara's face wore such a thoughtful, private look that I hesitated to speak to her. Even watching her, as I often did, felt like an invasion of her privacy. Instead I looked around me at this enchanted world while tales from my childhood played themselves out inside my head. I felt small and insignificant among these trees grown old and wise.

"Does it please you?"

Maara's voice startled me out of a daydream. I didn't know what she meant.

"The forest," she said.

It would never have occurred to me to ask myself such a question. The forest cared not a bit whether I was pleased with it or not, but I saw that Maara did care. She waited to hear my answer as a woman waits to hear her guest praise the beauty and the comfort of her home.

"I am humbled by it," I said.

Maara smiled.

We were traveling north and west, or so Maara said. I didn't understand then how she could tell direction when she couldn't see the sky or the horizon. From time to time she would stop and study the gentle rise and fall of the land or the way the leaves turned to take advantage of what light there was. More than once she seemed puzzled, as if she had expected one thing and found another. I didn't let that worry me. I had no doubts that she would find what she was looking for. If she had any doubts herself, she never let me see them.

In the forest it was impossible to know when the sun had set. The gloom deepened slowly, until the light was gone. When Maara disappeared, I thought it was the last of the light playing tricks on my eyes. We had been following a brook upstream, and I had knelt for just a moment to drink. When I stood up, Maara was a dozen yards away, standing still, gazing up into the branches of an oak tree. Then she took a step and vanished.

I cried out and began to run toward the place where I had last seen her. Before I had taken a dozen steps she reappeared, as if her body had distilled itself out of the air. I stopped. At that moment I believed all the tales of enchantment I'd ever heard.

Maara beckoned to me. Cautiously I approached her.

"Look," she said, gesturing at a deep fissure in the trunk of the oak tree.

I was beginning to recover from my fright, but I didn't understand what she was showing me. Then she stepped into the fissure and was gone. By now it was so dark that I thought she might be lost in shadow. I took a step closer.

"Come on," she said.

Her voice echoed in the air around me like the voice of a disembodied spirit. I had heard tales of portals that opened into another world. Perhaps this fissure in the tree was such a portal. I closed my eyes and stepped into it.

I found myself in deep darkness. After a few moments, I began to see a little. Dim light filtered down from above me, revealing the shape of someone kneeling at my feet. It was Maara. If I had taken another step, I would have fallen over her. She struck a spark that caught tinder and blew it into a tiny flame. Then I saw where we were.

"We're inside the tree," I said.

Maara looked up at me. "Of course. Where did you think we were?"

Although I felt a little foolish, at the same time I felt delight at being in the heart of this ancient oak. It was almost as good as being in another world.

Maara piled up some of the litter that lay on the ground and set it alight. "Bring some firewood," she said.

When I had a good pile of deadfall stacked outside, I brought an armload in to her. She was mixing batter for oat cakes.

"You knew about this tree," I said.

Maara nodded. "This was my hiding place."

We were sitting side by side, leaning against the smooth, warm wood, our bellies full of the best meal we had enjoyed since we left home. Along with venison, roasted on the coals, we'd had fresh oat cakes with bits of dried fruit in them. Now we were sharing a pot of fragrant tea.

My hunger satisfied, my body warmed, my heart at ease with Maara beside me, I was only half awake, so comfortable that I nearly missed the meaning of what she told me.

"Your hiding place?"

Maara sighed. "We don't have to talk about this now."

"Is it a sad story?"

"Not anymore," she said.

"Then tell me."

"I was an outlaw. I told you that."

I took her hand and waited for her to go on.

"It was just after harvest time. The weather was warm and fine. I felt safe in the forest, but every day I moved my camp, in case I was still pursued. After several months went by, I grew careless. By then winter had come, and I had made a shelter. One day when I returned home, I found my shelter torn to pieces, my food stores gone. The furs from animals I'd trapped, that clothed me and kept me warm at night, they were gone too. I had lost everything that made life possible. I was left with only what I had on me, my clothing, my bow and a few arrows, a rabbit I had snared that morning. They weren't satisfied with destroying the things I needed to live. They came after me. I had no time to hunt, no time to sleep. My pursuers hunted as the wolf hunts. They kept me moving."

"As the wolf hunts?"

"When wolves hunt an animal too large or too dangerous to bring down, like an elk or a boar, two or three of them together run ahead of the pack and give chase. When they tire, they fall back, and others replace them. Turn by turn, they press their quarry, until it can run no farther."

"Is that how the northerners caught Breda?"

Maara glanced at me, surprised. "Yes, I believe so. What made you think of it?"

"You said something at the time. You said they ran after him until they ran him down."

"Hunters learn from other hunters," she said. "I once heard that it was the wolf who taught humankind to hunt."

I remembered my fearful dreams of Breda running from his pursuers, and I saw in my mind's eye an image of those who had pursued Maara. In my mind they had the golden eyes, the lolling tongues of wolves.

"It was long past the time I wanted to give up," said Maara, "but my body refused to yield. I would stop to rest, intending to stay where I was until they caught me. As soon as I heard them coming, my body insisted on running away.

"When I came to the stream to drink, a bird began to sing. A songbird in the forest in winter is a rare thing. I felt it sang for me. I followed it for quite a distance, until it perched in the branches of this tree. I didn't see the fissure in the trunk at first. As I stood listening to the bird, a shaft of sunlight fell across it."

"The bird led you here?"

"The forest led me here. The bird was its messenger."

"There are tales like that."

"Are there? Will you tell them?"

"Of course."

I leaned my head against her shoulder, thinking pleasant thoughts of all the evenings we would spend together here. We would have time for talking, for storytelling, for lovemaking. I was perfectly content.

I don't remember Maara putting me to bed. I didn't wake until late the next morning. Oat cakes lay warming in the ashes of the fire, and tendrils of steam from a pot of tea coiled into the air. I was finishing the last oat cake when Maara returned.

"I hope you already had your breakfast," I said, "because I've just eaten everything in sight."

She laughed. "It's a good thing I found this," she said, and held up the body of a hare.

While Maara dressed the hare, I examined our new home. The hollow part of the tree trunk extended several feet above our heads. A dozen people might fit comfortably inside it. Cracks above us let daylight in and let the smoke of our fire out. Except for the place that Maara had cleared for our bed, the floor was covered with litter. I went outside and gathered several armloads of bracken. Some I bound together to make a broom to sweep the litter out. I tied the rest in bunches and hung it up to dry, intending to use it to make us a soft bed.

In a crevice I found a clump of feathers, tied together with a leather thong. I held it out for Maara to see.

"An offering," she said. "From the forest people."

I hardly knew which question to ask her first, so I asked them all at once.

"Who are the forest people? Is this a sacred tree? Will they be angry?"

"I doubt we'll ever see them," said Maara. "When I was here before, I knew they were close by, but they never showed themselves. Sometimes I left food for them, if I had anything to spare."

I put the feather offering back in the crevice where I found it. "If this is a sacred tree, won't they object to our living here?"

She shrugged. "I hope not."

"How long did you live here before?"

"Not long," she said. "My pursuers never found my hiding place, but they never stopped looking for me. I couldn't stay in the tree all the time. I had to find food. I had to make a fire. Eventually they would have found me. I had to move on."

"Where did you go?"

"I went to Merin's house."

62

THE PAST

All morning we spent on housekeeping. Maara made a meat safe out of hazel wands and set it in the branches of the tree. The air was cold enough to keep the meat for another week or two. What we couldn't eat in that time, we hung up to smoke.

It was a pleasant day, windless and a little warmer than the day before. After a dark morning, the sun came out to cast bright patterns on the forest floor. Maara made a fire out in the open, close by the brook, and we cooked and ate the hare for lunch. Then she brought both our packs outside and undid them, spreading our belongings on the ground. I watched with curiosity as she picked out a change of clothing for each of us. She had me do up our packs and put them away, while she made our clean clothes into a bundle.

"Let's go," she said, and got to her feet.

"Where are we going?"

She smiled. "You'll see."

For the best part of an hour we followed the brook upstream. The ground rose steadily until the gentle walk uphill became almost a climb. At last we reached a large rock that emerged from the ground beside the brook. It would be a lovely place in summer. The surface of the rock was flat, worn smooth by flowing water, perfect for sunbathing, and beside it a fall of water had hollowed out a swimming hole. This time of year it made me shiver just to think about it.

Maara stood on the rock, examining the ground beside it until she spotted something half-concealed under a pile of leaves. It was a wide plank, rough-hewn, made by human hands. I thought at first it must once have served as a bridge, although the brook was hardly wide enough to need one. Maara set one end of the plank on the rock's edge and slid the other under the waterfall, diverting the water so that it ran across the rock and began to fill a hollow where once the fall of water had scoured it. The hollow proved deeper than it looked, a dozen inches at the deepest part.

I thought I understood what Maara intended, but I was puzzled.

"Why did we have to come so far to do our laundry?" I asked her.

"We're not going to wash our clothes," she said. "We're going to wash ourselves."

I knelt and dipped my hand into the water, then quickly drew it back. "It's freezing."

Maara smiled. "Gather some firewood. Bring some stones. Like this."

She held up both hands to show me that she wanted stones the size of a loaf of bread. By the time I had collected half a dozen, she had a fire burning there on the rock beside the hollow. I knew what she was doing. It was a trick I had used to heat water when I didn't have a cooking pot. I would fill a leather bag—a water skin or even a carrying bag as long as it was watertight—and drop hot rocks into it. We heated the stones in the fire, then nudged them into the water.

Maara took a handful of tubers from the pocket of her tunic and shredded them on the surface of the rock.

"You first," she said.

I hated the thought of undressing in the cold. I wished I had worn my cloak, so that I could undress under it. As quickly as I could, I hurried out of my clothes and into the water. It was only lukewarm, but the fire helped keep me warm enough.

Maara wrapped the shredded tubers in a bit of cloth and soaked them, squeezing them until they made a lather. Then she began to scrub me. The tubers worked almost as well as soap. They had a delicate scent, like a meadow of wildflowers.

"Did you once bathe here?" I asked her.

"Yes."

"When you were an outlaw?"

Her hands paused for the briefest moment.

"Before that?"

She nodded.

At once I understood the implications of what she had told me. "How far is Elen's house from here?"

"Far enough."

"How many days?"

"We came here in summertime," she said.

"You and Elen?"

"Elen and her companions."

When I would have asked her more, she gently pushed me back into the water so that she could wash my hair. While she finger-combed the tangles out, she tried to talk of other things, but I was not so easily distracted.

"Won't you be in danger here?" I asked her.

"Not if no one finds us."

"What if someone does?"

"I told you," she said. "This forest is a boundary. No one comes here."

"Elen came here."

"Only in summer."

"If someone did come, would they know you?"

She shrugged. "They forgot about me long ago."

But the more she tried to reassure me, the more fearful I became.

"You shouldn't have come back here," I said.

Maara stopped what she was doing and met my eyes. "Where else should we have gone?"

"Anywhere else."

"There was nowhere else."

I couldn't argue with her. I was on the verge of tears.

"Hush," she said. "Let's not borrow trouble. I know this place. We can survive the winter here. We might even manage to live well and in some comfort. Should we have begged the mercy of the northern tribes, or challenged the mountains to the east or some other place where I've never been?"

She was right. Still I couldn't put away my fear, until her lips on mine broke the spiral of my worried thoughts and brought me entirely into the present moment. It was a long kiss. I was sorry when it ended.

Maara helped me to my feet and dried me with my dirty shirt. While I put my clean clothes on, she undressed and got into the water. Goosebumps appeared along her arms. The water must be cold by now. I resolved that next time she would bathe first.

While Maara shredded more of the tubers and wrapped them in the cloth, I built up the fire. Then I took the cloth from her and began to scrub her back. The water on her skin deepened its color. Although it was only midafternoon, the light had begun to fade, and Maara's body took on the dark colors of the forest.

I set the cloth aside and used my hands. Her skin was smooth, slippery with lather. As I ran my hands across her back, I found the scars, not many, invisible to the eye. As often as I'd bathed her, I had never noticed them before. Scars on the back are not a warrior's scars.

They should have made me angry. Instead they made me cry. Silent tears spilled down my face. I was behind her. She didn't see them. I kissed the nape of her neck and used her hair to wipe my tears away.

It was cold, now that the sun had gone. The walk home took longer, because of the dark. We had wrapped our wet hair up in our dirty shirts and wore our dirty trousers like shawls around our shoulders. I would have made fun of our outlandish costumes, if I had been lighthearted.

Safe inside the hollow tree, we dried our hair by the fire. Maara had hung the deerskin across the fissure in the tree trunk to keep out the draft, and the small space inside the tree warmed quickly. Soon we were in our shirt-sleeves. We hadn't spoken more than a word or two since our conversation at the bathing rock. Maara seemed lost inside herself, and I couldn't let go of the thought that we had fled a place where there was a price on my head, only to come to a place where there was a price on hers.

I hoped she was right about no one coming here. The signs of our presence were everywhere. We had washed the remains of our fire from the surface of the bathing rock, but it had left its mark. The places where we gathered wood, where Maara had dug the tubers, where we knelt beside the brook to fill our water skins, all remembered us. Maara had taught me to read the signs left by others. I was not blind to the signs we left.

Something else disturbed me. It felt almost like desire, though it was prompted, not by love, but by a hunger I had never felt before. I thought about her body, its shapes and textures, the way her wet skin had shone like bronze in the firelight. Her body kept her secrets, but my hands had searched them out. In her body was the memory of things her mind had long forgotten. Her body expected pain and was surprised by pleasure. Her body defended her, even against love.

"You might as well ask me now," she said.

I stared at her. I didn't understand.

"I was an outlaw. Haven't you ever wondered why?"

I had, of course, but one doesn't ask such a question lightly. I knew the danger of speculation, of thinking things that might not be true, yet the thought could make them seem so, and I had tried not to wonder.

"If you had asked," she said, "I would have told you."

"I knew you'd tell me when you were ready."

"Are you ready to hear it?"

"Whatever you did, it makes no difference to me," I said.

"I killed someone."

"So did I."

"No," she said. "I killed a man in his bed. I killed him while he slept."

"Why?"

"He was Elen's husband."

"What did he do?"

She didn't understand my question.

"Did he hurt someone? You? Or Elen?"

Maara's eyes glittered in the firelight. "Don't think so well of me. I killed him out of jealousy, I think."

Maara sighed and gazed into the fire. "She married him for the sake of an alliance. She still took me into her bed when he was away, and when he was at home, sometimes she came to mine. Even after she began to love him, she still came to me."

"How do you know she loved him?"

"She told me so."

How cruel, I thought, but I kept my opinion to myself.

"When I used to sleep among the other companions," she said, "I heard them whispering their secrets to one another. They talked of who had caught their eye, of who had offered them a flower or danced for them at the bonfire. Elen began to do the same with me. She would tell me things he said and did and ask me what I thought they meant. I knew what she wanted to hear. She wanted to believe he loved her. I told her that anyone would love her when they knew her, but of course I was speaking for myself."

Maara fell silent. I watched her eyes grow fierce as she remembered a time that had caused her so much pain. My heart ached for her.

"Time went by," she said, "and Elen didn't come to my bed anymore. At first she made excuses, although she owed me no explanation, but after a while it was as if there had never been any intimacy between us. She treated me as she treated the others, and that hurt most of all. More than the loss of her body, I grieved the loss of her friendship."

Now my heart began to ache for myself, and jealousy left its sour taste in my mouth.

"I did the unthinkable," said Maara. "I complained to her. I begged her to spare some time for me. I accused her of throwing me away." Maara glared at me, as she must have glared at Elen. "Worst of all, I spoke before others. I didn't care about the consequences. I spoke my heart. I had no right to speak to her like that. She was a married woman, and I was just a slave. She should have had me punished for it, but she treated me with kindness. She took me aside and told me she was sorry she hadn't spoken to me before. Her husband was jealous, she said, and she intended to keep herself for him, because she loved him. She was kind, but she made it clear to me that I had lost her."

There was so much pain in Maara's eyes that I wanted her to stop. As if she had heard my thoughts, she said, "I'll never speak of this again. Hear it now, or not at all."

"Go on," I said.

"Elen put me to bed that night and lay down beside me, although she wouldn't let me touch her. I kept my tears inside, but she knew they were there. She tried to comfort me, and while she was beside me, I was comforted a little. At last she fell asleep. I watched her until the lamp went out. The next thing I knew someone was shaking me awake. It was Elen, telling me I had to leave the house. Then I saw the blood. We were both covered with it, and the knife was still in my hand."

It took me a minute to put it all together. If Maara had killed Elen's husband, she had done it in her sleep. A fear I didn't understand crept into my heart. Maara saw it reflected in my eyes.

"You should have let me go," she said.

"No." I got to my feet and stepped over the fire to kneel beside her. "I never feared you, and I'll never let you go."

"You're afraid now."

"Not of you."

"What then?"

"Dear one," I said, "I'm afraid you'll break your heart."

"Too late," she said.

It wasn't true, but there was no use talking to her then. I regretted allowing her to awaken the past, until I understood that it had been awake in her already. Its ghost had found her at the bathing rock and followed her home. As an old wound, long healed over, can fester under the skin, this dreadful thing had slept in Maara's heart until the awakening of memory made it poisonous. It was best to let the poison out.

I remembered that we'd had no supper.

"Are you hungry?" I asked her.

She shook her head.

I wasn't hungry either. "Then come to bed."

I unfastened her leggings and helped her take off her boots. She would have gotten into bed in her shirt and trousers. I stopped her and reached for her belt.

"No," she said.

"I won't ask you for anything. I just want you close to me tonight."

Reluctantly she allowed me to undress her down to the skin. Then I undressed myself and got into the bed beside her. She lay on her side, with her back to me. I couldn't keep myself from touching her. At the first brush of my fingers on her shoulder, she stiffened, but she didn't draw away. I began to caress her back, first with my fingertips, very lightly along her spine, then with my whole hand. It was a healing touch my mother taught me, meant to comfort the heart.

Now I had time to try to understand my fear. I had never feared her, and I didn't fear her now, but I did fear what had awakened within her. What must it be like to believe oneself capable of murdering an innocent? Yet how could she hold herself responsible?

Little by little, the rigid shield of muscle across her shoulders softened under my touch. Perhaps now I could speak to her.

"It wasn't your fault," I said.

Her body grew still.

"You did nothing wrong."

"No more," she said.

I sent a prayer to the spirits of the forest for her healing.

Then I said, "You were asleep. You didn't know what you were doing."

"I said, no more."

"Surely you can't—"

"Enough!" she said.

"But you were blameless."

Suddenly she turned to look at me. I held myself steady against the anger in her eyes.

"Don't make excuses for me," she said. "I make no excuses for myself. I killed someone who had never done me harm, and I took from Elen someone she loved."

"You didn't mean to."

"No," she said bitterly. "I didn't mean to. Did you think that would make it better? That only makes it worse."

"Why?"

She didn't answer me. Was this a puzzle she meant for me to unravel? Something in her eyes reminded me of a time long ago, when we were hostages in Merin's house.

Now I understood why she had given me her knife. It was not to cut the thong binding us together. She had meant for me to use it to defend myself against her.

"Are you afraid you might hurt someone else?"

"What do you think?"

"In all the time I've known you, I've never seen you do harm to anyone. Except in battle," I added as an afterthought. "That's different."

"You don't understand," she said. "By my hand or not, harm comes anyway." She smiled at me, but her eyes were cold. "The god's curse falls on those I love. I would be wary if I were you."

There at her wound's heart was the true cause of her pain. For the first time I understood something my grandmother told me years before, that it's not our deeds that hurt us, but what they make us believe about ourselves.

"No curse will fall on me," I said. "To me your love has been a blessing. Your love is all I want, and I would say the same if I were to die of it tonight."

I recognized the pain in Maara's eyes. A healer's touch must fall upon the sorest spot.

"Listen to me," I said. "I don't care what you've done, because I know your heart. Nothing you might tell me about the past can change what I see now."

I felt her resist me, as she tried to push my words away.

"All right," I said. "Think what you want. If your love brings a curse with it, then I accept it."

"Hush," she said, and her fingers covered my lips.

I took her hand in mine and kissed it. Then I bent and kissed her mouth. I felt her yield, not only to my touch and to my kiss, but to the truth at the heart of my words, that I knew the price of love and had agreed to pay it.

I raised my head and smiled down at her.

"You won't get rid of me so easily."

She smiled back at me, but worry lines still creased her brow.

"Don't try to tell me this isn't my fault," she whispered.

"This? What?"

"Vintel was first my enemy before she became yours."

"Neither of us is to blame for Vintel's treachery."

"Nevertheless, if I had never come to Merin's house, you would be safe there now."

"If you had never come to Merin's house," I said, "I might have died of loneliness."

To that she had no answer.

I woke to her touch on my skin, a light caress along my shoulder and across my back that made me tremble, as if I had awakened from a dream of desire. I held myself still, thinking she might have touched me in her sleep. Then she leaned over me, lifted my hair away from my neck and kissed me there, just behind the ear. Another kiss brushed my temple, and another touched my brow.

I opened my eyes to darkness. No glow of firelight, no ghostlight of the moon showed me the shape of her. She was a dark presence I could feel but not see, as senses I never knew I had revealed her. My blind eyes saw color at the center, the crimson pain she'd kept from me, lost memory in twilight colors like the dark under the trees, the soft glow of her desire. Perhaps I was dreaming still.

No dream has this much truth in it. Her fingers at my throat reminded me. I felt her ask the question, not of me, but of herself. I felt no fear. No harm will come to me, not like this, not when love asks the question.

To my hands her body is familiar. Others have touched the surface, and some have left their mark. My touch will replace them. My hands will search out the wounded places and give them instead the memory of tenderness. Others have touched the surface. My touch will go deeper.

My body conforms itself to hers. The contours of her body define my shape. Her arms steal me from the world's embrace. My own words echo in my ears. *Your love is all I want, and I would say the same if I were to die of it tonight.* Will the world hold me to my promise? I spoke the truth.

The sweet fragrance of her skin and the scent of her desire lift me into her. My pores open, to breathe her in. My thigh rises between her thighs. Her breath sighs beside my ear. She speaks to me in whispers. I don't understand the words. There are no words for this, but I know her meaning. Her heart is a bright flame within a cloud of darkness. Now, if I'm careful, if I'm clever, I will thread the labyrinth and tread the secret pathway to her heart. The gate is open.

END BOOK II

When Women Were Warriors: Book III

A Hero's Tale

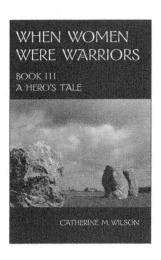

In Book III of the trilogy, Tamras must make her own hero's journey. She ventures into the unknown and encounters a more formidable enemy than any she has ever faced. Character is destiny, and the destiny of Tamras and all her people will depend upon choices that come less from the skills she has been taught than from the person she has become, from her own heart.

★ ★ ★ ★ ★ Being the third and last volume in a series I enjoyed immensely, I knew that I could expect this last book to deliver a happy and satisfying ending. What I didn't expect was the intricate and daring storyline of this last volume. It is bigger and broader than what has come before, and it is spectacular. This book takes up where the last left off but instead of merely working out the story conflicts already apparent, this time the story unfolds on to a whole new level. More characters, more intrigue, greater losses, wonderful reunions... There's no taking the easy road here—the story opened up into unimagined dimensions to tell a tale that really is that of a hero.
—from a review by Kate Genet, *Kissed By Venus*

Ebooks!

The trilogy, *When Women Were Warriors*, is available in multiple ebook formats from Amazon, Barnes & Noble, Kobo, Smashwords, the iBookstore, and other online ebookstores.

Book I of the trilogy is available for FREE in multiple ebook formats from many of these ebookstores and also from the Shield Maiden Press website, shieldmaidenpress.com, and the author's website, catherine-m-wilson.com.

Autographs!

Autographed paperbacks and/or free autographed bookplates can be ordered from the author's website, catherine-m-wilson.com.

ABOUT THE AUTHOR

This picture was taken in 1968, more than 40 years ago, so if you should happen to run across me in real life, don't be disappointed that I no longer resemble the young woman you see here. I have grown old, and although not so cute on the outside, I am much lovelier on the inside.

I chose this photo because in it I am standing by the entrance stone at Newgrange, a megalithic passage tomb in Ireland, built over five thousand years ago. If mysterious portals exist in the world, this is one of them. Many authors will tell you that their stories come from a mysterious place, and when I began to write my trilogy, *When Women Were Warriors*, I suspected that perhaps I had once stepped into another world without knowing it and brought back some ancient long-forgotten tale. Wherever the story came from, it came more through me than from me. I made it from my own life and from my own experience, but I also heard a voice whispering within me that was not quite mine.

Catherine M Wilson
December, 2008
catherine-m-wilson.com

Made in the USA
Coppell, TX
30 July 2023

19767367R00184